Bitter Winds

BOOK THREE IN THE
Tales of the Scavenger's Daughters

Also by Kay Bratt

Silent Tears; A Journey of Hope in a Chinese Orphanage
Chasing China; A Daughter's Quest for Truth
The Bridge
A Thread Unbroken
Train to Nowhere
Mei Li and the Wise Laoshi

TALES OF THE SCAVENGER'S DAUGHTERS
The Scavenger's Daughters
Tangled Vines
Bitter Winds

Bitter Winds

BOOK THREE IN THE

Tales of the Scavenger's Daughters

A Novel

KAY BRATT

lake union publishing

Text Copyright © 2014 Kay Bratt

Printed in the United States of America.

Published by Lake Union Publishing, Seattle

www.apub.com

ISBN-13: 9781477848999
ISBN-10: 1477848991
Library of Congress Control Number: 2013914051

To Lisa
my twin, more than just a sister

"A violent wind does not last for a whole morning;
a sudden rain does not last for the whole day."

—Lao Tzu

Prologue

Lily shivered as she pulled her Ye Ye's jacket tighter around the stiff clothes they'd made her put on. The sterile smell of the room mixed with what reeked of old urine was nauseating, and she filtered her breath through her mouth as she waited. She listened intently, hoping the sound of footsteps wouldn't come. She'd been crouching on the ice-cold floor in the corner for hours, ever since that nasty excuse for a man had slammed the door on her. The turning of the lock and his threats to return later that night still rang in her ears. She felt a wave of revulsion remembering how he'd taunted her, coming close enough that she could smell his rancid breath as he hissed what he'd like to do to her.

But she wouldn't let him touch her—he'd have to kill her first. If he thought because she was blind she wouldn't be able to defend herself, he was in for a surprise because she'd fight until there was no breath left in her. She'd pull from that place deep within her, the reserve that so far had kept her from becoming hysterical. Ivy would be proud of her for being so strong. When she'd wished for independence she hadn't meant this—being jerked away from her sister and sentenced for something she hadn't even done. She only wished she could go back and live the morning again, just start completely over.

Her face burned with shame. It was her own fault. Given another chance, she'd do it differently and stay within the protection of her family—she'd forget her *independence* nonsense.

Her ears perked as she heard the faint slapping of plastic slippers coming closer. She reached out and pulled the mattress from the bed, then crouched under it. If it was him, maybe he'd think she'd been moved to another room. As she waited, a high-pitched shriek filled the hall and then her room. A chill went through her at the sound, a scream that could only be triggered from complete torture or hysteria. *What were they doing to that poor woman?* She tried to still the new onset of trembling.

She would not let them break her.

She would not let them break her.

She would *not* let them break her.

Chapter One

Old Town Wuxi, China, two months earlier

She concentrated on the sounds around her, letting her instincts guide her forward. Under the anticipation Lily felt about the public performance looming ahead of her, she pushed away an underlying feeling of foreboding. She wouldn't tell Ivy her concerns, or her sister would refuse to guide her to the park.

She'd awoken at four o'clock that morning, on the fourth day of the month and then had dropped her boiled egg not once or twice, but four times! Only in China would such events involving the number four predict impending doom, but she would not let ancient superstitions ruin her day. She was sixteen—not sixty, and only the elderly held on too hard to the old ways.

"Curb coming," Ivy warned.

Lily stepped up patiently. She always tried to think positively. She knew being blind had its perks, though sighted people might argue the point. But really, there were many things she could do that some couldn't. Take her exceptional hearing, for instance. Or even the way she never judged someone by their looks, instead focusing on their personality. She'd tried to tell her twin sister to ignore the clothing people wore, or the cleanliness of their hair, or whether they carried a designer bag or a knockoff. From her viewpoint, sight just got in the way.

But today being blind gave Lily another advantage. She knew the rain was coming probably before anyone else on the street did. Even through the heavy layer of pollution she could feel and smell it. She moved her white cane back and forth faster in front of her to show her sister she was in a hurry. Ivy wasn't cooperating and her stubbornness was going to get them caught in the rain.

"Ivy, the rain's coming." She kept her voice calm and matter-of-fact. She didn't feel like arguing this morning.

She heard the irritation in her sister's reply. "No, it isn't. Ye Ye said it isn't supposed to rain today. You're just feeling the wind. Slow down. We can't go too fast or you'll break your neck. You should see all the piles of bicycles and electric scooters stacked up and down these sidewalks. It's a freaking obstacle course."

Lily didn't answer but picked up the pace anyway, even though her sister was supposed to be the one leading her. Holding tightly to her upper arm, she forced Ivy to walk faster, oblivious to the uneven sidewalks and the other obstacles in her path. She knew her sister wouldn't let her get hurt; Ivy was her twin and had been her eyes since birth. There wasn't another person on earth she trusted more. But she'd made a decision. No longer was she going to sit in the dark and wait for her destiny to come to her; she was going to go out and find it.

"*Aiya,* I hate it when you're right," Ivy said, and Lily felt her cringe into herself as the rain began to fall in big, slow plops. She felt Ivy juggle the violin case around as she dug in her bag for the umbrella and popped it open above their heads.

Lily smiled. "I told you, didn't I? Make sure Viola doesn't get wet! We're almost there, aren't we?"

Lily could feel the sidewalks crowding up with more people the closer they got to the park. And even though she couldn't see them, she could feel their stares and hear their voices trailing off to nothing as she and her sister walked by. Being blind wasn't a big deal to her—but obviously it was to others. Lily was glad she couldn't see the pity evident in their voices. She wished she'd left her cane at home, but these days Ivy insisted she take it everywhere. For her it was like a flashing sign to the public, I'M BLIND, LOOK AT ME, I'M BLIND!

This was one thing between them her sister just couldn't understand. Ivy always tried to tell her the hesitation people showed was because they were twins—not because she was blind. But Lily knew better and just wanted to be treated like everyone else.

"Zao!" someone called from the other side of the street.

Ivy returned the greeting, then leaned in closer to Lily. "It's old man Wong from the butcher's shop."

"Give Benfu and Calli my regards," the man called out again, and Lily waved her hand in his direction. She was surprised someone hadn't already stopped them. It was rare to walk anywhere without running into someone who knew their Ye Ye and Nai Nai.

"I still don't think this is a good idea, Lily. If Ye Ye finds out we did this, he's gonna pitch a fit."

Lily squeezed Ivy's arm as her sister guided her around a barrel of reeking trash. She could barely hear Ivy over the cacophony of street sounds around her. Cars and trucks zoomed by and even without touching, she felt carried away in the flood of other pedestrians crowding the walkways. She let the dinging of the bicycles horns, the chattering of pedestrians barking into their phones, and street vendors hawking their wares give her a moment to collect her thoughts for a response for her too-protective sister.

At sixteen years of age, they'd made it through most of their lifetime with very few disagreements. When a tragic fire had been the catalyst to have them taken from their birth parents, they'd landed in the care of a kind old scavenger and his wife—now their beloved Ye Ye and Nai Nai. Even as young as they'd been, it had made for a tumultuous time, but together they'd learned to deal with it.

But lately, they both seemed to be pulled in opposite directions. Little things were causing friction, stuff that normally wouldn't have been a problem. Lily felt it was because Ivy was growing more mature and wanted more freedom, though she knew her sister would never admit it. Lily hated being a shackle around her sister's ankle.

"Ye Ye and Nai Nai won't find out until it's too late for them to stop it. And don't think of it as begging—I'm going to put on a concert and if people want to pay to hear good music, that's up to them."

"Well, what if no one gives you anything? Then you're going to be in one of your moods all day," Ivy said.

Lily laughed. It was amusing how Ivy thought *she* was the moody one and Lily thought it was just the opposite—Ivy was definitely the one who slipped into her dark clouds when things didn't go her way.

"No, I won't. If I don't make any money today, I'll come back tomorrow and try again. It will just tell me I need more practice. Ivy, you know we need more money now that we have the new house and Ye Ye and Nai Nai are getting old. One of these days they aren't going to be around to make sure we're all okay. I have to find my way, on my own—or at least with your help for a while. Then you can go on and do what you want to do, without me." She hoped her sister didn't sense she was keeping a secret. The real reason she wanted to perform in front of strangers was because she was tired of being invisible. She needed to know and feel she was present in the real world. Her entire life she'd felt like an accessory on the arm of her sister, and she couldn't take it any longer.

"We need to get back by four o'clock or Nai Nai will have our hide," Ivy said.

"*Mei wenti,* stop stressing so much!" Lily was excited for the party. For a family made up of all adopted daughters until now, tonight was going to be a big event. Nai Nai and Ye Ye's long-lost biological daughter had finally been found and for the first time, they were going to be celebrating the birthday of her son—and their grandson—Jojo. All of them were supposed to help get the party ready. Lily didn't mind the extra work—so far Jojo had managed to steal everyone's heart.

Ivy didn't answer and Lily could feel her pouting. She hoped her mood wouldn't last long. She needed her sister's emotional support; this would be a fateful day. She'd find out if she really was good or if she was a total loser when it came to the violin. It'd be much different than playing for her family and neighbors in the *hutong.* Here, no one would know her or give her praise just because they loved her. Empathy in the public areas of China was rare to find. If they didn't like her music, they'd be sure to let her know. She felt a rock of nervousness settle in her stomach and took a few deep breaths.

Ivy guided her around the corner and Lily knew right away they were there. The sounds of laughter and festivity floated through the air. Her moment had arrived and she hoped the last year of intense practice sessions paid off. *Literally.*

Ivy watched her sister from a few feet away as she stood hidden under the low branches of a large banyan tree. The rain had stopped almost as fast as it'd arrived, so she didn't need the cover, but she didn't want people paying more attention to the fact they were twins than to her sister's concert. Anyway, it was her job to watch to make sure no one swiped Lily's money can and also to alert her sister if the *chengguan* came sniffing around. The officials who walked the city were supposed to be urban law enforcement and their job was to tackle low-level crime, but it was well-known they mostly harassed and blackmailed street vendors and beggars. Simply put, they were bullies. They shouldn't mess with Lily, since she wasn't technically begging, but Ivy didn't want to take any chances. She and Lily agreed if she saw one of them approach, she'd clap her hands slowly, then faster the closer he got.

So far Lily's music had brought in a few curious lookers but none had given any coins to the can. If Ivy could get away with it, she would've added a coin just to make Lily feel she was successful. But Ivy knew her sister would sense her—or smell her, or whatever it was she did to instantly know she was near— before she could get away with anything sneaky.

She had to admit, even without the clink of coins in a can, it was obvious Lily was doing a beautiful job of playing. With all of their Ye Ye's instructions, and a few months of his constantly correcting her bow placement along with hours and hours spent listening to recordings of classical songs, Lily had conquered the tremors her nervousness usually brought and had turned into quite the musician. Best of all was the look of peace that came over her sister's face while she was playing. Ivy was surprised to find she was actually a little jealous. She knew that was ridiculous, considering she had full vision and her sister was blind, but Lily had found something to excel at, and so far all Ivy was good at was being her sister's helper.

Movement in front of the bench where her sister sat caught her attention, and Ivy saw a woman stuff a rolled bill into the can at Lily's feet. Success! As she watched, others murmured their wonder at her sister and how she played without sight. Ivy felt her cheeks burn as she saw a few point at Lily's blank eyes and lean in to whisper. It embarrassed and infuriated her that people found Lily's motionless eyes strange. Why couldn't they just talk about how beautiful and serene she was? People were cruel and sometimes Ivy wished she couldn't see, either. Then she wouldn't have to witness the constant pity the sight of her blind sister evoked in others. Pity infuriated her.

Ivy heard a coin drop in the can and let herself get lost in her thoughts. Lily paused and then began to play a slow, somber song. Ivy immediately recognized it as Hu Kun's "Song of Homesickness." She sighed. The song was both a blessing and a curse. Since the first time Ye Ye had played it to teach it to Lily, Ivy had discovered it unearthed the memories she had of their mother. It was something she'd never told anyone, but the song somehow brought to mind the curve of the woman's face, a hint of a smile, and the lilt of her voice. The good things—before everything had turned bad. Ivy didn't want to talk about their past, and when her sister tried to bring it up, Ivy usually shut her down before much could be said. What Lily didn't understand was that Ivy held a secret. A secret that could change everything her sister felt for the woman who gave her life. But some secrets were too terrible to speak aloud.

Still, she'd always remember the words her mother had whispered in her ear as the police were dragging them away. *I'm sorry. Take care of your sister.*

So far, Ivy had done that. They rarely ever spoke of their time before Ye Ye took them in. They didn't even use their birth names. Doing so would've been too painful. But in the moments she didn't hate her, Ivy hoped her mother knew her plea had been heeded. Even as she wanted to forget the woman,

9

something in her still yearned to be reunited just once more so she could ask her *why* she'd done what she did that night. Lily may not have understood or remembered what went on, but Ivy would never forget.

The song ended and a few more people came forward to drop money into Lily's can. Ivy began to clap slowly. She didn't really see an official, but she didn't want Lily to tire out and, anyway, she was ready to go home. Lily quickly put her instrument and bow back in the case and buckled it, then stood waiting for Ivy. She clutched the can to her chest, smiling triumphantly.

"Come on, Lily, you did really well. I wish you could have seen their expressions."

"Oh, don't worry, I felt it," Lily said, grabbing Ivy's arm and moving with her toward the park gates. "Now, let's take it slow. I'm going to figure out the distance and landmarks so maybe next time I can come here without you."

"Lily, don't be ridiculous. You aren't ready for that yet." Ivy didn't know what was up with Lily lately and her new streak of independence, but there was no way she was going to let her try to get all the way to the park by herself. Traversing up and down the *hutong* alone was one thing, but taking on the city streets and traffic—no way.

She watched as Lily ran her hand along the concrete fencing surrounding the park, counting under her breath how many steps to each post, pausing to listen to the sounds around her and settle her sense of direction. She nudged her along, hoping Lily would get that idea out of her head.

They reached the intersection and Lily turned her head toward Ivy. "Don't lead me—I'll tell you when we should go."

"Lily, No! The traffic's terrible today, I'll guide you."

"No. Be quiet so I can listen." Lily turned her ear to the road and stepped out when she heard a slight lull in the traffic.

Ivy cringed but walked evenly beside her. Her sister was getting more stubborn every day. While the noise of pedestrians, car horns, and bicycles gathered around them, Ivy went back to her thoughts to take her mind off the looming vehicles as she let Lily win her tiny battle.

Chapter Two

Li Jin put the finishing touches on the birthday cake and poked in eleven candles. She could hardly believe merely months ago she and Jojo were alone in the world and now they would be celebrating his birthday with more than a dozen others. After so many years of being labeled as an orphan, she would never have predicted her birth parents would finally track her down. But here she was, suddenly—and miraculously—surrounded by family in a building that wasn't just a home for them, but had been converted to a shelter. Now Li Jin had her hands full taking care of not only her newfound family, but others from in and around town who needed a place to call home.

Coming to Wuxi hadn't been an easy decision, either. Li Jin had thought long and hard, but in the end her desire to have a real family won out over her long-held resentment of feeling abandoned. When Auntie Wan, the wise old woman she'd met a year ago when she'd been on the run from Erik, had taken her aside and reminded her of the old Chinese proverb, "Each generation will reap what the former generation has sown," Li Jin knew she needed to foster a change that would make her son's childhood much better than hers. She wanted to surround him with love and family, so hopefully he'd know very little of the pain of rejection she'd felt.

And Jojo had made the decision easier, as the few weeks in Hongcun getting to know his grandparents had brought out an obvious yearning in him Li Jin had never seen before. It wasn't so much that he *wanted* family—though he did—but it was plain to see he *needed* it. With the attention his newfound grandfather showered on him, Jojo had flourished.

So far the hardest part of their move was dealing with Sami. They'd bonded in Hongcun and pledged to stay together no matter what. It had taken some convincing, but Sami had finally agreed to join her in Wuxi and be a part of Li Jin's new family. But during the first few months of settling in, Sami had mysteriously turned up pregnant with no explanation to who the father was or even any clue that she'd been seeing anyone. Li Jin knew Sami was still struggling emotionally from her past, and she refused to judge her for her indiscretion. Sami had been on the receiving end of so much abuse in her life, Li Jin was determined to be her one unwavering source of support. Sighing, she still wished Sami would embrace their new surroundings more. With her sour attitude and unwillingness to get involved in any of the family events, she still looked miserable every moment.

Li Jin glanced at the table in the corner and smiled. Jasmine sat there, her brow creased in concentration over a sheet of paper as she drew the outline of a flying panda. The little girl had taken to following Li Jin everywhere and she couldn't say she minded. Jasmine was sweet and looked up to Jojo as if he were a big brother.

Li Jin put her finger to her lips and looked around the room. What else could she do to make the day special? Not only was Jojo getting a few red envelopes of money, but she'd also let her Baba know all his grandson really wanted was a yo-yo. One word was all the old man needed to hear and he was out the door and back in a flash, his wrapped gift taking center court among all the others. He'd also gotten Jojo a jade stone with the character for protection carved into it, to hang around his neck.

Now her Baba—*it was still so strange to have a real father*—had taken Jojo out to keep him busy while her new sisters decorated the gathering room. The sounds from both the family hall and the opposite hall that housed the shelter's residents all echoed around and surrounded her kitchen, which was located between the two. Li Jin never got tired of hearing the sounds of laughter and life around her. The party would be a great way to end a long week of hard work by everyone who'd lent a hand to the cooking, cleaning, and renovations of the place, but more importantly it would be one more event to cement her new family ties.

Some of their new residents would also join them and Li Jin hoped they'd feel comfortable. She'd stuck to tradition—other than the fancy cake—and made longevity noodles and steamed buns. The noodles, steamed in a savory stock of soy sauce, chicken broth, and sesame oil, were a tradition in Chinese families, as they represented long life. Jojo always enjoyed the challenge to eat the noodles without breaking them.

Li Jin put her hands on her hips and looked around the kitchen. *Her kitchen.* A safe place where she could use her hands and her taste buds to create comfort. She felt a sense of peace surround her. She'd finally found her calling.

Li Jin still thought it ironic she had found something to feel passionate about with the money she'd taken from her ex-boyfriend's drug cache the day she'd left him. She'd used it to buy an abandoned factory and, with her parents' help, they'd opened their own shelter. They'd named it Rose Haven, after the very first abandoned child who had come into her father's life. Li Jin looked around her kitchen and thought of Auntie Wan's kitchen in Hongcun, which had inspired her own. She'd tried to make the room just as inviting by repeating Auntie Wan's style of table, rugs, and decorations; she felt hers came close to carrying the same warmth she'd felt there. Although Moon Harbor had been strictly for abused women, Li Jin's place would be open to anyone who needed a home. Adults and children of any age; orphans, beggars, and even abused women could apply to live under their roof—but they had to agree to work as a team to make everything run. Things weren't perfect. The financial responsibilities were a challenge, but so far with small funds coming in from a few different areas, they were making do.

Li Jin still could barely believe the road her life had taken. The building that was once a shoe factory now housed at least fifty people who, like her at many times in her life, felt hopeless and alone. Some only stayed temporarily, until they could make other arrangements or be taken in by family, but others had nowhere else to go but the streets and were thankful to have a shelter they could count on long term.

With Nai Nai, Ye Ye, Sami, and all the girls pitching in, they were turning lives around and bringing hope back into once-empty eyes. Rose Haven was a family affair and, finally, Li Jin felt what it was like to be a part of a family.

"Li Jin?"

Li Jin looked up to see her mother come in, her arms full of red paper streamers. A line of girls trailed behind her, waiting for direction. Four of the six were now her sisters. Behind two teenage runaways were Ivy, Lily, and Peony, and all were eager to help. Little Maggi Mei rolled her chair behind them, smiling and ready for her orders. Li Jin was glad they'd arrived, as they needed to get the party done and cleaned up so she could start preparations for dinner. She'd discovered she loved cooking for so many, but it was indeed a challenge.

"Yes?" She wiped her hands on her apron and pushed a stray

hair behind her ear. Her mother came close and Li Jin inhaled the comforting scent of dough and freshly powdered babies that seemed to cling to her at all times.

"Come help us hang some of these, dear. I want Jojo's first party with us to be festive," her mother said, and smiled, her round face breaking into a million crinkly lines; a sight that in the last year of getting to know her own mother, never failed to warm Li Jin's heart.

She untied her apron and laid it across the counter. "Coming, Mama."

Li Jin wrapped her arms around Jojo and squeezed. Finally the party was winding down and he had settled into one spot to practice his yo-yo. Unlike the first cheap yo-yo he'd received from her ex so long ago, this one was top of the line with flickering lights and even sounds.

"Are you happy, *erzi*?"

Jojo nodded and squirmed to get loose. Li Jin could see him glance over to see if Sami was watching and she let go. Her son had a crush on Sami—that was obvious. Who could blame him? Even with the extra weight she'd put on, with her silky long hair and perfect features, Sami was still very beautiful. And Jojo didn't want to be treated like a little boy, especially in front of Sami.

"What was your favorite part of this day?" Li Jin asked as she sat back, forcing herself to stop touching him.

Jojo looked through the room and pointed into the brightly lit kitchen. Li Jin thought he would say his yo-yo, his cake, or that he got to eat as many noodles as he wanted, but no—her son never ceased to amaze her.

"Well, I think my favorite part is now I have two grandfathers."

Li Jin looked at the two men sitting at the table, then at the scene around her. She was happier than she'd ever been and was almost afraid to allow herself to feel it. It was all just about too good to be true and that scared her. What if it was all taken away?

But even if it all ended today, she'd at least know she was a changed person from having known them all, even for a brief moment. She'd already let go of her anger against her parents once she understood she hadn't been abandoned, but instead was abducted.

She'd even released the need for vengeance against her ex, Erik, for the way he'd abused her. Now she felt lighter and even healthier. She'd never imagined she'd be a part of such an amazing family, and looking toward brighter beginnings was easier now. Her father had taught her a valuable lesson in forgiveness. He'd allowed his own father—her grandfather—to be a part of Jojo's celebration. The old man had come bearing gifts, but most importantly, he'd begged Li Jin's forgiveness for his part in disrupting her life. She'd given him that easily. Li Jin was tired of holding grudges and *eating bitterness,* as the elders liked to say. And after all, it wasn't him; it was his wife, Li Jin's grandmother, who had taken her from her parents and sent her to an orphanage.

Two grandfathers—yes, Jojo was right. Now her Baba and Lao Zheng, father and son, both old men, sat together drinking oolong tea and somberly catching up on what they'd missed in each other's lives. Her mother fluttered around them, sometimes sitting for spells, then getting up to do something else for one of the girls. Even she had forgiven the old man, after telling him they didn't want to ever speak of his wife in their home, and with her mother's words of mercy, anyone could have seen the obvious change in Lao Zheng.

"You sure do, Jojo. Two grandfathers, a grandmother, and a whole pack of aunties! Now if you get into trouble, I have plenty of people who will help me straighten you out."

Jojo smiled up at her and she knew it was unlikely she'd ever have to call on anyone for help. Jojo had handled the last year of changes like a champ. No one would ever guess the trauma he'd been through. His grandfather had even pulled strings to get him a new *hukou* so he could attend school in Wuxi, and he was catching up on all he'd missed. Li Jin expected to hear he was at the top of his class any day.

Their moment was interrupted when Sky walked into the room holding a small red horn. In the few months since Sky had been introduced to her by Linnea as a close friend, Li Jin had come to realize how kind he really was. Jojo obviously agreed, as he jumped up and ran to him, giving him a high five. Li Jin felt her cheeks turn red when Sky looked over Jojo's head and waved to her. For some reason, her stomach fluttered a little every time he looked at her. Even with his strange sunset-orange flared pants and green shirt, he looked well put-together, and she wondered how he had such good style. She gave him a slight wave and then turned her attention to Jojo. From the corner of her eye she saw Sami sit up straighter and knowing the girl like she did, Li Jin could bet the sour look had been replaced with a seductive smile.

"Jojo! Happy birthday, little fellow." Sky handed him the horn. "Sorry I'm late. I had a hard time finding just the right gift for you."

Li Jin watched as Jojo looked at the horn, confusion clouding his face.

"This is what you found? A horn? Um . . . thanks, I guess. What's it for, Sky?"

Sky put his hand on Jojo's shoulder and guided him toward the door. "You'll see. Come out here with me."

Li Jin and the rest of the girls followed, with her parents bringing up the rear. Jasmine found her way to the front of the pack and held her arms up for Li Jin to hold her. She did, though the girl was really too big to be held, and they all gathered outside. They waited as Sky disappeared around the front gate, then reappeared pushing a blue bicycle.

"Well, I'll be," her Baba muttered beside her. "I should've thought of that myself."

"A bike?" Jojo happily squealed as he ran to Sky. "Really?"

The bike was obviously brand-new and Li Jin couldn't believe Sky had spent so much on her son's birthday. She and Sky had hit it off when they'd met, but a bicycle was a bit extravagant when they weren't even related.

"Sky, you shouldn't have done that," she said over Jojo's excited babbling.

He winked at Li Jin, acknowledging her concern, then held the bike for Jojo as he climbed on.

Li Jin felt her face warm and looked away from Sky. She peeked over at Sami to see if she'd noticed Sky's wink. If she had, it hadn't affected her, because she was now staring at the ground, her face emotionless.

Jojo straddled the seat. "Let me go. I want to try it!"

Sky beckoned Li Jin over. "We need to let your mama decide who is going to teach you to ride this thing. Hold on a minute, little buddy."

Li Jin put Jasmine down and started toward Jojo, then stopped. She turned back around and looked at her father. "Baba, I think this one falls under a grandfather's job title. You show him."

A big smile worked its way across Benfu's face and Calli gave him a gentle shove. "Go on, Benfu. Help your grandson. And don't you get hurt, you crazy old man."

Li Jin and her mother watched as Benfu took Sky's place behind Jojo and supported the back of the bike while the boy pedaled. The other girls called out directions, each of them offering their own advice on the best way for him to learn.

"Faster, Jojo—you need to keep up your speed," her Baba said, already panting from the exertion.

Sky clapped his hands and Li Jin could tell he was proud that Jojo loved his gift so much. He turned and caught her looking at him and smiled.

"That was really nice of you. *Xie xie,*" she said, reaching up to put a hand over her scar. She wished he wouldn't look at her so intently. She used to be pretty. Before Erik's last beating.

"Li Jin, you don't have to thank me. Just being included in the family gathering is thanks enough. And Linnea and Jet paid half—they were really upset they couldn't make it."

"I'll call her after the party." Li Jin already knew ahead of time it was unlikely her sister Linnea could make it, as Jojo's birthday fell the same week as the town festival and her shop was hopping from all the tourists. Jet had even been roped into working for her to help the customers with their purchases and arranging deliveries when needed. Li Jin understood completely and thought it nice Linnea still wanted to be a part of the celebration by helping with the bike. They were all spoiling Jojo.

"Benfu, you need to stop!" Calli called out. "You're going to wear out your lungs!"

Li Jin smiled at her parents. It was endearing to watch her mother constantly hover over the man she still called *her sweetheart.* Her baba's tuberculosis was under control, but her mother still watched him carefully to keep him from exerting himself. The two never wavered; they were the happily-ever-after story she knew she'd probably never find in her own love life.

"He looks just like he did at sixteen," Lao Zheng said, shaking his head and chuckling as he leaned on his cane and squinted through his glasses.

Li Jin and the others laughed and watched her father running behind Jojo, a proud grin on his face while his old legs struggled to keep up and his ever-rounded belly jiggled up and down. Even Sami let a few giggles slip at the funny scene they created moving recklessly down the sidewalk. Jojo's squeals of laughter could still be heard as the two disappeared around the corner.

"Lily, play something happy," Ivy said.

Lily sat on the curb and held her violin against her, then began to play a lively song. Poppy, the first to feel the music, started hopping up and down. Peony ran to her and took both her hands to help her dance. Jasmine joined in, twirling round and round them. Even Lao Zheng caught the excitement, and he made his way to Jasmine, slowly kicking out a jig with one hand on his hip and one on his cane.

"Lao Zheng, don't hurt yourself," her mother called out as she stood behind Maggi's chair, patting the little girl's shoulders.

Li Jin looked at Maggi and her heart lurched. Maggi sat watching, a small smile playing on her lips as she clapped her hands to the beat. Li Jin wished Maggi could shed the chair and, just once, be as mobile as her sisters. Suddenly Sky stood and covered the distance to Maggi's chair, then bent down and scooped her up.

"Let's dance, Maggi Mei," he said, cradling her in his arms as he moved to the center of the lane, then whirled her around in the midst of her sisters, causing her to erupt in a fit of giggles.

The sound of Maggi's infectious laughter filled the air, and Li Jin looked over at her mother, only to see the glistening in her eyes as she watched her daughters. *This is what I was missing in my life for so many years—love and laughter,* Li Jin thought as she jumped up and ran to Sami, pulling her up to make her join in the fun.

Three hours later, Li Jin sat on the curb under the dim, flickering streetlamp and dangled her hand in the dirt beside her. The silence, broken only by the song of the cicadas and the whir of Jojo's bike wheels, settled around them. Sami and Sky kept her company watching Jojo, while everyone else had gone in at dark to get ready for bed.

"'Scattered petals, withered leaves, a foolish man gives his heart to thee.'" Sami stood and stretched her arms over her head, then looked down at Li Jin.

"That's beautiful, Sami. What is it?" Over the last year Li Jin had gotten accustomed to Sami quoting poetry, but she still found herself impressed at how much she had memorized. She was truly a smart girl. She'd also heard Sky quote poetry before—suddenly it hit her how much Sami and Sky had in common.

"It's appropriate, that's what it is," Sami answered, snickering. "It means the party is over for all you flower children."

She looked knowingly at Li Jin, then turned her attention to Sky. "Do you want to take a walk?"

Li Jin knew Sami was making fun of their names besides trying to make Sky uncomfortable with her sarcastic remark about a foolish man. Even though Li Jin had decided to continue being called by the name she'd always known, her parents still slipped occasionally and called her Dahlia. Sami told her it was silly to have a house full of flower names and a man who referred to them all as his beautiful garden. Li Jin disagreed; she thought it was a sweet gesture by her parents.

Sky looked to Li Jin. "If you'll come along, Li Jin?"

Li Jin glanced over at Sky, then looked back at her feet. "No, you two go on. Jojo and I are going in shortly."

Sky looked back to Sami and shook his head. "No thanks, Sami. I think I'll stay here and watch Jojo a bit longer."

Sami shrugged her shoulders and walked away, but instead of going for a walk, she went directly into the house. Li Jin didn't comment on it, only continued to draw circles in the soft dirt.

"What are you thinking of, Li Jin?" Sky asked, his voice barely loud enough to hear.

That was another thing she liked about him. He was always quiet and calm, despite the flamboyant outfits he wore. She couldn't help but compare him to Erik, and she was amazed that with Sky she could relax and know she didn't have to watch his every move. In just a short time, he'd become a good friend. And she hadn't had a lot of those.

"I was thinking about how much our life has changed. This is the first birthday Jojo has been able to celebrate with someone besides me."

If it was anyone else, she wouldn't talk about her past. But Sky was the most nonjudgmental person she'd ever met. Over the last few weeks, she'd shared more with him than perhaps she should have. He probably thought she was a terrible person since other than a few places, she'd basically lived on the street for years. But even if he did think badly of her, she couldn't change the past.

"He looks happy, doesn't he?" Sky said.

Looking up, Li Jin watched as Jojo rode in circles on the pavement, and she felt a swell of contentment. Since their new home used to be a factory, they also now owned a parking lot. Her father had roped off half for public use to bring in additional revenue—and some of the residents made great parking attendants—but the half near their building was all theirs, and Jojo loved having a place to ride his new bike.

"Yes, he is happy. And I can't believe how fast he was able to learn to ride that thing!"

Sky chuckled. "You know what they say—the Chinese were born knowing how to ride a bike. And your father wasn't about to quit until he knew Jojo had caught on."

Li Jin looked at Sky. "I'm sorry you brought the bike but didn't get to be the one to show him how to use it."

Sky shook his head. "Li Jin, I didn't think a thing about that. I was just glad to see Jojo bonding with his grandfather. As much as I love being here with all of you, I'm not really family."

"Don't say that, Sky. From what I hear, you practically are family. And you should have brought your mother and grandfather with you. We would have enjoyed their company."

"Bai Ling doesn't socialize much these days. And my grandfather is set in his ways—he rarely leaves the shop. But thank you, I appreciate you inviting them. That means a lot."

"Linnea says under the grouchy act he puts on, your grandfather's no fiercer than a sleeping panda bear."

Sky laughed. "I don't know about that. I do know he took a shine to Linnea and treats her like his own. But they still battle it out with *xiangqi* and cards. Your sister is kind to take time out to keep him company, especially since she's so busy planning her wedding now."

That was true. Linnea had come by several times in the last month and delegated duties to the rest of them, things to get off her own list. The girl was amazing—her career as a designer was soaring, she was keeping up her own apartment, and she'd even declined her future mother-in-law's offer of hiring a wedding planner so she could do it all in her own style. It was a year away but there was a lot to do. Li Jin didn't know how Linnea kept it all under control but she was happy for her and Jet.

Because her parents' old house was so tiny, Li Jin, Sami, and Jojo had stayed with Linnea in her apartment until they'd all moved into the new place. While there, she'd come to realize what a cute couple she and Jet were. It was amusing and even a little inspiring how they appeared to be completely in love on the evenings that Jet visited and stayed for dinner. She wondered if Sky had originally liked Linnea—maybe romantically. After all, they saw each other frequently since her store was located across from the store that Sky managed for his grandfather.

That was an interesting thought. One that led to Sami. Li Jin would love to know what he thought about her best friend. "Sky, now that we're alone, can I ask you something?"

"Sure."

"What do you think of Sami?"

Sky didn't look at her. Instead he used his foot to kick at the small pebbles at his feet. "I'm not sure. She's hard to figure out. I don't know that I've heard her speak more than a few words. And I can't gauge her moods. She never shows any sort of emotion."

"True. But she's just been hurt a lot in the past. It makes her wary of people but she's different under that hard shell—a lot more human than she lets others see. She just needs someone to make her trust again. And you have to admit—she's gorgeous."

He nodded but he didn't look up. "*Dui,* gotta give her that. She's really pretty."

She wished Sky would say more. Did he like Sami? Because Li Jin was starting to get the feeling that Sami had her eye on him. Maybe he'd be good for her. If Li Jin could get Sami to open up and allow someone in, she just knew it would completely transform her. All Sami needed was someone to love her.

She returned to swirling her fingers in the soft dirt. They sat in the quiet, watching Jojo ride around until his face was barely distinguishable under the dim streetlights.

"Watching the evening unfold from here is so different than anywhere else I've ever watched it," Li Jin said.

"How so?"

She looked out toward the street at the few people left walking by. It was obvious which people were strolling as an evening ritual, and which were on their way to somewhere important. It was all in the abundance or lack of determination in their pace.

"Before, in different places I've been, I have always wondered what it would feel like to be part of a family. I spent a lot of time alone—then when Jojo came, it was just the two of us. Now, I know when I go in for the evening, I'll be surrounded by people who care about me. It's not just us against the world anymore. It's strange."

She suddenly wished she hadn't shared so much again. He'd always had a family. He'd never understand the complete feeling of isolation she'd lived with for so long. She saw Jojo's bike veer wildly when he swatted at the mosquitos around him. If she got him through the day without blood or tears, it'd be a miracle. She stood and stretched, realizing how tired she was.

Sky took her cue and stood, too. "Well, the bugs are getting bad out here, aren't they? I'd better go. Do you want me to help you get Jojo's bike in? I brought a chain and lock for it."

"No, we can manage." Li Jin stepped forward a few steps. "Jojo! Time to put it up. You need a bath for school tomorrow."

Jojo mumbled his reluctance under his breath but began to bring the bike in.

"Well, I'll see you tomorrow then," Sky said.

"Tomorrow?"

"Yes, aren't you all painting the animals on the walls in the playroom?" he asked.

Li Jin nodded. Linnea had offered to come and draw animals, and Li Jin and the other girls were going to help her fill them in with color. So far they had a small handful of children and wanted their gathering room to be stimulating and fun, anything to cover the drab walls.

"Yeah, but I didn't know you were coming."

Sky laughed. "Linnea already roped me into it. She said my sense of color was needed, but I think she just needed more muscle. I'm bringing the paint, and wait until you see what I've got planned."

Li Jin smiled. She knew now that she need not worry about how it would turn out. With Sky's unique sense of style, the room would probably be the most colorful in the house.

Jojo pulled up and hopped off the bike.

"Night, Jojo." Sky held his hand in the air and waited for his high five.

"Night." Jojo slapped his palm, then took off into the house, sending a small cloud of dust up at Li Jin as she stood holding the bike upright.

She shook her head. "Off to the next thing, I'm sure." She looked at the door he'd disappeared through and saw Sami staring at them before she moved out of view.

Sky took the bike from her and guided it into the small shed at the back of the lot. He pulled the lock from his pocket and attached it, then handed Li Jin the key. In the dirt at their feet a few pesky dandelions competed for space. Sky bent down and picked one up, then stood and pushed it through the hair over Li Jin's ear.

"Tomorrow then."

She smiled and looked away quickly. "Tomorrow."

Chapter Three

Benfu struggled to carry a load of diapers as he followed Li Jin into the storeroom. Jasmine trailed behind them, silently moving her lips to a song only she could hear. He dropped his boxes on the stack of others, then pulled his hankie from his pocket and wiped the sweat from his brow.

Li Jin had already stacked her load and stood waiting for him. His grandson's birthday a week before made Benfu wish he were at least a decade younger. He hated the way his body refused to cooperate with the pace of his mind.

To add to his worry, he'd awoken from a dream of ants crawling up his bedpost. Though he tried not to allow old superstitions to dictate his thoughts, he couldn't help but hope the symbolism the ants brought of impending bad news was wrong. Things were going well in his life and he wanted it to stay that way.

"We've got enough diapers to last until the end of the month," he said, counting the boxes once again. "That was a nice gesture those foreign ladies made. Their donated milk powder should last awhile."

"*Dui,* unless we get more babies," Li Jin answered, a twinkle in her eyes. "Have you seen our latest dark-eyed beauty? She's a keeper."

Benfu knew the one she spoke of—an infant brought to them after being found in a box outside the hospital. Poppy was no longer their youngest, but now a big sister. In their home, all incoming children were considered part of the family. The new child—Coral, they'd decided on—had a cleft lip, but even so, her complexion and beautiful eyes more than made up for that slight imperfection. He didn't know how just yet, but they'd find a way to fund her operation when she met the minimum age and weight requirement. For now Coral was being cared for by Auntie Rae, an elderly woman who'd found her way to the center after being on the streets for the last several years. After only a few weeks with shelter, regular meals, and a purpose in life, the woman already looked years younger and was proud of her position as an *ayi* to Coral. Benfu knew soon they'd probably give the woman another child or two to be in charge of. If his daughter would let them loose from her own care, that was.

It was obvious that Li Jin had a soft spot for all babies, but especially those abandoned. She wouldn't be able to turn any away. He'd try to counsel his daughter about taking on too much but what room did he have to talk? He'd taken in dozens of baby girls over the years. He couldn't turn any away, either!

"That reminds me, how's Sami doing?" he said as he began arranging the boxes in a neat stack.

Li Jin sighed. "Other than her feeling under the weather every day, I guess she's okay. I just wish I knew what keeps triggering her dark moods. She's told me a lot about her past but I think there's something more—something she can't speak of."

Benfu patted the top of a box and he sat on one next to it. "Have a seat, Daughter."

Li Jin sat down. Benfu took a deep breath.

"Jasmine, run on into the kitchen and see if your Nai Nai is ready for your lessons."

The little girl smiled at him, then turned and scampered out of the room and down the hall. Benfu shook his head. She was still his little shadow and had yet to say one word since the day she'd joined their family. He sighed. Maybe one day. He gave his attention back to his eldest daughter.

"Your mother and I have been talking. Now don't go getting all riled up, but we think maybe Sami needs to see a doctor."

He watched as Li Jin wrinkled her forehead, a look he'd come to know that she used only when deeply confused.

"She's seen a doctor several times now. You both know that."

"Not that kind of doctor, Li Jin, though I'm glad you finally talked her into seeing to the health of the baby. We mean someone she can talk to about her problems. I don't think you see what we do, and I'm afraid the girl might be in more serious trouble than you know."

Li Jin shook her head. "Baba, Sami's been through a lot and I think that if everything goes well with the birth, she'll be much better. A child will give her a purpose in the world, rather than just floating from place to place as she's always done. Just give her some time. Please."

Benfu watched his daughter closely. If she really believed a child would cure the girl of her constant melancholy, then she was hiding her head in the sand. And it was more than sadness he saw in Sami—it was something darker.

Li Jin continued. "And anyway, I think she and Sky would make a great couple. He'd be good for her. I'm working on that, too."

"She doesn't think I've noticed, Li Jin, but she's been sneaking out after we've gone to bed. She doesn't come back until just before daybreak sometimes." He avoided telling his daughter that he'd walked in on Sami cornering an uncomfortable Sky in the storage room the week before. The poor boy had looked relieved to see Benfu and had fled as if the emperor's ghostly army were after him.

"I know. I woke up one morning when she was climbing back into bed and she said she just likes to sit outside in the quiet. She's fine, Baba."

"And she does an awful lot of sleeping during the day, Li Jin. I don't think she's too fond of anyone here, except you."

"She's just shy. But you're right that she is really loyal to me." Li Jin moved away, fidgeting and turning her head.

Benfu wanted to say more. *Aiya*, he *needed* to say more. But it was such a touchy subject with Li Jin. She was overly protective of the girl and in her eyes, Sami was just temporarily troubled. But Benfu suspected her problems went much deeper than Li Jin knew, and from what he knew of Sky, even that young man wouldn't be able to break through Sami's icy wall.

"We should have a few more rooms available by the end of the month, too. Maybe we can move Sami out of your room, to give you both some privacy."

He was hopeful that they'd soon be done with all the construction. Already they'd filled six of the extra rooms and were busy converting one of the attached warehouse areas into smaller living accommodations. The walls were up and he'd arranged for a group of unemployed laborers to finish working on the plaster. They wouldn't be paid much, but in these times, a little would go a long way, and they were eager to get the job. Overall, the place was coming along fine. Even their first priority—a small private bathroom with a shower and bench for Maggi—had turned out much nicer than they'd thought possible with their tiny budget. Yes, their new house was fast becoming a home. And they even had another empty building once used for storage that they could expand into later, if needed. He still couldn't believe the terrible shape the property had been in when they'd first seen it, but luckily his daughter had seen the potential. It had been priced at just enough to cover the overdue government taxes, and he felt they'd gotten a steal.

Sometimes Benfu missed their little house where they had lived for so many years, but then he realized it wasn't the place that made the memories—it was the people. And anyway, his father was tickled to death to have moved into their old house and it was a perfect fit for the old man. Calli was glad to have someone in it who would take great care of the garden and flowers she'd left behind, and his father had even made a lot of new friends in the *hutong*.

"Your idea to have one adult to live with and oversee three children per room was perfect. And now that we're holding competitions for the cleanest kept rooms and children, everyone is working hard and things are falling into place," Li Jin said.

Benfu nodded. It was an easy plan. People wanted to have a home—that much was simple. Putting good, honest men or women in charge of rooms and giving them the responsibility of a few children in their care only brought out the best in people. And the ones who'd come forward so far were just regular citizens down on their luck. A few of the older women were simply forgotten mothers of grown children, left to fend for themselves without the security of a husband or family. It was a second chance for them and feeling needed was helping them improve their outlook on life again. The old women—and even some men—were seen smiling ear to ear, or laughing as they pushed their charges around the center to eat, play, or finish chores. The transformations of their personalities once they felt needed were amazing.

Li Jin sighed. "I wish the rooms could be bigger, but I understand. It's just that there isn't much space to accommodate people's belongings."

She was right, Benfu thought. Each room was outfitted with two sets of bunk beds and a small table and chairs. They had splurged on small propane heaters for each room, too. But that was enough and probably more than most of their residents were accustomed to. And material things were overrated—even Lao Tzu taught "to have little is to possess and to have plenty is to be perplexed." In all Benfu's years, he'd also known this to be true. In his life, he'd been blessed to have shelter, food, warmth, and most of all, family. That was all he needed and he'd tried to give the same to others out there walking the world alone. When Li Jin had approached him with the idea, her selflessness had made him proud. In their room that night as they'd marveled over it, Calli had only nodded and told him of course his own daughter would've inherited his altruistic tendencies.

So far their shelter hadn't been approved as a welfare institution, meaning Benfu couldn't get the financial help he really needed, but they were making it work with donations—and a bit of bargaining and bartering. Li Jin had mostly used her own money to buy the property, but from what he could gather, her funds were also running low. He wasn't even sure why her ex-boyfriend had given her the large amount of cash, as she'd said, but that wasn't his business. He was just glad the purchase meant she'd probably be in his life permanently.

"Did you hear that our latest teen boy, Jace, is painting the inside of a store downtown and they're going to pay him with some secondhand high chairs?" Li Jin smiled triumphantly.

Benfu was taken aback. Jace's disability usually resulted in others not giving him a chance in the outside world. That was how he'd come to them—tired and defeated from life on the streets, being ostracized because of his deformity. It hadn't taken long for word to spread about their shelter, sending the boy their way. And despite only having one arm, he could paint! He was a really nice kid and the best painter they had. Benfu was proud that Jace had taken it a step further and gone out to see what he could do to help his new family. He was proving his loyalty, and a few high chairs would come in handy, to be sure.

He held his hand in the air and Li Jin slapped it. "See! That's what I'm talking about! We all use our strengths and connections and we can make this place run like a finely tuned machine."

More than anything Benfu was full of pride. Rose Haven was even more special because he and Calli were creating it with their daughter. It was Li Jin's dream they were helping her fulfill. The project had given him a burst of energy he hadn't had in a long time, and it was amazing how coming together to make decisions, organize rooms, and run the place had done wonders to mend the fractured relationship with their daughter. Slowly Li Jin was beginning to trust again, and Benfu hoped with all his heart that one day she'd forgive all the transgressions that had been done to her. He didn't have much time left on this earth—he was an old man—but he planned to spend it helping this daughter and the others get on track for their futures. He knew he needed to slow down. His aching legs told him so each morning as he traveled his usual route to look for abandoned or lost children on his side of town. The gods had been good lately—no recent discoveries of little ones left behind.

"You're right, Baba. And it doesn't even feel like work. I love being able to spend most of my day in the kitchen."

Benfu tucked his handkerchief back in his pocket. "Well, this new place sure has made your Mama happy, too. I thought she'd never leave that tiny house. But she flutters around here like a mother hen making sure everyone's doing their chores and showing up for classes. You'd think she would stop at teaching the children their reading and writing, but now she's even making more quilts and knitting winter gear. I've never seen her so busy."

He watched as Li Jin smiled. If he never saw another beautiful thing in the world he wouldn't care, as her smile was worth more than any sunset or painting he'd ever laid eyes on. He couldn't get enough of seeing it.

"Li Jin, do you think it's time for you to get out a bit, maybe make some new friends?" He didn't say what he really wanted to, that maybe she should get acquainted with some gentlemen her age.

Li Jin laughed. "No, I have more than enough to do for now."

Benfu stared at her. He couldn't help it; he wanted his daughter to know the kind of love he'd known with her mother. Didn't every father want that for his child?

"What about male friends? Wouldn't you like to start seeing what's out there? I have a few comrades who have unmarried sons your age."

Li Jin's face fell. She busied herself over a box, pretending to count diapers.

Benfu felt ashamed that he'd pushed too hard. Her romantic life—or lack thereof—wasn't a subject they'd yet broached. Li Jin had been through a lot, and he only wanted to see her happy, but he'd have to be more patient. "Li Jin, I'm sorry. Is it still too soon?"

She nodded, not turning around.

"*Hao le, Nuer*. But remember, every broken heart will lead you to your true path. You are only stronger for the trials you've been through. In time, you'll see the lessons you are meant to learn from them." And speaking of time . . . that reminded him of something else. He looked down at his watch.

"Isn't it time for my grandson to get home from school?"

Finally she stood and turned to him, a small forgiving smile on her face. "I think he's already in the courtyard with the girls."

Lily stood at the counter, an apron wrapped around her waist. She'd carefully braided her hair to keep it out of the way, and now she was ready to go. She could feel Ivy staring holes in her back and wished she'd go on and do something else. She didn't mind if Ivy wanted to learn, too, but she didn't want her there if she was just going to be difficult. Behind her, she could hear Maggi sitting near the table, chattering about new ribbons for the spokes of her wheelchair. Beside her, Jasmine colored quietly, but Lily still knew she was there by the soft sounds she made as she moved around.

"Have you already washed the celery?" Li Jin asked, then reached around her and gently put the large knife in Lily's right hand.

"Yes, that was the easy part." Starting at the handle, Lily explored the length of the knife with her left fingers, taking care not to touch the sharp side of the blade.

"Okay then, the onion is a few inches from your knife, and the bunch of celery beside it," Li Jin said, her voice low and calm. "Maggi, you come over here and wash the carrots, please."

"The onion is at one o'clock and the celery at three. You need to use a clock reference so she can visualize it. But she's going to cut her fingers off," Ivy said. "Don't let her use that big knife."

"No I'm not, Ivy. I can do this." Lily was trying to keep her voice steady; she didn't want to fight with Ivy in front of Li Jin. It was embarrassing. It was ironic that her sister was usually her most vocal advocate when people tried to treat her differently because of her disability, but lately she was worse than strangers. She of all people should know that Lily just wanted to be treated the same.

"Ivy, I'd like for you to pull the chicken off the bone, but first cut off the feet and drop them in the broth. You can find the bird in the wire basket in the sink."

"Gross, I don't want to touch the chicken." Ivy wrinkled her nose and stepped back from the counter.

Lily snorted. "She doesn't want to learn to cook, Li Jin. She's only in here because she thinks she has to watch out for me." Lily used her left hand to line up the onion, then began to chop through it carefully, feeling along the top of it each time to see where to make the next slice. It was no secret that her sister acted as if she were Lily's own private security guard.

Lily heard the sound of a zipper; then Li Jin spoke. Lily noticed her voice didn't change a bit, even after Ivy's defiance.

"Ivy, please go to the corner store and buy two dozen pears and a bag of dates. We'll have a special dessert tonight."

"Steamed pears? What's the occasion?" Ivy asked.

Lily stopped her carving and turned halfway around. "The occasion is I'm going to put together the entire evening meal and I want to finish it right. Please go, Ivy," she pleaded.

"Fine, Lily, but if I come back and you're missing digits, don't cry to me." Ivy's voice trailed off as she left the kitchen.

Lily breathed a sigh of relief. She felt Li Jin move to stand beside her.

"Wow, is she overprotective or what?"

"She's bossy," Maggi added under her breath.

Lily smiled weakly. "I know. But she means well. It's just that she's been perfecting her position as my bodyguard all our life. It's embarrassing."

She felt Li Jin's arm move around her shoulder and give a quick squeeze. "Don't be embarrassed. You should feel honored to be loved that much. Your sister would move mountains for you, I'm sure of it. It's hard for her that you are learning to be more independent. Here, stop cutting for a minute. See, you left some of the onion peel on." She guided Lily's fingers to the half of the onion still intact. "Feel the papery peeling?"

Lily did feel it and began to pick at it until it came off. She felt Li Jin put another onion on the board. She didn't tell her, but she'd been peeling and chopping onions for a while now in her Nai Nai's kitchen.

"Remember, we're doubling everything to feed so many people. And Sky's coming over, too. If it was just a small family, you'd need to scale way back. It's important that we learn how to make a lot of soups for the upcoming winter as there might be weeks we won't have rice."

Lily nodded, taking in everything Li Jin said. She loved the kitchen, and best of all, Li Jin didn't treat her differently just because she was blind.

"Looks like you'll be doing the chicken-picking, so hurry up with the onions and celery," Li Jin said, and Lily heard her sweeping the floor. She really wasn't going to help her cook! Lily felt a rush of anxiety, then pushed it back.

"I can do it." She'd been helping her Nai Nai in the kitchen for years, though admittedly it was with only simple tasks. She was ready to move on and show everyone she wasn't helpless.

Li Jin's broom stopped moving. "I know you can. And while you're cutting up vegetables, I'm going to tell you how to make the steamed pears. I'll only say it once, so you'd better listen up. In a real kitchen, everything moves fast and there's no time for teaching it twice."

Lily perked up to full alert as she pushed her pile of onions to the corner of the cutting board and felt around for the celery. Li Jin sounded confident in her abilities to do this, so she'd have to show her new sister she was right.

Li Jin talked as slow and steady as she swept, and Lily took in every word. "First, you'll need to wash and dry the pears. Then you'll need to cut the tops off. After that, take out the cores and make a small slice at the bottom so the pear will stand up straight."

Lily began carefully chopping the celery while listening to the instructions for the pears.

Li Jin continued. "Then put two teaspoons of honey in each pear along with one date; then put the top back on the pears. You'll steam them for thirty minutes. That's it, Lily, and we'll have a delicious dessert that everyone will think I made—if Ivy can keep her lips zipped."

Lily laughed. Li Jin really was getting to know her sister well.

"And don't tell her we were talking about her, Maggi Mei." Lily reached over and felt for the girl, then ruffled her hair.

"I won't," Maggi said.

Lily heard Li Jin rustling around again.

"Here's ginger, chives, and some other herbs—all grown from my own windowsill. I'll even let you add my own version of Chinese five-spice powder. I used to hear about this stuff in every foster home. Now I've made my own with a strong addition of dried ginseng. After we let them rave about dinner for a few minutes, we'll tell them who the real chef is," Li Jin said.

Lily tried to suppress the smile she felt spreading across her face. It wouldn't do to look so proud. She moved her knife even faster to cut the celery; she was getting the hang of it and couldn't wait to tackle the chicken, and the pears. Tonight was going to be her show, this time a performance without a violin propped under her chin.

Chapter Four

Li Jin pushed the hair back away from her eyes and joined Sami on the sidewalk. The walk from the old factory—their new home—to the street leading to the local shops of vegetables and other staples was short. It was after dinner and in their neighborhood while many people were settling down to prepare for bed, Sami was like a bubbling pot of water on the brink of boiling over.

"Where do you want to go?" Li Jin asked. She was bone-tired, but Sami had pleaded with her for some alone time and after all, everyone had been competing for her attention lately, leaving not much for Sami.

"I don't care—anywhere that we don't have a bunch of your family members or any of the others in the house tailing us," Sami answered, waddling quickly up the walk.

She sounds bitter, thought Li Jin, and that concerned her. She wouldn't admit it to her father, but she'd also noticed lately that Sami was even moodier than usual. She knew one thing for certain; Sami's moods were getting worse the closer her due date came. Everyone in the house avoided her as much as possible, afraid to set her off. Li Jin was relieved that today her mother had shooed them out, offering to spend the evening with Jojo and get him into bed. No doubt she hoped a few hours away would settle Sami a bit.

"Sami, what's going on with you? We're finally alone, so talk to me. We've only got about a week to go and you haven't prepared anything for the baby. We need to get things ready!"

"I don't want to talk about that right now." Sami guided Li Jin to the curb where a taxi sat waiting for its next fare. "Let's go have a drink, Li Jin."

Li Jin stopped. Sami never wanted to talk about anything—that was the problem. Or at least it was one of the problems. Along with sleeping too much and having huge mood swings. One day she was euphoric, the next so sad she looked suicidal. Li Jin couldn't keep up anymore. "I don't want to go have a drink. I have to get up at five in the morning to start preparing breakfast for two dozen hungry people. You shouldn't be drinking, anyway."

Sami opened the taxi door. "Just one drink, Li Jin. One. You do everything for everyone else—can't you do anything just for me anymore? We'll just go down to Kiko's and have a drink, then come home."

Li Jin had never heard of Kiko's, but maybe it would be a good idea to go somewhere with Sami that would make her comfortable enough to talk. Li Jin was tired of walking on eggshells around her and they needed to get some things straight.

"One drink, Sami. And mine is going to be cola. You can order juice." She climbed in and slid over to make room. "This Kiko's place better not be in the red-light district."

Sami got in and Li Jin watched the smirk spread across her face. *The girl loved to get her way.* Sami told the driver where to go and he took off, sending all of them backward in their seats from his heavy foot.

"It doesn't matter where we go, I just want it to be you and me again, like it was in Hongcun."

That disturbed Li Jin. She looked at Sami and saw the girl was completely serious.

"Sami, the only reason it was just you and me at that first shelter is because Jojo was taken from me before we got there. I was never meant to be there alone."

"You weren't alone, Li. You had me," Sami said quietly.

Li Jin fell silent. She didn't know what to say to Sami anymore to make her understand that there was room in her life for *everyone*. She watched out the window at the crowds of people that got thicker the farther they went from their own corner of Wuxi. Many were still probably trying to get home to their families, tired from their long days. The electric scooters and pedestrians all competed for their piece of space in the narrow bicycle lane that ran parallel to the busy street. The vendors took up the sidewalks with their street stands, and they moved quickly to pack up, their early-morning masks of cheeriness and goodwill removed to reveal their exhaustion and impatience.

The driver finally stopped in the middle of the block. From what Li Jin could see, there were bars and clothing shops lining the street, but they weren't too far from the red-light district. The neon sign in front of the small building marked Kiko's flashed, a few of the bulbs burned out but the others a tacky pink.

"You want to go *here*? Have you been in there before?" Li Jin asked. She really wished she could turn around and go home.

"Yes, I've been here before. Come on." Sami opened the door and jumped out.

Li Jin could see a sudden change in her as soon as they stepped onto the colorful street. Sami looked more alive, full of anticipation. She was practically jumping up and down, she was so excited to be there. Li Jin handed the driver the fare before following Sami out.

They entered the bar and Sami led her to a small booth on the far wall. There were only a few others there, a couple playing pool and a few locals who sat in purple velvet chairs around a small table, sharing a huge platter of French fries. On the other side of the long mahogany bar, a tall young man was drying a glass with a ragged towel.

She followed Sami. The music was loud and Li Jin didn't recognize it but guessed it was one of the new Hong Kong superstars that were always on the radio.

They sat down and a waitress came over.

"*Ni hao,* what can I get you?" The girl pulled the pencil from behind her ear and a pad from her pocket.

"A cola for me, please," Li Jin said, and smiled. The girl didn't even look old enough to be working, much less in a bar. She held her tongue and didn't ask her what her situation was. While she'd love to give the girl some advice, she had to face the reality that she couldn't save everybody.

"Suntory," Sami answered quickly.

"No, she wants orange juice," Li Jin said, giving Sami a scolding look.

Sami returned her look with a glare, then directed her attention back to the waitress. "Don't bring me juice. I want beer."

Li Jin reached for a piece of popcorn from the dish on the table. She wasn't hungry, but she felt awkward arguing in front of the girl.

"Okay . . . an orange juice and a Suntory." The girl looked at Sami's stomach, then quickly back down at her pad. She scribbled, then headed back toward the bar.

"Sami, can we have a serious talk?"

"Again?" Sami said, looking around quickly, her attention everywhere except on Li Jin.

The way she was acting made Li Jin think of Jojo when he was too excited and having trouble concentrating. Sami looked ready to spring at any notice of action. It was obvious that first of all, her mood was all over the place, and second, she had been at Kiko's many times before.

"Do you like living here in Wuxi?"

"Not really, but it's just temporary, right?" Sami said, finally looking directly at her.

"Temporary? What makes you think that, Sami?" Li Jin was confused. Didn't spending all her money on their new home mean anything to the girl? Did she think she'd just up and leave it all behind?

"I thought you and I were going to take a trip?" Sami's face changed and suddenly she was back to looking moody and withdrawn.

"I did tell you that I'd go with you to your hometown, Sami, but that was before I met my family—and before we knew about your condition. Can't we let all that go and just enjoy a new start?"

Li Jin watched as Sami's face turned hard and unyielding. "No, I can't let it go. And you shouldn't, either. I want revenge. And don't you want to make Erik pay for everything he did to you, too?"

Li Jin sighed. "Well, I think *you* should go to see about the sister you left behind, Sami. But I can't come with you. I have too many responsibilities now."

The girl returned with their drinks and set them on the table. "Fifteen reminbi."

Sami looked away and Li Jin pulled the bills from her purse. She wasn't happy about it, as she needed to watch every penny, but someone had to pay and obviously Sami didn't have any money. The waitress took her money and went back to stand at the bar.

Li Jin lowered her voice. "Sami, listen to me. About Erik . . . once and for all, I don't want to ever see or talk to him again. He's out of my life and it's going to stay that way. Erik is dangerous and I don't want him near me or Jojo. What did you think I could do to him?"

Sami gave a sly smile and Li Jin felt a shiver of foreboding. She wished now that she'd never told Sami all about Erik and the things he'd done to her. Sami knew everything—and that could be disastrous.

"I have plans for Erik, just like I do for my father and uncle. When I'm through with them, they'll never hurt another little girl again," Sami said, glaring into the space above Li Jin's head.

Li Jin reached across the table and grabbed Sami's wrist, bringing her attention back to her.

"No, this has to stop. Erik can make big trouble for me and Jojo. He dragged me into doing things I'm not proud of, Sami. Things I don't want my family to know about and definitely things that can get me thrown in jail. Just let it be."

A well-dressed businessman approached their table and smiled down at Sami. "Care to share a drink?"

"*Zou kai,*" Sami answered. She barely looked at the man, dismissively waving her hand in the air at him.

Li Jin was embarrassed. She didn't want to be approached, either, but the guy looked nice and she felt bad for him and knew he'd really be embarrassed if he could see the swollen belly Sami kept hidden under the edge of the table.

"Thank you, but maybe another time," Li Jin answered to soften the blow, even though he clearly wasn't interested in her. He wandered off quickly, with red-tipped ears.

"See, Sami. You're a beautiful woman. You attract attention everywhere you go. Why don't you let yourself enjoy life again and just forget about this revenge trip you keep hanging on to?"

Sami shook her head. "It's just an illusion. Just because they see pretty on the outside, they think a woman will be sweet on the inside, and that's not always the case, Li Jin. Or sometimes they just hope to use me and my pretty face. I'm done with men and wish they wouldn't approach me at all. I'll use *them* if *I* want something. I just wish I had the scar you have on your face, then maybe they'd leave me alone."

Li Jin took a long sip of her cola. Sami knew she didn't like to talk about her face—she was just trying to get a reaction, but Li Jin wouldn't give it to her. Sami had a serious chip on her shoulder about men that she might never get over. It was clear she was bored with her new life and was craving more action. Li Jin hated seeing her so unhappy, and the honest truth was she just didn't think family life and the day-to-day operations of the center were going to be enough for Sami. She was unsettled, and Li Jin wished she knew how to make it right.

"What about you, Li Jin? Are you going to fall for the crap that some man will feed you?"

"What do you mean, crap?"

"A man will say anything to win you over but they all only want one thing."

Li Jin reached up and touched her scar. "Sami, I doubt we'll have to worry about that. What man is going to look past what Erik did to me? I wasn't much to look at before but now I'm almost nothing."

"What about Sky? I see the way he looks at you," Sami said in a teasing voice.

Li Jin felt the heat rush up her neck. "He's just being nice. I don't think he really thinks of me like *that*. But back to you—you have a chance at real love if you'd learn to let go of your past hurts. There is possibly someone out there just perfect for you."

Sami rolled her eyes at Li Jin, then drained her beer and beckoned for the waitress to bring her another. Li Jin slapped her hand on the table and the empty bottle wobbled, almost tipping over before Sami reached out and steadied it.

"Now you're crossing the line, Sami."

"I'm just relaxing, Li. *Dan ding.* Chill out with me." Sami laughed, throwing her head back. "Anyway, maybe I'll take Sky for a little test run, tell you how it goes?"

Li Jin didn't even look up. That comment didn't deserve a response, and she couldn't keep up with Sami's moods tonight. And she sure wasn't going to sit and watch the girl get drunk. Sami was acting like a spoiled brat. Li Jin needed to get out of there before she said or did something that couldn't be taken back. She stood and put a ten-reminbi bill on the table. "I'm going home, Sami. I have to get up at the crack of dawn. Please be careful coming home."

"That place means more to you than I do, Li Jin." Sami's smile disappeared and she stared down at her empty bottle.

"No, Sami, it doesn't. But I care about the people who live under its roof. And I care about you . . . too much to sit here and watch you act like this."

On her way to the door, Li Jin walked past a couple making out in a booth. She was going to need a hot bath to feel clean enough to climb into bed tonight.

Li Jin wished she'd skipped the long, hot bath and gone straight to sleep before everything had gone wild in the Zheng household. Just as she'd drifted off, Sami had returned and jerked her awake, reeking of alcohol and crying with the pain of her labor. They'd now been at it for hours and it didn't feel like much progress had been made. It was too late to get her to the hospital; a home birth might be common in the country, but most city women were frightened of childbirth and scheduled their Cesarean sections way ahead of time.

Sami screamed again, making Li Jin jump. She could see the veins in her neck bulging, and worried Sami would faint from the exertion. The room around them was a wreck. Sami had gone through it like a madwoman once the contractions got unbearable. Li Jin had finally gotten her mother to help calm Sami enough to get her undressed and into the bed.

"We should've taken her to the hospital, Li Jin. I tried to tell you," her mother whispered, wringing her hands at the foot of the bed.

"No!" Sami screamed. "No more hospitals!"

Sami squeezed Li Jin's hand even harder. The contraction passed and she flopped back on the bed, gasping for breath. She was already exhausted, her strength having been drained in the last four hours of struggle.

"What is she talking about?" Calli said. "When has she been in a hospital?"

"I don't know." Li Jin sat next to Sami and stroked her forehead. It was covered in sweat and her hair was pasted around her face. She looked horrible, and Li Jin was worried Sami was going to let her hysteria get out of control and that it might hurt the baby.

Li Jin pleaded with her. "At least let us call someone, Sami. We aren't midwives. You might need a Cesarean." Li Jin couldn't believe they'd gotten into this predicament. Sami had returned from the bar well past midnight and woke her to tell her she was in labor. She'd refused to go to the hospital and because she was staggering around reeking of alcohol, Li Jin had relented. But now she wasn't so sure she'd made the right decision.

"No. No. No," Sami chanted, then sat up and began rocking back and forth.

Li Jin looked to her mother. "Mama, please *do* something. She's in so much pain."

Calli had just peeked under the sheet and she straightened, her face a mask of concern. "Hand me those trash bags, Li Jin. It's too late for a hospital—I see the head crowning. She's going to have this baby *right now!*"

Li Jin helped her rip open a few large bags and tuck them under Sami's bottom half. She flashed back to her own labor so many years ago. She'd been alone in the world, surrounded by strangers in a small hostel room. Those girls had helped her bring Jojo into the world and it wasn't a pleasant experience. She knew this would also be hard, but like with Jojo, so worth it once Sami finally held her baby in her arms.

"Are you sure you can do this, Mama?"

Calli ran out of the room. Sami wailed and yanked at her hair. Li Jin reached over and stopped her, then smoothed the tangled locks. She lowered her voice and tried to talk soothingly, "Sami, you need to calm down. You're going to be a mother tonight!"

"Get. It. Out. Of. Me!" Sami spat out through gritted teeth.

Calli returned with a sharp knife. When Sami saw it, she shrieked and tried to push herself farther back against the headboard.

"It's just to cut the cord, child! Stop it. You are going to terrify the girls in the hall. They already think you're dying, the way you've been carrying on."

"I *am* dying, old woman!" Sami screamed.

Li Jin could see that Sami didn't care whom she frightened, or that the entire family was up and pacing the hall from worry.

Sami's only concern was to fight against the intense pain that consumed her.

Li Jin felt sweat break out on her own forehead. She was scared. Sami was so small. Her petite frame looked unnatural with the huge mound she'd carried for the last few months. Li Jin knew it had to be difficult for her to go through childbirth. She crawled onto the bed and behind her friend, bracing herself against the headboard with Sami directly in front of her. She put her arms around her and reached down to grab her under the knees. She pulled Sami's knees up even with her own.

"Okay, this is it, Sami. We'll do it together. I'll help you push."

Sami whimpered like a small child. "You won't leave me alone, Li?"

"No! Come on, I've done this and you can, too. When Mama says push—you bear down and push with all your might. I've got you back here. We're about to have you a nice, healthy baby, Sami. You're going to be a mother!"

"Noooo . . . ," Sami wailed, throwing her head back.

Calli draped the sheet until it was propped over her knees. Sami tried to push it down again and Li Jin pulled her hand back.

"Leave it, Sami. Mama has to be able to see."

"Ivy!" Calli called out toward the door. "Get in here and get the baby blanket ready. I need you."

Ivy ran in just as Sami began another contraction. She looked from Sami to Calli and up to Li Jin, her eyes huge with fright. Li Jin lowered her voice to try to calm the girl.

"It's okay, Ivy. Just help Ma—"

She was interrupted by Sami's most bloodcurdling scream yet. She could feel the waves the contraction made as Sami writhed in pain, her head thrown back onto Li Jin's shoulder.

"Stop holding your breath, Sami. Breathe." Li Jin blew in her face until Sami gasped.

"Push now!" Calli yelled, her head disappearing under the sheet. "Hard!"

Sami bore down and her face turned a mottled purple as she pushed.

Li Jin helped her pull her knees even closer to her chest. "Push, Sami. This is it, it's almost over. Push as hard as you can!"

Sami pushed one last time; then her body shuddered and went limp against Li Jin. The baby was out.

"You did it! I've got her!" Calli called from her end of the bed. Li Jin could hear the tears in her voice.

"Her?" Sami asked with absolutely no emotion. "It's not supposed to be a girl."

So far Ivy had only stood there helplessly but with Sami's hurtful words, she looked up and locked eyes with Li Jin, her mouth dropping open. The long-ingrained cultural preference for males in China was a sensitive one in their home. Calli passed Ivy the child and after staring at her in awe for a moment, Ivy used the corner of the blanket to wipe her tiny face.

"Shhh, Sami. Just be glad you have a healthy baby girl," Li Jin murmured in Sami's ear. The child let out a loud cry and Li Jin felt tears of relief wet her own cheeks.

Sami shook her head adamantly. "I don't want a girl."

"Hand me the knife, Ivy," Calli said. "And Sami, I don't want to hear any more of that kind of talk. Motherhood is a blessing, and if the gods hear those words, they'll take this one away."

Sami turned her head toward the wall, ignoring everyone around her as she slipped into one of her moods.

Li Jin had never heard her mother so cross. She watched as Calli cut the cord, releasing another baby girl into the world, a world where she would surely face a lifetime of struggle because of her gender. It shocked her that although Sami had suffered most of her abuse because she was a girl, she still fell right into the age-old tradition of wanting only a male child. Those attitudes needed to be abolished. She looked down at the little infant. *Maybe soon, little one . . . maybe soon, things will change.*

"Okay, Sami. You aren't done yet. It doesn't look like you'll need any stitching, but push some more and let's get you cleaned out." Calli shook Sami's knees, breaking her out of her stare. "When you're finished, we'll put the child to your breast so she'll know who her mother is."

Li Jin felt a shiver of foreboding as Sami shook her head. "I don't want to. Let someone else feed her."

It was going to be a long night. Li Jin disentangled herself from Sami and climbed from the bed. She was soaked with sweat, weak, and felt as if she'd just given birth herself. Her legs wobbled as she struggled to stand upright. Finally, she got her footing and stood straight.

"Can I help you, Mama?" she asked, cringing at the bloody mess on the bed, thankful they had spread out the plastic bin liners.

"No, I got it. This placenta will need to be boiled and made into a broth. Sami can drink it to improve her nursing milk. You look over that baby and make sure everything is where it's supposed to be. We might need to take her down to the clinic." Her mother gathered up the corners of the plastic and tied it all in a knot, then carried it out of the room.

Li Jin was glad from the reprieve. She'd much rather deal with the infant than the mess the child had left behind in her journey out of her mother.

"Here, Ivy, let me hold her. I'll clean her up and make her a bottle." Li Jin looked down at the perfect infant who mirrored her mother's exquisite features. She gave a low appreciative whistle. "Sami, are you sure you don't want to try feeding her? These first moments are important for bonding."

Sami shook her head. "No, and tell your mother not to waste time boiling that mess. I won't need it."

"Okay, but this little one is going to be just as gorgeous as her mother." Li Jin left the room, ignoring the glare from Sami as she watched them handle her daughter.

Chapter Five

enfu stood at the head of the table and tapped his chopsticks against the glass. All around him the room buzzed with chatter and laughter in celebration of Sami's child's one-month birthday. His heart was full as he scanned the room filled to every corner with people he loved. Toward the back, Auntie Rae caught his attention, waving and beaming with pride, showing off baby Coral's first tooth. It wasn't hard to see as there was such a gaping hole where her top lip should be. But no one paid any attention to the imperfection; instead it was impossible not to be drawn to the baby's shiny black eyes as they danced with excitement from all the attention. Benfu held up his hands.

"*Anjing.* Quiet please!"

He was satisfied that his daughters and the other residents stopped talking and looked to him. Even Jace put his finger to his lip and encouraged little Poppy to hush. It was a special day for Sami's child. Though they couldn't afford to have a big party at a local hotel or restaurant, they would still celebrate the baby's birthday in their own way. Even without a lot of money, the ceremony would be complete with red eggs to symbolize the renewal of life, and Li Jin had worked for hours on creating intricately designed turtle-shaped cakes to wish the baby a long life.

His eldest daughter wasn't the only one who'd worked hard to make the day special. Ivy, Lily, Peony, Maggi, and even little

Jasmine had spent hours making and hanging red lanterns, giving the room the air of celebration they felt the baby deserved. Benfu was proud of his girls; they were all so selfless.

He gestured toward Sami and her daughter.

"Today this little one is one month old and we will be giving her a name. A name her mother will choose." Benfu nodded at the girl. If Sami were home with her family, more than likely the child would've been given a milk name upon her birth—something temporary until the one-month party when the baby's grandparents would have done the honor of choosing her official name. But today, unless she said otherwise, it would be up to Sami to give her child a name that would honor her future.

He saw Calli head over and take the Zheng family book from the cupboard. They'd talked about it the night before and even though Sami's baby wasn't officially family, they were going to add her to the book. Li Jin and Sami were so close, it was like they were sisters, and if Sami would allow them, they'd consider her and her child as family. So far she had resisted their attempts to embrace her. And if he had to guess, with the way Sami had been treating her child for the last month, the baby girl was going to need family. Even now, Sky held the baby in his arms as Sami sat alone in the corner, picking at her nails. The lad had rocked the baby to sleep, and Benfu was touched at the way he had softly sung to her, unafraid of looking less than manly.

Sami stood and went to Sky. She took the baby from him, tossing down the embroidered blanket that covered the tiny red set of clothes she wore—the blanket Calli had worked nonstop for weeks to have ready for this special day—and it fell to the floor. Sky picked it up, shook it off, and folded it over his leg.

Linnea reached over and plucked the blanket from Sky's lap and held it up. "Look, Jet, another masterpiece made by my Nai Nai."

"And my Maggi Mei made a matching pillow," Benfu said, pointing to the end of the table where Maggi sat in her wheelchair. She beamed from ear to ear and held up the small embroidered pillow from her lap. On it Maggi had sewed a panda, complete with shiny black marbles for eyes.

"Whoa, Maggi! That's some nice work! Maybe one day you'll be making baby stuff for us," Jet joked, then put his arm around Linnea and squeezed.

Benfu smiled at the two lovebirds. Despite a few obstacles—one being Jet's mother—they'd really stuck it out together in the last year, and to see his Linnea so happy was a comfort to his soul. With her vintage shop and Jet's business degree, the two would go far and she'd be one daughter he'd never have to worry about.

Benfu watched Sami straighten the baby's clothes and took a deep breath. The tiny garments reminded him of long ago when his own daughter was snatched from his life. Li Jin had insisted that her own unused one-month outfit be worn to erase the bad luck of that terrible day. The clothes fit Sami's baby perfectly, almost as if they'd been made for her. Benfu looked at his Calla Lily and nodded, giving her an encouraging smile. He hoped today would be the salve that finally soothed the wounds from Li Jin's abduction.

"Wake her up!" Ivy called out, and clapped her hands. The other girls and residents joined her and Benfu saw the baby flutter her eyes until they remained open. She didn't cry—he'd give her that. She was a tough one and it was a good thing, as Benfu didn't see much motherly love coming from Sami. This baby girl was going to have to be strong in spirit.

"I say we call her Quchong, the name our elders gave the newborn girls," Sami said, a defiant look coming over her.

Benfu wanted to cross the room and shake the insolent girl

but instead he shook his head. The name literally meant maggots in the rice and was given to baby girls by farmers who only wished to have boys. "No, we'll have no girls under this roof considered unwanted. Give us another name."

Sami sat down and held the girl in her lap. "I have no other name. Li Jin, you can name her."

Li Jin got up and went to them. Sami scooted over on the bench to make room for Li Jin to sit down. When she did, Sami passed the baby to her, then went back to studying her nails.

Benfu caught Calli's eye again and knew what her look meant. Sami was an unhappy girl, to say the least. But today was the baby's day and he'd not let her own mother ruin it. Naming a child was a very important part of their future, and even if they couldn't afford to pay a traditional name-finder, the child should still have a name that was picked especially for her.

"Okay, Li Jin. What name do you have for this little beauty?"

Li Jin held the baby up until she was looking her straight in the eye. The baby's head bobbled back and forth. Li Jin quickly caught her behind her neck and steadied her.

"What should your name be, little one? You sure are a pretty girl," she said to her, then laughed when the baby smiled back. Even from a distance, Benfu could see the child's dark eyes sparkle at the sound of his daughter's voice. His daughter had spent more time with the baby than her own mother had, and an attachment between them was already showing.

Jasmine climbed down from her chair and joined Li Jin on the bench. She put her finger up and the baby wrapped her fat little fist around it, making Jasmine giggle.

"What do you think, Jasmine? Do *you* have a name for her?" Li Jin looked down at Jasmine.

Benfu waited hopefully.

Jasmine shook her head.

"Well, I think we all need a hero, so I would like to call her Lanying, our orchid hero. What do you think, Sami?" Li Jin asked.

Benfu clapped his hands together. Perfect. There weren't any legends involving a heroine named Lanying that he knew of, but maybe this little one would write her own story.

Sami looked up and shrugged her shoulders. "Fine with me. Whatever you want, Li Jin."

"Then she is officially Lanying, and we'll call her Lan," Benfu said. He wasn't sure what surname Sami would give her child, as she'd never even told them her own full name, so Benfu didn't address it in front of everyone. But they would need to know it for their records, and he hoped Calli would talk to her about it. He looked up to see his wife scribbling in their family book and knew she was already jotting down every detail for the child's new page.

As he watched, his girls took turns gathering around little Lan, bending to kiss her on the head. After watching the first few kisses and well wishes, Sami stood.

"I'm not feeling well. I'm going to lie down."

Li Jin looked up. "Oh, Sami. I'm sorry. Do you want to take Lan with you?"

"No, she can stay out here and enjoy her party." Sami turned to leave the room.

Benfu followed her out of the dining room and into the hall. Once again the girl seemed jealous of her own daughter. And she sure did a lot of sleeping. He would've thought she could at least stay awake for her daughter's birthday party. "Sami. Wait."

Sami stopped and turned around, her expression impatient. "Yes, Lao Benfu?"

Benfu pulled a red envelope from his pocket and held it out. It contained several hundred reminbi—much more than he could really afford to give away. "I know that if you were around your own family and old friends, you'd receive many of these. I'm sorry you are so far from home. But here is one that I hope you can use."

Sami looked down at the red envelope and Benfu was touched to see that tears filled her eyes. Finally, some emotion. She reached out and took it from him.

"*Xie xie.*" She murmured her thanks and turned away.

Benfu watched her walk down the hall toward her room, her shoulders down and her entire body slow and sluggish. He was worried about her and a part of him thought maybe she needed to find her way back home. Perhaps being around family would bring her out of the dark cloud she constantly buried herself in. He would talk to Li Jin about her again, and this time he'd make her listen.

Chapter Six

"Watch out, Lily. We're entering a disaster zone," Ivy grumbled as she guided her sister around another row of electric scooters. "Yesterday this whole block was cleared out, but today the bikes are back. *Aiya,* they don't give us any room to walk without falling into the street!"

It was expected. The local police took trucks around Wuxi every day and confiscated thousands of bikes parked illegally. People had to pay fines to get them back, but then the next day or so the trucks moved on to patrol different areas and the bikes were right back where they started. Ye Ye was saying more and more that there simply wasn't enough space in the city for all the commuters—bikes or cars. With their new place, they were no longer protected by the quaintness of Beitang. Now they were in the busier area and Wuxi was bursting at the seams. With all the new foreign companies coming in, expansion would only continue to happen until one day it would be in the leagues of Suzhou and Shenzhen.

Ivy tried to slow down, but Lily continued to drag her along, oblivious to the many obstacles in their path. Ivy was glad they lived on the quieter side of town, but even so they still moved within a constant state of chaos from so many people squeezed into such a tight space. There were times that Ivy dreamed of seeing the sparsely populated mountains and villages that others were able to visit on national holidays. One day—she swore to herself—one day she'd also have the money to travel and see the world.

Lily gave Ivy's arm another tug. "Come *on,* Ivy. We're wasting half the day just getting there. I don't have to move so slowly. You're supposed to be my eyes . . . so do your job."

Ivy could tell her sister was teasing her again. They'd called a truce only a few days ago after Lily had awakened screaming from another nightmare and Ivy had comforted her. Now each of them was trying not to set off the other. Ivy just wished that Lily would slow down. But almost overnight, her sister wanted to experience everything. For years she'd been content being sheltered because of her blindness, but in the last few months she'd turned into a different person. Ivy felt like she was losing her sister and she didn't like it. Without Lily, she was nothing and would serve no purpose in the world.

"Do you think there will be other musicians there?" Lily asked.

"I don't know. From what I remember of last year's festival, it'll mostly be vendors. I think the religious ceremony for the Wuxi founder, Taibo, was yesterday. But today they're having a huge erhu display. I saw in the paper they'll show how the instrument is made and even give lessons on how to use it." Ivy nudged her sister. "Want to learn a new instrument?"

"No. I've barely grasped this one. I sure don't need to move on to a new one."

Ivy knew that wasn't true. Her sister was a born musician and played like an angel.

They arrived at the bus stop just as it pulled up to the curb. Ivy guided Lily to get in line behind the others waiting to board. She was glad they were at the back so no one would shove them to move faster. They were headed to the Wuxi Wu festival and Lily had brought her violin, trusting it to Ivy for safekeeping.

With so many little street thieves around, Lily wasn't safe holding it.

Ivy wished they didn't have to go to the festival. They'd told Nai Nai they were going to help Linnea at the shop, and she hoped they didn't get caught in a lie. Lately in her quest for experiencing new adventures, Lily was getting her into too many possible snares.

Finally everyone in front of them had boarded the bus and Ivy led Lily to the steps. She quickly placed her hand on the handrail.

"We're at the door. It's three rungs. Up now."

Lily stepped up and paused.

"And again," Ivy said, coming up right behind her.

Lily stepped again.

"And one more time and turn left."

Ivy looked around the bus to see it was jam-packed. There wasn't an empty seat to be found. People looked at them curiously and Ivy felt her cheeks flush. It was obvious to them that Lily was blind from the white cane she carried, even if they hadn't noticed her eyes that stared out at nothing.

But did anyone offer up their seat? *No, of course not.* Ivy felt like cussing all of them as if they were dogs but she kept her voice even for her sister. "Lily, the bus is full. We'll have to stand." She guided Lily's free hand to a handgrip hanging from the ceiling. "Here, let me hold your cane." Lily handed her the cane and Ivy juggled the violin case as she folded the cane and tucked it under her arm.

"Hold on to the back of this seat with your other hand." She ignored the look of disgust the guy in the seat shot at them and held back the urge to tell her sister wasn't contagious. Instead she put Lily's hand securely on the headrest behind his neck just as the bus driver stomped on the gas, almost throwing both of them off their feet before they caught their balance.

Lily laughed but Ivy didn't. She bit her lip to keep herself from going up and knocking the driver upside his head for his careless driving.

The passenger who'd given them the disgusted look was now staring rudely at Lily. "So, can they fix her eyes?" he asked.

Ivy felt the heat rush up her neck.

"Um . . . my eyes are—," Lily started to answer, but Ivy put her hand on her shoulder and interrupted, directing her anger at the stranger.

"Forget about her. What about you? They might be able to fix her eyes someday, but you're out of luck because they can't fix stupid." Ivy glared at the man, daring him to say another word. Luckily he looked away.

Lily leaned her head toward Ivy. "You don't have to get so worked up, Ivy. It really doesn't bother me."

Ivy didn't trust herself to answer. Some people were so inconsiderate. And stupid.

A few stops later and finally the bus pulled up in front of the pavilion.

"We're here," Ivy said, and put her arm out for Lily to grab.

Together they got off the bus and Ivy led the way to the gates. All around them music blared and people crowded together, slowly moving through the many stands of foods and collectibles.

"I smell some good street food. *Mmmm* . . . is that turnip dumplings?" Lily said, shuffling along. She put her nose higher into the air and sniffed. "I can smell all the different treats, but tell me what you see."

Ivy looked at her sister and saw the smile on her face. She couldn't believe she wasn't overwhelmed. It was crowded, loud, and hot. But Lily was enjoying it! Her sister was nuts. She sighed. "I see too many people—that's what I see."

Lily laughed. "What else, grumpy?"

"Besides the hordes of people, there are vendor stands selling everything. Cricket cages, hand-carved whistles, stick candy— oh, there's a woman over there selling sunglasses." Ivy turned her sister in that direction. "Come on, we're getting you a pair."

Ivy hurried Lily over to the table and picked up a pair of knockoff Ray-Bans.

"How much?" she asked the vendor, a small woman wearing a huge red apron and a wide-brimmed straw hat to keep the sun off her face. The woman stood behind the table, straightening the rows of sunglasses.

"Fifty reminbi."

"Tai gui le," Ivy said. "These aren't even real!" She wasn't paying that, but she hoped the woman would come down to something she could afford. She was tired of all the stares Lily's blank eyes attracted. They'd never needed to shield her eyes before, but now that they were venturing out more every day, Ivy wanted her to have some privacy.

"You say how much." The woman put her hands on her hips, starting the bartering game.

"Fifteen," Ivy answered.

"Just forget it, Ivy. I don't need them," Lily whispered to her.

Ivy felt a rush of irritation. Leave it to Lily to wimp out. Her sister hated conflict, even if it was only a means of negotiation. Ivy thought briefly about the story their Ye Ye always told them when they asked how he'd chosen their names. He'd chosen her name because she was strong and stubborn like the vines growing on the side of their home. But Lily was named for her delicate and quiet nature, just like a lily swaying in the wind. She had to admit, he'd pegged them just right.

The woman took the sunglasses from Ivy's fingers and put them back on the table. "*Aiya*. You're too cheap. Go away."

"Fine. I'll give you twenty." Ivy was losing patience fast with the woman. How dare she think she could get a foreigner's price when it was obvious she was a local.

"*Hao le.*" The woman picked up the glasses and handed them to Ivy, holding her hand out for the money. She studied Lily's face. "*Aiya*, your sister, she looks just like you but she's blind, *dui*?"

Ivy ignored her question like she did every time she heard it. She pulled the money from her pocket and laid it in the woman's hands, then walked away, Lily beside her. They moved to a place out of the way and Ivy put them on Lily's face.

"Now you look like a celebrity." She'd used up a lot of her money, but it was worth it. She'd just have to put more hours in at Linnea's store to earn more.

Lily smiled. "You should have gotten some, too."

"You're the star, not me. So let's go find a place for you to give your concert so we can get out of here."

As they walked around the pavilion, the music got even louder until it was almost too loud to even hear each other. Gradually they found themselves enveloped by the crowd gathering around the stage.

"It's the Wuxi Dance Troupe. They're doing a number," Ivy said loudly, bringing Lily closer with her to read the sign that named the group and listed their accolades.

Ivy smiled when Lily started moving her head to the beat of the music. It amazed her how much more her sister got into the events around her when all Ivy wanted to do was go home and get out of the chaos.

"What are they wearing?" Lily hollered her way.

Ivy sighed. Even without their usual twintuition, she recognized the longing showing on Lily's face, and Ivy knew she wasn't going to budge until her curiosity was satisfied. "There are six women and they're wearing long yellow satin skirts, as bright as the sun. They have on Western-style hats—you remember the kind with the big bills that Ye Ye told us cowboys in America wear."

"What else? Are they pretty?"

"*Dui*, they're really pretty. They're wearing crisp ivory jackets trimmed in a pink as soft as the petals of a rose, and they have knotted lucky-tassels tied around their waists. All of them wear their hair long and straight. They look enough alike to be sisters!"

The girls all kicked, then jumped in unison, and those in the crowd yelled their appreciation at the precise choreography, some even whistling loudly. Ivy used her elbow to nudge back the couple moving in closer next to them. The crowd was getting thicker and she needed to get Lily out of the middle of it.

"They must be wearing slippers made of the softest leather. I can't hear their feet hitting the stage," Lily said.

Ivy nodded, forgetting for a moment her sister couldn't see her. She watched as one by one, each girl dropped to the floor in a dramatic dying pose until the last one did one more pirouette around the stage, then joined them, the music ending abruptly. The crowd erupted in applause. The perfectly synchronized movements were so mesmerizing—Ivy wished Lily could see them.

"Come on, Ivy. It's over." Lily was the first to turn away, and Ivy took her arm and together they continued on.

"Okay, we're at the resting park. Is this where you want to play?"

Ivy asked. They'd carefully worked their way through the rows of vendors, shows, and all the exhibits until they'd found the small grassy area at the back of the pavilion.

Lily listened to the noise around her for a second, then nodded. "This'll be fine. It's much quieter here. Take me somewhere I can sit."

Anywhere was quieter than the area of the festival they'd just left, but even here in the park area, Ivy was overwhelmed with the number of people spreading out picnic blankets, walking, flying kites, or just lounging around.

"At least here there aren't so many beggars, so maybe those with a little jingle in their pockets will help you out," Ivy said, thankful that most of those looking for handouts usually tended to stay around the busiest part of the festival, hoping for a more generous take for the day. She didn't begrudge them their efforts, as she knew without the interference of her Ye Ye, she and her sister might have easily been among them, begging for their dinner each night.

She looked around, trying to find a suitable place for Lily. Somewhere out of the sun would be good but the only bench in sight was already taken by what appeared to be another beggar—this time an old man. Ivy saw him lean over and pull a few pieces of trash from the can next to him, then grin when he shook a bag and discovered it wasn't completely empty.

She leaned her head toward her sister. "Lily, there's a bench about twenty feet in front of us, but someone already has it. I'm going to ask that man if he'll move. I still have a few coins."

They approached the man. Ivy decided to first try to play on his sympathies, even though it was usually something she didn't do. But Lily played better when sitting.

"Laoren, my sister cannot see. Could you be so kind as to let her have your bench to take a rest?" Ivy asked.

The old man shoved his hand back into his bag of seeds, grabbing a handful and pushing them into his mouth. The seeds that found their way out of his mouth were quickly plucked from his shirt and sent back to where they came from. It was obvious he was consumed with hunger—too consumed to think of offering a simple kindness. *"Bu."* He spat the word out and looked away.

Ivy sighed. "What if I give you a coin?"

That got his attention and the man quickly stood. Ivy pulled a coin from her pocket and tossed it to him, then led Lily to sit before someone else could slide in and grab the empty seat.

Lily reached up and pulled the violin case from Ivy. She held it to her chest for a moment, then placed it on her lap and fumbled with the brass openers. Ivy saw her hesitate, then look up at her.

"You can go walk around for a while. I'll do better if you aren't standing over me watching."

"Fine. I will." Ivy felt a rush of irritation at her sister's brisk dismissal. Lily was taking her new streak of independence too far. If she wanted to be that way, Ivy would just leave her to watch out for her own money—if she was able to earn any. Anyway, she wasn't in the mood to battle the emotions that Lily's songs always brought out of her.

She gave her sister one last look and turned away. She'd be okay for a little while. Maybe Lily would miss her and next time wouldn't be so quick to dismiss her. Ivy would just take a walk around the festival; then hopefully when she returned, Lily would be tired and ready to go home.

Lily heard Ivy walking away and could tell she was slipping into another bad mood. These days, anytime they went out in public, the atmosphere around Ivy turned heavy. Lily knew it was because of her blindness and she wished with all her might that her sister could come to terms with it. But instead, Ivy got angry because people stared and were curious. Which was one of the reasons Lily wanted her to leave. She didn't need the heavy vibes affecting her ability to play. Ivy didn't understand that playing for strangers was less about money than receiving the validation she craved. She wanted people to see she had worth in the world and wasn't just a blind girl dependent on her sister to guide her through life.

Lily was irritated with Ivy, too. Only the night before she'd tried to talk to her sister about their birth mother, but Ivy had refused to cooperate. Lily didn't understand why Ivy was so angry with the woman. They didn't even know why they'd never been returned to her care after the fire, so how could Ivy still be angry with her for all these years? It was clear that the unfortunate accident had led to their separation. Lily just wanted to be able to compare and maybe share any good memories they could piece together. But Ivy refused.

Lily took out her violin and laid the case open beside her. After her last concert, they'd figured out it was better to use the case to collect any donations. A bigger target to toss coins, and they could quickly grab the case and leave if they were in a hurry to take off.

Again today she'd felt the now-familiar sense of foreboding but shook it off. Nothing had happened the last few times they'd been out, so she knew nothing would happen today. It was just nerves, she told herself. She was a performer and all performers had stage fright.

Putting the violin to her shoulder, Lily felt a welcome wave of peace wash over her. Her body and mind knew what was to come. She picked up the bow and made her first swipe slowly, then burst into the sweet but sad song she'd been practicing for weeks. Slowly, she pulled the deep, mournful notes from her violin, the bow feeling like a feather beneath her fingers.

As she moved into the second section of verse, she heard a few people coming close to drop coins into her violin case and murmurs of appreciation. Their acceptance made her play even harder, and she dug deeper to find the emotions and pour them out of her fingertips and onto the instrument. She approached the crescendo and was lost in the storytelling of the notes. She didn't hear the small commotion until she felt someone jerk her arm.

"Who's there?" She tried to pull back but was gripped harder, this time a steely clamp around her upper arm.

"You're going to join the rest of them and be put somewhere out of the way," a strange man snarled at her as she was dragged forward.

Lily had never been manhandled before and it left her disoriented. "Please. My sister. Where's my sister?" She struggled to find the violin case around her but the man had already dragged her far from the bench. She held Viola and her bow tightly, scared he would try to wrench them away.

"Shut up. No talking. If you're lucky, you'll be released at the end of the day when the festival is over."

Lily felt panicked. Released? From where? Where was he taking her? She suddenly knew by the whispers around her that she had been caught by a *chengguan* officer. She tried to pull her arm back but he kept her close to him—close enough for her to smell his rotten breath and the stench of cigarettes. Her senses were knocked off balance and Lily lost her bearings.

How would Ivy find her if they took her away? She felt the first tears start to slide down her face and she began to tremble. What would they do to her? She stumbled again as her feet hit something; she wasn't sure what. If the man hadn't had such a tight grip on her, she would've fallen but instead he jerked her upright and cursed her for slowing him down.

"Ivy!" Lily yelled as loud as she could. Surely her sister wouldn't have wandered too far. "Ivy! Help!"

"*Anjing!* I said shut up!"

Lily felt a slap across the side of her head and her ear started to ring loudly. She immediately stopped struggling and walked easier. She didn't want to get hit again. If she passed out, someone would surely steal her violin. She cradled it close to her body and prayed that Ivy would be along soon to find her, before this animal took her too far away.

The officer half dragged, half walked her through the festival. Now that she'd calmed down, Lily could tell when they passed the stage, and then, by the smells, she recognized the path she and Ivy had walked through with the food vendors. Was he taking her completely out of the pavilion? Was she going to jail? She thought of Ye Ye and Nai Nai and how ashamed they'd be when they found out their daughter was taken away by a policeman.

He continued to escort her to what she thought was the entrance. The noise got less intense and the crowds started to be less packed, but then he made a sharp left, causing Lily to stumble again.

"How about some warning?" she said, realizing immediately that she'd also left her cane behind at the bench.

He ignored her and walked her for another few minutes until they came to an abrupt stop. Lily listened for some clue as to where they were, but all she heard was more people.

Then he released her arm and she stood still, waiting for him to speak. She heard a large chain rattle, then the creak of a heavy door. The officer grabbed her arm again and pushed her through what felt like an opening. What was it? They were still outside, so she couldn't understand where she was that would have a door. As she passed through, she tripped on what felt like a bar under her feet. The violin flew from her arms and she heard it skid across the cement as she reached out to break her fall. With both palms and knees slapping the cement, she heard others around her laugh loudly.

They were laughing at her. She felt her cheeks burn as she reached frantically around to find her violin. Where was it? Her fingers touched shoes, legs, and even what felt like small metal bowls, but she couldn't find her instrument. There were other people around her. What were they all doing there?

"Here. It's right here, child," an old woman's voice called from a foot or so away.

Lily felt her violin being put next to her hands, and the bow resting near her feet. She grabbed the instrument and quickly ran her fingers over every inch of it to be sure it wasn't hurt. Finally she breathed a sigh of relief.

"Where am I?" She reached out and felt what she thought were iron bars going from the ground all the way up over her head.

"It's a large metal jail cell, brought out just for us beggars."

"Jail? But how? Why? I wasn't begging. I was giving a concert." Lily moved her head left to right, trying to pick out if she could hear her sister's voice among the crowd outside.

"If you were taking money from strangers, you were begging. This year the local officials decided to put us all together behind bars so we can't dirty up their festivities. They say we're an *embarrassment* to the city."

Lily could still hear the music and crowd, though they were now some distance away. From the outside of the bars, she heard people pausing to comment on the plight of those imprisoned. Only rarely did she sense any compassion in their voices as they spewed their opinions and then moved on. Her face burned with shame and she bowed her head.

She hoped Ivy would be able to find her and straighten things out. She sat up on her knees, squatting in a more comfortable position. At least they hadn't taken her violin, and for that she was grateful. But the humiliation of being put into a cage like a wild animal was overwhelming, and her heart began to pound again. She'd heard the *chengguan* was cracking down on street begging, but to be imprisoned in public? What kind of cruelty was this?

The excitement built around her again and Lily heard the chain, then the door creak open. Another body was flung through and the door slammed. Their newest visitor was breathing heavily.

"*Aiya!* If I'd known this was happening here today, I'd have stayed on my own side of town," he said between ragged breaths.

"You aren't the only one. I thought the festival would be a great place to make enough for the whole week. Now my family will go hungry tonight," another defeated voice said.

Lily inhaled and discovered that she was indeed with some of the poorest of the poor. Her nostrils filled with the smell of unwashed bodies and musky clothing. She didn't want to judge but she also didn't belong with people like them. What if they tried to take her violin? Just when she felt she'd explode with a sob of fear, the door was opened again and another person was thrown in. The official—a different one by the sound of his much younger voice—barked at all of them to quiet down. She felt someone come near her.

"Lily? What are you doing here?"

She recognized his voice immediately. "Sky?"

"Yes, it's me."

She felt him slide close to her and put his arm around her shoulders. He smelled clean—comforting, even—and she inhaled his familiarity.

"Oh, Sky. I'm so glad you came. But how did you know I was here? Have you seen Ivy?"

She heard him hesitate. "Lily, I didn't know. They've thrown me in here for passing out brochures. I had no idea you were here. Where's your sister?"

Brochures? What was he talking about? "She walked away for a few minutes and the *chengguan* got me. I was only playing my violin, but because my case had donations in it, he said I was begging."

Beside her she heard a repetitive slap of metal against the concrete and felt something brushing up against her, back and forth.

"What is that?"

"*That* is begging. The old woman next to you has her bowl against the bars and is kowtowing to the people as they walk by. She's hoping her pain will get her some pity and a few coins." Sky squeezed her closer. "Well, don't worry. They'll let you go at dark. They've been doing this all week with the beggars. It's their new idea to clean up the city during peak tourist times."

"But what about you? What kind of brochures were you handing out and why do they care?"

She felt him tense up.

"Lily, I don't know if you know this, but I'm a Falun Gong practitioner. The government doesn't approve of it and they're doing their best to try to squash it out of the country."

She wasn't sure but she thought she heard everyone in the cell with them move to the far side after Sky's statement. She wrinkled her forehead. "Falun what? I don't understand."

Sky laughed quietly. "It's just a way of life. We use physical exercise and discipline of the mind to cultivate higher qi energy.

In simpler terms, it is a peaceful way of life completely opposite that of the cruel communist ways."

Lily shrank back. She wasn't into politics but she knew enough to never publicly bad-mouth the government.

"Sky, please shh . . . ," she whispered.

She'd always known that Sky and his mother, Bai Ling, were different. Her family had often teased him about his laid-back attitude and starry outlook on life. He was so different from other men his age. While most men were driven to gain success and money, he was always talking about peace and contentment. Now it all made sense. But was it some sort of cult?

Sky cleared his throat. "Lily, I can see those wheels turning in your head. Let me just say that this is not something scary. While we wait for either the sunset so you can be released, or your sister to come find you—whichever comes first—I'll explain it. Come on, let's lean against the bars. I'll hold your violin and promise you it will be safe."

Lily was physically and emotionally exhausted from her world being turned upside down. She reluctantly handed her violin to Sky, hoping he'd keep it safer than she could. She'd never admit it, but this time she was glad for someone to take over and tell her what to do. She let Sky lead her to the bars and she sat down where he guided her. He sat, too, and she laid her head on his shoulder, thankful that someone she knew was there with her. For the hundredth time since the official had put his dirty hands all over her, she wished for Ivy to come find her and take her home.

With the lingering aroma of fried tofu and the pork-filled steamed buns still teasing her senses, Ivy sauntered slowly along the lane to tables lined with yards and yards of the famous Suzhou silk. She admired the purses and pajamas, and trailed her hand along the smooth uncut bolts of every color and pattern imaginable. She wished she had the money to buy some of it for her Nai Nai and thought perhaps she'd return to find Lily's violin case overflowing enough that she'd want to splurge and spend some of it.

In front of her was another lane with racks of winter scarves, hats, and mittens. Ivy considered having a look but thought to peek at her watch first. *Aiya!* She'd been away from her sister longer than she'd meant to be. Surprisingly, once she'd started looking at all the pretty things for sale, she'd realized she hadn't gotten to linger like that in a very long time. Usually Lily was on her arm, putting her in protective and defensive mode. She felt a little guilty but she had to admit, she was enjoying some freedom, too.

Ivy turned around and headed back toward the resting park. She needed to hurry. Lily would be worried about her. She noticed that the crowd had really thinned out and many vendors were packing up their wares. She practically ran through the few remaining pedestrians and turned the corner, looking out over the hill toward the tree where she'd left Lily.

She wasn't there! The bench was there but instead of her sister, a small group of boys were lounging on and around it, one of them holding the violin case. She ran to them, looking all around to see where Lily had gone.

"Hey! That doesn't belong to you!" She reached them and snatched the case out of the hands of the biggest boy. He stood and she realized he was at least a head taller than she was.

"Give that back. I found it," he said, glaring down at her.

"It's my sister's violin case. Where is she?" Ivy held on to the case. She wasn't backing down. What had they done with Lily?

"I didn't see no girl 'round here. The case was layin' there on that bench."

"Liar." Ivy twirled around, looking in every direction. Maybe Lily had gone to the bathroom? She didn't see her near the public restrooms building, or anywhere else.

The boy jerked the case back and tucked it under his arm. Two of the other boys stood beside him. The three of them crossed their arms, defiance on their faces. They were a ragtag little group, but Ivy decided it wasn't worth getting bloodied to a pulp over.

"Fine. Keep it. I need to find my sister." She turned to go, then saw Lily's cane lying under the bench. She picked it up and folded it as small as it would go, then put it in her pocket. She started to leave.

"Hey—I saw your sister. She looks just like you, but she's blind, right?" one of the smaller boys offered.

She stopped. For once it didn't bother her to have someone point out that Lily was blind.

"Yes! That's her. Where did you see her?"

"The *chengguan* got her."

Ivy felt the blood drain from her face. Today she'd been so preoccupied that she hadn't even thought about the local officials getting her sister, even though she'd seen them all over the pavilion herding up the beggars. Just once she'd let her guard down and now Lily was in danger.

"Do you know where they took her?"

The other boy stepped up and laughed. "They got 'em in a big metal cell outside the North Gate. Last I saw, there was about fifty of 'em in there waiting to be released."

Ivy didn't wait for them to finish. She bolted forward, grabbed the violin case from the shocked boy, and kept running.

"Wait! Give that back!"

She ran harder until their voices were far behind. Holding the case close to her, she resisted the urge to shove everyone aside, instead zigzagging around vendors, a couple with a trailing toddler, and even a few seniors strolling along slower than turtles.

Struggling to catch her breath, she rounded the corner outside the North Gate only to see a line of beggars leaving the huge metal room. She bobbed around, trying to see Lily and as she got closer, she saw two officials pushing her into a white police van.

"Wait! Stop!" she cried, running faster.

One of the officials slammed the door and turned around. "What do you want?"

Ivy looked behind him and through the window. Sky was with Lily! She almost fainted with relief. He'd help her.

"You"—she bent over, grabbing her side with one hand—"have my sister. I'm here to take her home. She wasn't begging, I swear!"

The other official rolled his eyes, then went around and climbed into the passenger seat. The official in front of Ivy shook his head.

"She's not being taken in for begging. She was going to be let go, but then we discovered she was with the other one that was spotted handing out propaganda. He's a stinking Falun Gong follower and she's with him! She fell asleep lying on his counter-revolutionary shoulder!"

Ivy gasped. Sky was a Falun Gong? She'd read about Falun Gong in the newspapers and online when she surfed the web on Linnea's computer. And she knew without a doubt her sister had nothing to do with the forbidden practice. Sky—she wasn't so sure—but wouldn't be surprised if he was involved with it. She looked around the officer to see Sky waving his hands around to get her attention. Ivy felt sick. What had he gotten her sister into?

"Find out where they're taking us!" he mouthed.

Ivy stood as tall as she possibly could and puffed out her chest. She had to make them see. "Our guardian is a very important man. You must let my sister go; I can assure you she knows nothing about this Falun Gong stuff."

The officer laughed in her face and gave her a shove backward. Ivy stumbled, almost falling before she caught her footing. The officer waved his hand at her in dismissal, lit a cigarette, then opened the driver's door and climbed in.

"Where are you taking her?" Ivy stepped to the van and clung to the door handle. It was locked but she jerked it back and forth anyway until he rolled the window down.

"She'll be processed at the local precinct and then most likely taken to People's Hospital Number Seven of Wuxi, where all the Falun Gong followers are examined before sentencing. You can sort it out there tomorrow." He ended his statement by spitting out a large blob of phlegm, almost hitting Ivy with it. He started the motor and stomped on the gas. The door handle was yanked out of Ivy's hands, and she fell to her knees on the sidewalk.

"Lily!" she screamed, tears running down her face. "I'll get Ye Ye! We'll come find you!" The van quickly pulled away until it was no longer visible in the mess of cars on the road.

Lily was gone and they were taking her to a horrible place. Ivy knew what institution the number seven hospital was—the local mental hospital. She'd failed to protect her sister for the first time in her life.

Chapter Seven

The van careened around a corner and Lily fought a wave of nausea. She let go of her violin and bow in her lap for a moment to wipe her clammy hands on her jeans. She was embarrassed that she couldn't stop her body from trembling.

"Lily? Are you okay?" Sky asked, squeezing her around the shoulders.

"No. I think I'm carsick." She had ridden in a car only a few times and those had been with Jet. He was usually very careful with them and didn't drive like a maniac. Sitting in a car was so much different than riding on a bus. She could feel every bump in the road. Now both of the officials were puffing on their cigarettes and their smoke filled the van. Even though Lily couldn't see anything, she still felt her world spinning.

"Just take deep breaths. You're white as a ghost!" Sky lowered his voice. He was so close, she could hear him lick his lips every few seconds, a gesture she knew people made when they were nervous. "You need to listen to me, Lily."

Lily didn't understand why everyone else was let go except them. Sky had talked to her a bit about the Falun Gong he was accused of, but it didn't sound like anything dangerous to her.

"I'm listening."

She heard him inhale deeply and felt him lean his head closer to her.

"Talk quietly. The officials don't seem to be paying attention to us but you never know. I just heard them say it's too late to take us by the precinct. So when we get to the hospital, they're going to say you are a Falun Gong follower. You must deny this vehemently."

"But I'm not! Of course I'll deny it—I don't even know what it is!"

"Listen, Lily! This is important. If they don't believe you, they'll take you to another place. What they call a reeducation center. You do not want them to do that. There they'll punish you and even try to brainwash you."

Lily started to tremble again. What he was talking about sounded like the camps they used during the Cultural Revolution, and she knew plenty about those from stories she'd heard from Ye Ye over the years. He was right; she didn't want them to take her there.

"But what do I say? How can I convince them?"

Sky tapped his foot in the floor. She could tell he was very nervous. "What I hope will happen is that Lao Zheng will get there before they interrogate or move you. He'll get you out. And you know your sister is on her way to him right now. Try not to worry."

Easy for him to say, Lily thought. He could see what was coming at him before it hit. For once in her life, she felt at a severe disadvantage for being blind. She'd always been protected and guided, and this feeling of vulnerability was new to her. She didn't like it at all.

"I'm so sorry, Lily. I shouldn't have even come near you in the holding cell. It's all my fault, but you looked so scared. I just wanted to let you know you weren't alone in there."

Lily could hear the guilt in his voice. He was right again. If he had left her alone, she'd have been released with the other beggars. But she couldn't hold it against him that he'd only wanted to comfort her.

"Do you think they'll take my violin?" she asked, unable to control the quiver of her lower lip.

There was a long pause before he answered. Around them other drivers blew their horns in impatience and the van jerked left to right, changing lanes faster than she could keep up. She heard Sky lick his lips again.

"I'm not going to lie to you, Lily. It's a good chance someone will take your violin. I'd hold it for you but honestly, they're more likely to take it from me immediately. If you can, try to hold on to it until your family comes, then maybe you can pass it to them."

She couldn't let anything happen to her violin! Her Ye Ye's violin! He'd kept it safe during the most tumultuous years in China and now she might lose it because she wanted to play a simple concert in the park. He'd never forgive her if they took it. She gripped it tightly, holding it and the bow to her chest. They'd have to peel it from her dead fingers first. She promised herself that.

"How do you know so much about all this, Sky?"

She heard him give a long sigh before he answered. "I've been arrested for this before, Lily. They've unsuccessfully tried to rehabilitate me a few times, so I know the drill. I'm just so sorry I dragged you into it."

The van came to a screeching stop and Sky gave her another reassuring hug.

"Be strong, Lily. They'll probably separate us immediately. I'll be close, though."

Lily didn't answer. She was frozen in fear from the unknown of what awaited her.

The door jerked open. "Come on, get out."

Sky scooted away from her and she heard him shuffle out of the van. She still couldn't move.

"You, too!" the rough voice ordered, and there was no doubt he was talking to her. She felt hands grab her arm and she was jerked toward the door, bumping her head on the frame. She reached up and rubbed at it. By the time she got through this day, she'd probably be black and blue.

"Okay, okay. I'm coming. Let me do it." She didn't know how she'd find her way out of the van and into the building without a guide, but she'd rather fall on her face than have him touch her again.

"You can't see your hand in front of your face—how are you going to do it?" He roughly pulled her from the van onto the sidewalk. With his hand tightly gripped around her arm, he led her to what she guessed was the hospital. They climbed the stairs and entered the doorway, then turned down a long hall. Their footsteps echoed hollowly around them and the strong smell of sanitizer overwhelmed her senses.

"I'm still right here, Lily," Sky called back from somewhere in front of her.

"Not for long, jackass," the official muttered under his breath. He took out his phone and dialed a number, then barked at the person on the other end that he'd be home in an hour and to have his dinner ready. Lily felt a pang of pity for his unfortunate wife.

He snapped the phone shut and she heard the sound of Sky being led toward the left while her captor turned her right. She knew that now, other than the occasional nurse or random other person in the hall, she was alone with him. She fought the urge to sprint out of his grasp and instead gripped her violin and bow closer to her chest and concentrated on keeping her footing. She didn't want to fall and take the chance of landing on Viola. She also tried to take note of where they were going, but the officer pulled her along so fast that she couldn't keep up with how many paces or turns they made as they traveled through the building.

For the first time in her life, she wished she could see.

Chapter Eight

Sami paced the bedroom like a caged tiger. She was alone again because Li Jin was busy, as usual, in another part of the building—probably painting, cooking, or some other ridiculous chore in her attempt to make everything at Rose Haven just perfect. Sami tried to stay away from contributing to the makeover of the old place, but now with even more people moving in, it was getting harder to find somewhere to mull over her thoughts without the incessant noise and nosiness of everyone who lived under the same roof.

Her room—actually, *their* room—was no longer one of peace and tranquility, for the baby had disrupted it. Li Jin had offered to move them into a separate room but Sami had rejected that idea. She didn't want to be alone with the baby. She didn't even know what to do with her! Li Jin was better at comforting her than Sami was, so in the night when the baby cried, she just pretended deep sleep and let Li Jin tend to her. She'd also found that slipping Auntie Rae extra treats during the day got her a few afternoon hours alone while the old woman kept the baby in her room. No one knew it; she'd made sure the old woman would keep her mouth shut. And with her secret outings, Sami was beginning to build up a nest egg that she hoped would soon be enough to start over with.

She walked over to the cradle and stood staring at the little thing they called Lan. Those dark eyes of hers sent chills down Sami's spine; they always seemed to be pleading with her for something she didn't have to give.

Sami hesitated. One hand over the tiny face for just a few moments and it would be over. Women used to do it all the time in the old days. Why not now? So many times she wondered why she herself hadn't been dumped upside down in a water bucket, or suffocated with the same cloth used to clean her mother—her life snuffed out like so many infant girls before her. Why was she granted life?

Now here she stood over another useless girl, but this one her own. It was ironic. If she had her way, she'd have terminated the child before it had ever drawn its first breath. But Li Jin had ferreted out the truth that she was pregnant before Sami could handle it. Once discovered, there was no way out. Li Jin had wanted to know who the father was. But Sami couldn't even be sure she knew exactly which man had spawned Lan. For her, they were nothing but strangers she used to try to fill the empty void inside her soul, but it never worked. The sex only consoled her momentarily; then hours later the same discontent and some- times startling rage filled her again.

Six long weeks since she'd given birth and Sami felt she would go insane if she didn't get out of the house and away from the baby again today. She needed male attention and needed it now. Sure, she hated men and all they represented. But she did so love the long looks and infatuation-fueled offers they made her.

Hopefully in a few weeks, Li Jin would be tired of working her fingers to the bone and be ready to travel. They could leave the baby with one of the elderly nannies and take off on their own adventure. It would be like old times, just she and Li Jin.

Sami went to the closet she shared with Li Jin and rummaged through until she found what she was looking for. Li Jin had gotten a shimmery red blouse as a gift from her mother, and Sami was going to borrow it. It was just right to cover up her tattoos and was still eye-catching. Li Jin would probably never even miss it. All she wore these days were aprons anyway, hiding her beauty in her crowded kitchen. Sami just didn't get why Li Jin wanted to be treated like a servant, cooking and cleaning for so many people for nothing in return.

The baby stirred and let out a low cry. Sami gave the cradle a shove and walked over to the mirror. Peering at herself, she smiled. Li Jin was right—she *was* beautiful. As the baby fretted behind her, she worked through her long hair and gave it one hundred strokes. Then she picked up her powder and brush and started the transformation. The child grew impatient and wailed loudly, and Sami found herself grinding her teeth together.

Tonight, if Li Jin was busy, she'd find someone else to tend the little banshee and she'd go see what trouble she could drum up. If the gods were in her favor, she'd quickly fill her empty pockets, even if she couldn't fill the hole in her heart.

Benfu stood back and admired the handiwork while he stretched the kinks out of his back. It had been a hard project but he was pleased with the outcome. Earlier he'd excused everyone else to their regular chores so he and Jace could finish the trim work together. Linnea and Sky had worked together for weeks to paint a mural of exotic animals, gardens, and rainbows, and now, with the trim a crisp white, the playroom was perfect. All the kids in the center would have a place to come and experience fun and learning, in a safe environment free from bullying and abuse.

He looked down at his hands. His fingernails were covered with white paint. He reached in and pulled out his pocketknife from inside his jacket and popped it open. He needed to get some of the paint out from under his nails before Calli fussed all over him.

Picking at the stubborn paint, he felt a lump come up in his throat as he thought of all the children—*his flowers*—who had come through his life and would've benefited from a home like the one they were building here at Rose Haven. But even without all this room and resources, he had given them a roof over their heads and more love than they knew what to do with. He and Calli had raised an entire garden of flowers, so he guessed they'd done all right after all.

"Everything okay, Lao Zheng?" Jace asked, his expression hopeful.

Benfu looked at the young man and smiled at the streak of white paint in his hair and over one eye. The boy had worked harder than anyone, as he always did to try to prove his worth to the family. He always looked as if he expected to be kicked out at any given moment. The boy obviously craved attention.

"More than okay, Jace. You've done a wonderful job." He clapped him on the back.

Jace beamed with pride at the compliment. Benfu shook his head. He couldn't imagine anyone putting such a good boy out on the street. Even if he was a little slow moving, he more than made up for it in his eagerness to please everyone around him. There were so many children like him out there, just waiting for someone to give them a helping hand, a word of encouragement. China had come far, but not far enough. There were still too many forgotten children. When he was gone, he hoped his daughter would continue to take up his work and make an even bigger mark on the world.

"Now we can bring in the tables, chairs, and the shelves. If I know my daughter, she'll want to direct where everything goes." He didn't dare try to tell Li Jin how to arrange anything—and rightfully so. It was amazing how with a little money and a lot of creative energy, she'd made what was once an abandoned old shoe factory unrecognizable—but in a good way. With her vision and all their work, the place was now worth at least double what they'd paid for it. He didn't know where she got it, but his daughter was one clever girl.

Jace laughed. "*Dui,* Li Jin is very bossy."

"Now, Jace. *Bossy* isn't a word she'd appreciate. But go get her and tell her she can start making it pretty."

Jace took off and Benfu looked around again. He couldn't wait to get all the new goodies out and see the children's faces. Now they'd been accepting more children and they had an even dozen, in addition to their own girls. The kids would be surprised; they didn't know the center had received a donation from the members of the local women's club. Benfu was shocked at the generosity of the group of women. More than milk and rice, they were now bringing monthly donations of used clothing, books, and even toys.

Benfu looked up when he heard footsteps pounding down the hall toward him. Who was running in the house?

Ivy slipped through the door and before Benfu could even ask her what was going on, she was across the room and draped around him like a spider, bawling loudly, her hair stuck to her face in sweaty strands. She looked as if she'd been running for miles. Benfu looked over her head into the hall but didn't see her sister. He quickly closed his pocketknife and dropped it back into his jacket pocket.

"Ivy! What is it? Where's Lily?"

"Ye Ye, they took her! They've got her!" Ivy sobbed, looking up at him with red-rimmed eyes.

Benfu felt his heart constrict, as if someone had reached in his chest and taken hold of it, and was squeezing the life from it.

"Who took her? Ivy! Tell me!" He gave her a little shake to try to calm her down and get her thinking straight.

"The police took her. They're on their way to the People's Hospital Number Seven of Wuxi. Please, Ye Ye, we've got to get there now!" She started pulling him toward the door.

Benfu didn't need to be told twice. Like a bitter wind, fate had turned and decided to upset the contented life he was leading. He pushed Ivy ahead of him. They needed to get outside and find a taxi quick. He didn't stop to tell Calli. He could call her from the car. Ivy would have to explain what happened once they were on their way. They had to move; there was no time to stop—someone had one of his girls. And the thought that she was in the clutches of the police, or any kind of official, was one that threatened to paralyze him with fear.

Chapter Nine

Lily stood on the other side of the huge metal door, still shaking from the admitting process into the mental ward and from the little cold rivulets of water that ran down her back, left over from the shower she'd been forced to take.

The official had taken her to the sixth floor and roughly handed her over to a nurse. During the entire exchange, they'd talked about her like she wasn't even there, as if her blindness made her incompetent to understand anything at all. As they talked, Lily tried to get her bearings. But all she could feel was a heavy emptiness around her.

"She's either a Falun Gong member herself, or a lover of one. Either way, same thing. We'll probably have to beat it out of her," the official had said as he handed her over.

She slowly began separating her hair into three sections, squeezing the water from it as she went. She'd braid it to get it off her back. She heard what they said but she'd try not to focus on it. After all, they couldn't beat out of her what wasn't there. She had hoped when she'd heard the woman's voice that she would be more merciful than the official, but the nurse had proved just as nasty. The first thing she'd done was pry Viola and the bow out of Lily's arms and strip her watch from her, then tell her personal belongings were not permitted. Lily had begged to keep the violin, but her pleas went unheeded. They'd allowed her to keep only the sunglasses after Lily had pleaded that the hospital fluorescent lights hurt her sensitive eyes. Lily hadn't really needed them but thought maybe she might use them to barter for something later.

"I would say she was the youngest we've had but just last month they sent us a fourteen-year-old. By the looks of this one, she's at least sixteen."

If they wanted to know how old she was, Lily wondered why they didn't just ask. Instead the nurse had escorted Lily to a large, cold shower room and made her undress. Lily had tried to cover herself, especially when the nurse had begun to cackle and make fun of her small breasts. After hosing her down from head to toe, the nurse had personally dried her with a rough towel and made her bend over to prove she wasn't hiding any weapons. Lily's face had burned with shame but she'd followed instructions, too afraid not to.

Then the nurse handed her a thin gown and told her to put it on. She wasn't given underclothes and when she'd asked about them, the nurse had only laughed again.

"What do you need underwear for? You aren't going anywhere."

Lily ran her hand down the gown again, reaching behind her to make sure it was still tied. The material smelled like it had been soaked in vinegar and Lily felt her stomach roll. She moved her foot and the slipper fell off. She reached down and, after searching for a second, found the wandering shoe and slipped it back on. She hoped they hadn't lost her clothes or shoes, but she especially worried about her violin.

After the humiliating bathing process, the nurse had brought her into the small room and pushed her up against the bed.

"Please, can you give me back my violin? I just want to hold it," Lily pleaded.

"Stay here and don't make any noise or we'll have to strap you down," the nurse answered, ignoring her plea. She'd then turned and left, slamming the door behind her. Lily heard the lock click into place and she was finally able to take a deep breath. She wondered what time it was and remembered they'd also taken her watch. Ye Ye would be angry—he'd splurged on the watch for her birthday. It was her first talking watch and finally knowing the time throughout the day without having to ask made her feel so much more independent. Now she was once again unaware of how long she'd been there, or even how long before night would come.

She felt around her and could tell the bed was bare, no sheets and not even a pillow. Even the mattress was sparse, only an inch or so thick. She wished for something to cover herself with to ward off the cold chill in the air. Her searching fingers finally found what must have been the straps. They were strong with metal prongs to fasten up with. Lily couldn't imagine them across her body. She didn't need straps. She wasn't crazy and she'd done nothing wrong!

Thinking of staying there through the night, she felt a wave of panic. She couldn't sleep here! Where was Ivy? She'd lost track of time but surely Ivy had already had time to get home and bring her Ye Ye back to get her out? A ragged sob tore through her and she took another deep breath. *Stay calm, Lily. Do not call attention to yourself.*

She heard a loud clatter in the hall and nearly jumped out of her skin. What were they doing out there? Were they coming to get her? Lily felt the moisture gathering under her arms and soaking her palms. She blinked rapidly and, in her state of fear, couldn't stop.

The clatter continued to come closer until it stopped right outside her door. She heard the rattle of keys, and then the door opened.

"*Ni hao.* Arrived just in time, eh? I think you could have found a much easier way to get a free dinner, eh?" a male voice called out, letting Lily know the noise was from a food cart.

Lily stared straight ahead without moving. What did he want her to do?

"Hey—here's your congee. Get off your lazy ass and come over here and get it."

Lily stood and shuffled forward a few feet, reaching her hand out to ward off any unsuspecting obstacles. She didn't want the congee but she didn't want to disobey, either. She felt she should just try to do what she was told.

"*Aiya,* you can't see, girl?"

She didn't need to see. She could feel—and smell—him waving his hand in front of her face like an idiot. She shook her head, then reached up to pull her sunglasses down over her eyes. She didn't move again, afraid of what she'd run into. She wished again for her cane and wondered if it was still under the bench in the park.

"Now they didn't tell me we had us a blind girl, no they did not!"

Lily froze, not sure how to answer. She could hear the man lean even closer until he was only an inch or so away, so close she could feel and smell his rancid breath on her face. His scent was revolting—a disgusting mixture of garlic and sweat. She tried to keep herself from flinching but it was impossible.

"I've never had me a blind girl before," he whispered. "And you is a pretty one, too. When lights-out comes tonight, I'll be back for a little visit. Tell me, are you still a cherry girl?"

She felt his spittle spray across her cheek. She shivered and backed up until she was against the bed. She tried to resist but couldn't and slowly reached up to wipe her face with the outside of her hand.

The man erupted into loud laughter. "Oh, see—I forgot already! It's always lights-out for you!"

She heard him set what was probably the bowl of congee on a table next to her bed and retreat from the room, still laughing as he let the door slam behind him.

She let out the breath she was holding only when she heard the lock click again. The clattering started back up and she heard him pause, guessing he must be in front of another room.

Lily climbed up on the bed and pulled her legs underneath her. She crossed her arms over her chest and began rocking back and forth, then stopped when she realized that was what a crazy person would do. She uncrossed her arms and sat on her hands. She thought of Viola and a tear started to slowly creep out of her eye. She ferociously brushed it away. If it were Ivy, she knew her sister would not cry, so she would be just as brave. She had to. Now she knew one really should be careful what she wished for—as now she was finally on her own.

"Come on, Ivy and Ye Ye, where are you?" she moaned. "Where are you, where are you, where are you. . . ."

She kept up the mantra under her breath, sure that when she'd said it a thousand times, they would be there to take her home. She only hoped it would be before the orderly came back to her room.

Chapter Ten

Benfu rapped on the large plastic shield that separated them from the man behind the wheel. Most times when he got into a taxi, the drivers were maniacs on the road. It was just his luck that today of all days, he'd get the one driver in the city who wanted to cruise along and actually follow the speed limit.

"Kuai yi dian!"

The shaggy-haired driver nodded and pressed his foot to the gas. Benfu tried to slow down his breathing. He could feel a coughing fit wanting to come on, tickling its way up his throat. Usually the only time he remembered he had tuberculosis was when he was upset and his body decided to revolt. He was glad he'd finally been educated on the disease, so he didn't have the stress any longer of thinking he was still contagious.

"Now, Ivy, tell me exactly what happened. What were you doing at the festival?" He put his arm around her and squeezed. He'd never seen her so upset in all their years together, but then he'd never seen her separated from her sister, either.

"We—were"—she struggled to speak through the sobs—"going to walk around. But Lily wanted to give—a—a concert."

"A concert? If she was just playing music, why did they take her?"

"Because she had the case open for people to drop money in! I guess they thought she was begging."

She started a batch of fresh tears and Benfu shook his head. He knew of many beggars who'd been pushed around by the local *chengguan*. Even another musician only months ago was hassled, and in the middle of the ruckus the police had manhandled him so much, they broke his nose! Benfu prayed that Lily was unhurt. He could only imagine how frightened she was. But what he didn't understand was why she was playing for money at the park. They didn't need the money that badly—these days most of their needs were met.

"Ivy, do you girls need money for something I'm not aware of? Is there something you aren't telling me?"

Ivy sniffled and shook her head.

"No. Lily said she just wanted to know if she was really good at the violin or not. She thinks everyone at home and in the neighborhood just tells her she is because they have to. She said with strangers, if she wasn't good, they'd let her know it."

Benfu gave a long, low sigh. His girls were always searching for confirmation that they were loved, or pretty, *or just simply good enough*.

"I tried to tell her, Ye Ye! But she's gotten so stubborn lately!"

He squeezed her shoulders again. "It's not your fault, Ivy. It was expected that your sister would start wanting more independence one day. Because of her blindness, she's been sheltered her entire life. Now she's rebelling against that. I've seen signs of it at home, too."

Ivy shook her head frantically. "But it *is* my fault! I walked away and left her there alone. I was angry at her, Ye Ye! I know she told me to go, but I shouldn't have listened—then they wouldn't have taken her!"

Benfu squeezed her close. "It is not your fault, Ivy. But listen, what about Sky? Tell me again, what was he doing?"

"I don't know. They said he was a Falun Gong follower. If

it wasn't for him, they would've let Lily go with the other beggars."

Benfu was puzzled. He thought he knew Sky well enough, but if what the police had told Ivy was true, he obviously didn't know enough about him. But even if he was a part of the Falun Gong crowd, Benfu didn't think he should be arrested for it. From what he knew of it, Falun Gong was just a new approach to life using Qigong along with morals and philosophies of peace. The people weren't committing crimes. Benfu felt the persecution for their beliefs was just another way for the government to exercise its control over the people.

The driver took a sharp right and came to a quick stop signaling they'd arrived.

"We're here. Don't worry, we'll fix this. Let's see what we can do about getting her home." He slipped a few bills through the crack of the partition to the driver and then scooted out of the car. Ivy followed.

Benfu looked at the front of the hospital and took a deep breath. Somewhere in there they had his daughter. He hoped they were ready for a battle, because he was going to give them one. He straightened his shoulders and led the way up the steps.

Benfu brought the cup of tepid tea to his lips. It was just one more in over a dozen he'd drunk since they'd arrived. They'd asked for Lily and had waited, pacing back and forth, for more than two hours in the lobby waiting area until the nurse had escorted them to a room on the third floor. There they waited another hour and instead of Lily being brought to them, an official had swaggered his way through the door and beckoned for them to sit.

The official, Delun, his badge read, stroked the long hair sprouting from the mole on his chin. He pushed at the documents in front of him until they were within Benfu's reach. "Because she's young and was probably led astray by the older fellow, I'll cut you a deal. If you agree to sign her into the psychiatric ward for three weeks and also sign this agreement, we'll handle this as an internal case among citizens and that will be the extent of her punishment. When it's time to discharge her, you pay a small fine, then she goes. Otherwise we'll make it an official case and we'll sentence her to a few months in the reeducation center."

"I've heard about those. Your so-called reeducation centers are nothing short of prisons. Have you lost your mind? My daughter is sixteen and has done nothing wrong. She's going home with me *tonight*. I'm not signing your agreement." Benfu pushed his chair back and stood up. He would not let them do to Lily what they'd done to him so long ago!

Ivy immediately jumped to her feet, too.

The official glared at them from across the table. "Your *daughter* was with a known Falun Gong practitioner—one who has been arrested before for spewing nonsense about their so-called philosophy. She was even seen holding one of their handouts. Just having possession of such literature is grounds for arrest. We must teach our younger generation the rules of society, and loyalty to country."

Benfu leaned on the table with both hands, bringing his face nearer to the official.

"My daughter is completely blind. Why would she be holding a piece of paper that she can't even read?"

Delun tilted his head and smiled. "To give out to other citizens at the festival, of course." He stood and spread his arms wide. "Let me make something clear, Lao Zheng. Falun Gong preaches idealism, religion, and superstition. It disturbs social stability and the people."

Benfu shook his head. "I don't care about what Falun Gong is or isn't. But I can promise you this—my daughter is *not* a part of that practice! That's what I'm trying to tell you!"

"Let me finish." Delun held his hand up. "Falun Gong has brainwashed followers and caused years of death and destruction. The so-called practice threatens our society, and any threat to the people is a threat to the Communist Party and our government. We take these cases very seriously and will make an example of anyone caught with the despicable propaganda."

Benfu felt the blood rise to his head. From what he knew of Falun Gong, the man was completely wrong. Basically, he felt the government had turned against the practice only because it was afraid so many had formed groups to be a part of it. But he didn't care either way. He just wanted Lily back. But in all his years, nothing had changed—the police and government would still twist any and all facts to suit their agenda. He wasn't about to sign a piece of paper acknowledging that Lily was something she wasn't. The label would stay on her record for her entire life and who knew what they'd do with it? They couldn't be trusted.

He was getting nowhere with this man and the tension was making it worse. He needed to calm down and try another tactic. He took a deep breath and tried to still the pounding of his heart.

"Can I see my daughter?" He spoke calmly, camouflaging the churning inside his chest.

"No, it's late and the staff is busy."

"Please," Ivy pleaded. "*Please* let us see her!"

Benfu held his hand up for her to be quiet. Officials like this one didn't have pity or compassion. They responded only to one thing. He reached into his pocket and pulled out his wallet. He laid four one-hundred reminbi bills on the table. It was the money he'd set aside to pay their monthly electricity bill, but he'd have to figure that out later.

"Now, can we see her?" he asked.

Delun looked at the bills and then reached out and slid them off the table. He quickly stuffed them in his pocket, then gave them a disturbing grin.

"Ten minutes."

After a silent ride up to the sixth floor in the slow, creaking elevator, Benfu followed Delun down the hall, with Ivy steadfast behind them. It was now nearing eight o'clock and it looked like the entire floor had gone to sleep. A bedraggled orderly pushing a food cart and a few empty stretchers lined the walls, but there were no patients to be seen. Benfu had always wondered what the psych ward was like inside, but he sure hadn't wanted to find out this way.

"So, twins, eh?" The official turned his head and looked at Ivy, then at Benfu. "You must have very potent qi, to have twins in your family."

Benfu ignored his comment and Delun chuckled. They passed a nurses' station, and a young woman wearing a crisp white uniform and cap looked up. Benfu noticed her name tag: *Nurse Guo.*

"Can I help you?"

Delun leaned over the counter. "What room is the blind girl in? The one they just brought in this afternoon?"

"The doctor said she is very agitated and shouldn't see anyone tonight."

Delun put both hands on the counter and leaned in even closer to the nurse. "I'm not just anyone—can't you see my badge?"

Benfu could see the nurse hesitate, then look at the badge the official wore. Behind them the quiet was broken by a loud, animalistic scream. It sent a chill down Benfu's spine, but at least he could tell it wasn't Lily.

The nurse clicked the keys on her computer. "She's in a holding room. On the left, the last room, down that hall." She pointed to the hall opposite her desk. "You'll need a key. I'll come with you. She's very frightened."

"No, just give me the key." Delun held his hand out.

Nurse Guo hesitated again, then pulled a set of keys from her pocket. She put them in his palm. "It's the red key."

Delun closed his fist over the key, then turned and led the way. Benfu looked at Ivy and nodded reassuringly. He fought to keep the tick in his cheek under control.

As they passed each room, he looked through the small glass windows. Some of the rooms were empty but in the ones that weren't, most of the patients he caught glimpses of were curled on their beds in a fetal position, but he did see a few strapped down straight as a board, staring emotionless at the water-spotted ceilings. He gritted his teeth. If they'd done that to his daughter, someone would pay.

At the end of the hall Delun stopped in front of the door and then turned to them. "I'm going to stand out here. Do not give her anything or it will be confiscated."

Ivy took Lily's cane from her pocket and set it on the floor in front of the door.

Benfu nodded and Delun unlocked the door. He walked in with Ivy struggling to get around him.

What he saw broke his heart.

In the corner of the room Lily had pulled the mattress from the bed and propped it in front of her as she huddled behind it. Her feet stuck out one end and just one look at her short, stubby toes sticking out of the top of an unfamiliar blue slipper told him it was her.

"Lily?" he called out. He took a few steps closer.

"Ye Ye?" she answered, her voice sounding more frail and weak than he'd ever heard it.

Ivy ran around him and sprinted across the room. She threw the thin mattress to the side. Benfu felt a catch in his throat when he saw Lily behind there, cowering in the corner. Wearing only a ragged hospital gown, she looked bewildered and cold.

"Lily, it's me! I'm so sorry!" Ivy wailed, dropping to her knees and throwing her arms around her sister. At her touch, Lily began to cry. She didn't make any noise but tears rolled down her face as she clutched her sister.

Benfu crossed the room and knelt down in front of his girls. "Lily, we're trying to get you out of here. Are you okay? Has anyone hurt you?"

He sensed her hesitation, but then she answered.

"No one has hurt me—not really. But Ye Ye, please get me out of here." Lily struggled to free herself from her sister, and Benfu reached out and pulled her into his arms, standing up to hold her close. He felt her trembling. She was so cold! Why didn't they allow her more clothes or a blanket? In that moment he felt more helpless than he'd ever felt before.

They heard a rapping on the glass and Benfu turned to see Delun pointing his finger and shaking his head. "*No* contact!"

He let go of Lily and struggled out of his jacket, then draped it around her shaking shoulders. "Here, wear this. Now listen to me, Lily. We only have a few minutes. But I want you to know I'm doing everything I can to get you out of here."

Ivy ignored the warning and put her arm around her sister. "Those damn officials! They don't know what they're talking about."

"Ivy, watch your language. Don't stoop to their level. We're better than that," Benfu scolded gently. He couldn't blame her; Ivy had every right to be angry. Lily looked shaken, cold, and terrified. He was angry himself, but it wouldn't do any good for him to lose control.

"But Ye Ye, I haven't done anything. Why did they arrest me? Sky was the one with that paper they were talking about, not me." Lily stared straight ahead but even without looking into her eyes, he could see the anguish and fear across her face.

"I know you haven't done anything. And you aren't actually arrested—they're just holding you here until they decide what to do with you."

"And they took Viola from me!" Lily wailed, a fresh batch of tears falling.

"I'll talk to them about the violin, don't worry," Benfu said. He asked her some questions about how she was transported and where Sky was taken. He asked and she confirmed she hadn't signed anything. She wanted to know about the Falun Gong and Benfu told her what little he felt she needed to know. He didn't want her to know too much, as the more she knew, the more they'd assume she was a follower if they questioned her.

Delun rapped on the window again. When Benfu looked, the man pointed at his watch. "Time is up."

"Wait, don't go yet!" Lily pulled the jacket closer around herself and reached out for Ivy. Her sister moved in closer, putting her arm around Lily.

Benfu swallowed the lump in his throat. "Lily, I'm going back down to talk to them. But right now they're saying if we don't agree for you to stay here for a few weeks as punishment, you'll be transported to their reeducation center."

"They are not taking her!" Ivy said, her eyes flashing. "They can call it reeducation all they want, but we all know it's nothing more than a prison."

Lily whimpered but Benfu had to give her credit; she was acting braver than he'd thought she would.

"Let's see what they have to say. I can maybe negotiate them down, but, Lily, I don't want to lie to you. I might not be able to get you out tonight. Can you hold on?"

They waited as Lily hesitated, then nodded slowly. Benfu felt sick inside. He didn't want to even tell her that, but the truth was that he might not be able to get her out and he didn't want to mislead her. His honesty with his daughters was one thing they'd always been able to depend on.

"I'll make some calls. I'll get Linnea on the phone to Jet so he can let his father know what's going on. If that gets us nowhere, maybe Lao Gong, my old friend, can help." Lao Gong had retired from his position with the government many years ago, but he still had connections, if his stories could be believed. Benfu was willing to try anything.

"Ye Ye, that's a great idea. Call him now," Ivy urged.

"I can't get a signal in here. I'll see what the last word is from the official first, then I'll have to step outside." He moved over to the girls and put his arms around them both. "Don't worry. We'll get this sorted out."

The door opened and Delun beckoned for them to come out.

Benfu started toward the door but looked back and Ivy hadn't budged. She still stood with her arms wrapped tightly around her sister, her mouth a straight white line.

"I'm staying with her," she said.

Benfu shook his head. "Come on, Ivy. You can't stay—you know that."

"Out." Delun pointed his finger at Ivy.

"Just arrest me, too! Please!" Ivy insisted.

At that, Delun pushed by Benfu and started across the floor toward Ivy. Benfu stepped forward and got between them. He didn't want the man to lay his hands on either of his girls.

"Ivy, you heard me. We have to go. Let's go see what we can do to get Lily out of here." He gently pulled her from her sister as they fought to keep their hands clasped. Benfu thought it might just be one of the hardest things he'd ever done. Twins weren't supposed to be separated in such a way, and the turmoil on both of their faces proved it.

"And put this mattress back on the bed!" Delun yelled as he shuffled them out the door.

"*Zai jian,* Ye Ye. Bye, Ivy," Lily whispered from the corner where she still stood, looking shell-shocked and tiny in his oversized jacket.

"We'll be back as soon as we can, Lily. Hang on," Benfu said. "Remember, they cannot take away your dignity. Be strong."

"Lily, I won't leave this hospital until you do. I'll be downstairs—I promise I won't leave you!" Ivy called out, trying to look around the official.

He pushed them out of the way and slammed, then locked the door. Ivy cursed and Benfu looked at the back of the official's head, wishing he could tear it from his shoulders. But at least the man hadn't made Lily take off his jacket. Benfu hoped it would give her a small sense of comfort. He shook his head, trying to shake away the visual of her shaking in the corner. How was he going to tell Calli? He knew his wife and she would be devastated to know one of her own was locked behind the doors of such a place.

Chapter Eleven

Inwardly, Sami tingled with anticipation but outwardly she looked calm as she carefully peeled her orange. She'd been good long enough and it was time to live a little. She kept her gaze on the comings and goings of the Wuxi Hotel across the street. Several lanes of traffic separated her from the two young doormen flanking the revolving doors. They stood at attention—the only time they moved or changed expression was when a patron arrived or departed. She popped a juicy section in her mouth and watched them salute a finely dressed businessman as he strode into the building.

She spat the too-sour orange slice out onto the sidewalk, then set the remainder beside her on the bench. She continued to watch the hotel. Sami had been around establishments such as these many times and knew the boys were probably working their first jobs, proud to be wearing crisp, clean uniforms instead of dusty day-laborer clothes like their fathers. Most likely they even made more money than their hard-working parents who probably came to town as migrant workers. She thought back to a time long ago when one such boy had held her attention for a quick night or two. He'd told her all about his luck at snagging a doorman position, his salary (that he'd burned through quickly with her), and his aspirations to move up in the hotel and bring his family out of poverty. Sami had let him ramble on as he awkwardly fumbled with her body, trying to appear as if he'd done that sort of thing often—but she'd known his position as doorman was a short-lived career that required youth; and as soon as he started showing some age, he'd be back out on the streets hauling bricks like the rest of the men in his family—and when she was gone, she'd only be a wisp of a memory. He'd never be able to afford anyone like her again.

Tired of watching, she stood and unbuttoned her blouse a few buttons, but not so low the tattoo showed. Reaching behind her, she pulled her hair loose from the rubber band and let it fall. The borrowed red shirt and black leggings weren't bad, but a pair of heels could have set them off nicely. She hadn't planned to land where she was, but then, she hadn't considered the magnetic pull of this part of town. In her hurry to escape the suffocating atmosphere of her new home, she'd just instinctively ended up there. But even without looking her best she knew it would be easy to get past the young doormen, and into the hotel. She just wanted to take a look; at least that was what she told herself. Li Jin and her family would never know. She snorted as she thought of how horrified they'd be.

As she debated what she'd say to the doormen, an old woman shuffled up and quickly dropped onto the bench, settling plastic bags around her to claim the unoccupied space. The woman gave a gasp of delight as she grabbed Sami's uneaten orange and tucked it into her pocket. Her leg touched the back of Sami's, an indication she wasn't going to wait politely for her to move.

"Excuse you, *Laoren*," Sami said as she glared down at the old woman. How rude of the old hag. Maybe Sami wasn't done with the bench yet; maybe she'd planned to sit back down, and maybe she was going to eat the rest of her orange!

"Dui bu qi," the woman mumbled in apology under her breath, and then turned her body and pulled her legs onto the seat. Stuffing one of her bags under her head, she curled into a ball and closed her eyes as if she couldn't wait another second to fall asleep.

Scrawny bare ankles showed up pale against the cold metal bench and Sami could see from her mismatched clothing and lack of socks the woman was most likely homeless. She reminded Sami of Auntie Wan in Hongcun; that old woman was nothing more than a peasant but somehow she'd made all the girls love her—*everyone except Sami.* And this woman wouldn't be getting any sympathy from Sami, either. She was just a *qi gai*—a beggar scourging on the kindness of strangers.

She looked at her once more and thought of her own grandmother. She'd been a hardworking seamstress until her fingers refused to cooperate. Then she'd had to resort to begging kindness from her own son, Sami's father, and he'd not made it easy.

Sami reached in her pocket and pulled out a few coins and laid them on the bench near the woman's feet. "You're still an old raisin-face," she muttered over her shoulder as she walked to the edge of the sidewalk.

Sami was glad she was alone. If Li Jin had been with her, no doubt they'd have one more rumpled resident living under their roof by nightfall.

She waited on a lull in the traffic and when none came, she stepped out into the street and held her hand up to the oncoming taxi as it barreled toward her. She didn't look at the driver. He had two choices; either stop and let her cross, or run her over and face criminal charges. Sami knew he'd make the right choice and smiled slightly when the sound of his screeching brakes followed the repetitive horn blares. Without looking at him, she continued across the street and stepped up onto the curb. Lifting her chin higher, she strode to the hotel doors.

The first doorman—he really should be called a *doorboy*—reached out and stopped her as she started to go in. He licked his lips nervously before he spoke.

"*Wo keyi bang ni, ma?*" he said, asking her if she needed any help.

Sami knew the drill. They'd been trained to watch out for street prostitutes trying to make their way into the hotel. The management allowed escort services, but only those quietly arranged by the hotel staff so they could take their cut.

Sami smiled up at the young man and was rewarded by seeing two bright spots of scarlet appear on his cheeks. "I'm meeting a foreign client in your lobby so we can go over some design plans. He's staying at your hotel while his office is being built."

"You're a designer?" the boy asked, straightening his jacket, his stern expression changing to curious respect.

"Didn't I just say that?" Sami tilted her head and winked at the boy. Of course she wasn't a designer. What an idiot he was. Did she look like a designer? Was she carrying a portfolio? "And I must hurry. You don't want to make a *laowai* angry if I'm late, do you?"

She was proud of herself for her last-minute idea of throwing a foreigner into the mix. These boys were young and probably still overwhelmed at the thought of dealing with *laowais*—especially angry ones.

"Um . . . no . . . *hao le* . . . go ahead." The boy stepped aside and Sami walked through the revolving doors.

Once inside, she let her eyes rove over the lobby, taking care not to be too obvious. She didn't want anyone to know she wasn't familiar with the area. From the first look, Sami thought she'd picked the right hotel. The lobby was big, but not too large. Elegant, but not too fancy. Ignoring the front desk, she made no noise with her soft heels on the ceramic tiles as she crossed over to the seating area and sat under a magnificent crystal chandelier. A man sat on one of the leather couches, tapping away on his laptop while his cigarette sat in the ashtray and burned down nearly to the filter beside him.

Sami studied his face. A businessman obviously, but his harried look and the nervous shaking of his leg told her he wasn't as successful as she'd like. She also didn't like the taste of tobacco. He was dismissed.

She crossed the lobby, entering the posh hotel bar. A quick look around told her it was too early. The bartender used a cloth to polish glasses as he looked over the room. This hotel knew what they were doing—instead of the usual inexperienced but attractive young fellow behind most counters, this bartender, with his buttoned vest and lines of character crisscrossing his face, could have passed for a professor. His eyes met Sami's and he raised an eyebrow. *Maybe it wasn't too early.*

She nodded and he nodded back. He was giving her permission, obviously assuming she was an approved escort. One lone customer sat before him, nursing what appeared to be a tomato drink with a stalk of celery as a garnish. Sami quietly sat a few seats down from the other patron.

The bartender approached her and set a napkin on the counter.

"What can I get you, *Xiao Jie*?" A small smile played at his lips until he twitched and it disappeared.

"*Yi bei cha.*" She asked for a cup of tea. She knew it was the cheapest thing on the menu but would be surprised if he really made her pay for it. They both knew why she was there.

The bartender turned away, and from her peripheral view Sami examined the man next to her: nice suit, Rolex watch, clean fingernails with steady and calm hands. Probably no diseases, she thought, then shook her long mane of hair over her shoulder, hoping the almond scent reached his nose. At least it was shiny clean and, even better, it was longer than most women kept their hair these days. Sami couldn't get over the trend of short hair taking over the cities. Didn't the women understand their hair was an aphrodisiac? For centuries it was the same—the men loved their feet first, then their hair. The current fad had girls resorting to short hairstyles framing their faces. Ugly. And unfeminine. Sami would never do it.

The bartender brought a tiny glass teakettle and cup, and set them before her. Sami poured the Longjing tea, holding her delicate fingers out to appear even more fragile. She lifted the cup to her nose and closed her eyes as she first savored the sweet aroma. Then she slowly sipped the steaming tea as she concentrated on using her mouth to its best advantage, even tracing a wayward drop of tea from her top lip with her tongue. She made it slow and sensual, an obvious tease.

She could feel his eyes on her. Instead of acknowledging him, she slowly uncrossed and recrossed her legs, then shifted in her seat. She didn't want to look too eager. Pensive and mysterious, that was how to hook them.

She suppressed a smile when he got up and moved into the seat beside her, sliding his glass of tomato juice over. She noticed he didn't wear a ring, not that it would have made a difference, but it did make her curious.

"*Xia wu hao,*" he said, wishing her good afternoon, his voice deep and throaty.

Sami nodded demurely. She could feel his eyes roaming her body from head to toe and was glad she'd opened a few buttons on her blouse. Just enough to give him a peek.

"What's your name?" he asked.

She finally granted him her attention. "What do you want it to be?"

A wide smile spread across the man's face. He reached into his pocket and pulled out a wad of cash. Quickly he laid a bill on the counter and waved at the bartender. "Close out my bill, sir. My date has arrived."

Sami felt her heartbeat accelerate at the sight of the money, but her expression remained indifferent.

He stood and held his hand out to her. For an instant she hesitated and thought about Li Jin. They'd met only the year before and had instantly felt connected at the heart. Together, they'd taken an oath to start over and live a clean life. Sami hadn't realized that would mean traipsing across China to live with Li Jin's recently found family under the roof of their so-called community shelter. The faces of Li Jin's parents flashed before her eyes. Such good, moral people out to save the world. What would they think of her if they could see her now? They'd probably throw her out into the street, where she belonged.

Sami looked down at her lap and a wave of revulsion hit her. But she needed this. No one would know. She needed something to take her mind from her situation; something to make her feel real again, not like this invisible person she'd become.

And it wasn't like Li Jin's family was paying her to stick around. Unlike the other girls, she wasn't really considered family and could be out on the street in a minute. *She needed the money as a backup plan.* She hung on to that thought and repeated it in her head as she climbed off the bar stool and accepted his hand, allowing him to lead her from the room.

Li Jin readjusted the wrap that held Lan tightly against her back, then wiped the soapy rag across the counters for the third time, grateful for the peace after such a long and eventful day. The unexpected news of Sky and Lily getting picked up earlier that day had really rocked the center, making everyone on edge as they scattered to their own corners to whisper and speculate. When her Baba and Ivy had returned without Lily, a pall had been cast over the center. First Ivy, then her parents had disappeared behind their bedroom doors. Dinner had been eerily quiet.

"What can I do to help?" Auntie Rae peeked inside the kitchen door as she bounced baby Coral on her shoulder. The concern on her face made her look ages older than usual.

Li Jin looked around as she continued to sway back and forth. She knew the room was sparkling only because of all the nervous energy she was exploding with. Already she'd scrubbed the row of high chairs, scoured the stove top, mopped the floors, and even rearranged their growing pantry twice. Usually she had help with kitchen duty, but today she'd run everyone out of there, knowing she wanted to be alone. Well, alone except for her Jojo. And of course, Lan.

"Nothing, Auntie Rae. It's all done, but thanks. You take Coral and go for a walk or something to get ready for bed." Li Jin couldn't get over how sweet the woman was, and how sad it was that her own grown daughter couldn't help care for her. Many years ago, the woman had been a matchmaker descended down from a long line of matchmakers in her family. Rae had finally told her about her hard times since her husband's death. With the younger generation's stubborn resistance to the old ways, she'd had to resort to a multitude of small but difficult jobs she'd worked just to make enough to eat. They'd been jobs like sweeping highways, planting flowers for the government complexes, as well as other tasks that an elderly person had no business trying to do. Li Jin was glad she'd found her way to them.

Auntie Rae smiled, showing the wide gaps in her teeth. She pointed at Li Jin's back.

"That baby looks good on you." She winked, then disappeared down the hall.

What did she mean by that? Li Jin rolled her neck, glad the center was quieting down for the night. Peony had been the most difficult to settle down—as she'd received a new postcard from her mysterious mother and was teetering between excitement that the woman had figured out where they'd moved and again reached out to her, but sad because she still didn't know who or where she was. Li Jin had spent over an hour talking with the girl and reassuring her that if it was meant to be, her mother would come forward one day. Li Jin's heart ached for her. Not only did the girl have to deal with being from mixed heritage, but she also had to overcome the deep feelings of rejection from being abandoned.

Finally Peony's exhausting roller coaster of emotions had led her to bed. Li Jin had peeked in on her and was moved to see the girl still clutching the postcard to her chest, even in her sleep.

Thankfully, even Lan had finally tired herself out and was sleeping bundled against Li Jin's back. Earlier in her bedroom, she'd caught their reflection and laughed, realizing she looked like a peasant mama working the rice fields with an infant tied around her. But Li Jin wouldn't leave her in the nursery or with anyone other than her own mother, so the wrap was the next option to allow her to still get around and run the place.

Sami had taken off again. Usually Li Jin didn't mind her short disappearances, but today with the terrible situation of the twins, it was an inconvenience. Still, she couldn't be irritated at Lan; the baby girl was starved for attention and she wasn't getting any from her own mother. Li Jin had tried to tell Sami that the infant's colic would settle if she'd hold her more and walk with her, but Sami acted as if she couldn't be bothered with motherhood. It was so frustrating to Li Jin. She'd heard of women having postpartum depression and she hoped that was the explanation—but something told her Sami's problems were much deeper and more permanent. Even before she'd gotten pregnant, her emotions were on a constant roller coaster of change.

"Ma, tell me again, what's going on? Why was Nai Nai crying?" Jojo asked from his place at the table. He was doing his homework and Li Jin was really missing her father's usual assistance. Since they'd moved into the new place and Li Jin was so busy with running things, he had taken charge of Jojo's education. Her father was a great teacher, but today they were on their own.

She walked over and ruffled her son's hair. He'd been so helpful all evening, especially after her father and Ivy had come with the bad news. Her tightly run kitchen and even the usually smooth-running evening chores had been overturned for a short while. Everyone was concerned. Even though her father had said very little, they all understood something dreadful had happened to Lily.

"Lily was detained for playing her violin at the festival in town," Li Jin said.

"What is detained? Music isn't allowed there?"

Li Jin could see Jojo wasn't buying it. He was a smart boy and knew something else was in the air.

"Tomorrow I'll know more, Son. Let's just wait until then to talk about it."

She felt Lan stir and went to the cupboard for the canister of milk powder. She'd get a bottle ready. Maybe rocking the little girl back to sleep would settle her own nerves and put her mind on something else. She couldn't stop thinking of Lily and how terrified she must be. Lily had never been without her sister as a guide, and now she was alone in a strange place, unable to see anything that might endanger her. With her hand on the cabinet she paused to bow her head and say a short prayer to the gods to protect Lily. Jojo saw her getting the bottle out and came to stand beside them. Lan had been with them so much lately that even he was growing attached to her. "I'll help you feed her, Ma."

"Put the kettle on to boil."

He ran to the stove top and checked the kettle to make sure it had water; then he turned the knob as Li Jin had taught him. He was always eager to help her. Maybe it would take his mind off Ivy, too. She was just glad he hadn't also overheard her father tell her that Sky had been detained as well. Like her, Jojo had grown attached to Sky and she knew he'd worry.

"Okay, it's on. I'll get the bottle ready. I know . . . she gets two scoops of powder." He went to the canister on the counter and peeled the lid from the top. Li Jin paced the floor, waiting for the kettle. As long as she walked, Lan wouldn't fuss, so she'd keep going until the bottle was ready.

Along with worrying over her sisters, she'd spent the last few hours going over and over what she knew about Sky and how he fit into the puzzle of the Falun Gong practitioners. Having spent so much time on the streets, she knew what they were—at least a little. As far as she knew, it was a practice similar to Qigong or Tai Chi, but with more of a spiritual responsibility. Interestingly, the founder introduced it to the people back in 1992 and the party declared it illegal to practice by 1999. She'd heard the new law hadn't stopped the most devout followers but Sky hadn't ever shared with her that he was a part of it. It didn't make much difference to her either way, as what she knew about the practice was minimal but she did know they strived to lead a peaceful life. She tried not to think of Sky being roughed up by the local officials, but her imagination taunted her. She hoped her father didn't think she was overstepping her boundaries, but she'd called Linnea and asked her to go over and let Sky's grandfather know what had happened. Hopefully someone was working to get him out, as her parents were working to free Lily.

Sky was totally different than any man she'd ever known—the complete opposite of Erik, that was for sure. Li Jin had to admit that when Sky was around, there was also a measure of peace and contentment. She would miss that if he was gone for long. *Aiya,* she already missed it, if she was being honest with herself. She hoped he was okay. She had big plans for him to help her get Sami back to a better mental place, if she could only get Sami to see in him what she did.

A loud whistle sounded, making Li Jin jump out of her daydream about Sky and Sami.

"I got it, Ma," Jojo said.

"No, you don't. It's too hot for you to handle. I'll pour and you can shake the bottle."

She headed toward the stove and looked down at her watch. They'd been gone three hours. She wished she'd hear something about Lily and Sky.

From her back, Lan let out a small cry. She was getting hungry again but she'd have to wait a few minutes until her bottle cooled. Once again Li Jin thought of the argument she and Sami had over breast-feeding. No matter how much Li Jin tried to convince her it was best for the baby, Sami had refused. Still, they were lucky the baby still had a mother, when so many at their center didn't.

She poured the water into the bottle and Jojo popped the nipple on, then shook it up and down, grinning from ear to ear.

Lan saw it and let out a lusty wail, unlike her usual meek cry.

She instantly felt guilty when the baby caused her and Jojo to laugh. It wasn't a time for that, not until they could get Lily home. She hoped Ivy hadn't heard them.

"Go put a splash of cold milk in it, Jojo. I don't think she's going to wait patiently for it to cool this time."

She headed to the rocking chair in the corner. She was glad Jace had built them a fire in the pit earlier and she pulled the chair a bit closer to it. Not only was the kitchen her favorite place to be because of the cooking, but it was also the warmest room in the house.

"Come on out of there, Lan. Let's fill up that little belly of yours so you can sleep through the night." She gently pulled the baby around to her front and untied the wrap from her neck. With the new movement, the baby quieted. Li Jin snuggled her against her chest and, smiling down at her, was rewarded with a sideways grin that just about melted her heart. Her Mama said Lan's smiles this early were because of gas, and that might be the case, but they were still sweet.

"I'm coming, Ma! You said I could feed her." Jojo sprinted across the room.

Chapter Twelve

Lily stirred and reached out to pull the blanket over her legs. *Why was she so cold? Where was Ivy? Why had she moved so far away in the night? And who was making so much noise in the kitchen? Was Li Jin up already, so early?* She reached farther and farther, trying to find the quilt, but her fingers felt nothing.

Then she remembered. She sat up and listened.

She was still in the hospital room. It was morning and the hall outside her door had come alive with the sounds of patients yelling for attention, nurses making rounds, and the clattering of metal plates—most likely breakfast being served.

She'd finally fallen asleep after trying to force herself to stay awake, listening as long as she could for the footsteps that might belong to the returning orderly. He'd said he was coming back and she'd believed him. But he hadn't. She was proud of herself for not telling Ye Ye and Ivy about him. Even though she'd been terrified, she didn't want to pass that worry on to her family. They were doing what they could to get her out and didn't need to know how dangerous it really was.

She pulled her knees to her chest and wrapped her Ye Ye's coat tighter around her legs. The slippers had come off during the night and she reached around until she felt them, then slid them back on her cold feet.

She hadn't put the mattress back like the official had told her to; instead she'd remained in the corner, hidden in case the orderly came back. She'd dreamed of her mother again, hearing her voice in her ear telling her not to be afraid. Now her legs hurt from lying on the cold floor all night. She needed to use the bathroom and the pains shooting through her gut warned her that her bladder wouldn't wait much longer. She stood, uncertain if she should try to knock on her door, yell out, or just wait. She didn't want to anger anyone. She remembered her sunglasses and felt the top of her head. They were gone. She bent down and reached around but couldn't find them. Giving up, she considered yelling out again.

As she debated, she heard the sound of plastic shoes slapping lightly against the ceramic tiles, coming closer to her room. Keys jangled, the lock clicked, and the door opened. Lily held her breath, praying it wasn't the orderly.

"Zao." A soft voice called out good morning.

Lily breathed a sigh of relief.

"Zao," she returned. "Can I please use the restroom?"

The voice came nearer and Lily cringed. What was she going to do to her?

"I'm Nurse Guo. Don't worry, I won't hurt you. Come on, let's get you to the bathroom." She took Lily's arm and guided her toward the door. "Wait, let me just check off that I asked you the morning questions."

They stopped and Lily heard paper shuffling.

"Do you feel like you want to hurt yourself this morning?" the nurse asked.

"No!" Lily answered. Why would they even ask that?

"Then are you homicidal—meaning will you be a danger to staff or other patients around you?"

"I know what homicidal means, and no, I'm not." She sighed. This felt like a bad dream.

"Sorry, it's procedure. Let's go. The breakfast cart is making its way to your room. We should be back before they get there. Oh wait—do you need these?"

Lily felt her sunglasses being pushed into her hand. "Thank you. I couldn't find them."

"They were just a few inches from you in the corner, girl. You didn't look too hard!"

Lily put them on her face and then the nurse awkwardly guided her out the door. In the hall, Lily paused. She just remembered what the woman had said before she found the glasses. The nurse was nice, and for that she was grateful. If the breakfast team consisted of the orderly, she hoped the nurse would stay with her.

"Can I show you how it would be easier for me to walk?"

Nurse Guo chuckled. "Of course. I must apologize. I've never had a blind patient before."

"It's okay. Just let go of my arm."

The nurse let go and Lily grabbed her arm just above the elbow. "See, I hold *your* arm, and you just walk and make sure nothing is in my path. If you hold my arm, it's too confusing for my senses."

They started again and moved up the hall. The nurse broke the awkward silence.

"There was a bedpan in your room. You didn't see it?"

Lily was taken aback. A bedpan? She wasn't bedridden; why would they give her a bedpan? "Um, no. I didn't."

The nurse chuckled. "Oh, I'm sorry. Of course you didn't see it. But from what I can tell, even if you'd known it was there, you're too independent to use it."

She was right. Lily wasn't squatting over a bedpan. That was ridiculous.

"Do you know if my family is still here?"

"We're making a left turn here, then the bathroom door is on your right. No, I haven't seen them, and I'm pretty sure I'd have noticed if they were here. You and your sister are identical and that sort of stands out, you know. But I did hear this morning that you're going to be transferred soon, maybe even this afternoon. We'll get you into some real clothes. Hospital issued—but at least you'll have pants and a shirt. You can keep your jacket, at least until someone else takes it from you."

They came to the bathroom door and the nurse stopped.

"Transferred? To where?" Lily turned to her.

"The reeducation center on the outskirts of town. Let's hurry here; I have other patients to see to. I don't mean to rush you, I just don't usually personally escort everyone around." The nurse guided her through the door and stopped. "Here is the toilet directly in front of you. One step up and turn around, then squat. Be careful, don't fall in."

Lily felt tissue being pushed against her hand and she grasped it. She was silent but she could hear her heart pounding in her chest. *She wasn't going home.* Her Ye Ye hadn't been able to get her discharged. She wanted to cry but she wouldn't. She would not show weakness. If she did, she'd be like a wounded animal in the wild and who knew what could happen to her. Here, in this place, she was vulnerable more so than she'd ever been in her life. She needed to at least appear strong.

She climbed the step and felt around with her toes for the lip of the ceramic toilet. Finding it, she backed up to it, lifted the gown and jacket, and squatted. Relief. Finally. When she stood, she felt a wave of dizziness and reached out and grabbed the wall.

She was determined she wouldn't look weak but she needed food. She realized she hadn't eaten since before she and Ivy had gone to the festival. She'd not touched the congee left by the disgusting orderly. So she'd missed lunch and dinner, and now if she didn't hurry back to her room, she'd miss breakfast. But had the nurse left her?

"Are you still there?" she called out, adjusting her clothes.

"*Shi.* I'm here."

The nurse reached out and led her off the step, then let go and waited for Lily to take her arm. When she did, the nurse hesitated, then leaned her head toward Lily.

"What's your name? I haven't looked at your chart too closely."

"Lily."

"Okay, Lily, I know you're scared. But if you use your Falun Gong breathing exercises, you'll feel calmer. No one can really hurt you. They might inflict physical pain, but they can't touch your spirit if you don't let them. Be strong," she whispered.

Lily's mouth dropped open. Was the nurse trying to trick her into a confession?

"But . . . I'm not Falun Gong. It's a mistake that I'm here."

The nurse reached down and patted Lily's hand. "Please don't tell anyone I spoke of it. There are a few of us here, carefully planted among the staff. And we try to do what we can to help without calling attention to ourselves. As Falun Gongs, we believe in acts of compassion to all living things. The next nurse up for duty will not be so sympathetic. She's a true Falun Gong hater—which is what we're all supposed to be on this floor. But because of your illness, you are in a different circumstance than others. So I wanted to let you know you're not alone."

Her illness? It took Lily a minute to realize the nurse meant her blindness. She wasn't sure how to respond.

"Can I go back to my room, please?"

The nurse stepped forward and together they made their way back down the hall. When they arrived at her room, the nurse led her to the bed.

"Just wait here quietly and you'll get some breakfast. I'll go find you some clothes. You're smaller than most who come through; I hope we've got your size. It'll be hospital-issued pajamas, but warmer than what you have on."

"Okay."

"And I'm keeping the door open until you get your tray. Don't go near it or you'll get an infraction."

With that she disappeared and Lily was left alone again. She heard the rattling of the food cart coming closer and was torn between anticipation to feed her hunger, and dread of coming in contact with the orderly again.

Lily sat as quietly as possible and listened to what sounded like an argument between a patient and another nurse. It wasn't Guo—she could tell by the loud, abrasive voice. Lily heard a woman commanding someone to get back into the bed, then heard what sounded like a man whimpering. Farther down the hall a loud scream pierced the air. She concentrated on the footsteps coming close and tried not to think about the other—possibly insane—patients.

Finally the cart was in front of her door. Lily took a deep breath and waited.

"Congee or boiled egg?" a man's voice called out.

She sighed in relief. It wasn't him. At least not this time.

"Um, can I have both?" She hated to ask, but the truth was she was starving and she knew she needed her strength for whatever lay ahead.

The orderly didn't answer but he noisily removed a tray from his cart and brought it in, then set it on the bed beside Lily. He quickly turned and left the room, slamming the door behind him. Lily heard the lock click into place but she wasn't disappointed. She felt safer with it locked.

Lily settled farther up on the bed and crossed her legs. She pulled the tray closer to her and then set to touching it carefully to find out where everything was situated. When she found the hard-boiled egg, she picked it up and took a big bite. The middle was mushy and it definitely didn't taste like the eggs from home, but she was grateful for anything. She set it down and felt around until she found a spoon, then tasted the congee, forcing herself to swallow the first bland bite.

She reminded herself that she wouldn't act like a spoiled child. She quickly began shoveling the congee into her mouth before her brain could tell her how tasteless it was. She could get through this if only she concentrated and went with the flow.

Benfu was exhausted. Though he'd stayed late the night before, no agreement could be made and he'd been forced to leave Lily there all night. But now they were back, having arrived just before daybreak, after he and Calli had lain awake all night, worrying and trying to figure out what to do. He'd tried to sleep, he knew he needed the rest, but he just couldn't get past the thought that he'd failed Lily—she'd had to stay the entire night above him in that cold room. He felt horrible about it.

Calli squeezed his hand under the scarred wooden table as the official once again lectured him on signing the agreement that would grant Lily's release. He could feel his wife trembling and he worried for her health. Across from them, Lao Gong, his old friend, watched every move with eagle eyes, taking his role as an adviser seriously. Beside him, Benfu's father, Lao Zheng, also sat loaning his emotional support to the situation. He'd brought both his father and his old friend because at one time, they'd both had many connections. Even though they were now elderly, sometimes those connections could still help move things along and he was willing to try anything.

They'd been brought to the same small room, and the air was still stifling and stale with the scent of filth and nicotine. Benfu tried to suppress the urge to cough and he hated that he'd even brought Calli to such a place, but she'd insisted on returning to the hospital with him. Unfortunately the same official was there to meet them.

This time Delun had banned Ivy from the room and she waited in the lobby. The evening before she had even refused to go home with him, preferring to stand by her promise to Lily that she wasn't leaving. He had to get stern with her to finally get her into a taxi and she didn't speak to him all the way home.

Delun lit another cigarette and thumped his finger on the top document. "She is already set to be delivered to the reeducation center. Once she is signed in there, the length of her stay will depend on her compliance and willingness to renounce Falun Gong. But if you sign this, I can arrange for her to be kept here in the psychiatric ward at the hospital for a short time instead."

Benfu weighed the options—a short time in the hospital versus a stint in their reeducation center, which amounted to either a brainwashing facility or a prison, from what he'd heard.

He didn't particularly like either choice. He wanted his daughter back under his protection immediately. He reached across the table to pull the papers closer, but Lao Gong put his hand out and stopped him.

"Benfu, don't do it. It's basically acknowledging that she is a Falun Gong practitioner. And we all know she's not. If you sign it, it'll remain on her private file forever and she'll be persecuted in whatever she does in the future—schools, jobs, even if one day she tries to buy her own home."

Benfu looked at Calli, then at his father. This time their names weren't opening any doors. Delun hadn't blinked an eye when he'd introduced them. But they had given him good advice on the way over, and one useful tidbit was for him not to mention Sky's name or acknowledge that they even knew him.

Now the man tapped his dirty nails against the tabletop. "You have to decide now. I'm tired of trying to help you people. I need to wrap up her paperwork and confirm her transfer or her stay here. What's your decision?"

Benfu looked back to Calli. How could he decide? Either way, Lily would be terrified. Should he take his chances and sign the documents that would keep her in the hospital, but might brand her forever as a counter-revolutionary? Or continue to deny the charges and hope she could get in and out of the reeducation center unscathed? He knew what he wanted to do. He wanted to reach across the table and put his hands around the filthy swine who had trumped up the bogus charges against his daughter. He'd heard of this happening more and more to the people, but never had he dreamed such a thing could touch his own family.

"Benfu, what should we do?" Calli asked, bringing him out of his murderous thoughts.

He shook his head. He couldn't do it. He couldn't say which one was better. What if by his choice, something happened to her?

Delun snorted in contempt. "She was with a man who had previously been arrested for distributing Falun Gong materials. There is no doubt she was involved."

"She was *not* involved!" Benfu slammed his fist on the table and everyone jumped.

His father stood and put his hand on Benfu's shoulder. The official sat straighter in his chair and waited. Even as an old man, Lao Zheng still garnered respect.

"Benfu, my son, I know you are struggling and I will take this burden from you. I'll make the decision." He looked down at Benfu, his head cocked questioningly.

Benfu felt relief wash over him. He nodded to his father.

Lao Zheng pulled his shoulders back and raised his chin a notch. "We will not sign anything that says Zheng Lily is involved in Falun Gong. My granddaughter has done nothing wrong and we demand her release immediately."

Delun stubbed his cigarette out in the overflowing ashtray. He reached out and pulled the papers back toward him, then picked them up and shuffled them into a neat pile. He scooted his chair back and the screech of the legs on the ceramic tiles made Benfu jump.

A smirk of self-satisfaction spread across his face. "Then you've decided her fate. She'll be transported to the Jiangsu Provincial Reeducation Center," Delun said.

Beside him Calli began to sob and Benfu gathered her close. He wanted to stand and demand someone listen to them—to see reason—but he knew that from his position as no more than a street scavenger and no direct connection with anyone of authority, he would be lucky if he wasn't thrown in jail for disrespect. He looked up and met his father's eyes. He didn't have to even speak his question; his father knew he was asking if there was anything more they could do.

"Calli, please don't cry. I'll see who I can call to help us get her out of here." Lao Gong reached over and patted Calli's shoulder. "This isn't over yet."

"Can we see her again?" Benfu asked. He wanted to explain

to Lily what was happening and why she wasn't coming home yet. He knew it would be a hard conversation, but she deserved to know from him.

"*Bu*. No more visits until she is fully processed." Delun turned to leave.

"Wait!" Lao Zheng put his hand up to stop the official from going out the door. Benfu wondered what else he could say.

The official halted.

"By law you have to give us any of our granddaughter's possessions that she cannot take with her to the reeducation center. She brought in a violin and you need to turn that over to us at this time," Lao Zheng demanded, glaring at Delun.

Benfu had forgotten all about the violin. He was glad his father had thought of it, as he knew how much it meant to Lily.

"I know nothing about a violin," Delun said.

Benfu stood and helped Calli out of her chair. "Then you'd better bring down the hospital administrator, because we aren't leaving without it. The violin isn't worth much, but it's a family heirloom."

His father nodded. "Yes, a family heirloom and one we will not let your staff's sticky fingers get ahold of."

Delun stomped out of the room, almost running into Ivy on the other side of the door.

"I'll see what I can find out but I'm not spending all day looking for any secondhand junk," he called behind him as he went down the hall. "I've been here all night and I have a wife and son at home waiting for me, you know."

Benfu led Calli out and the others followed them.

Ivy pulled on Benfu's sleeve. "What did he say? Is he going to get Lily and let her go with us?"

He looked at her and put his hands on her shoulders.

"No, Ivy. She can't come with us right now. They're transferring her to another location."

He watched as the emotions played across her face and the air seemed to deflate out of her. His heart broke for her; he knew she was still carrying the guilt that she'd left her sister alone in the park.

"Come on, Ivy. Let's sit down for a minute." Calli put her arm around Ivy and led her back to the row of green plastic chairs.

Benfu pressed his knuckles to his temples and rubbed. He could feel a heavy headache coming on.

"Benfu, you've done all you can do for now," his father said.

"I'll start making some calls as soon as we get out of here—see if I can catch anyone before they leave for the weekend," Lao Gong added. "But everyone will be back in their offices on Monday. Maybe we can pull some strings."

Benfu realized he was right; it wasn't over yet. And Linnea had also told him that Jet was doing his best to contact his father to see if he could help. The man still held a position in the local branch of government. Though it wasn't a part of the Criminal Department of Affairs, perhaps he could still do something. He sure didn't want Lily to have to spend the entire weekend there.

They all turned around when they heard the official's loud stomping coming toward them from down the hall. Ivy jumped up when she saw he was carrying a plastic bag. The scowl on his face told them he wasn't happy about having to hand it over.

"Is that Lily's violin?" she asked.

Delun ignored her and handed the bag to Benfu. "This is all she had with her. And we're taking her to the main Wuxi Township police station for processing."

Calli put her hand over her heart and gasped. "What will they do to her?"

"Fingerprints. Photos. But she won't go yet. Might be

morning or it might even be a few days before we take her. They'll do a chest X-ray and a cardiogram here before they let her go. They wanna make sure she's not carrying any disease into the next facility. You never know, she might be blind from something that's contagious to others."

Benfu could see the spark of anger in Ivy's eyes and he put his hand on her arm. When she turned, he handed her the bag with the violin in it, then addressed Delun. "So help me, if I find out that one hair on her little head has been harmed by anyone here or from your station, I'll personally bring everyone involved to their knees."

"Are you threatening me?" Delun puffed out his chest. "I can have you thrown in jail for that."

Lao Zheng cleared his throat and stepped between Benfu and the official.

"Now, see here. You can probably understand my son's concern. My granddaughter is blind. You need to take special care of her and make sure she is in a safe environment at all times."

The official spat a long stream of tobacco on the white ceramic floor and turned to leave.

"All of you get out of this hospital now before I write you up for disturbing the peace."

With that he disappeared down the hall. Benfu looked at everyone around him. They all appeared as devastated as he felt. But it was still early; maybe he'd be able to get Lily out before she had to spend another night there. He went to Calli and put his arm around her. She looked too weary to even move. He moved to help her out of her chair.

"Come on, Calli. We've done all we can here—let's leave so we can make some more calls."

He led her out the main hospital doors and the others followed quietly behind, even Ivy, who could be heard crying softly as she clutched the violin and bow to her chest.

Chapter Thirteen

Ivy opened her eyes slowly and stared at the ceiling. It was too quiet and Lily wasn't crowding her like usual. Then she remembered. She sat up and put her feet on the cold floor beside the thin mattress in their room. She'd had to spend two days and three nights without her sister and still her Ye Ye had not been able to find a way to bring Lily home. She'd marched back to the hospital with him each time, pacing the lobby as he negotiated, and they hadn't even let them in to see Lily again! Her Ye Ye and his old friend, Lao Gong, had made dozens of phone calls, and her Ye Ye had been to see every official he'd ever made contact with over the years but no one would help them.

The nights had been agonizing for her lying in the bed alone, staring wide-eyed in the dark as she tried to send Lily messages of encouragement. It was the first time they had ever slept apart and after so many years of fighting for bed space, Ivy couldn't wait to let her have all the room she wanted.

To be honest, she hadn't gotten much sleep; since no one else could do anything, she'd decided she wouldn't close her eyes again until she'd figured out what to do. It was well after midnight when something had finally come to her. Then she was so excited to have a plan that she couldn't fall asleep for several more hours.

Now it was time to put her plan into place.

She slipped her feet into her slippers, then stopped to listen but didn't hear any movement down the hall in the kitchen. It was still dark but she'd have to hurry if she was to get out of the house before anyone would know. She stood and went to the rod hanging on chains suspended from the ceiling. On it were the few outfits she and Lily shared. She reached out and touched their *fire sweater,* as Lily called it. It was the nicest and softest piece of clothing they owned. Lily had claimed it as her favorite when Ivy had told her it was red, her favorite color.

The sweater reminded her how much time Ivy had spent describing everything in their life to Lily. People's faces, surroundings, and yes—even colors by comparing the colors to things Lily could actually feel for herself. She'd used the warmth of the sun to describe yellow, the coolness of water for blue, the softness of a flower petal against Lily's cheek for pink, and even held her hand over the heat of a burning fire to describe red. So many things could represent a color. And Lily had long ago chosen red as her favorite because to her it represented the rush of heat and the excitement that always followed.

She pulled the garment off the hanger and slipped it over her head, keeping her nightshirt on underneath. She hoped the sweater would bring her luck. She was going to need all she could get if her plan was going to work.

She slipped on a pair of dark jeans and wrapped a scarf around her neck.

From the overturned barrel that served as their makeshift dresser, she took a brush and pulled it through her unruly hair. As she worked, she eyed the violin propped against the barrel. The instrument seemed to stare at her accusingly, until Ivy finally reached over and turned it to face the wall.

She needed to hurry. She didn't have a mirror, but even if she did, she wouldn't have cared what she looked like. She put the brush back, careful to make sure it was in its designated spot.

Lily would scold her if she came home to find everything out of place. Or *not* find anything, because it was out of place.

She bent down and pushed the barrel up a few inches, just enough to pull her small silk drawstring bag out from under it. The bag was her and Lily's secret stash—just a small amount of cash they'd saved from holiday red envelopes and small jobs. She pulled out the money and separated a few bills. She picked up the fifty-reminbi bill and folded it in half. The twenty she folded in half and bent the corner. The rest of the cash she stuffed back in the bag and into her front pocket, but the ones set aside for Lily she slid into her back pocket. She hated to spend their money but this was an emergency.

They'd been saving to buy a real bed for their new room—a frame to put the mattress on and maybe even plump new pillows. She looked at the colorful quilt on the mattress and sighed. Bedding was something they wouldn't have to buy because it was just perfect. Her Nai Nai had made it for them when they found out they were moving and would no longer be sleeping separately on the floor. The quilt was big enough for two and Nai Nai had used many different styles of material and textures to make it attractive to Lily's sense of touch as well as visually appealing for Ivy.

Lily's favorite squares were the soft silk and flannel ones, while Ivy preferred the tougher denim and corduroy squares. Nai Nai had even sewed in a few things for each of them. A corduroy heart over a square of wool for Ivy, and prickly stars made of threads around a velvet moon for Lily. A few squares even had pockets on them from their outgrown jeans and sometimes Nai Nai surprised them with candies or little notes tucked down deep inside. At night they liked to "claim their squares," a game that usually helped them to unwind and fall asleep.

She thought about the tall institutional bed in Lily's room at the hospital and wondered if her sister had really slept in it, or if she'd stayed cowering in the corner all night. Unfortunately, she thought she probably knew the answer to that question. She pushed the silk bag into her pocket, then went out of her room and crept quietly down the hall. At the front door, she hesitated when she saw Lily's slippers placed so neatly in their usual place. She took a deep breath and pushed her feet into her shoes, picked up Lily's cane, then froze when she heard a sound.

It was Jojo. She saw him shuffling down the hall toward his Mama's room, tripping over his long pajama pants. Ivy held her breath, hoping he wouldn't look up and see her.

But he did.

At the sight of her hovering at the door, he stopped rubbing his eyes. "Ivy? Where are you going so early?"

She hesitated. What could she say? If they were at their old house, she could say she was going to feed the neighbor's chickens. But here—there weren't any chickens. Not yet.

Jojo walked down the hall and stopped in front of her.

"Are you going to see Lily? Because if you are, can you tell her I miss her?"

Ivy smiled down at him. He was a cool kid. She put her finger to her lip to tell him to be quiet.

"Yeah, I am, Jojo. And I'll be sure to tell her. Now go back to bed."

He turned around and went back the way he'd come. Ivy slipped out. She looked around, a little nervous about being out alone before the sun had even come up, but she kept going.

She jogged up the long driveway to the street and stopped at an early street vendor setting out his wares on a large blanket over the sidewalk. He was arranging necklaces pulled from a box beside him.

"Excuse me, do you have sunglasses?" she asked, startling him.

He rose up on his haunches, surprised to have a customer so early.

"*Dui,* but it will be half an hour before I get to them." He waved his hand over to another stack of boxes behind him.

"If you can get to them now, I'll pay you fifty reminbi. I'm in a hurry."

The man jumped to his feet and went to the boxes. He moved the first one out of the way and opened the flaps on the second one, reached in, and pulled out a pair of sunglasses. He handed them to Ivy.

They weren't exactly like Lily's, but they would do. She propped them on her head, then got her money out and paid the man. He held the bill up to the sun and examined it closely.

"It's real." She felt a stab of impatience. Obviously, just because she was a teenager, he didn't trust her. Why didn't people just judge individuals—not age groups?

He nodded, then tucked the bill into his shirt pocket and turned away, restacking his boxes the way they were.

Ivy hailed a taxi. The car screeched to a stop at the curb and she climbed in and slammed the door. She rubbed her sweaty palms on her jeans. This was it. No turning back.

"People's Hospital Number Seven," she told the driver, then leaned back and took a deep breath. She wasn't sure she could pull off her plan, but her fear wasn't going to make her give up trying. Lily needed her like she never had before, and it was her responsibility to get her out of the mess she was in.

Almost an hour later after weaving through stop-and-go morning traffic, she climbed out of the cab. It was now light outside and more people were out and about, on their way to jobs, school, or wherever it was their day would take them. *Seven steps from the curb to the hospital stairs, then eleven steps on the stairs leading to the double sliding doors.* Ivy held her head high and walked through the already crowded lobby, passing by the girl at the reception window as if she were not even there. The girl barely glanced up. *Thirty paces from the double doors, through the lobby and to the elevator.* The path from the doors to the elevator was clear, no chairs blocking the way.

So far, so good. She went to the elevator and pressed the button quickly, then shoved her shaking hand in her pocket. She used her foot to slide the tall ashtray a few inches to the right, well out of the way of anyone trying to exit the elevator. With the other she held Lily's cane close to her body. From the corner of her eye, she looked to see if there were any exits other than the front one, but if there were, they were well hidden down the long hall.

The elevator arrived and the doors opened. A couple shuffled out, a disheveled man holding a toddler as the woman pushed along the IV pole behind him, careful to stay close to her baby to keep slack in the line attached to the tiny bald head.

Ivy stepped aside. "Excuse me."

She felt a quick stir of respect for the parents, poor but obviously sticking with their sick child rather than abandoning her to the hands of strangers.

She stepped into the elevator and held the door for the few people who'd lined up behind her. They all crowded in and she pushed the button for the sixth floor. The button had braille. She was impressed. Many city elevators didn't. Lily had just started learning braille and so far she knew numbers, but that was about all.

Ivy didn't look around after hitting the button, knowing the others would be giving her strange looks. What the sixth floor represented was well known, and in China most people didn't talk about mental issues. Like physical disabilities, they pushed the subject under the rug and pretended as if it didn't exist.

People reached around her and pushed the buttons they needed. No one spoke and Ivy tried to ignore the tingling in her toes and fingers. She opened her mouth slightly, trying to quiet the sound of her breaths. She wondered if everyone could hear her heart pounding as she could.

Finally the bell chimed and the faceless voice announced the sixth floor. The doors opened and Ivy took a deep breath, said a prayer that fate would go her way for once, then stepped out.

The hall was much louder than it had seemed before. She could hear crying over the noise of someone banging metal against metal. She looked to one side and saw a young man cowering in the hall, rocking back and forth with his face to the wall. Looking the other way, she saw the nurses' station with a few nurses huddled around it and behind it. She crossed her fingers and started toward it.

Twenty-three paces to the station.

She stopped at the station, and the chattering nurses all quieted and looked at her.

"Can I help you?" a rounded, elderly nurse asked, her voice unfriendly.

Ivy licked her lips. Her mouth was as dry as the Gobi desert.

"Um, I'm here to see my sister, Zheng Lily. I was here a few days ago and forgot to leave her walking cane. She can't move around without it." Ivy held the cane up so they could see it.

The nurse looked down at her watch. "It's not visitation hours right now."

"But, if I could just see her for a minute."

The other nurses watched her and Ivy thought she saw a flash of sympathy in the eyes of one of them. She looked closer and discovered it was same nurse who was there the night Lily had been admitted. She directed her attention to her.

"Remember me? The official named Delun said I could visit her in the mornings. You heard him, didn't you?" She stared deeply into the woman's eyes, silently appealing to her.

The nurse squinted at Ivy. "Hmm . . . I do remember you. You two are twins, that's hard to forget."

Ivy decided to gamble. "If you don't remember him saying that, you can call him."

Nurse Guo, as her tag read, shook her head and looked to the first nurse.

"Yes, it *was* Official Delun. He works the afternoon shift, so I don't think he'd appreciate being woken up at the break of dawn, but you're in charge, so that's your decision. I do remember him saying something like that, though."

The elderly nurse tilted her head to the side and pursed her lips.

Ivy held her breath, waiting for the woman to answer. Finally she pointed at the smaller nurse.

"Fine. You take her in and watch her closely, Nurse Guo. But I'm not going to allow the walking stick. It can be used as a weapon and I'm not letting anything happen on my watch. We can guide the girl around where she needs to go." She pointed at the stick in Ivy's hand. "You take that back home with you."

Ivy let out a shaky laugh. "I can understand that. And thank you, I'll make our visit short. I just want to make sure she's okay."

The old nurse snorted and went back to scribbling on her clipboard. "As okay as you can be in a loony bin like this one, I guess you could say."

"Follow me," the nurse said, coming around the desk and heading toward Lily's room. "I don't know what's going on with her transfer—her paperwork is a mess and Official Delun needs to get it straightened out."

Ivy followed closely behind, almost running into the woman when she stopped abruptly. *Thirty-seven paces from the nurses' station to the door of her room.*

She noticed the farther they got away from the nurses' station, the stronger it reeked of urine and other putrid smells around her. She wrinkled her nose and put her hand over her mouth.

Nurse Guo turned to her and chuckled when she saw what she was doing.

"Sorry about that—mornings are rough on the senses around here until we can get all the pans emptied and the patients cleaned up. You'd be surprised how many grown-ups are not potty trained." She turned back to the door.

"Can my sister and I have a few minutes alone?"

The nurse shook her head, then held up the key that hung around her neck. "That's against regulations." She opened the door and swung it wide.

The scene in the room filled Ivy's eyes with tears. Lily was sitting on the bed next to a tray with an empty bowl, picking at her nails like she did when she was the most nervous. Gone was the threadbare hospital gown and in its place her sister wore a pair of blue-striped oversized hospital pajamas, with their Ye Ye's jacket still layered on top. Ivy's first thought was how tiny she looked. And frightened.

"Lily, I'm back." She walked toward the bed.

At the sound of her voice, Lily's face lit up.

"Ivy!" She quickly moved off the bed, knocking the entire tray to the floor.

The noise was like a gunshot in the small room. Lily froze and a look of terror Ivy had never seen before crossed her sister's face. In that moment, Ivy knew she'd come to do the right thing.

Now she only had to somehow get the nurse out of the room so she could convince Lily.

Benfu sat at the table and sipped at his tea, watching Calli bounce little Lan on her knee. The baby girl was always her most cheerful in the mornings. He and Calli were first up as usual and had heard her fussing down the hall. Calli had peeked in to see no one paying her any attention, so had scooped her out of her cradle and brought her with them. One dry diaper and a full belly later, Lan was happily gurgling her gratitude.

Benfu tried to muster up a smile for the two of them. It was a sweet moment but soon the kitchen would come alive with Li Jin and whoever was scheduled as her helpers to get breakfast ready. Because they were currently housing over a dozen residents, in addition to their own family, meals were a huge production every day. So far though, Li Jin had kept it all running smoothly. He wondered if her knack for organization came from living an institutional life. He wasn't sure what scars she carried from her life in and out of the orphanage, but he knew it hadn't damaged her spirit of compassion. Li Jin was loving and giving to everyone under their roof. Even when she looked ready to drop from exhaustion, he never heard a cross word from his daughter. In that, Benfu thought, she took after her Mama.

"And what did Lao Gong say to do next? Can you tell me again?" Calli asked as she balanced Lan with one arm on her lap so she could take a sip of her own tea. Benfu was fine with explaining everything over again, as Calli wasn't able to come to the last few meetings. They still hadn't made any progress to free Lily, but this morning he was determined to make some headway or he just wouldn't leave the hospital. He put his cup back on the table and reached over for the child. Calli handed her off and Benfu laid her over his shoulder.

"He still thinks Lily is safer in the hospital than in the reeducation center, but if we sign the papers, she'll forever be marked as Falun Gong in her private citizen file." Under the table he jiggled his leg up and down, trying to burn away his nervous energy.

Calli reached up and rubbed at her forehead. Benfu wished he could take her fear away and carry the burden alone. They were so unsure of what would happen to Lily. It was always a big question mark when trying to predict what the local government would or wouldn't do.

"Are you taking Ivy up there with you this morning?" she asked.

"Yeah, I need to go wake her. Poor kid—she was a wreck. I thought I'd let her sleep in a little." Benfu had thought she looked sick with worry before she'd gone to bed. They'd all been up late the night before, the family coming together for an update on the situation. Even Linnea had come over and pledged to do anything she could. He had hoped whatever Lily was doing at that moment, that she had felt all of them gathered and sending good thoughts her way.

He heard footsteps and Li Jin popped through the door, already looking fresh with her hair pulled back neatly and a clean white apron tied around her middle. Jojo trailed behind her, his face puffy from sleep. He crossed the room and came to stand beside Benfu's chair. With one arm holding Lan and one wrapped around Jojo, Benfu felt blessed. If he could only get Lily back home and out of the clutches of those in power, he would once again be at peace.

"Hey, Jojo. You don't look too awake yet." He squeezed him tighter.

Li Jin began pulling her large metal pots off the hooks and setting them on the stove top. Calli got up and went to the counter to start gathering ingredients for the congee.

"He sure is grumpy. He crawled in between Sami and me early this morning. He said he couldn't sleep," Li Jin said. "Sami will be mad as a hornet when she gets up, so thank you, Mama, for getting Lan. At least Sami will get to sleep in some with the whole bed to herself."

Benfu snorted. "Seems to me like she sleeps in every day. I see this baby on your back much more than I see her in her mother's arms."

Li Jin stopped moving for a moment. "Baba, I know. But you have to understand. Sami's had a hard time of things. She'll get on her feet. We just have to help her until she finally releases all the anger she's holding."

Benfu held his tongue. He didn't turn around but if he had, he knew Calli would be shooting him a look that told him to hush it up. Talking about Sami never went well; their daughter was just too loyal to the girl. But he did hate to see Li Jin taken advantage of so much. Sami was getting free room and board without lifting a finger. And now Li Jin was practically a full-time nanny to her child! But he didn't have the time or energy to worry about it right now. He needed to focus on Lily and how he was going to get her home.

"Calli, Lao Gong said it would be best if we go ahead and work on getting some money together for when they set Lily's fine. There's a small chance we can pay it and possibly just bring her home."

Calli came back to the table and sat down. "How much money are you talking?"

"A lot more than we have at our fingertips, that's all I know." He gave Jojo a gentle nudge to the chair beside him.

Li Jin came to stand behind Jojo as he laid his head on the table. She stroked his hair while she talked. "I'm so sorry, Baba. You've put most of your money into this place along with mine."

Benfu held his hand up. "No, Li Jin, don't even think like that. This place is a blessing—not only to us, but to a lot of other people. No one knew when we started this that we'd run into an emergency. We just have to figure out another way."

Calli put her head in her hands. "I just don't know how, Benfu. We've been blessed with a lot of kindness lately, but when it comes to paying the bills, we're still just living month to month."

"Don't worry so, Calli. With the allowance they started giving us last year and the stipends we're receiving for some of the girls, it's stretching enough to get us through. But first things first. I'm gonna go wake up Ivy and we'll go back to the hospital. I promised her I wouldn't go without her. We need to hurry—maybe something has changed."

Jojo looked up quickly. "Ivy's not here, Ye Ye."

"What do you mean, she's not here? She's asleep," Benfu said.

"No, she's not. When I came to Mama's room this morning, I saw her leaving."

"Oh dear," Calli said, wringing her hands. "Benfu, you know she's on her way to the hospital. I hope she doesn't cause any trouble and get herself arrested."

Benfu got up quickly. What was his daughter up to? She was capable of just about anything when it came to protecting her sister. He needed to get there, and quickly. "She'd better not. These officials don't play around. We sure can't afford to have two girls in their clutches. I need to go. I'll call you when I get there." He didn't wait on a reply as he stood and headed for the door.

"It's me. I'm here, Lily." Ivy crossed the room, set the cane on the bed, and enveloped Lily in a tight hug. She felt her sister trembling under the coat. She turned around to face the nurse.

"Can't you turn some heat on in this place? You treat people like animals in here! I think this is considered cruel and inhumane treatment."

The nurse chuckled and moved around her. "Not quite, dear. Cruel and inhumane would have been if I'd left her in here for hours until she finally wet herself, like the other nurses would have done. Tell her, Lily. Tell her I come for you early every morning."

Lily nodded. "She does, Ivy. She even brought me these pajamas. I'm a lot warmer than I was before. It's freezing in here at night."

The nurse closed the door behind her. "Listen, we need to talk. Maybe you can help prepare your sister for the reeducation center. I'm on your side, but there's nothing I can do other than warn you of what to expect. You think sleeping in a cold room with no covering is bad? Wait till she gets over there. It'll be hard—especially since she can't see."

Ivy narrowed her eyes at the nurse. "What do you mean you're on our side?"

"Shh. Not so loud. I also follow Falun Gong. But you must keep this quiet or I could lose my job, or worse. I'd be jailed or sent to a labor camp. I took this job to help as much as I can."

"But we're not Falun Gong followers," Ivy said.

"I tried to tell her that," Lily whispered. "But she *has* been nice to me, Ivy."

The wheels started turning in Ivy's head and she got an idea. She crossed her arms and lifted her chin. She was glad she did know a bit about their practice; it just might work to their benefit.

"So, if you are Falun Gong, you are committed to living a life of compassion, right?"

The nurse nodded.

"Then you know, as you've already said, that my sister will have a rough time in the reeducation center because she is blind."

Lily put her hand on Ivy's arm. "Ivy, I'll be fine. Don't worry about me."

"Yes, I've already said she'll have a rough time. But I can at least tell her a bit about what to expect, if we hurry. I need to get back out there before they get suspicious." She turned and peeked out the window.

Ivy decided it was her only chance just to lay it out there.

"Then you can help me trade places with Lily. I can go to the reeducation center and Lily can go home."

Lily gasped and the nurse turned around to face them. Ivy steeled herself. She'd definitely gotten her attention. Now how she'd answer was a different story.

"No, Ivy! I won't let you do that. And we'd never get away with it."

The nurse nodded her agreement. "Right, how do you think they wouldn't know? It's fairly obvious your sister is blind and you aren't."

Ivy felt a rush of excitement. The nurse was asking questions, so it wasn't a no just yet.

"I can pretend to be blind. See, I came in with sunglasses, too, so no one will suspect anything. And I've watched Lily so many times, I can act just like she does when she's walking, talking, or doing anything. We can do this."

Lily shook her head and Ivy felt a surge of irritation. "Dammit, Lily! You *are* going to do this!"

They'd argued before but Ivy had never cursed at her and she could see the surprise cross her sister's face. She immediately felt guilty. Lily had been through enough. "I'm sorry, Lily. I just want to get you out of here *today*. But you've got to let me help you. It's you and me. That's all it's ever been. Please."

As Lily hesitated, the nurse clucked in sympathy, then put her finger to her mouth. "Enough talk. If we hurry before the morning staff change, we might really pull this off."

Ivy turned to Lily and put her hands on both her shoulders. "Lily, you have to let me do this. Nai Nai is just sick over you being here. I can handle it better—because I can see what is coming at me. Please."

Lily didn't look completely convinced. Ivy knew what her sister was thinking; she wanted to go but didn't want to leave Ivy in her place. Loyalty and responsibility went both ways in their sisterhood.

"Please, Lily. If you love me as your twin, you'll let me do this." She knew Lily wouldn't like her saying that. Their twin ultimatum had only been used in dire circumstances before, but this *was* a dire circumstance! "And Ye Ye is already working on getting you out of here—so I won't stay long. You'll see. Okay?"

Before Lily could answer, Ivy was shocked to see Nurse Guo jump into action.

"Let's do this. Your sister's right, Lily. Your blindness puts you at a serious disadvantage. There are some scary things to watch out for here, but even more so over there." She came closer. "Ivy, what's your plan?"

Ivy quickly kicked off her shoes. "Lily, get undressed. We'll trade clothes and then I'm going to tell you exactly how to get out of this hospital and to the taxi line. Remember how you taught yourself to count paces?"

Lily didn't answer but she shrugged out of their Ye Ye's jacket and let it pool around her feet on the floor.

"Well, I listened when you rattled on and on, and wouldn't shut up. Guess what? I actually learned a lot." Ivy pulled the sweater off and tossed it to Lily. She forgot to warn her and it settled over her head before Lily grabbed it off and pushed her arms through.

"Here's some money for the taxi, and don't let the driver know you're blind or he'll cheat you!" Ivy tucked it into Lily's hand.

"Ivy, I'm blind, not stupid," Lily mumbled as she reached up and smoothed her hair down.

Ivy was relieved to see her sister snap out of her quietness. She almost smiled at the sassy tone she'd used. It showed she wasn't completely broken from the experience.

"I know that. Oh, and I have your cane. You'll have to just carry it out until you get outside, but then you can use it to get the rest of the way home."

"Hurry up, you two!" Nurse Guo said, peeking out the window again.

Lily paused at the door and took several deep breaths, blowing out her chest and dropping her shoulders. She could do this; she knew she could. She knew one other thing, too; other than the worry and guilt over leaving her sister behind, she felt a sense of relief to be dressed in familiar clothes and about to find her way home.

"That's right, Lily. You have to look relaxed. Usually when you walk around, you're stiffer because you are hyperaware. This time you can't be that way."

Lily shook her body and practiced a more relaxed stance. It was hard to relax when she was scared to death. She couldn't believe she was actually doing this. She could only imagine how Ivy felt, dressed in the hideous hospital clothes and plastic slippers that Lily had quickly discarded. She felt torn—she wanted to go home but she didn't want Ivy to have to take her place.

Nurse Guo came to stand beside her. "I'll get you to the elevator. You just walk next to me and I won't let you collide with anything. We'll pretend I'm scolding you and making sure you leave. Ivy—put those sunglasses on before someone comes in here and notices you aren't blind."

Lily heard Ivy fumble with the glasses and felt butterflies in her stomach. Could her sister really make people think she was blind? "Ivy, are you sure about this?"

Suddenly Ivy was beside her and her arms were wrapped tightly around her. Lily could feel the soft texture of their Ye Ye's jacket and was glad that Ivy at least had that for comfort. Having it the night before had made all the difference and she'd gone to sleep clutching the lapels over her nose, inhaling her Ye Ye's familiar scent.

"I'm sure. Now get going before the other nurses get suspicious. Don't worry—Ye Ye will get me out of here before you know it. And Lily, thank you for letting me do this."

Lily felt Ivy's arms fall away and her sister stepped back. This was it.

Nurse Guo opened the door and Lily stepped out. The nurse nudged her gently in the right direction and Lily began walking. Ivy had said it was thirty-seven paces to the nurses' station, then twenty-three to the elevator. With more confidence than she felt, she counted silently in her head as she walked briskly.

"Now I told you only a few minutes! Next time—if there is a next time—you and your sister will have to keep it shorter,"

Nurse Guo chattered in her ear as she walked beside her, supposedly to make sure she got on the elevator. "And who wears sunglasses inside? You kids all think you're so cool. It's *ridiculous*."

As they approached the nurses' station, a familiar voice called out. Lily stiffened. It was surly and rough. She'd never forget it.

"Where's she going? Her time up already?" he asked, his voice just as bitter as the night before. "We were just getting to know each other."

Lily stopped when the hair on her arm stood up. It was the orderly. She'd forgotten to warn Ivy about the orderly!

"This isn't our patient—this is her sister," the nurse answered, then nudged Lily to start walking again.

Behind them the orderly whistled. "Well, I'll be damned if she ain't the spitting image of that little mouse you got back there in that room. Except it looks like she can see by the way she's swaggering around. And she isn't a mouse like her sister—I think this might be a little firecracker."

"Nurse Guo, I must go back. I need to tell Ivy something," Lily whispered, hoping no one else was near enough to hear.

"No, you're getting on the elevator and don't come back until this time tomorrow," Nurse Guo said, raising her voice, obviously so everyone could hear.

"But—" In the confusion, Lily lost count and was unsure how close she was to the elevator. Without her cane, or any reference or guidance, she felt a wave of panic and her steps faltered. Where was the wall? The elevator? How far behind did she leave the nurses' station?

Nurse Guo grabbed her upper arm. "I'm going to make sure you leave right now. We have work to get done around here and don't have time to babysit you two."

Lily tried again to stop but the nurse was surprisingly strong.

She let herself be guided toward the elevator and then they stopped. The nurse pushed the button.

"Is anyone else around us?" Lily whispered.

"No, but they're watching. Keep your mouth shut."

"That orderly harassed me last night. Please keep him away from my sister."

"Shh. Your sister will probably be transferred out of here before nightfall. Don't worry about her. She's a tough one. And old Cho won't hurt anyone—he's all talk."

Lily was silent. She wasn't so sure about the orderly being harmless but it was true; Ivy was a tough one. She prayed that this time her sister's forceful personality would be a benefit in keeping her safe.

The doors opened and Lily felt the nurse give her a soft push.

The nurse threw one last hint her way. "Lookie there, you got the entire elevator to yourself. See you later. We'll take care of your sister!"

Lily stepped in and turned to face the door. The button panel was supposed to be right there. She reached out and found the bottom row of buttons and pushed what she thought was the one for the first floor. The doors closed and the elevator moved with a sharp jolt.

Now all she had to do was find her way out of the hospital, into a taxi, and to their home. If she pulled that off without breaking her neck, it would be no less than a miracle. Then she needed to round up the troops to help her get her sister out of there.

"Kuai yi dian." Benfu tapped his fingers on the door rest and urged the driver to go faster. As much as he hated the usual

kamikaze recklessness of the city taxi drivers, this time he appreciated it. He didn't know what Ivy was up to, but knowing his daughter, it couldn't be good.

As the driver stomped on his brake, rammed the gas, then pounded out a vicious litany of horn blasts, Benfu once again wondered how they'd stumbled into such bad luck. Everything had been going well, and now this. He couldn't deny that finding Li Jin and opening Rose Haven were still a blessing, but why did such a blessing have to mean his other daughters must suffer? Couldn't the gods let all his children be happy at once?

The driver finally pulled up to the curb in front of the hospital.

"Eighteen reminbi," he said, without turning his head. He held his hand up to receive the money and Benfu put a twenty on his palm. He opened the door and scooted out.

The area around the hospital was already starting to get busy. Beggars, vendors, and people seeking medical intervention clogged up the walkway and hurried around him. Benfu paused to put his money clip back in his pocket—he didn't want to fall victim to a pickpocket. When he looked up again, his jaw dropped.

There was Lily coming out of the automatic doors of the hospital with no cane and no one to guide her! What was she doing free already? And where was her sister? He watched as her lips moved silently and she paused at the top of the concrete stairs, then took her cane from under her arm and began to unfold it.

"Lily! Wait!"

Her head jolted up at the sound of his voice. "Ye Ye?"

Benfu hurried across the walk and up the stairs. He gave her a quick hug, then stepped back. "What are you doing out here and where's Ivy?"

Lily bit her lip. A sure sign she didn't want to tell him something.

"Lily? What is it?" He guided her out of the way of the many people coming in and out of the doors. They stood next to the hospital wall. Benfu watched as she took a few hard swallows, then pulled her shoulders back.

"We switched places," Lily said quickly, then flinched. "Ivy made me do it. I swear."

Benfu shook his head. He should've known. He'd watched as Ivy had made it her life goal to protect her sister since the day they'd arrived on his doorstep. While he should've been angry, he wasn't—he was just relieved to have one of them to take home.

"I can't say I'm surprised. That sister of yours is more than a little protective of you. I'm surprised she didn't take the entire hospital staff hostage to get you sprung." He sighed as he looked at the glass doors behind her. "Well, what's done is done. Now we have to get her out of there. But first, I need to get *you* home. You've been through enough and I think you need some time to pull yourself together."

Lily nodded. "They're working on the transfer and might get to it before this evening. Do you think we can get her out before then?"

Benfu put his arm around Lily and guided her down the stairs and to the line of taxis.

"I'm going to do my best, Lily."

He opened the door of the first taxi and gently nudged Lily until she climbed in. He leaned down and told the driver their address, and threw a twenty-reminbi bill at him.

"You, my dear daughter, need to go straight home and into your Nai Nai's arms." He watched as one tear found its way out from under her sunglasses. He was proud of Lily—she'd been courageous long enough. Now he could see she was close to losing her composure and probably would once Calli started mothering her.

"Okay, Ye Ye. But please, see what you can do for Ivy."

Benfu bent his head lower until he could see the driver in the front. "Make sure you drive very carefully. This is precious cargo you got back here." He patted Lily's hand once, then closed the door securely. He turned back toward the hospital.

Now, on to see what he could do for his other daughter. It was only early morning and his joints ached from the stress and uncertainty his body held. He knew one thing for sure—he was getting too old for all this turmoil.

Chapter Fourteen

Sami sat across the table from Li Jin and Calli, painting her nails a bloodred. The blind twin, Lily, had shown up alone an hour before and shook everything up. She'd told quite a story of switching places in the psychiatric ward with her sister. *More drama from the precious flock*—and again Sami was left alone while they comforted the girl and finally put her to bed. It was the middle of the day and they were letting Lily sleep! If she was the one who wanted to sleep in, she'd have to put up with their disapproving looks and such, but because Lily was theirs, she could do what she wanted. It was unfair.

"Did you see how much she was shaking?" Li Jin said, reaching down to rub her feet. Sami knew she had to be tired; she'd fed everyone breakfast and lunch, and supervised all the cleaning involved. Li Jin wouldn't admit it, but her family worked her way too hard.

Calli nodded and *tsked* her lips for the fifteenth time. "And I peeked in just a minute ago and she was sound asleep, cradling her violin. It's going to take her a while to get over this."

They were really throwing a pity party for the girl, Sami thought as she held her nails up and blew softly on them. The only bright spot of the afternoon was the baby was taking an extra-long nap, meaning Sami could finally relax awhile.

"I wish your Baba would come home or call and let us know what's happening with Ivy. That girl! Only she could come up with such an elaborate scheme. I'm not surprised at it one bit," Calli said.

Sami looked up to see the old woman taking a long swig of her green tea. That was another thing. They talked about budgeting and rationing their supplies all the time, but she and the old man could always be found in the kitchen, stalking Li Jin and drinking up all the tea. Sami could barely get a moment alone with her own best friend.

"I didn't want to ask her before she got rested up, but I hope nothing horrible happened to Lily while she was there. She's more delicate than Ivy. And I can tell she's been crying," Li Jin said.

"Oh, they said she was locked in her own room. So hopefully she was protected from those who are truly mentally ill," Calli said.

Sami snorted without looking up. These people had no clue what kinds of things happened in the local hospitals. They'd be shocked right off their fairy-tale rockers if they did.

"Sami, did you have something to add?" Calli asked.

"Uh—not really. I just find it entertaining that you both think you know so much about mental wards and you've never really been in one. The blind twin probably saw more without her sight than you two will ever understand about hospitals."

"Don't call her that," Calli said. "But anyway, you think you know more than we do about the hospital?"

Even without looking up, Sami could feel the disapproval forming on the old woman's face.

Li Jin, of course, butted in and tried to smooth it over. "Sami just probably knows a lot from street talk."

"No, that's not where I know it from," Sami said. She'd give them a little to chew on.

"What do you mean?" Li Jin looked perplexed, amusing Sami even more.

"I've been in a few mental wards." She held both her hands up and wiggled her fingers. "Not 'cuz I'm crazy or anything—just because when you aren't a part of an upstanding family or have government connections, you can get thrown into a mental hospital for just about anything."

"Like what?" Li Jin persisted.

Sami started painting the other hand. Now that she had their attention, she was going to draw it out. She finished all five fingers before answering.

"Like . . . I knew of a man who was committed for six months just because he complained to the owner of his company about their treatment of employees. The owner knew someone who knew someone and there you go—he did months locked in the psych ward and his wife had to pay a big fat fine to get him sprung."

"That's awful!" Calli said, holding her hand to her heart. "But what about you, Sami? What did you do to get put in there?"

Sami fought the urge to roll her eyes. This family was just too much. She could really shock the old lady if she wanted to but she wasn't telling them anything about her past troubles.

"What else were other people in for?" Li Jin asked.

"Hmm, I also met a woman in the same ward as me who tried to divorce her husband. Unfortunately he held a position in the local government section. He had her committed and she'd been there for years. The last time I saw her, they were shooting her up with some injection. She was screaming that it felt like she was being attacked by a swarm of bees as the juice went in. They gave that juice to anyone who refused to be compliant and quiet."

"Isn't there some kind of law to keep the government and

hospitals from committing normal people? And from giving them drugs they don't need?" Calli asked, shaking her head.

"I've heard they're working on one now." Sami held her hand up and examined her work. She was pretty good at it, if she did say so herself. "But I doubt they'll ever get it passed. The government will always do what it wants to do. Even if a law *is* passed, it won't do much good. If a person with a little power wants you removed from society, you'd better say your good-byes and pack your bags."

"Those poor people," Li Jin said.

"You think *they're* in bad shape? That's nothing compared to what your pretty-boy Sky is probably going through if they've transferred him. Falun Gong practitioners are beaten, starved, and even tortured if they resist long enough. There're even rumors of organ harvesting for the black market."

Li Jin gasped.

Sami tried to hide the twitching of the corner of her mouth. She didn't want Li Jin to see her smile. It wouldn't do for her to know how much the thought of Sky's punishment brought her joy. The best part of this whole situation was she thought maybe they'd gotten rid of him for good. It was much easier this way, as Sami had even contemplated seducing Sky to turn Li Jin against him. Now he was out of the picture without any help from her.

She heard Lan's cries from the hallway. *Great, the kid was up.* So much for her anticipated long afternoon break. And she'd hoped the old woman would go find something to do so she and Li Jin could talk. But no, she sat her plump bottom right down at the table, probably even knowing that Sami wanted to be alone with Li Jin. Lately nothing went her way.

"I'll get her." Li Jin pushed her chair back and stood. "I need to get out of here anyway."

Sami watched her leave the room. Li Jin could run but she couldn't hide from all the troubles being a part of a family and being attached to someone would bring. It was Sami's job to make her understand that. Then maybe she'd agree the best thing to do was hit the road with her.

Speaking of the road—Sami was headed out again later but first she needed to talk Li Jin into keeping the baby for the evening. Or, if she was careful, she could just sneak out again while her back was turned and then she knew Li Jin would watch Lan. But first she needed to take a bath and do up her hair and makeup. She hoped she'd have a profitable night. She couldn't have love and didn't want family—but damned if she wouldn't one day have riches.

Li Jin changed Lan's bottom and took her outside. She needed to get some air and she was sure Sami was probably still working on her nails—or even her toes by now, and wouldn't take kindly to an interruption. Li Jin didn't care; she could handle the baby all night if she had to. Anyway, something about Lan's quiet nature always made Li Jin calmer.

And right now she needed any diversion she could get. All she could think about was Sky and if he was being mistreated. She knew Sami didn't mean to, but her comments had really upset Li Jin.

She looked at her watch and wondered what he was doing right now. *Is he pacing in a cell? Looking out a window? Is his grandfather fighting to get him out? Is he hurt?*

She went to the bench in front of the door and sat down. She balanced Lan on her lap, facing her out toward the yard so she could look around. The little girl was getting more curious every day and she loved to be outside. Jojo would be home any minute from school and Li Jin knew from experience that when the baby saw him headed down the sidewalk, she'd ball up her little fists and punch the air with excitement.

Li Jin kissed Lan on the top of her head. Even with the comfort of the baby's downy soft hair touching her lips, she couldn't stop thinking about Sky and what he might be going through. She felt guilty that everyone's focus was on Ivy and hardly anyone mentioned Sky's predicament.

She felt helpless. Not only was she tied down at the shelter, unable to be gone for long periods of time, but she didn't have any money left to even try to help. She didn't even know if they were asking for a fine to be paid for her sister's release yet. She needed to get Linnea to call Sky's grandfather and get some news on him, too, but she didn't want anyone to think she was more concerned for him than she was for her own sister. She sighed. Yes, they needed to just concentrate on getting Ivy home. She didn't want to upset her parents any more than they already were.

Chapter Fifteen

Benfu walked through the *hutong* lane and picked up his pace when his old home came into view. On the way over he'd collected a stack of old newspapers and at least half a dozen plastic bottles. Calli wouldn't be pleased to hear of him picking up rubbish again, but every penny was needed now. He shifted the large plastic bag over his other shoulder and wished again for his bike. But he hadn't known when he had left home that morning he'd be trekking across town.

Being back in the neighborhood was bittersweet and he waved at his neighbors as he made his way to the gate of his old house. He couldn't deny the connection he felt to the community that had embraced him so many years ago when he was a young man without direction.

"Benfu! So nice to see you!" Widow Zu called out from across the way. She had her hand deep into a bucket of chicken feed, getting ready to sling it across her yard as her hens strutted around her.

Benfu smiled at her and held his hand up. "You, too, Widow Zu. How are you feeling?"

"I'm just finer than a four-star general on opium. Are you going to be visiting your father for a while? I'll get some eggs ready for you to take back to Calli."

Benfu nodded. "I'll be here for at least a half hour or so. *Xie xie,* Lao Zu."

He swung open the gate and walked through. He looked around at the yard and shook his head in wonder. If even possible, it looked better than it had when they'd moved away. His father had quite the green thumb, it appeared. The flowers swayed in the wind, the grass was clipped and manicured, and even the water in the koi pond was crystal clear. From one of the tree branches a wicker birdcage hung with a bright yellow bird hopping around inside.

Benfu went to the door and gave a soft knock. He hoped his father wasn't trying to take a mid-morning nap. But on second thought, maybe it would be a good thing if the man didn't answer and Benfu couldn't ask the question he'd come to ask.

The door swung open. "Benfu! Come in, come in."

His father stood aside and Benfu walked in. He looked around the large room that had been his home for decades. While the outside was neat and trim, the inside looked like a totally different house. And as expected from a bachelor, it was a bit dusty and cluttered.

"Sit down. I was just shucking some corn. You've got some mighty generous neighbors around here, Benfu. It's been a year and they still keep me fed. I'm getting fatter than a swine."

Benfu chuckled. His father was far from plump and actually still kept himself fit and dressed as if he were going to teach at the university every day. He had a suspicion that many of the widows in the area probably had their eye on him, maybe even Widow Zu. It was no surprise he was flooded with vegetables and other tasty home-cooked treats almost on a daily basis.

"I'm glad they're taking care of you, Baba." He sat down at the small table and picked up an ear of corn. He tore at the husk, dropping the pieces into a bucket at his father's feet.

Letting his father move into the house was the final gesture that seemed to have melted away all the bitterness between them. It was Calli's idea, as were most of the good things he'd done in his life. He wondered what she'd think of her little home now. Just behind his father he saw the metal bed that had replaced his and Calli's bed. It looked small and uncomfortable, at least not as comfy and inviting as theirs had. Also gone were the colorful quilts and braided rugs from the room, leaving behind a dreary living area. But most of all, the difference was in the atmosphere. To put it simply, the house felt lonely. Benfu could only surmise it was the absence of the girls' laughter and incessant chattering that had turned a once-vibrant home into a quiet and somber house. He felt sorry for his father.

"So I can tell by your face that you've had no luck getting Lily released," Lao Zheng said as he stripped the husk from his ear of corn.

Benfu sighed. "Lily's at home. But now Ivy has taken her place."

Lao Zheng laid his ear of corn on the table and looked up at Benfu. "Now tell me how in Buddha's nation you managed that?"

"I didn't manage anything. It's that stubborn and protective streak that girl possesses. Ivy snuck out this morning and went to the hospital without me. When I got there, Lily was standing outside and Ivy was in custody on the sixth floor. They switched places!"

Lao Zheng chuckled. "I'm sorry. I know it's not funny. But I can just see Ivy sitting up all night concocting a plan to spring her sister from that hospital. That girl has spent her life protecting her sister; we shouldn't be surprised at her latest maneuver."

"No, I'm not surprised, either. But I put her in a taxi and sent her home; then I went up to talk to them about releasing Lily—*I mean Ivy*—but they refused."

"Is there anything we can do at all?"

"I'm getting to that. But I've got one piece of good news first. They were unable to transport Ivy to the reeducation center. Each patient has to pass a physical and Ivy had a fast heartbeat and felt faint—or at least that's what they told me. I'm not going to tell Calli about that part because she'll worry herself to death. I supposed it was Ivy's adventures of the morning that got her heart rate going. She was probably terrified they were going to be caught. But from what I've heard, she's better off in the hospital than she would be at the reeducation center they've sent Sky to."

"Well, that is good news then."

Benfu sat up straight in his chair. It was time to come out with it. "I've come to ask a favor."

Lao Zheng returned his steady gaze. "Anything I can do, I will. You know that."

Benfu nodded. "They've set a fine. If I can get the funds together, they'll release her in two weeks and won't note her as a Falun Gong follower in her file—her sister's file."

"How much are they asking for?"

Benfu hesitated and took a deep breath. "Ten thousand reminbi."

Lao Zheng's eyebrows rose quickly and he whistled. "That's a lot of money, Son."

"I've come to ask you if I can borrow it." Benfu waited, hoping that for once, his father would come through.

Lao Zheng stood and wiped his hands on his trousers. He crossed the room and went to the window, looking out over the yard. Finally he turned around.

"Benfu, I'm sorry to say I can't loan you the money." His shoulders slumped and he looked at the floor. "There's nothing left of what your mother and I had saved. We used most of it for doctors when she got sick, and the rest of it was used to make her comfortable in her final days."

Benfu sighed. Even though he still had some buried resentment against his mother for her actions against Li Jin, he didn't like to think of her suffering. But everything? His parents were well-off at one time. Could it all be gone?

"Everything? Your entire life savings?"

Lao Zheng nodded. "I live off my teacher's pension from the state now. It's a pittance, but I don't need much."

Benfu felt defeated. And tired. But he couldn't go home to Calli yet. He had to keep trying. "Well, I guess I need to go talk to Lao Gong. He's probably in the same boat as you, but he's my last resort."

"Jet's father couldn't help?"

"No, he tried. I called him from the hospital this morning. But he's in a different branch of the city government and couldn't pull any strings. These officials who are in charge of keeping the streets clean of beggars and Falun Gong practitioners act like they're untouchable. It's so frustrating."

Benfu stood and tried to ignore the feeling of panic threatening to envelop him.

"Wait. Before you go, I do have one idea. Please, sit back down."

Benfu sat down, waiting. Hoping.

"The violin."

"What do you mean, the violin?"

"It's a special violin, Benfu. The reason we sent it with you all those years ago was because it was worth more than any of our antiques or pieces of art. At that time, the houses in Shanghai were all being ransacked by the Red Guards faster than anyone could keep up with. So many valuable items and antiques were demolished—it would have been crazy to try to hide it there. My biggest hope through our years of estrangement was that you were keeping it safe. Son, it's very valuable. We can find some-one to buy it."

Benfu stood quickly. He couldn't imagine the violin was worth enough to bail out Lily, but even so, he could never part with it knowing that it was his daughter's most prized possession. For a family like theirs, finding and affording another instrument of that caliber and that held so many memories would be next to impossible. There had to be another way. "No. It no longer belongs to me, Baba. That's Lily's violin and it's the only thing she has, her one link to independence. I can't take that away from her. I don't want her to know we even spoke of it."

Lao Zheng held his hands up. "Okay, okay. I just thought—"

"I appreciate the idea, but no, I just can't do that. We'll find another way." Benfu crossed the room and opened the door. "You can come for dinner tonight if you feel like crossing town."

Zheng nodded. "We'll see. My joints are screaming today, but maybe."

Benfu left through the door and closed it behind him. Across the lane he saw Widow Zu sitting on her short stool, waving him over.

"Benfu, I have your eggs! But you have to promise me you'll come visit more often before I hand them over. I miss those girls, too! Next time you'll bring them?"

He headed over to make his promises. At least Widow Zu didn't know he'd failed his family. So far they'd been able to keep the gossip contained, something important to a proud old man like himself. Widow Zu and the rest of his old neighbors still thought he was a hero to all his daughters and didn't know he'd lost track of one. He didn't look forward to the day they found out otherwise and lost faith in him.

Chapter Sixteen

Ivy felt ridiculous. She used one hand to hold up the baggy pajama bottoms and one hand to hold together her jacket over the hospital-issued shirt that gaped from too many missing buttons. To keep the cheap plastic slippers from sliding off, she shuffled along beside the nurse, barely lifting her feet from the floor. The nurse—a different one altogether from Nurse Guo—gripped her arm tightly, leading her down the hall at a pace faster than her shoes could keep up with. All around them Ivy heard and felt a sense of chaos. Obviously the rest of the patients had woken up and now many of them were vocally letting their needs be known.

"Hurry up, we don't have all day. I've got to start med rounds," the nurse scolded as she picked up the pace.

Ivy was glad for the sunglasses so the nurse couldn't see the way her eyes flashed with anger at the way she was being pulled down the hall like an ox on a rope. She wouldn't be transferred to the reeducation center, at least she knew that much. By some miracle she'd wound herself up so tight that her heart rate was almost double the normal, according to the nurse. When the woman asked if she'd felt okay, Ivy had lied and said she'd been faint several times. With a few chops on her—well actually, Lily's—file, Ivy was spared from a new adventure at an unknown place because she'd failed the physical exam.

A win for her but now she was going into the women's ward. Ivy concentrated on taking deep breaths. She wasn't exactly thrilled to be put into the general population with a bunch of crazies, but she was thankful she was the one, rather than Lily. At least she could see and take care of herself.

At the end of the hall, the nurse unlocked another set of double doors and gestured for Ivy to come through. On the other side was another long hall with many more closed-off rooms, probably private patient rooms, from what Ivy could tell.

"Don't start trouble with anyone. Don't touch anyone else's bed or belongings. Don't be aggressive. Don't make eye contact—oh, sorry, that doesn't apply."

Ivy shook her head at the woman's ignorance but didn't reply as she rattled on.

"Dinner will be at five o'clock. Showers are only weekly and you'll have to get on the schedule. Lights-out will be at eight, and if you're found out of your bed, you'll be strapped in until morning."

They arrived at the end of the hall and the nurse stopped in front of yet another set of doors. She reached over and pushed a black buzzer on the wall, then held her identification card up to a camera mounted over the door.

"What about visitors?" Ivy asked.

"Visitors have to be approved by the attending doctor, but he won't have a chance to look at your file today and maybe not tomorrow. We'll let you know."

After a few more seconds, the doors slowly opened and instead of another hall, they stepped into a small office enclosed in glass with a view over a huge room. The attendant, a young woman dressed from head to toe in what looked like a pink running suit, jumped up and stood before them.

Ivy reminded herself not to appear as if she was seeing anything, so she looked around as far from one side to the other as she could without moving her head.

"Zheng Lily, patient 877, transfer approved by Wang Yisheng."

"History of violence?" the attendant asked.

"No, not yet. Falun Gong."

"Anything else I should know?"

"She's blind."

The attendant took in a deep breath. "*Aiya!* Now I know why you've let her keep her sunglasses. I was wondering if you were getting soft in your old age, Nurse, letting some teenager come in looking like a Shanghai starlet."

They continued to discuss her as if she weren't there, giving Ivy time to look out at her new living arrangements. Other than one small sitting area with a couch and television, and a station against the wall that looked to hold tea and water, most of the room was taken up by three rows of beds with at least ten beds in each row. Mulling about the room, and some lying on their beds, were patients dressed exactly like her, minus her jacket— though some of them wore tattered sweaters over their pajamas. It was eerie how everything and everyone looked the same.

The nurse handed over the file. The attendant set it on her desk, then took Ivy's arm.

"Time to introduce you to your new family, Lily."

She opened the door that led to the main room and led Ivy to the last row of beds, and the farthest bed on the end. Ivy stopped when she stopped and remained still, waiting on instructions.

"This is where you will sleep." She guided Ivy to the bed and Ivy began to run her hands over it as if examining it.

"You can smoke if someone brings you cigarettes. Make sure to put them out in the ashtray—if you drop them on the floor, you'll smoke no more. You're allowed to wander around in this room as long as you don't bother anyone. This is a low-security ward, so if you cause trouble, you'll be transferred to a high-security area and will be isolated to your own small space. *Mingbai?*"

"Yes, I understand."

A small, athletic woman and a tall, wiry girl approached and walked in a circle around Ivy and the attendant, examining Ivy closely. They looked like a couple and they obviously bought the blind act, for Ivy didn't think they'd be so openly curious if they thought she could see. Or maybe they would.

"You probably feel someone around you. They're just checking you out. Pay them no attention and they'll leave you alone." The attendant lowered her voice to a whisper. "Bother them and they'll tear you limb from limb. And I won't be jumping in to save you."

Behind her glasses, Ivy's eyes opened wide at the attendant's words. The two women were definitely of the threatening, scary type and Ivy was careful not to turn her head their way.

The attendant turned her loose, and Ivy backed up and sat on the bed. The strong scent of urine wafted up from the mattress and she tried to put it out of her mind. She'd rather sleep on the floor than the soiled bed, but she would deal with that later.

Her arrival had definitely stirred things up, and as she watched without seeming to do so, others stopped what they were doing to peek from where they were, or they came closer. Across the room, one girl sat on the couch primly with her legs crossed, taking a deep drag from her cigarette while watching Ivy. She looked scary with her stringy black hair hanging in her face and her blank expression. Though her eyes were rimmed with dark circles, she didn't appear to be much older than she was and Ivy wondered what could have brought her to a mental ward. *Was the girl really crazy?*

She felt her stomach rumble and remembered that she'd missed the lunch rounds while she was in the doctor's office. Not that the nurses on her hall had cared; they'd just shrugged and told her she'd get dinner. Ivy wasn't sure what to expect but she knew it most likely wouldn't be anything like Nai Nai or Li Jin's cooking. At that thought she felt her first longing for home and the protection of her family. Turning, only slightly, she found her eyes lingering on the mesh-covered windows beyond the beds, windows that showed only glimpses of a hazy China sky and the world outside that kept right on moving, even without her in it.

Chapter Seventeen

Lily listened to them talk from the hallway where she'd crept after she'd heard her Ye Ye come in. She could tell by his slow gait and the heavy dragging of his feet that he carried bad news. He'd gone straight to the kitchen and now he, along with Li Jin, Sami, and Nai Nai, sat around the table discussing how to get Ivy out. Lily knew he'd talk more openly if she didn't join them.

"My father didn't have the money. I have no way to pay the fine to bring Ivy home."

"Oh, Benfu. How can they just keep her like this? She's just a child."

Lily heard more movement; cups clinking together, tea being poured, Lan gurgling from her basket near the fireplace.

"It's that official—Delun—he's a tyrant," Benfu said.

"Baba's right, Mama. Most of the officials are egotistical bullies," Li Jin said. "And Sami said the mental hospital is a common place to put people to get them out of the way, even if they don't have mental issues. It's just another way for corrupt officials to make money under the table. Isn't that right, Sami?"

Sami mumbled something about Linnea that Lily couldn't make out, so she stepped closer.

"No, I can't ask her," Ye Ye said. "Linnea used her savings to pay for Maggi's surgery last year. She didn't want me to tell anyone it came from her, but that's why I can't ask her for a loan. She emptied out all she had. She even put the wedding off for another year to do it."

"That was very generous," Li Jin said.

"And you went over to your father's house today, Benfu. Right? How did that go?" Nai Nai asked.

She heard her Ye Ye sigh deeply before he spoke again. "My father only had one idea but it wasn't something I'll do."

Lily leaned in closer. Any option was now their only option, right? What would her Ye Ye possibly refuse to do that could get her sister home?

"What did he say?" Nai Nai asked.

"He said the violin is worth a lot of money, that we could sell it."

Quiet settled around the room and Lily felt her breath catch in her throat. Her violin? Viola? Sell it? She swallowed. It wasn't really even a hard decision. Her Ye Ye had said it was hers when he gave it to her. That meant only she could decide.

"But I told him that wasn't an option," Ye Ye said.

Lily started to back away, but then Li Jin spoke. She stopped. "There's another option, Baba."

"What is it?"

"I have the deed to this place in the safe. It's free and clear. We can use it as collateral for a loan."

Lily held her breath, waiting to see what her Ye Ye would say.

Her Nai Nai beat him to a response. "No, Li Jin. This place is yours—it's the only thing you'll have when we're gone. We don't want you to put it in jeopardy."

"It wouldn't work anyway. A bank's not going to loan us any money, even with collateral, when we don't have an income to pay it back with. These days the government still controls the banks, and loans are hard to come by," Ye Ye said.

"I wasn't talking about a bank," Li Jin said, just as Lan let out another squeal.

Lily could hear her get up and go to the baby. She stepped back another foot or so, in case Li Jin looked her way. But what was she talking about? Who else would loan them money?

"Then who?" Ye Ye asked.

"Shadow lenders," Li Jin whispered, so low that Lily almost didn't hear her over Lan's noises.

"Do you mean loan sharks?" Nai Nai said, and Lily could hear the alarm in her voice.

Lily heard a chair being pushed back and Sami spoke. "A loan shark is different from a shadow lender. The loan sharks are small-time and usually connected to something illegal, while the shadow lenders have cropped up all over China to give loans to people for small businesses, medical bills, and other things that the government-owned banks won't touch."

"That sounds like something we can possibly do, right?" Nai Nai asked. Lily heard the hope in her voice.

"Maybe," Li Jin said. "But we still have the issue of no way to prove to them we'll pay it back. We'd have to make up a different reason than using it for Ivy—maybe invent a small business so they know income will be coming in."

"Speaking of paying it back, you do realize that these organizations charge anywhere from eighteen to twenty percent interest? That's robbery," Ye Ye said, and Lily heard him move farther away and guessed he was going to stand in front of the fireplace, or to take Baby Lan from Li Jin.

"Benfu, you're going to have to stop being so stubborn," Nai Nai said. "We need to just listen to Li Jin and go to one of these shadow lenders. We'll get the money, and get Ivy home. Then we'll figure out where to go from there."

Li Jin spoke. "And we can all work together to find a way to pay it back. Linnea and Jet will help. We'll all scour the streets for collections, and maybe we really can start our own small business. I can bake, or we can grow tea leaves, or—I don't know . . . something."

"Better be careful who you borrow from. . . ." Lily heard Sami trail off with a warning tone.

"I don't know. I've always felt that borrowing is only a step up from begging. But let me think about it today. Sami's right— we need to be careful when it comes to underground money-lenders. They're usually the scourge of society. There must be some other way," Ye Ye said, his voice getting louder and footsteps moving toward Lily. "And it's not a good solution, but we might just have to let Ivy finish Lily's sentence while our application for a review to overturn her fine is being processed."

Lao Gong had walked him through the steps to apply for a review the day after Lily had been taken, but so far they'd heard nothing from the panel of so-called patient advocates.

Lily backed up another few steps and then turned to head back to their room. As her fingers trailed along the wall, she weighed her options. If her Ye Ye wouldn't go to the shadow lenders, it would be up to her to find a way to get her sister home.

Li Jin stood at the counter drying the freshly washed pots. Dinner had been a somber affair and she'd urged most of the others out, wanting the room to herself. Even her Baba and Nai Nai had left, saying they were going for a walk to discuss the situation. Lily, the pitiful thing, was sitting outside with Jojo as he rode his bike. Li Jin had asked her to go out with him, knowing she needed to be doing something to keep her mind off Ivy. Only Sami had stayed to help her clean. Or at least what Sami thought cleaning was. Together they'd worked silently until Li Jin couldn't stand the silence any longer.

"Sami, I need your help."

Sami stopped and looked up, one hand on her hip. "I'm sweeping your floor, looking like some scullery maid, what else do you want?"

"Not that kind of help. Serious stuff. You know more about these things. I need you to help me find a shadow lender. Baba doesn't want me to do this, but I need to get enough to pay both fines and get Ivy and Sky out of custody."

"Sky?" Sami pushed the broom around the room, and Li Jin noticed she still ignored Lan's fussing from the cradle near the fireplace. "You haven't said a word about him lately."

Li Jin stopped what she was doing and put both palms on the counter, leaning forward toward Sami.

"How could I? My parents are worried sick about the twins. I'm not going to bother them about Sky. But I *am* worried. I asked Linnea and she said his grandfather won't interfere, since he doesn't agree with the Falun Gong philosophy. His mother doesn't have any means to pay his fine, so Sky's on his own. I don't think anyone has even been to see him."

She watched Sami's face to see if she showed any concern over Sky. It was so hard to tell; Sami was so stingy with her feelings.

"And you're willing to put up this place"—Sami waved her arm around the kitchen—"this happy little hovel—for them? I thought this was your dream to have something like this?"

Li Jin dropped her head and sighed. "It is. I don't know what I'd do if we lost it. Jojo loves it here—I love it here, too. But I can't just sit back and do nothing. Ivy is just as much their daughter as I am. I have to get her home. And after all, they put everything they had into helping me get this place."

Lan let out a loud bellow and Sami returned to sweeping, ignoring the baby. "It would be nice to see Sky come home," she said.

Li Jin watched her closely; yet she couldn't tell if Sami really meant that or was just baiting her. Sometimes Sami acted like she was interested in Sky, but sometimes she didn't. It drove Li Jin crazy but she would not ask her. She knew if she showed any interest in him at all, Sami would be on him like flies on pig dung.

Sami stopped and put both hands over the broom handle, propping her chin on top. "I'll see what I can find out, but remember, if you don't pay them back, they'll have no mercy. They'll evict you and all of your little beggars so fast it'll make your head spin. Are you sure that's what you want to do?"

Lan let out a heartier bellow and Sami went back to sweeping.

"I'm sure." Li Jin felt a weight lifted from her. She'd made a decision. For once in her life someone besides her son needed her, and she was going to do what she could to help. It was scary, yet felt good. She just hoped she could come through. She put the last pot away and took off her apron, then crossed the kitchen to Lan. Lifting her, Li Jin held her to her shoulder and soothed her until the baby once again closed her eyes. She sighed with contentment as Lan relaxed to snuggle against her. *Sami didn't know what she was missing,* she thought as she inhaled the little girl's scent and headed for the bedroom to lay her down.

Chapter Eighteen

Ivy stood quietly in line, waiting her turn to use the bathroom. The nurse on duty had brought Scary Girl over to her when it was time for dinner rations and officially given the girl the responsibility to lead Ivy around, telling Ivy to call her Yao Mo before turning around and leaving them standing there. That was a shock, because in their local dialect *Yao Mo* was used to refer to someone from the dark underworld. Was the girl a witch? Ivy had felt a chill run up her spine when the girl didn't object to the name, but instead stood staring at the floor in front of her, an eerie expression on her face.

Yao Mo had stayed sullen until the nurse left and even through their meager dinner of cold congee, but at least now she was attempting to act human. From the middle of the room, Ivy saw a woman making circles around the card table, moving quicker than seemed possible for her age. She panted heavily as she ran, never taking her eyes from her shoes.

"What is she doing?" Ivy said, then remembered she wasn't supposed to be able to see. "I mean, I hear what sounds like someone running around the room?"

"We call her Crazy Coco. She thinks her shoes are talking to her. She makes circles around the table all day and when she gets going fast enough and she makes that sound you're hearing, she says her shoes are telling her what to do to get out of here."

Ivy looked from the corner of her eye without moving her head and immediately agreed with the nickname they'd given the woman. She *was* crazy.

"After bathroom break they'll come in and give us our meds," Yao Mo said. "Then we have an hour of free time before lights-out."

"But I don't take medication."

"You will here. You either take it willingly or they'll give it to you in a shot while three of the gorillas hold you down."

"They'll really do that?" Ivy felt the girl nudge her forward and she took a step closer to the door, stopping an inch or so behind the elderly woman in front of her.

"You'll see. There are always a few here who want to do it the hard way. The attendants enjoy it, too—gives them their dose of power for the day."

Finally it was Ivy's turn and she held the door to allow the elderly woman out of the bathroom, then slowly went in.

"Do you need some help?" Yao Mo asked.

"No. I can find my way around," Ivy answered, closing the door behind her. First the heavy smell of urine and feces took her breath. She slapped her hand over her mouth and nose and looked for a lock, but the knob didn't have one. Glad to finally drop the blind act for a moment, she turned around. The bathroom was sparse, only a raised platform with a sewage drop in the floor, and a small pedestal sink. No shower and no mirror. Ivy grimaced at the mess left around the sewer hole. Unlike the bathroom she'd used in the other wing earlier, this one was filthy. Couldn't the women hover over the hole? Did they have to just let their bowels go wherever?

Sighing in disgust, she held her pajama bottoms high enough not to touch the mess around the ceramic rim, and quickly did her business. She stood and waddled off the platform and away from the toilet to straighten her clothes. She turned on the spigot at the sink and ran her hands under the tiny stream of cold water, then shook the droplets off just as someone banged on the door.

"Kuai le!" someone hollered, telling her to hurry, and she quickly opened the door.

"It wasn't me," said Yao Mo, her hands up as if she thought Ivy could see them. She nudged Ivy to the wall. "Just stand right here, and I'll get you back in a second."

Ivy let her eyes wander around the room, thankful again for the sunglasses as a camouflage hiding her curiosity. She had to admit, there were several women in the bathroom line and around the room that looked like they should be there. But to her surprise, there were also women who looked as sane as she or her Nai Nai, their eyes and expression like any Ivy would see on a daily basis in the outside world. What were these women in here for and where were their families? It was hard to take in, and she wished once again that someone would come for her and tell her she'd been sprung.

Yao Mo came out of the bathroom and took Ivy's arm, then led her to her bed.

Surprisingly, Yao Mo said, "Wanna talk?"

Ivy wasn't sure if she needed a friend who was branded as a witch, but she didn't want to be left alone again. "Sure."

She backed up and sat up on the bed and Yao Mo climbed up beside her.

"First, just call me Mo. Now, how did you end up here?" she asked.

Ivy took a deep breath. She had to be careful to tell the story as if she were Lily. She didn't know Yao Mo enough to trust her.

"I was playing my violin in the park and got picked up and accused of being Falun Gong."

Mo nodded. "There are plenty of your people in here. They're a weird lot, never complaining about anything, even if they're treated roughly."

"They aren't *my people*. I'm not part of that. I was wrongly accused." Ivy couldn't keep the irritation out of her voice. Just thinking about the way her sister was treated made her flush with anger.

"*Aiya*, fine. Whatever. I really don't care. They call me worse, as you know."

"So, *are* you a witch?" Ivy asked. Her curiosity outweighed her good manners.

Mo laughed quietly. "Let's just say if I were a real witch, I'd cast a spell and get myself out of here. But I am interested in the subject. Enough that my father decided to put me in here to teach me a lesson."

"Teach you a lesson?"

"Yeah." Mo used her fingers to draw circles on the coverlet. "He said I needed to get help to get sorcery out of my head. He was suspicious about the black cat I made my pet last year, but when he found me reading a history book about the soul stealers scare in the eighteenth century, he flipped out. He's very traditional."

"Soul stealers?"

"It was started by a peasant who went to a mason known as a sorcerer to ask him to punish his nephews for terrorizing him. Word got out and the peasant was arrested for dealing with the occult. The mason disappeared, and soon the townspeople panicked and began to accuse anyone without a real place in society of being sorcerers."

"That's ridiculous," Ivy said, picking at her nails.

"But it's interesting—which is why I was reading the book. The townspeople went village to village and persecuted beggars, wanderers, trash collectors, and even monks. It was the first official Chinese witch hunt."

Ivy's eyebrows rose when the girl mentioned trash collectors. "And your Baba really thinks you're a witch?"

Mo laughed as she played with her ponytail. "Probably now he does. I told him if he put me here, I'd curse him and his grandsons. And he doesn't even have any yet."

Ivy thought that was a little harsh, considering the superstitions of the elderly and their high hopes for future generations to do well, but the father should've tried to work out their disagreement rather than sending his daughter to a mental hospital. Ivy bet if it had been a son, he'd have received a slap on the wrist or been branded a scholar, instead of being sentenced behind bars.

Keys against the metal door saved her from responding and a nurse pushed a large cart into the room. Three muscular men dressed in white followed her in and stood behind her, arms crossed as if daring someone to defy them.

"There's the Gang of Four," Mo said, snickering quietly.

"That's an ominous nickname," Ivy mumbled low enough for only Mo to hear. The Gang of Four were what Mao's personal team were called during the revolution. Composed of his wife and three of her most trusted cadres, they wielded extreme—and cruel—power for a time. When the revolution fizzled out, they were all arrested and died in disgrace for the way they treated the people during their short reign of terror. Usually their names were only invoked in terrible circumstances.

"They've earned it." Mo slid off the bed and pulled at Ivy, urging her to her feet. "Let's get it over with."

Ivy let Mo lead her to the cart where they stood behind several patients already shuffling forward in a line. When they got to the nurse, Ivy pretended to stare right through her. Mo pushed her a little bit closer.

"She's a new patient," Mo said to the nurse.

"Name?" the nurse asked, obviously bored as she picked up her clipboard and pencil.

"Zheng I—Lily," Ivy said.

The nurse skimmed down her paper, then marked it and picked up a small white paper cup of water and handed it to Ivy. Mo guided her hand to take it.

"Open up," the nurse said without an ounce of compassion.

Ivy stood there, ignoring the command. Instead she held out her hand for the pill.

"Until they get to know you, they'll put the pill in your mouth and then check to make sure you swallow it. Open your mouth." Mo nudged her.

Ivy sighed. She didn't see any way out of it. She was about to be drugged. She opened her mouth. The nurse put a tiny blue pill on it and then used her hand to quickly push Ivy's jaw closed.

"Hurry up."

Ivy turned the tiny bit of water up and swallowed, then opened her mouth and stuck her tongue out. The nurse nodded.

"Come on." Mo grabbed her pill and water and guided Ivy back to her bed.

"What's that going to do to me?"

"You'll sleep through the night. Makes it easier for the staff if we are all drugged."

"*Hao le*, are you ready for Mental Madness 101?" Mo crossed her legs Indian style and leaned against the metal frame that served as Ivy's headboard.

"What do you mean?" Ivy sat opposite her, where Mo had led her after they'd gotten their medication. Around them the other patients—except for the lady still chasing her shoes around the table—were obviously winding down. Mo had brought her a cup of lukewarm tea and explained they weren't allowed hot water because the manic patients might throw it on someone. Ivy drank the tea, but without the heat the tepid liquid didn't bring her any comfort. She couldn't help but feel a rush of anxiety at the thought of being locked in for the night with a bunch of strangers. She wished they'd left her in the room Lily had started in. At least there she'd have been alone behind a locked door.

They wasted a half hour or so talking back and forth and Ivy thought she felt the meds working. Either that or the excitement from being in a new place had just drained her. From the bed beside her a series of low snores began. Someone was already asleep. That fast!

"So now what?" she asked Mo, ignoring the sudden wailing from a woman who sat squatting in the corner, reading over a tattered letter in her hands. Ivy could only imagine what brought on such anguish—a breakup maybe, or words from her son, or maybe even her parent had died while she was committed. Ivy didn't want to think about it or even look at the woman again. It was too heart-wrenching.

Mo laughed at her.

"What?" Ivy asked.

"Your face. You look terrified. We've got a few minutes before lights-out. And you said this is your first time in a mental ward. So let me give you some tips that'll make it easier for you. Stuff I wish someone had told me on my first few nights."

Ivy nodded. Mo sure had pepped up and no longer carried the somber expression she'd started with. Now she acted almost as if they were at a sleepover and Ivy were her best friend. *Weird.*

"First, stay close to me. Especially since you're blind you won't be able to tell when someone is totally going off their rocker. One minute your new friend might be playing cards with you and smiling, the next she'll start talking in a low voice as she uses the sharp edge of a card to slit her wrists. Don't panic, just get the attendant. And for sure don't ever try to talk sense into someone who's gotten ahold of a sharp or blunt object, even if you think you know them."

Through her sunglasses Ivy studied the serious expression on Mo's face. She wondered if that went for Mo, too—would the girl turn on her and suddenly become a raving lunatic? She shook her head and Mo's face went in and out of focus. Everything was starting to feel surreal.

"You get all sorts in here. Some will be screaming at imaginary friends and others will curl up in a corner with a blanket and suck their thumbs."

Mo held up her hand and pushed down one finger, then held up another.

"Now, second, don't show fear or the crazies will be on you like flies on shit. Most of the really violent patients are on another floor, but we get one or two in here and you never know when they'll explode. Just carry an air of confidence and they'll leave you alone." She paused. "For the most part."

"For the most part?" Ivy said.

"Yeah, and really, you're more likely to be harmed by the staff than the other patients. And that leads me to the next rule. Avoid getting restrained. They'll hurt you and hurt you bad. Just do what they say, take the meds they give, and never make eye contact with them. They want us to know they have all the power and they're always ready to make an example of anyone who challenges that."

Ivy really didn't want to take the medication. What if it made her crazy? She thought of Lily and how glad she was her plan had worked and her sister had gotten out. There was no way Lily would've been able to survive what Mo was describing.

Mo lowered her voice. "The fight equals flight rule. If you're only here a few days, you might not even see one, but if a fight breaks out, just get out of the way. Even an eighty-pound granny hiked up on meds here can cause some serious damage, and it's not your job to restrain her or protect anyone but yourself."

"You don't have to worry about that," Ivy muttered, struggling to keep her eyes from fluttering closed. "I don't care if they all beat the crap out of one another here, it means nothing to me."

Mo laughed. "Oh yeah—you reminded me, if you get to go outside tomorrow with some of us, do not and I repeat—do not try to pet the geese."

"Geese?"

"*Dui le*. Unless you get chosen for laundry or food duty, it's your only chance to leave this room. We have a small courtyard with a pond and it never fails, the newbies always think the geese are *so pretty*." Her voice went high and squeaky, then back to low again. "They go up to them and those geese have special powers that allow them to know when someone is mental. I'll just tell you this—they'll beat the hell out of you. If we go out tomorrow, even if everything in you is drawn to those geese, don't listen because they'll give you a flogging you'll never forget."

Ivy felt her head fall to the bed and wondered if she was dreaming. Something about geese and flogging, or maybe it was laundry, but she thought she heard someone say she could leave tomorrow.

Mo's voice dropped to a whisper. "Wait, Ivy. Before you go to sleep, I have to tell you about one orderly to look out for. He's more dangerous than all the rest."

Ivy was so tired. More tired than she'd ever been. And now Mo's voice was too far in the background to make out her words. But she'd said something about tomorrow. *Tomorrow*. She'd get to go home tomorrow. Home. She smiled, then gave up and let herself drift into a deep sleep.

Chapter Nineteen

Li Jin and Sami climbed out of the taxi and stood before the tall building. The sign over the door advertised it as a karaoke bar, but they'd found out from Sky's grandfather the top floor was the so-called reeducation center where Sky was being held. That was all the help he'd been, though. If it wasn't for her Baba's friend, Lao Gong, calling in some favors, they wouldn't be getting to see Sky at all.

"This is it." Li Jin situated the bags to one hand and opened the door, holding it wide for Sami to enter.

"Let me do the talking," Sami said, taking the lead and strutting as if she were much taller than her petite five feet.

Gladly, thought Li Jin. Since Baba was back at the hospital to see if he could visit Ivy, Sami had been nominated to accompany her. Li Jin hated dealing with officials. Ever since her many years in and out of the institution, she got very nervous around anyone connected to the government. When she was growing up, she'd seen directors and vice directors smile and play nice in front of visitors, then turn nasty and vile the minute they were behind closed doors. Some memories would never fade. And in her experiences, power was usually connected to something ugly. But Sami—she acted as if she were ten feet tall. She was impressive; Li Jin had to give her that. Nothing scared her.

They passed quickly through the lobby, ignoring the plush couches and blinking lights, a few Japanese businessmen laughing it up with some girls, and went straight to the elevator. They'd been told to go to the seventh floor, where the Jianghan Brainwashing Center was located. When the doors closed, they didn't speak. They'd already discussed taking extra precautions in case they were watched or recorded.

Li Jin set the bags at her feet. She hoped she'd be able to leave the items with Sky to bring him just a tiny bit of comfort. His mother, Ling, had sent him slippers and a warm jogging suit, saying the last time Sky had been through this, he'd just about frozen to death. She'd thanked Li Jin repeatedly for going to visit her son, stopping to cry every few minutes when they'd dropped by on the way to pick up his things.

Li Jin had also brought fruit and bottled water, and some instant-noodle bowls. Sami even had a good suggestion and Li Jin had packed a few books, something for Sky to do during his long hours being detained. She hoped he could have them.

The bell rang for the seventh floor and Li Jin took a deep breath. It was silly, but she was nervous—especially standing beside Sami, who always looked perfect. Li Jin self-consciously reached up and pulled her hair over the side of her face, trying to cover her scar.

"Let's go," Sami said, reaching down and grabbing one of the bags.

Li Jin grabbed the other two and followed Sami out of the elevator. They were in a long hall of shiny ceramic tiles, but the first thing she noticed was each door was made of steel. She guessed no one would be escaping from these rooms.

They went to the one marked with an A-1 and rang the buzzer. They could see the camera directly over the door, pointed at them.

A sliding slot opened and Li Jin could see the eye and part of a cheek from what appeared to be a pimply-faced young man.

"Ni yao shenme?" he said, asking what they wanted.

Sami held up the piece of paper from her pocket, and the young man paused, checking to see if it was properly stamped for approvals, then slid the slot closed. They heard a series of dead-bolts click and the door opened.

"Step inside." He moved and allowed them through.

Li Jin looked around. It was a big room with a long black counter running the length of it. Behind the counter were a few scarred metal desks, an out-of-date television with an antenna, and a refrigerator. A rusty old fan oscillated on top of the fridge, emitting a low buzz in the otherwise quiet room. A few girls sat at the computers, typing rapidly and lost in concentration. At the end of the room was a door with a window that showed a hall-way on the other side. Long iron bars ran the length of the wooden panels, reinforcing the door. So that was where the prisoners were kept, she thought.

"Has your pass been officially approved?" The young guard took the paper and laid it on the counter, examining it.

"Yes, chopped by His Highness himself," Sami said, her voice sarcastic but as confident as Li Jin had ever heard it.

His Highness must have been some other official in the Wuxi government, Li Jin thought. And obviously someone with some influence, because the young guard quickly stood at attention when he saw the characters representing the man's name.

"I'll show you to the visitor's room. You'll be searched there." He turned and led them to the barred door. Sami followed closely and Li Jin stayed behind her. She felt a bit light-headed but knew it was just nervousness.

He led them to a room and opened the door. They walked through and he shut it behind them, leaving them alone.

"Searched?" Sami said. "I hope he does the searching."

Li Jin rolled her eyes. "I don't. Lao Gong said they'd search us but they probably have women to do that." She set the bags on the table and began pacing. The air was getting thinner, harder to breathe. She forced herself to calm down, taking deep breaths.

"Settle down, Li Jin. It's fine." Sami crossed the room and placed her hand on Li Jin's back to stop her from pacing.

Li Jin didn't care what others thought about the girl. She knew in her heart Sami was like a wounded animal. She just needed kindness and understanding until she could trust people again. Look at how good she was to her; did crazy people do that?

"Thanks, Sami. I'm sorry I'm being such a baby. This place reminds me of the orphanage administration area. Nothing good ever went on when we were called to that building."

The door opened and a guard came in. At first Li Jin thought it was a man by the haircut and swagger, but then she realized it was just a tough-looking woman. The guard walked brusquely to the table and began pawing through the bags. She took the books and put them to the side, then the bowls of noodles.

"Will we be able to leave those with my brother?" Sami asked. Their cover story sounded far-fetched to Li Jin but Gong had insisted they'd only get in if they were family.

The guard shook her head without looking up. "No uncensored books. No outside packaged food. He can eat fruit while he is visiting with you but cannot take it back inside."

Sami looked at Li Jin and raised her eyebrows. Li Jin wasn't arguing—the woman was built like a man, with a disposition and mustache to match.

She finished rummaging in the bags and turned to them. "Who's first?"

It was obvious when she pulled a pair of plastic gloves from her pocket what she wanted.

"Here?" Li Jin asked, looking around the large room.

Sami pointed at another door on the other side of the room. "What about in there? Is that a bathroom?"

The guard shook her head. "That's where they'll bring the prisoner in from. Either undress or leave. I don't have time to fool with your modesty."

Li Jin felt a moment of panic and she looked to Sami. They held eyes and Sami slipped her feet out of her shoes. "I'll go first. It's nothing, Li. Pretend she's a doctor."

The woman snorted. Sami quickly stripped down to her underwear and bra and stood brazenly in front of her, looking unashamed of her curvy body half covered with the elaborate tattoo.

The guard shook her head in disgust, then told Sami to turn around. Sami did and the guard put her finger inside the waistband of Sami's underwear and peeked inside. She took the pencil from behind her ear and stuck it down Sami's backside crack, making her jump.

"*Aiya,* won't you buy me a drink first?" Sami said, her voice laced with sarcasm.

Li Jin almost smiled, but then remembered she was next. The she-man yelled over her shoulder, "You. Undress. Hurry."

Li Jin began to undress as the woman reached into Sami's bra to check underneath her breasts.

"Clear. You can get dressed." She turned to Li Jin and sneered. She pointed the pencil at her. "Now your turn, Scar Face."

The guard was finally satisfied all their cracks and crevices were clear of propaganda, drugs, weapons, and whatever else they suspected, and Li Jin and Sami were left alone. Now dressed, they sat at the table and waited for Sky to be brought in.

"That was awkward," Sami said, looking up at the camera. "I wonder if we'll be paid for that?"

Li Jin appreciated her attempt to lighten the heavy mood. She'd also wondered who had watched them undress and assumed somewhere in the building Sami had caused quite a stir with her body. "To say the least. I think I may have pencil lead in my nether regions now."

Sami pushed at the pile of clothing and fruit. "At least he'll have something familiar to wear. And some fruit."

Li Jin tapped her fingernails on the table and looked at the clock over the door. The guard had left them at least a half hour ago. What was taking so long? She looked at Sami again. At least she wasn't spouting anything mean about Sky. Since the whole situation had happened, Sami had been unusually nice about Sky. Maybe there was still a chance of getting them interested in each other after all.

"I hope Auntie Rae can handle Lan and Coral together," Li Jin said, thinking about the way Lan had cried out when they left. For the last few days she'd been coughing and Li Jin was starting to think they needed to take her to the doctor.

"She'll be fine," Sami said, rolling her eyes.

Li Jin sighed. She'd have to take Lan herself the next time Sami was taking one of her marathon naps. It'd be easier that way anyway, without Sami there to dismiss everything Li Jin would try to tell the doctor.

Finally the door opened and the young male guard who had let them in appeared, holding the arm of his prisoner.

For a split second, Li Jin thought they'd brought out the wrong man. She'd never seen Sky without his colorful and eccentric clothing, and in the gray pajama-like pants and shirt he looked like an old man. Then he lifted his head and his eyes met hers. It was Sky, but it was a much different Sky than she'd last seen. He looked exhausted and was missing the spark she remembered. She felt her stomach drop and found herself unable to form words.

Thankfully Sami never had that problem.

"Sky, you're looking ravishing," she said as the guard brought Sky to the table and pulled out a chair, then shoved him into it.

"Half an hour and then visiting time is over. You'll be watched." The guard tilted his head to the camera mounted on the wall and then left the room.

Sky ignored the guard. "I guess I've been better. But tell me, what about Lily? Is she home? Is she okay? I'm so sorry for dragging her into this."

Li Jin found her voice. Sky needed normalcy. "Yes, she's okay. She's home but it's complicated. Ivy took her place and is still at the hospital. They've set a fine."

Sky shook his head. "Typical. They know she's too young and inexperienced to really be a Falun Gong practitioner. I told them so, but this is just another example of extortion of the people. We need a law to regulate the acts of hospitals and the government, and to prevent them from jailing normal people in mental hospitals."

"We're trying to take care of getting Ivy out, but let's talk about you. How are you really?" Li Jin asked.

Sky looked up at the camera and winked. "Oh, they're treating me like the little emperor in here. Besides being forced to attend brainwashing sessions every day to watch their ridiculous videos and listen to their lectures, I have to write thought reports before they'll let me sleep. Their education helpers—meaning the brainwashing assistants—might force me to read material that slanders Falun Gong. But they know I won't bend."

Sami pushed the fruit toward Sky. "We brought more food, but you can only have this, and only in here, so start eating."

Sky grabbed a handful of the longans and peeled one, then popped it in his mouth. Li Jin reached across the table and picked up a few. He needed to concentrate on eating, not peeling. Their time was slipping away fast.

She pretended not to see the many pin-sized scabs on his arms, though she wondered what had caused them.

He nodded toward the pile of clothing. "Thank you. Did Bai Ling send those?"

"Yes, she also sends her best wishes. She's very upset," Li Jin said.

"I know she can't come here. She's too delicate. But tell her the clothing is much appreciated. In addition to making me go entire days without relieving my bladder, they also make my room frigid cold. It's their mental persuasion to make me cooperate."

"What do they want you to do?" Li Jin asked.

"If it was me, I'd say whatever they wanted me to in order to get out of here," Sami said.

"They want me to renounce Falun Gong, of course," Sky said nonchalantly. "But I've been here before and I know the drill. I wasn't even allowed to sleep the first thirty-six hours I was here, but they still didn't break me."

He looked so sad Li Jin felt her heart stir. "Are you homesick?"

Sky looked up. "Just like the poet Zhu Yufu did, I feel the loss. 'Dark falls between the bars and I think of home, missing the warmth of a mother's hand, yet here I lie against the wall, an accused man in a foreign land.'"

Sami snorted. "It's not like you're in a foreign land."

Li Jin would've kicked her under the table if she could've reached her. She truly had no compassion sometimes. Sky didn't seem to mind her sarcasm. He went back to eating his fruit, filling the cheeks that had looked so hollow. He'd definitely lost weight.

"Are you at least allowed to do your exercises?" Li Jin asked.

He shook his head. "Absolutely not. They have someone watching me at all times. They think taking away our exercise is the real torture for us practitioners. But they don't understand, Falun Gong is not just about physical exercise—that's just a misconception many Chinese have. Ours is different than other practices because we place greater focus on the mind than anything else." He pointed at his head. "They can hurt my body, but they won't touch the peace I have stored in here. And reciting poetry all day and evening keeps me sharp, despite the lack of sustenance in here."

Li Jin watched him talk and saw some of the old spark return to his eyes. She didn't really know anything about Falun Gong, but if it brought him happiness, who was she to judge?

"Is there anything I can do?" She didn't tell him she was already working out a plan to get him sprung. She didn't want the camera to catch her words. But she needed to know how much his fine was.

"Not for me. My fine is too high because this isn't my first offense. Twenty thousand reminbi, if you can believe that. But they'll let me go in a few months. If I say what they want, I'll be sent to the cells on the second floor where the so-called *transformed* are kept. They're sentenced to months of slave labor until they fulfill their sentence. But since I won't fold, I'll either be kept here or they'll move me to another detention center outside of town."

"Maybe you'll be out of custody before then." Li Jin looked at him and tried to convey the message with only her eyes.

Sky looked at the clock. "We don't have much time before the guard takes me back. Listen, I need to tell you a few things you can do to help Ivy. First, go to the Public Security Bureau and fill out a grievance. They may possibly let you have an evaluation by a panel of doctors to prove that Ivy doesn't need to be there, but you'll have to push hard."

"The bureau hasn't been very helpful so far," Li Jin said. That was putting it mildly. Her Baba had barely been able to see Ivy in the past week. She couldn't imagine what the poor girl thought about her lack of visitors.

"They won't. But you have to be strong. The authorities don't follow the rule of law and they have friends everywhere. You can also ask for a diagnostic review from a psychiatrist who isn't involved in the initial assessment. You might luck out on that but it'll cost you."

As he talked, Li Jin studied his face. He wasn't even concerned for himself. He was more focused on giving them pointers on how to help Ivy.

"Li Jin . . . are you listening?" he asked, tapping the table and bringing her out of her daydream. "This is important. Bad things happen to people accused of being Falun Gong. You've got to get her out of there before she becomes a statistic."

"Yes, I hear you, and hurry up and eat more of the fruit." She pushed an orange at him. He needed vitamin C; he looked pale and sickly. But he was still handsome.

He grabbed the orange and grinned up at her. "Watch how fast I can do away with all this fruit."

Sami laughed at Sky shoving the pieces in his mouth. Li Jin watched them joking with each other, feeling like an outsider. But she wouldn't let it bother her. She needed to keep a positive outlook and then maybe everything would work out okay.

And it just had to. Her family was depending on her to do something to help Ivy and Li Jin didn't want to lose their trust. To finally have a family to call her own and then have it break apart or forever be heavy with the sadness the corrupt city officials had caused, was just too much to fathom.

Chapter Twenty

Ivy sat watching from her bed as the oily-haired doctor distractedly pushed his glasses farther up his nose, then stuffed a cloth-covered metal ruler in the woman's mouth. The orderlies had spread her out on the stretcher and were trying to hold her steady, but even with so many hands bracing her, the woman continued to thrash and buck, her eyed darting around wildly in a silent plea for help.

"Why are they putting that in her mouth?" Ivy cringed and felt her own jaws tighten. She'd admitted to Mo, after the girl had pretty much figured it out, that she wasn't blind. And then the whole story came out. Since then Mo had treated her as if she were some sort of hero, as well as helped her keep the charade going.

"They don't want her to bite her tongue off." Mo sounded bored from the bed beside her as she took a long drag on her cigarette. The girl had given away her dinner ration two days in a row to trade beds so she and Ivy could be next to each other. Over the last week they'd forged somewhat of an unlikely friendship, and Ivy was finding out her Ye Ye and Nai Nai had kept her and her sisters sheltered from so much of the world. That life was tough out there was the most consistent lesson Mo was giving her.

"Why can't they just leave her alone? She was fine until they came after her."

"Remember the first day when I told you it was easier to just take the medication they hand out? This is why—refuse enough and they'll restrain you. Keep it up and they bring out the zapper."

Ivy watched in horror as what she had at first thought was a blood pressure machine was wheeled closer and the doctor attached electric needles to both sides of the woman's head. He turned the knob and called out for everyone to step back. When they did, he hit another switch and the machine sent out an electric shock that caused the woman to shriek as if she were being slaughtered. Her head went rigid and she thrashed only once more, then went limp. Her eyes stared up at the ceiling but Ivy didn't think she was seeing anything.

"Next time, don't refuse your medication!" the doctor bellowed down at her, then turned and stomped from the room. He called out to the staff still standing around the stretcher. "One of you stay here to monitor her. Unhook the machine, and if she still won't take her lithium, come get me."

The woman had avoided the morning meds line and huddled into a corner when they'd tried to order her to take the pill. It wasn't long before her resistance had brought out the rest of the gorillas.

Ivy was thankful she at least wasn't required to take any medication during the day. So far, they'd only made her take the nightly sedative along with everyone else on the ward. And Ivy didn't give them any trouble about it. Now they no longer made her stick out her tongue or even checked to see if she'd swallowed the pill. She'd given them no reason to suspect she was anything but drugged each night.

The pills were strong and literally minutes after taking one each night she fell into a dreamless sleep until Mo woke her the next morning. She was glad she didn't have to take the lithium, as many who were on it acted as if they were out of their minds.

Mostly they sat around staring or drooling, but sometimes they went into crying jags that were unbearable to listen to.

She sighed. She'd had only one visit from her Ye Ye and he'd told her to stay out of trouble, for they were still working on getting her released. So Ivy hadn't seen a familiar face for days and she'd had plenty of time to think about her last conversation with Lily.

"Ivy, listen. You shared your secret with me and now I'm going to tell you something." Mo crept across the space separating them and huddled next to Ivy's bed. Secrets. Was that all there was? *Her mother's secrets. Her secrets. Mo's secrets.*

"*Hao le.* What do you want to tell me?"

Mo stuck out her pinky and Ivy joined it with hers.

"Okay, you know the orderly named George?"

"The skinny one with the shaggy hair over his eyes?" Ivy asked.

"Yeah, he's cute, isn't he?"

Ivy squinted at Mo and shook her head. "Mo, what are you trying to tell me?"

Mo laughed quietly. "He's going to leave the door unlocked after he finishes his rounds tonight and I'm going out to meet him in the laundry room. He's promised me a pack of cigarettes if I come."

George had just started working their room that week and Ivy had noticed he'd had his eye on Mo from the first day. He was older than Mo's eighteen years, and not what Ivy would consider cute, but definitely an improvement over most of the men who wandered in and out of their room. Still, Mo was her only friend and if she got discovered, Ivy would surely be alone again.

"Please, Mo, don't do this. You can't trust him and what if you get caught? You know they'll send you to a higher-security ward."

Mo smiled slightly. "Can anyone ever really be trusted? You have to take chances in life to ever say you lived a little. And I'm dying to get out of this room for a while. You have to remember, Ivy, I've been here for months. If I don't get out, even for an hour or so, they're going to be passing me the lithium—not because they want to but because I'll need it."

Ivy shook her head. It was useless—Mo was too stubborn. No matter what she said, the girl was dying for a diversion from their boredom and would do whatever it took to get it.

"And anyway, I'm almost out of cigarettes," Mo said, sending Ivy a mischievous grin.

Ivy wondered but wasn't about to ask how she'd gotten her supply so far. She could only imagine. While Mo talked about escaping for just an hour, Ivy couldn't help but think she would also like to leave the room. At least Mo had been allowed out into the courtyard a few times. So far they said Ivy hadn't earned that privilege. More than anything Ivy wanted to see the crazy geese Mo told her tales about. She knew she was lucky to have found the girl, because if there was one thing Mo had, it was an abundance of stories of chaos involving those called The Crazies, previous patients who'd entertained others with their antics.

Her eyes wandered over to the woman on the stretcher and Ivy was again glad for the anonymity of her sunglasses to hide the pity she felt. She knew it wasn't right that people were treated worse than farm animals just because they were depressed or confused. She'd never seen this much cruelty in her life.

"Hurry up, lights-out time," Mo muttered from beside her.

"Are you sure you'll be okay?" Ivy had a bad feeling about what might happen.

"I am. Orderly Cho worked the day shift today, so I don't have to worry about him. And I promise I won't stay gone longer than an hour. That should be all I need to talk George out of more than just one pack of smokes. And I might even get a rise out of him."

"Rise?" Ivy wrinkled her forehead.

Mo laughed. "Yes, rise. Sex. You do know what sex is, right?"

Ivy felt her cheeks flame. Of course she knew what sex was. But George wasn't much more than a stranger! She knew Mo was eccentric, but now she wondered if she wasn't really a little crazy after all. She ignored her question anyway.

Mo finally stopped giggling at her and got serious again. "You just watch the attendant while I'm gone and if she wakes up and starts to head over to my bed, you'll have to cause a scene or something to distract her."

Ivy definitely didn't like the sound of that. She didn't want to be punished for acting out or causing a scene. She bit her lip and looked at Mo. The girl was doing her best to hide the excitement threatening to spill out of her. Even if no one else could tell, Ivy could see it in the sparkle of her black eyes. Mo had better get herself back safely, too. Ivy didn't want to have to deal with the crazy place all alone.

Hours later Ivy lay under her thin cover and waited for Mo to return. It had been a long day of passing time lying about or shuffling around the room, bored out of her mind. Finally Mo had left her to go to the table and play cards, and Ivy wished she could drop the blind charade and play with her.

The staff members had teased them with promises of a courtyard visit if they were good, but eventually the patients had given up and most—at least the ones who were lucid enough to know what was going on—had slipped into quiet and even angry moods until meds were passed out and then everyone was ordered to bed.

Now Ivy listened to the sounds of snoring around her. This was the first time she'd been awake this late since her arrival on the ward. Mo had made her promise not to swallow her sleeping pill in case she should need to divert an attendant's attention away from her empty bed. Ivy had been nervous they'd catch her hiding it under her tongue but everything had gone smoothly and she'd been able to slip it out and crumble it under her pillow.

When the lights officially went out, and the attendant laid her head on the desk behind the glass and closed her eyes, Mo had slid quietly down to the floor to wait, and thirty minutes later she was gone out the door George had left unlocked.

Now Ivy was nervous. *Really nervous.* Mo had said she'd only be gone for an hour at the most and that had passed thirty minutes ago. What was she doing? Was she okay? What if she'd escaped? Or been caught? The more Ivy waited, the sicker she felt.

She looked at Mo's bed. The girl had used both hers and Ivy's pillow to form what looked like a body under the cover. Hopefully no one would notice she was gone.

More minutes ticked by and Ivy felt her heart would explode with anxiety if Mo didn't come back. Finally, frustrated she was being pulled into it, she slipped from her bed and squatted on the floor.

She waited another five minutes to see if anyone stirred and when they didn't, she quickly scampered across the room, keeping to the edges of the beds until she got to the door. She looked once at the sleeping form of their attendant through the glass window, then slid out the door and left it cracked open as she crouched on the other side of it.

Outside in the hall the lights glared brightly, making Ivy feel like a rabbit caught in a trap. Luckily, she didn't see anyone around, but which way was the laundry room? She could only go forward, so she slowly and quietly moved along the hall, listening for any sound. Around the curve another hall led the opposite way. Ivy strained and thought she heard the sound of machines, so turned and headed toward the noise.

She covered the last few feet and slipped through the door. Several machines on the far wall of washers were running, but they couldn't mask the sound of Mo giggling from the other side of a line of dryers. Ivy also saw a tendril of smoke making its way toward the ceiling.

She crept over there, irritation filling every pore. When she turned the corner, she put her hands on her hips and stared down at Mo entwined in the arms of George, all unkempt six feet of him. Ivy was thankful he was wearing pants, but she still looked away from his bare chest.

"Mo. You're late and you scared me to death! I thought you were caught."

Mo startled and sat upright, almost as fast as George. "Ivy!"

"Who the hell are you?" George asked, standing to pull his pants higher and tie the drawstring.

"Don't worry, that's just my roomie," Mo said, and laughed nervously. She took one last drag on the cigarette and let it drop to the floor, where she ground her slipper against it to put it out.

"Damn. You told her we were meeting? You're going to get me fired," George said. "I'm out of here. You two are on your own. You get caught and I'm saying I don't know you."

With that he slipped his feet into the strewn slippers, pulled his shirt on, and stormed out of the room. Mo glared at Ivy.

"Thanks a lot." She smirked. "But at least I got these." She pulled a pack of cigarettes from her pocket and held them up just as they both heard the shuffling of plastic slippers coming down the hall.

"He's coming back," Ivy said.

Mo turned toward the door. "No, that's not him. He walks heavier than that." She put her finger to her lips and beckoned Ivy to follow her. They quietly slipped behind the rolling cart piled high with soiled bed sheets. Ivy winced at the overpowering smell of urine.

The door swung open and a woman came through, softly humming a song. Ivy could see a reflection in the glass door of a dryer and from the same striped clothing she wore, she appeared to be a patient, too. Ivy wasn't surprised, the staff took any opportunity to get out of their work, even if it meant delegating chores to the patients—the ones who could be trusted.

The woman opened a washing machine and began unloading wet sheets and carrying them to the dryer. For such a small woman, Ivy thought she was exceptionally nimble. She poked the sheets in, still humming, then made another trip for another armload.

"She's got night-shift laundry duty," Mo whispered just as the washer that had been running stopped.

Ivy didn't answer. That the woman had wash duty was obvious and now she might have heard Mo speak. Suddenly, the woman stopped. She cocked her head, listening. Then she looked down and her eyes landed on the ground-out cigarette.

Ivy and Mo didn't move a muscle. Ivy even held her breath.

But it was too late. The woman turned and came around the bin. Crossing her arms, she glared down at them.

"What are you two doing here? And what idiot has been smoking around these hot dryers?" she demanded. Even with her hair wild around her face and standing in baggy patient garb, she looked completely lucid—and angry.

Mo stood and Ivy slowly joined her. She reached up and quickly pulled the sunglasses down over her eyes. She'd only just remembered she was supposed to be blind. She had a good mind to pretend to be mute as well.

"Um . . . we—um—were lost. But we weren't smoking," Mo stammered, and swayed from one foot to the other.

For once Ivy saw Mo as an equal. She was no longer the fearless leader she'd made Ivy think she was. They were in a lot of trouble and Mo knew it.

"Lost? How did you get out of your rooms? I've been doing wash here every night for at least a decade and I've never seen either one of you." The woman blew the hair out of her eyes, then reached up and pushed it farther. More of her face showed, causing Ivy to intake a sharp breath.

That face. It was so familiar. But it couldn't be. Could it? Something like ice water entered the tips of her fingers and tingled up her arms to her neck. She stood there, shaking her head in disbelief.

Mo turned to her. "What's wrong?"

The woman squinted at Ivy, then reached over and plucked the sunglasses right off her face. Ivy reached for them but she was too late; the woman held them over her head. Then she leaned in and studied Ivy even closer.

"Lai Song?" the woman said, her face incredulous. "Is it really you?"

"What? Who is Lai Song?" Mo asked, looking from Ivy back to the woman.

Ivy sighed.

"Lai Song is my sister. I am Lai Sun. And that—that lunatic"—she pointed at the woman—"is the woman who gave birth to us."

Ivy felt a wave of dizziness, as if the very earth shifted beneath her feet. After so many years how was it possible to be facing her own mother—the woman who tried to take her sister out of this world?

The woman's face broke into a huge smile and Ivy stepped back, narrowly avoiding the thin arms that reached for her. The outstretched arms held for a second, then dropped to her sides. "Lai Sun, my *nuer*, I've tried to find you for years. I can't believe it, you're here!"

Ivy swallowed and clenched her shaking hands into tight fists. She would not let *her mother* see how her appearance had affected her. That face—that same face Ivy had woken up to see twisted into a determined grimace the night of the fire.

"Don't pretend with me. You didn't want us. I saw you that night," Ivy said stiffly.

The woman visibly flinched. "I don't know what you think you saw, but I wasn't responsible for that fire. Since that night I've appealed to the social welfare department repeatedly with letters asking for your whereabouts."

"You weren't responsible? You're such a liar. I may have been just a little girl, but I saw you with the oil—and the matches," Ivy said, her voice raised a few notches to match her long-bottled anger.

"Shh . . . ," Mo hissed at them. "You two are going to draw the floor supervisor's attention. Quiet down. Ivy, could you be wrong? You were really young, right? Maybe you've forgotten."

Ivy would never forget. Her mother had carried her out of her room in her sleep, separated her from Lily by laying her on the couch. She hadn't known Ivy had opened her eyes to see her in the doorway of their bedroom, then a loud *whoosh* . . . and it was ablaze.

"I know what I saw," Ivy said, glaring at her mother.

"No, Lai Sun, you are wrong. You were having a bad dream. And please tell me, why are you here—in this horrible place? And where is your sister?"

From her memories Ivy could almost smell the smoke and even feel the heat of the fire against her skin again. She took a step toward the woman. "Don't call me that name. I'm not that girl anymore. But was I having a bad dream when I ran toward the room and you blocked me with your body? When I kicked and screamed until Lily woke up? Was it all a nightmare when I got around you and pulled my sister out of a burning room? I don't think so, *mufu*."

The woman backed up until she was against the wall, then slid down it to the floor. She covered her face and sobbed. "I'm sorry. I didn't want to do it. It was your father! He called her *the blind one* and said he wouldn't come back unless I got rid of her. He thought she was a curse on our family. It was for us, *Nuer*. I did it for you, so you could have a better life—a life without your sister around your ankle like an anchor."

Ivy felt a rush of rage. "Don't even say that to me. Taking Lily from me would've been the worst thing anyone has ever done. Don't you understand anything about twins? About sisters? Her blindness means nothing to me. She's just Lily! She's my sister!"

From behind her hands the woman sobbed. "I've paid my penance. I haven't seen the light of day or breathed fresh air since that night. This has been my punishment, to let them believe I am mentally ill, rather than face the truth that a sane person—*a mother, even*—would do such a thing."

Ivy stepped back. "I almost do feel sorry for you. You've missed out on raising two daughters, and one of them is an accomplished violinist and even an aspiring chef. Look at the talent you walked away from."

Her mother lowered her hands. "I've wondered about you for years, *Nuer.* You can play an instrument? And cook?"

Ivy glared at her. "No, I can't. But Lily can. You know, *the blind one?* The one you and your husband wanted to be rid of? Yes, *she* is the better half of us."

"Does Lai Song know?" the woman asked, her eyes hopeful.

Ivy sighed. She knew what the woman was asking, and she felt like lying and telling her Lily *did* know her own mother tried to murder her. But what good would it do now? The truth was that Lily didn't remember much about their mother, and both of them remembered even less about their father, other than his constant stomping about and clear dislike for them.

"No, she doesn't know. She thinks it was an accident. She believes we were taken from you because the house was too damaged to live in and you had no means to keep us together. Unlike you—*and my so-called father*—I care what burdens she has to carry. It's hard enough to be blind but does she really need to know her own parents wanted her dead because of it?"

The woman put her hand to her heart and gasped.

"Don't you dare act like the victim here," Ivy said. She felt the rage surge through her veins. She just couldn't take that—of all they'd been through, and what this woman had tried to do to Ivy so long ago, she'd better not insinuate she was the one to be pitied.

At that the woman looked over Ivy's shoulder. Mo followed her gaze and gasped. Standing there, his chin propped on a push broom, was the orderly, Cho.

"So what do we have here?" he asked, his eyes flashing. "I think we got us some trouble brewing."

Chapter Twenty-One

Lily took a deep breath and stepped out of the house. Everyone else was busy and she'd slipped away after telling Nai Nai she was going to lie down for a short nap. Since she'd come home they'd been treating her like she was an invalid—as if without Ivy she couldn't manage anything. Only Li Jin understood that though she felt lost without her sister, she could still do everything she'd done with her there.

Today she'd prove it. She planned to make her own way to Linnea's store.

The night before she'd sat up again for hours as everyone else slept, just thinking of how to get Ivy home. Something had changed and she felt in her heart that her sister was in danger. Call it twintuition, or just a sixth sense, but something was wrong. With the heavy feeling upon her, Lily had panicked, wondering if her sister was sick or in trouble. Something was different and she just hoped Ivy was okay.

As she'd stroked the neck of her violin, she'd suddenly remembered the grand opening at Linnea's store a year ago when one persistent customer had slipped his number into her hand and told her if she ever decided to sell the instrument, he was interested. Lily had poked it down into the lining of her case, and luckily it was still there. Now the paper was in her pocket. Linnea would help her either find a buyer or call the man to see if he was still interested—she'd understand Lily had to do something to get Ivy back.

After she'd made a plan, she'd spent the hour before drifting off to sleep going over and over the route to the store in her mind. She and Ivy had gone many times together, and Lily had each step of the way memorized. But she wasn't naive—she knew traversing it alone would be much different, as well as scary the first time.

Now at the sidewalk, she paused and took a deep breath. *She could do this.* Rule one, clear an area and step into it. That was the first thing she'd learned when the tutor came to teach her how to walk with assistance. The woman had barked at her each time she'd forgotten to use her cane. "If body in motion, cane is in rhythm!"

It had taken a few weeks but Lily had learned to use it. She still didn't like it—but in some cases agreed it was necessary. Now she swung the stick wide back and forth, feeling for obstacles or step-offs. It was her first time off their property alone except for the short walk from the taxi to the door when she'd come home from the hospital, and the sweat dribbling between her shoulder blades proved her nerves would take some adjusting.

She knew by the sounds of the horns and the whishing of cars that she was getting closer to the intersection. A man called out to her, asking if she wanted to ride in his pedicab. She shook her head and kept going.

As her grip on her cane tightened, she reminded herself she'd crossed the same juncture many times before, with the only difference being she'd had Ivy to tell her when to go. So just like she'd done with her sister, she quickly sidled up behind the waiting crowd and when she felt them surge as a whole, she went with them.

Her first step into the street was terrifying. Her worry was she'd be in the back of the cluster, but soon she felt others on her footsteps and breathed a sigh of relief. Ironic, but in the crowd she felt protected from any wayward vehicles.

"You're walking crooked," a male voice said from beside her.

Lily wished he'd tell her to straighten to the left or straighten to the right, but her pride wouldn't let her ask. Instead she went with her gut and adjusted. When she didn't bump anyone, she figured she was back on track.

"Step up," he said when they reached the other side.

"I got it. *Xie xie.*" She thanked him impatiently and moved ahead, feeling for the curb with her cane, then stepping up. *She didn't need someone telling her what to do.* That was why at almost seventeen, she was now out for the first time on her own. Today was a new beginning of independence and she wanted to do it herself. She walked faster to put distance between herself and the helpful stranger.

She followed the sidewalk, pausing right before she approached what she remembered as a low spot. She felt for it and smiled when her cane hit it exactly where she remembered it. All of a sudden, she felt a burst of confidence. She was prepared for this! She knew halfway down this block she'd pass a woman selling steamed turnips, a fruit stand where an old dog always lay in the middle of the walkway, and a series of overcrowded bicycle stands she'd need to be careful of. That would bring her to the bus stop. She'd climb aboard, just like she'd done a hundred times before with Ivy. Then she'd have a few minutes to catch her breath before she had to tackle disembarking the bus and traversing to the shop street to find Vintage Muse.

As she picked up her pace she heard a woman in heels rapidly come up behind her and then pass her. She didn't care. It was fine. She walked slower than some and faster than others. Just like everyone else did! She brought her cane in a little closer, hoping she wouldn't trip someone up with it.

"Do you know where you're going?" The question came from the same male voice she'd heard earlier.

Her moment of giddiness was gone as she realized he'd been behind her for quite a ways and she hadn't even picked up that someone was keeping pace with her. She'd heard walking all around her, but she hadn't recognized it as him.

Lily could feel he was tall, and he moved easily, making her think he was thin and wiry. She stopped abruptly and felt just a touch of him before he caught himself and moved back a step to keep from colliding into her. "Yes, I actually do know where I'm going. Do you?"

He chuckled. "You're blind, right?"

Lily couldn't help the sarcasm, though she flinched as the words came out nastier than she'd planned. "No. I just like to wander around with a white cane so I can draw attention from strangers like you."

His chuckling stopped. "That's fair. I've just never seen a blind person walking around alone before. You caught my attention."

He sounded apologetic and Lily felt bad for her attitude. It was just that she'd been warned of strangers and how easy it was to get into a bad situation. She'd begun to distrust anyone who wasn't in her family, and she knew that was no way to be.

"Look, I'm sorry. To be honest, this is my first outing without my sister. It's a bit daunting and I'm trying my best to appear confident." She cringed again. If Ivy were there, she'd tell her she shouldn't be so open with her thoughts. *But Ivy wasn't here, was she?* She started walking again.

"Sounds like we have something in common. . . . I strive to look confident every day."

He was making a joke. She could hear it in his voice. She could also feel him move up beside her. He wasn't giving up and she felt a bit uneasy. What did he want with her? As she hesitated, a pack of young boys passed by. One of them hurled an insult at her and told her to get off the sidewalk if she couldn't see. She felt a moment of insecurity as their voices moved away.

"Seriously, you're doing great. Don't listen to them," he said. "If I were blind, I'd be falling on my face right now."

Lily sighed and kept walking. "Thanks." Her cane bumped up against something hard, at least as big as a brick, but it sounded as if it were wrapped in a bag.

"Whoa! Watch out, don't step on that," the stranger said, and Lily felt him cross in front of her and bend to pick up the item.

She carefully stepped around him as she heard plastic rumpling.

"What was it?" Her curiosity got the better of her as she continued on.

The guy caught up with her and was fumbling with something. Lily tried to concentrate on her path, but he was very distracting.

"Nothing," he mumbled.

Lily smelled something putrid and heard him making smacking sounds.

"It was food! You found food on the ground and ate it?" Her stomach turned. "That's really gross."

The guy continued to keep step with her, but he didn't answer.

Immediately she felt heat fill her cheeks. There was only one reason someone would eat food left as trash—he had to be very hungry. He was a street person, a beggar, or someone really down on his luck. She was so embarrassed for calling him out on it.

She walked faster. It was time to put some distance between them. "It was nice talking to you."

Finally she arrived at the next corner where she and Ivy always waited for the bus. She wished again for her watch, but the hospital had kept it. She moved slowly until she felt her cane touch the back of someone's foot. She knew it by the way they moved it immediately.

"Is this the line?" she asked politely. She didn't know why she bothered; as far as she knew today was like any other and no one would queue up. They'd stand in a group, then all try to cram on the bus at the same time, and she'd hold back and hope there was still a seat for her when she boarded last. But she knew most likely she'd be left standing in the aisle.

Someone ahead of her grunted and she stood quietly and waited. She listened to the chatter around her. A few people discussed an accident that had happened on their way on another street. A man a few feet from her talked quickly on the phone, obvious by the one-sided conversation he was having as he bellowed instructions to someone on the other end. Lily smiled grimly when she heard the rustle of a newspaper and a mother telling her toddler to squat over it to do his business.

Usually she and Ivy would listen to those around them and send silent messages to each other with a bump of the elbow or some other nonchalant gesture. Today the antics of strangers weren't so funny without Ivy to share them with.

Finally she heard the familiar braking of the bus and the crowd surged forward. As she shuffled toward the bus door, Lily held her cane close to her to keep it from being broken or torn from her hands. She breathed through her mouth, filtering out the smell of sweat and perfume as people closed in on her, invading her personal space. Again, she missed Ivy and the way she'd always shielded her from too much contact.

She didn't know she was as close as she was until her shin banged into the first step of the bus. Biting back a yelp of pain, she stepped up and grabbed the handrail. Two more steps and she knew she was in the aisle. She listened, but now nothing would tell her if there was an empty seat, other than touch. She knew from experience some people didn't like to be touched, so she was wary.

She passed the first few seats and could tell just by the rustling and settling in that they were full. At the third set of seats she carefully put her cane where the feet would be. Nothing. She'd found an empty seat! She pushed it a little farther to be sure and felt feet.

"There's still room on this seat."

It was him. The one she'd humiliated. He'd somehow gotten ahead of her and boarded the bus.

And he'd saved her a seat.

Lily thought about moving on but what if there wasn't another spot open? She was exhausted from the challenge of getting this far—her shaky legs screamed at her to take the seat. So she took a deep breath and did the exact opposite of what Ivy would do.

She sat down.

It was hard for Lily to concentrate on what was going on around her as well as the conversation, but by the time the bus had gone the four long stops and two short ones to the corner where she needed to get off, the guy had given Lily most of his life story. He'd competed in the Olympics! But now Dawei—the name given to him by his teammates meaning *greatly accomplished*—was retired. Lily had been astonished, then sympathetic as he'd told his tragic tale. At the height of his career, he'd competed and won bronze in the Olympics as a gymnast. But then a torn ligament had ended everything only a few years after it had started. Lily felt a rush of sympathy when he told her since then he'd been forced to live a life of performing and begging on the streets.

"So why are you on the bus?" Lily asked, still sad yet completely fascinated about his rags-to-riches-and-back-to-rags story.

"After mornings performing, I sometimes ride the bus all afternoon just to have a place to sit out of the weather. Other times I spend ten yuan to stay in the Internet café and surf the net. Today I hadn't decided which I'd do—until I saw you."

Lily blushed. She wasn't sure who he was or even if he was some sort of criminal feeding her a phony story. But she had to admit she was flattered she'd caught his attention.

"What do you look like?" she asked.

Dawei slapped his leg. "I'm so glad you asked. You would not *believe* how handsome I am."

Lily laughed. She thought about how many times she'd warned Ivy not to judge by appearance and here she was asking someone what he looked like. He was an Olympic hero, for goodness' sake! What did it matter what he looked like?

"Didn't you get any compensation from being in the Olympics?" she asked.

He hesitated, then spoke so quietly she had to lean in closer to catch his answer. From experience, she knew his sudden change in volume could only be for secrecy or shame.

"I did. But I've sold my medals, and the retirement compensation the administration of sports gave me was big at the time, but that has gone fast in the last few years. I spent some foolishly before I realized I'd become the sole supporter for my grandfather."

"How big?" Lily couldn't help herself, then slapped her hand over her mouth. "I'm sorry. You don't have to answer that."

He laughed. "I don't mind. Everyone eventually asks. They gave me sixty thousand reminbi. It lasted for a while, at least long enough to make sure we always had a roof over our heads until my *waipo* died. Now it's just me."

Lily could only shake her head at having access to that much money. Here she was on a quest to try to sell her violin just to try to earn a fraction of that amount. She wouldn't share her story with a stranger, but if she did, she felt he might think it was just as far-fetched as his. Meeting him reminded her everyone has a story, with some more tragic than others.

"No more roof over your head?"

"*Bushi*. Just me sleeping under the stars each night, or wherever I find a safe place. I miss that old house we had—on Yellow Lane Street. I left a lot of memories back there."

Lily thought of home and wondered if she should tell him to come by and talk to her Ye Ye about a room at Rose Haven. She knew they were full at the moment, as all the construction was still going on, but surely they could find him somewhere to sleep. But should they trust him? He didn't sound like a teenager. This was someone who had been around.

"*Ni ji sui le?*" she asked.

"I'm nineteen. And you?"

Before she could answer, the bus hit the brakes and the driver announced they were at the shopping street. Their talk was over. Lily stood and unfolded her cane.

"Have a great afternoon," she said. At least he'd been a distraction and she'd barely felt her nerves getting the best of her as they'd talked.

"Can I walk with you? I don't have anything else to do," Dawei asked from his place on the seat.

Lily hesitated. If he came, Linnea was sure to see them together and it might worry her. But then, they all had to realize sooner than later she wasn't a baby. If she wanted to make a new friend—her first ever, actually—she could do it and shouldn't have to hide it.

"You can walk with me but don't try to guide me, tell me what to do, or help me in any way. If you can manage that, come on." She turned and began to walk toward the door.

"*Kuai, kuai,*" the bus driver said, hurrying her along.

"I'm coming," Dawei called from behind her. "And I promise not to say a word, even if you're about to run into a raging ox barreling down the street. I'll just keep it to myself."

Lily smiled as she carefully climbed down the bus steps. When both feet hit the ground she heard the familiar sounds around her and felt a surge of triumph. She was on Linnea's street. Dawei stepped off the bus and stood quietly beside her.

She'd made it. *On her own.* She only wished Ivy were there to share her victory.

"Can I talk now?" Dawei said from beside her.

Lily turned right, easily maneuvering around the large mailbox she knew was there. "Sure, as long as you don't tell me where to go."

"How would I do that? I don't know even know what your destination is. You planning on doing some shopping today?"

That was a valid assumption, Lily thought.

As she walked on determinedly, the midday sounds of the city settled around her, bringing a familiarity she craved. Grandmothers cackled at their toddlers, shop owners hawked at passing people, and beside her the cars and trucks competed for space and blared their horns, creating a cacophony of chaotic impatience.

As they passed each doorway, Lily counted silently in her head.

"Five, six, and we're here." She felt the familiar rubber mat under her feet and knew she'd arrived at Linnea's store. She put her hand on the door handle, only to feel Dawei's hand cover it.

"You won't even let me be the gentleman and get the door?" he asked.

She hesitated.

"It has nothing to do with sight or no sight. It's called good manners—drilled into my head by my grandfather," he added. "He'd turn in his grave if he thought I wasn't opening the door for a lady."

Lily dropped her hand and stepped aside. She felt foolish. In her stubbornness to be independent, she was making herself look ridiculous.

Dawei opened the door and Lily walked in.

"Lily!" She was greeted with Linnea rushing up and throwing her arms around her, so tight she could barely breathe.

Lily inhaled her familiar scent and smiled. Linnea represented safety and trust, something Lily needed to feel right now more than ever.

Linnea stepped back and Lily sensed her sister was looking behind her, taking in anything she could see. "What are you doing here? Where's Nai Nai, and who is this guy? *Aiya*, did you come across town alone?" Linnea asked, all in one breath.

Lily felt a rush of relief. She'd accomplished something on her own. She could be independent later; for now she was glad to have her big sister take over for a while.

Lily rolled her shoulders a few times, then picked up another pod. Home sweet home. It was three hours later and she was exhausted from her adventurous day. She sat at the table shelling peas while behind her Linnea told everyone the story of her little sister showing up at the store with a tall, handsome stranger.

All around her she could hear exclamations of astonishment at her new streak of independence, though her Nai Nai wasn't so thrilled. Lily had only one consolation and that was her Ye Ye wasn't home to hear the exaggeration from Linnea. But he would come later and Lily knew she'd have to answer for sneaking away.

"Lily has a boyfriend!" Peony chortled.

"No. I do *not* have a boyfriend." She felt her cheeks redden. "He just wanted to walk with me."

"I couldn't believe it when she came through that door. But at least she let me escort her home," Linnea said.

"Lily, I hope you understand what you did was dangerous," Nai Nai said, her voice disapproving.

"But—I—" Lily started to defend herself, but Li Jin interrupted.

"Mama, Lily has to begin doing things alone sometime. She's more than old enough to start having a life of her own."

Lily smiled slightly. She knew Li Jin would defend her. Now she had two allies—Li Jin and Linnea. She went back to concentrating on the pod in her hand, searching for the string, then releasing it like a zipper, opening the case. She then used her thumb to push the peas, allowing them to fall into the bowl. She'd learned long ago to let gravity do the work, as more than the lightest touch would ruin their perfect shape.

"Yes, but she let some strange boy walk with her? He could've done anything. No one even knows of this boy. And why, Lily, did you decide to go to the store anyway?" Nai Nai said.

Lily heard her thump down the bowl she was kneading dough in for the evening noodles and knew she was upset. She could tell by the way she dragged her feet around the kitchen her Nai Nai was not only irritated, but tired.

"Nai Nai, here—let me take that. You go put your feet up," Linnea said. "Maybe Lily just needed to get away on her own for a while. And I have to admit, her friend was really nice. He sort of reminded me of Jet—though definitely not from the same mold."

Aiya, here it comes, Lily thought. But at least it had moved the subject away from what she was really doing, and Linnea had promised to keep her secret about the violin.

"What's that supposed to mean?" Nai Nai asked.

Lily pushed the bowl of peas away and stood up. "I'm going to my room. But what she means is Dawei is poor. Really poor—as in homeless. But he's still nice."

"Lily, I'll clean this up."

From beside her she felt Peony take the bowl and bag of empty pods. Lily felt gratitude to her little sister for knowing she was at the end of her rope. She just wanted to be alone. She returned her chair to its proper place under the table and moved toward the door, her arm outstretched, reaching for the doorway. Almost out, a few more steps, she told herself.

"Homeless? He's sleeping on the street?" Nai Nai asked.

Lily sighed loudly. "Yes, but before you offer, he didn't leave me a number or any way to contact him. So even if you have room, we can't find him."

With that, Lily turned and left the kitchen. She was tired of the talking and teasing. She hadn't had any luck with selling the violin. Linnea hadn't wanted to leave Lily alone with Dawei, so she'd accompanied them up to her apartment to use the computer. Her new friend had scoured websites to find a quick buyer, but so far no luck. And the number from the stranger Lily had kept had turned out to be disconnected. She was back to square one with no other way to find the money needed to get Ivy released. Knowing she had failed made her feel as if her body had gained a hundred pounds over the last few hours—making her limbs heavy and awkward. And for someone who rarely questioned being blind, suddenly she felt like cursing the heavens for the predicament it had caused her and her sister. She bit back an urge to open her mouth and scream—and scream—and just scream. She'd never before felt so helpless and frustrated.

Holding her hand against the hall wall, she quickly covered the few feet to their room and closed the door behind her, just in time for a tear to travel unseen down her cheek.

She picked up her violin and began to play the song Ivy had declared her favorite. It was a sweet, slow song that made her feel even more homesick for her sister. Still, out of respect for Ivy, she finished it, then put the violin aside. She was going to go to bed, even though it was the middle of the day, and she didn't want to even get up for dinner. What was there to get up for? She prayed she could sleep. Just sleep until Ivy came home—that was all she wanted to do.

Ivy blinked her eyes rapidly. The room was pitch-black. So black she had reached up more than a few times just to make sure her eyelids were really open. Now she could understand possibly just a tiny bit of what Lily saw most of the time. Knowing her sister lived it every day made it a little easier, and though Ivy couldn't even see her hand in front of her face, she decided she would not cry. Instead, she spent her time doing what Lily would do. She explored the room with her hands. But in every corner she found the same thing—nothing.

Her stomach growled loudly, reminding her she'd missed dinner. She thought of Mo. And wondered where they'd taken her. *So much for getting back to their room safely.* One minute she was standing under the hum of the washing and drying machines, arguing with the woman who'd given her life; the next minute the orderly had rung the alarm bell and accused Ivy and Mo of trying to escape the hospital. Then all hell had broken loose. And not surprisingly, her birth mother had done nothing to try to save her, just scurried out of the laundry room like a panicked rat once the head nurse came rushing in with her gorillas in tow.

Ivy leaned back against the padded wall and slid down until she was sitting. *Her mother.* What were the odds after all these years she'd see her again and, of all places, in a mental hospital? But then, she thought, it made sense from that angle. Maybe the woman really was crazy, because how many mothers tried to set their own children on fire?

She reached over and rubbed at her left shoulder. Moving around on the thick padding released a swirling smell of urine that reached her nose. The mat felt dry but must have had many patients lose their bladder on it over the years. It was an overwhelming and stomach-turning stench—so much that it almost made her forget her aching shoulder. If she wasn't mistaken, the orderly had dislocated it when he took so much glee in dragging her down the hall and throwing her in what he called the Dark Room. With one shove from him, Ivy had landed on her knees, palms slapping the mat and her sunglasses flying from her head. She hadn't even had time to look around before the light had disappeared with the slamming and locking of the door behind her.

Most of all, the head nurse's parting statement still burned in Ivy's ears. When her Ye Ye found out, he'd be so disappointed in her. Even in the dark of the tight room, she felt her cheeks flame for the additional strain she'd surely brought onto her family. The nurse had tried to hide her small smirk as she'd scribbled on her clipboard and led the way to Ivy's punishment room. Just before they'd tossed her in, she'd given one last sucker punch.

You, little blind mouse, have just added another ten thousand reminbi to your fine. Your family will never be able to afford to get you out of here.

Chapter Twenty-Two

The taxi stopped and Sami climbed out, then held the door for Li Jin. Immediately a dark-skinned fellow lounging on his bike in the line of *sanlun ches*—bicycle taxis—tried to wave them over.

"*Wu kuai,*" he bellowed, specifying a price, then spat a long, black stream of tobacco sailing across the walkway.

Sami shook her head. The locals in Wuxi were so irritating. *Didn't he just see them get out of a taxi?* Why did he think they needed another one before they'd even taken a step away from the last one? What an idiot. She waved him away and the others around him chortled at the brush-off. Sami turned back to Li Jin.

"Just let me handle everything. Did you bring the papers?"

Li Jin followed her out of the car and stood on the sidewalk, then patted the bag slung over her shoulder. "I've got it. But I still don't understand why we had to come after dark."

Sami laughed. Li Jin was spooked. You would think she'd never spent any time on the streets. She was getting soft.

"How many loan sharks or gang members do you see conducting business in the light of day?"

"I don't know, Sami. I've never been around loan sharks or gang members. You tell me."

Sami could hear Li Jin's fear hidden under her sarcasm. She reached over and squeezed Li Jin's arm. Sami hadn't even told her they were meeting with the Bamboo Boys, who were rumored to have close ties to the famous United Bamboo Gang in Shanghai. The less she knew, the better. "It'll be fine. I know how to handle these kinds of people and I got your back. Just remember we aren't here on a social call. At least the scar on your face gives you a harder look. Try to match it with your expression. Don't look so blasted nice."

Sami led the way down the street, checking her map as she went. Li Jin kept pace with her, babbling on and on about leaving Lan with a dripping nose and the hacking cough, nagging her that the baby needed to see a doctor. Sami found herself biting the inside of her mouth so hard she tasted blood. She was so tired of hearing about Lan—Lan—Lan.

"*Anjing*. I need to concentrate," Sami said. She'd been told to turn down the alley between the Wuxi Noodle Shop and the shoemaker. She looked ahead and didn't see it, then back down at the scribbled notes. "Come on, the taxi didn't go far enough. We've got to go to the end of the street."

As it was late, and it wasn't a popular part of town, there weren't many people out and about. They continued to walk, passing a few open shops scattered among those closed for the day. A block down, a gap-toothed old man came toward them, carrying a chubby-cheeked toddler over his shoulder. Sami grimaced at the boy's round bottom protruding through his red split trousers.

"*Gei wo qian?*" the man said, asking for a few coins.

"*Meiyou.*" Sami shook her head, telling him she didn't have any. Before she could stop her, Li Jin was digging through her bag and had come up with a ten-yuan bill and held it out. Sami tried to slap her hand down. "Li Jin, stop it! You'll have every beggar on this street following us and we'll have to turn around and go home. We can't be leading them to the money house."

The man's hand shot out like a striking snake and grabbed the bill; then he nodded a few times and backed away, his grandson never moving a muscle as he slept through the exchange.

"I know, Sami. But look at him. His grandson is fat but the old man looks as if he hasn't eaten in a week."

Sami shook her head and grabbed Li Jin's arm, pulling her along faster. They passed more closed shops until she saw one with a large sign hanging in the window with an amateurish drawing of a bowl of steaming noodles.

"This is it." They turned and found themselves in a labyrinth of alleys between the buildings, fire escape ladders hanging around them like unattached streams of a spiderweb. Sami looked down at the paper, then turned around in a circle. "I don't know which way to go next."

Li Jin clutched her bag closer. "Sami, I thought you had the directions already down? Maybe we should just go and come back tomorrow."

Sami stopped and turned to Li Jin. "If we don't show tonight, we can't come back here. Is that what you want to do?"

Li Jin hesitated, then shook her head. "No. I really want to get the money we need to bring Ivy home. It's tearing at my parents that she's in that place."

Sami started walking again. She knew Li Jin wouldn't give up. She just needed to be able to make the decision. Sami pulled out her cell phone and began to punch in the number she'd been given. She was going to have to get some better directions.

Suddenly a man stepped out of the shadows, and both she and Li Jin jumped.

"Ni hao." He nodded, looking them both up and down from head to toe.

"Ni hao." Sami figured there'd be one of them waiting to lead them in. She checked him out just as closely as he did her, and she wasn't impressed. His flat haircut and the soiled tank top he wore did nothing to improve his looks. His stout arms were heavily tattooed and Sami could see the symbol of a Shanghai street gang, and wondered how he managed to leave there and end up in Wuxi. He was what was typically called a bruiser.

"You come to see the boss?"

"Dui."

The bruiser jerked his head and turned. "Follow me." He swaggered down the alley, obviously assuming they were right behind him.

Sami looked at Li Jin and raised her eyebrows. Li Jin shrugged, and they began to follow as he led them through more dark, smelly lanes piled high with discarded junk and trash. There was evidence of people living there, as they also ducked under several lines of clothes left out on lines stretched from window to window.

A few minutes later he led them straight to a set of wooden doors centered in a concrete wall. He knocked two sharp knocks, then three slow ones, and the doors opened. He waved at them to come through.

Sami squared her shoulders and erased the expression of uncertainty from her face and walked through the gate, Li Jin close behind her. The doors opened onto a large, well-kept courtyard—worlds away from the slummy look on the opposite side of the wall.

They looked around and the bruiser stood talking with another guy dressed identically as he was with a soiled white shirt and the same haircut. In hushed voices they talked and shot Sami a few interested looks.

"Where to now?" she asked.

The bruiser held his hand up, silencing her from more questions. Sami sighed impatiently. She hated his type—men who thought women were beneath them and could be silenced with just a look.

"Just hold on," Li Jin hissed at her. "Don't be so testy."

The bruiser grunted in frustration, seeming to have lost the battle to hoist them off on the other guy. He returned to them. "Mobile phones." He held his hand out.

"What about them?" Sami asked.

"They stay down here." He pointed at his buddy and Sami looked to find the other guy smirking back.

She sighed and dug in her bag, pulled out her phone, and put it in the beefy outstretched hand. Li Jin tossed hers in, too. The bruiser threw them both to his buddy and the guy caught first one, then the other in midair, and slipped them into his pocket.

"I hope we get those back," Li Jin muttered.

"Oh, we will. If I have to, I'll take 'em from the guy myself."

The bruiser pointed at the bags. "Let me see inside."

Sami held her bag open wide while the guy looked in, then stuck his hand down and felt around. He grunted in satisfaction and did the same with Li Jin's bag. Then he turned and beckoned for them to follow once again.

He led them inside the house and they entered a big room, empty except for a few randomly strewn couches and chairs. In the corner of the room was a huge, winding wooden staircase, almost like something Sami might see in an old movie. They went to it and followed the bruiser up to the second landing that overlooked the first floor they'd left behind.

Unlike the courtyard and the bottom floor of the house, the landing was outfitted in classic teakwood furniture and even an antique emperor's bed loaded with lavish silk pillows, taking up the far wall. Next to the bed was a table and much to Sami's astonishment, it was covered in pink stacks of reminbi. Sami had never seen so much money in her life and marveled at how trusting they were to leave it unattended.

Scattered around the room were other bruiser-type fellows, as well as a few more studious types perched on the couches hunched over laptops or their mobile phones. Everyone appeared busy and until they walked farther into the room, no one even looked up. Sami saw one fellow had a row of colorful credit cards lined up next to his laptop and he thumped one with one hand as he used his finger pad to scroll the computer screen with the other.

Their guide cleared his throat and a few men looked up, a buzz going through the room quickly until most eyes were on them. Sami saw their gazes flicker from her to Li Jin and back to her. She knew she and Li Jin were probably the best-looking women the men had seen in those parts, as most likely they were accustomed to street girls tending their needs.

She held her hands up. "What are you looking at? Have you never seen women before?"

The men answered with laughs and guffaws, obviously surprised at her spunk. Sami looked at Li Jin and saw by the stiffness of her spine and the paleness of her face she was even more nervous now that they were in the house.

The bruiser gave her a not-so-gentle nudge and pointed to a small group of chairs near the balcony. "The boss man will be here in a minute. You sit."

Slowly, to show him she wasn't afraid of him, Sami led the way to the sofa and gracefully sat down, crossing her ankles as she leaned back and pretended to savor the softness behind her.

"Sami, this is making me really nervous," Li Jin said, and Sami saw her nod just a tiny bit toward the corner of the room where the money was stacked up.

"We're here now. Let's just get it over with." She'd already explained to Li Jin on the way over that money lending was only a small part of the racket this gang had going. The nerdy types proved her prediction, as it was clear they were engrossed in some sort of online activities. If what Sami had heard was true, this gang had their hands in everything from credit card fraud to online phishing endeavors.

As they waited, a girl who looked to be in her late teens wobbled into the room, carrying a tray of plastic cups. Despite the short red dress and spiked heels she wore, the girl was timid, barely attempting to peek out from the fringe of bangs that hid most of her delicate face. As she moved, the long black curtain that was her hair swayed along in rhythm with her hips. She came to Sami and Li Jin and set the tray on the table in front of them.

"Cha?" she asked them.

"Tea would be great. *Xie xie,"* Li Jin answered first, picking up a cup and wrapping her hands around it.

Sami grabbed one and held it to her nose, hoping it was jasmine tea or another famous type, but the ugly green leaves had a putrid smell and Sami knew it was cheap everyday tea. She returned the cup to the table untouched.

The girl set one more cup down and turned to leave. Sami watched her and just before the girl scooted out the door, she glanced back. Their eyes met and Sami saw the naked vulnerability the girl closely guarded. It brought back one of her most deeply buried memories and as though seeing a shuffle of photographs in her head, Sami was taken back to the night her uncle had sent her to an official's promotion party. Years ago, she'd been obedient and that night she'd served men tea and food. As the hours had passed she'd felt a relief she wasn't there for more—until the guests began to leave and one by one, men bid on a night with her. Still no more than a child, she'd stood horrified while the top official had bantered back and forth with the men, selling her for the highest price as if he owned that right instead of her uncle. She'd learned that night that evil came in every package. Rich, poor, insignificant, important, dirty, and clean. The night had been one of many she was ashamed of—a collection she kept inside her just waiting to spring up and give her courage when she finally got her day of vengeance.

"Sami—Sami . . ." Li Jin's voice brought her back to the present and she looked to the door to see who must be the big boss come swaggering through.

Taller than most of the men in the room, the one who had drawn Li Jin's attention carried himself with an undeniable air of authority. He wore what looked like to Sami a very good copy of a sapphire blue Armani suit. His jet-black hair was longer, barely tickling the collar of the silk shirt peeking from his jacket. If she'd seen him on the street, she might have thought he was a well-respected, handsome man, but experience told her he was probably a twisted soul with a lust for money and power, and he would stop at nothing to get it.

At his appearance, the room quieted and most of his men kept their concentration on whatever was in front of them. Sami sat straighter and squared her shoulders. The leader of the ragtag gang wouldn't intimidate her. She'd dealt with men just like him and as she'd seen so many times in the past, they were all controlled by their male anatomy and would ultimately do anything it told them to.

He looked at her squarely in the face, and Sami met his gaze with a steely look of her own. First his eyes were some of the hardest she'd ever seen, but then he smirked, almost causing the ashes to fall from the cigarette dangling from his lips. Sami didn't flinch, but she watched him as he strode right past them and went to sit on a red velvet couch near the far end of the room. He snapped his fingers and one of the men pretending not to watch jumped to his feet and went to him, bending his head to hear his instructions. Then he quickly left the room and Sami could hear him bellowing orders to someone as he pounded down the stairs.

"Is that him?" Li Jin asked.

"*Dui*. His name is Chenzi. And doesn't he think he is some sort of kingpin." Sami couldn't keep the revulsion out of her voice. She thought he'd probably grown up on the streets, collecting favors and growing his gang, one displaced boy at a time, playing the big shot until he finally made his fantasy a reality. Underneath all his pomp and bravado he was probably an insecure little punk.

But still, they needed him. Li Jin needed him. So Sami would play the game. She consciously made an effort to relax. She smiled, crossed her legs, and leaned back on the couch. When Chenzi looked up again, Sami locked eyes with him and this time, she used the feminine wiles she'd spent years perfecting. And of course, he took the bait. His chest suddenly swelled and a creepy leer crept across his face.

"*Guo lai.*" He waved them to come over.

They stood and Sami led the way across the room, turning heads as she went. Li Jin followed quietly behind her, her wariness almost palpable. Sami hoped she'd pull it together or they'd be kicked out on their cute little asses. These kinds of men didn't deal with anyone who sent up a signal of alarm. Confidence. It was all about confidence, Sami thought as she sat down on the smaller sofa across from Chenzi and made room for Li Jin beside her.

"*Ni hao,* and thank you for seeing us," Li Jin said, the shaking in her voice immediately giving away her nervousness.

Sami felt a rush of irritation. Where was the tough girl who used to live on the streets? The one who'd had the gall to pack up and make a new life? Why was Li Jin acting so afraid and for that matter, what was she doing taking over? The shark in front of her would eat her alive and spit her out to have her again for breakfast. And Sami didn't want the man thinking Li Jin was his customer. Sami didn't want her exposed that way in case something went wrong. She had to take back control.

"I'm Sami. I spoke to your comrade on the phone and he assured me you were interested in taking me on as a client. I'm in need of some funds and it's fairly urgent."

Chenzi nodded but before he could speak the hostess girl returned with a tray that held a steaming bowl. She quickly crossed the room and set the bowl down on the table in front of her boss, as well as a small teapot and a cup. Sami's stomach turned at the aroma of the spicy tofu and garlic-coated green beans.

He put his cigarette out in the ashtray and Sami couldn't help but stare at the discolored fingernail on his pinkie finger, grown out so long it looked like a spoon or scoop. She wondered what would possess a man to do that. She'd seen it before and still didn't understand it, though one time her uncle told her it was a status symbol separating the business men from the working class. Whatever it was, Sami found it disgusting.

One of the other men crossed the room and removed the ashtray, obviously a task he knew to do when Chenzi was ready to eat.

The girl finished arranging the treat for her boss and quickly left the room, looking even more nervous than she had before. Again, Sami felt something for the girl—could it be compassion? She didn't want to deal with it.

"So? Can we talk?" They didn't have all night to sit and watch him be waited on like some sort of emperor.

"You said you have a property deed?" Holding the bowl close to his mouth with one hand, he used the other hand to shovel a large clump of tofu into his mouth with his chopsticks.

"*Dui.* It used to be a shoe factory and the land covers two acres. The building itself is twenty-five thousand square feet of space. The family is using it as a home and a shelter for displaced people. They've spent a lot of money in renovations; I'm sure increasing the value."

Li Jin pulled the papers from her bag and laid them on the table. Chenzi put down his bowl and chopsticks.

"Displaced people? You mean homeless beggars. And they stay for free?"

His jaw dropped, making him look more like a boy than the leader he was.

"*Dui.*"

"What a waste. If they were smart, they'd use the building for a hostel and people would pay good money to stay there—even foreigners passing through. Wuxi's getting a lot more tourists and many can't afford hotels."

Sami could tell that ruffled Li Jin's feathers immediately and before she could answer, Li Jin had to open her mouth.

"We aren't interested in being rich. My family works in the community to provide relief for people who need it. My father has been rescuing children for decades."

"Children. Another lucrative business," he said with a derisive snort.

"Are you saying you're interested in legitimate enterprises, in addition to loan-sharking, extortion, and whatever else you got going on here?" Sami waved her hand around the room.

Chenzi ignored her baiting. Instead he took a few more bites, then set the bowl down again. Finally he looked up at Sami.

"I'm a businessman. I see potential in the property. You don't because you don't use your brain to get ahead—your female heart gets in the way. So yes, I'll loan you the money. But the terms will be strict and if you don't meet them, I *will* take your deed. I don't fall for the whimpering of any fools who claim fate is cruel to them. In my world—it's thrive or just survive. No handouts."

Sami held her own tongue and put her hand on Li Jin's arm, squeezing it to give her a signal to stay silent. They waited as Chenzi picked up his bowl and raked the rest of the food into his mouth, then sat back and pulled a linen cloth from inside his coat. He dabbed at his face, then put it away. Reaching in again, he pulled out a pack of cigarettes and shook one loose, then lit it and took a deep drag. Finally, he looked at Sami.

"You said thirty thousand. I'll loan it to you and hold your deed. You have four months to repay the note. With interest." He snapped his fingers again and a tank-topped guy came over. "Set them up with thirty."

With that he stood and left the room, all eyes following him. Sami looked at Li Jin and saw her face fall. Shrugging her shoulders, she leaned over and whispered, "Don't look so upset. We did it."

Li Jin should be looking relieved, Sami thought. But she was most likely already thinking about how they were going to pay back the money so they didn't lose Rose Haven. Sami had helped her solve one problem, but Li Jin still looked as if she carried the weight of the world on her shoulders. Sami wished she could feel more compassion, but she'd done what she could and if she was perfectly honest with herself, she didn't give one little whit about Rose Haven—or Ivy and Sky, for that matter. She only cared for Li Jin. Unless . . . maybe she could find a way to break Li Jin's infatuation with Sky.

As they waited for Chenzi's assistant to get them the money and give them their papers, the wheels in Sami's head began to turn again. Something the boss man had said might have just triggered an idea.

Ivy paced the four corners of the dark room and bit her lip to keep from yelling again. Since she couldn't hear anything from the other side of the door, she assumed no one could hear her, either, so she saved her energy. She felt as if she'd been dropped onto another planet—a very cold planet—and was the only life-form left.

By now she didn't even have to use her hands to keep from walking into the opposite walls; she'd memorized the distance. She needed to keep moving to keep her joints from freezing up. She also knew she'd been in there for two days because she'd been fed a boiled egg for each meal, and so far she'd had four eggs. The first night they'd finally brought her an egg, and now she assumed it was night again as she'd had three more eggs, each at different times; breakfast, lunch, and finally dinner.

They'd also taken her to use the bathroom only three times, and the nurse had said she was scheduled for a bathroom break every twelve hours. She'd been given only a tiny bit of water so far, so other than an unquenchable thirst, the lack of bathroom access didn't bother her. She'd been warned if she soiled her room, there would be consequences, but by the stench around her, Ivy knew others had not heeded the threats.

The first time they'd opened the door and led her out, Ivy had thrown her hands over her eyes to shield the light. She'd shuffled down the hall with the nurse clutching her arm to keep her from running away. As if she would. Where did they think she'd go?

She no longer wore the sunglasses and no one mentioned her blindness. She figured since she'd stopped being treated as human, they'd stopped caring whether her story matched up or not. She'd barely slept, and the times when she did manage to nod off, she was awakened very shortly after by bursts of night-mares. She was exhausted.

She'd begged each nurse to tell her where Mo was, but they'd only shaken their heads and told her to stop talking non-sense. Ivy hoped the girl was being treated better than she was. Being in the dark had stopped being so creepy and now she almost favored the deep black void over the brightly lit hospital hall and bathroom. At least in the dark she could avoid facing what she'd become. With her scraggly hair and rumpled, soiled clothing, she knew she looked like a genuinely deranged mental patient. Now she could see how some people entered the hospital as sane but quickly lost all senses. The staff had a way of breaking your spirit so you no longer felt like yourself. More than once, she'd prayed for Nurse Guo to be assigned to her, for just a moment of kindness. But since she'd switched places with Lily, she'd not seen the woman.

Her stomach growled painfully. It seemed like a long time ago they'd brought her egg; it hadn't been nearly enough to fill her up. She felt like her belly was eating through itself. She'd even welcome their tasteless congee if they'd only bring her a bowl. But more than anything, the isolation was driving her crazy. She wasn't used to being alone. All her life she'd had her sister by her side and now the seclusion was crippling. She needed someone to talk to, to lean on—someone to help her get through this nightmare.

She slid down against the wall until she was seated again. Her eyes felt droopy, so maybe it was time to get some sleep? Her hours were so turned around she was really unsure.

Suddenly she heard a slight movement that sounded like someone turning the doorknob. She waited. Were they going to give her an extra bathroom break? It hadn't been twelve hours, she knew that much.

In the dark she turned to watch the area where she knew the door to be, and slowly she saw a tiny sliver of light. Someone was opening the door. Usually it was snatched open loudly and quickly, but whoever it was this time was being extremely quiet and careful. The sliver of light gradually got bigger until it widened enough for Ivy to see a few inches in the hall. Then the area filled with a body and in stepped her birth mother.

The woman quickly but quietly closed the door behind her, extinguishing the light again until Ivy could no longer see her face.

"What are you doing in here?" Ivy asked. She wasn't happy to see her—if it weren't for her, she probably wouldn't even be in the punishment room and accused of trying to escape. She and Mo would be safely back in their ward, laughing over the whole experience.

Ivy heard the rustling of a bag, and then felt a blanket tossed at her.

"Here's a blanket. I know they keep the temperature frigid in here as punishment. I brought you something to eat, Lai Sun."

Ivy pushed the blanket away from her. She didn't need the woman's charity. Next a cardboard carton and a set of chopsticks were pushed into her hands and Ivy inhaled the sweet smell of rice with pork. She hadn't had meat since she'd arrived at the hospital, and though she would have liked to have shoved it right back at the woman, her willpower evaporated and she began shoveling it into her mouth instead.

"I have milk for you when you finish eating."

Ivy didn't reply. She couldn't reply if she'd wanted to—her cheeks were bulging with the delicious food she knew couldn't have come from the hospital cafeteria. The pork with its tasty spices and sauce was some of the best she'd ever eaten and she couldn't imagine how the woman had gotten it.

Finally she managed to get a few words out. "How did you know where they put me? And how did you get in here? That door was locked."

"I have keys. I'm a trustee. They give me a lot of freedom around here as long as I keep up all my duties and never give them any trouble. They think I'm collecting laundry and won't even know I've been here."

Ivy didn't understand how they'd allow a crazy person such freedom, and if she knew nothing else, she knew her mother was crazy. Only someone seriously insane would try to kill her own child. Still, she felt a seed of gratitude begin in her heart. She appreciated the food especially, but if she was being honest, she was thankful most of all for the company of another human being. She didn't care who it was—just having someone to fill the darkness with her was a comfort.

The awkward silence felt heavy as Ivy got to the bottom of the carton. She couldn't think of what to say that wouldn't completely wipe out the small spark of gratitude she felt. Even through her thankfulness, she still felt anger.

"Do you want me to go now?"

Ivy hesitated. She should say yes at least out of loyalty to Lily. But she didn't want to be alone again so soon. She heard the woman moving.

"Wait," Ivy said.

The woman stopped. "*Hao le*. Do you want me to stay? I still have some time before I'm due back to my ward."

It was hard, but she managed to get the words out. "Yes, can you stay?"

She heard the woman settling herself down on the mat. For a moment, Ivy wished she had had more time to study the woman's face before the light had been extinguished. Would she have seen the same contours and features she saw in her own mirror each day, or on the face of her sister?

"Do you know what's going to happen to you?" she asked.

"They said they were going to add ten thousand reminbi onto my fine," Ivy said, then heard a gasp from the other side of the room.

"That's a lot of money. Does your family have access to those sorts of funds?"

Ivy gave a quick laugh. "Definitely not. I'm the daughter of a scavenger."

"A scavenger? They let a scavenger adopt you and Lai Song?"

"My Ye Ye is not just any scavenger. He's rescued many girls over the years, raising them as his own. He and my Nai Nai have done it together, and expected nothing in return."

The woman didn't reply and Ivy felt a rush of possessiveness about her life details. The woman didn't deserve to know what had happened to them. But try as she might, Ivy couldn't stop the silent questions from entering her mind until she finally had to ask.

"I don't remember much about our life with you. Can you tell me about when we were little?"

"Of course, Lai Sun. The memories of you and your sister have kept me alive all these years. I try to do good things, too, for people of all types—just like your Ye Ye and Nai Nai do. I guess I've been trying to outweigh the bad I've done. I've spent years in a quest to redeem my sins."

"What's your name?" Ivy had always wondered her mother's name but had not wanted to ask her Ye Ye or Nai Nai if they knew it.

"Fengniao."

"Hummingbird?" Ivy said, her voice laced with doubt, but the truth was, the name *did* fit her. From what she'd seen in the laundry room and in the brief light of the doorway, the woman was small and flitted around gracefully just like a little bird. Suddenly, she felt something tickle the end of her nose and she jerked her head back, fighting a sneeze.

"It's a tiny blue feather. I always carry it for good luck. And yes, Fengniao was only meant to be my milk name—a nickname until a proper one could be found—but it stuck and I was never given a formal name. My own childhood wasn't so wonderful, Lai Sun."

"All about you, huh? How did it circle back around to you again?" Ivy couldn't help the irritation from entering her voice.

"No, it's not all about me. I've got plenty to tell you about your early years. Hmm . . . let's see. What I remember most was how protective you were of your sister. From the very beginning you two had a connection that couldn't be broken. I remember when you girls were born, the doctor released me and you a few days later, but Lai Song had to stay for more tests on her eyes."

Ivy didn't know that and couldn't imagine she'd been separated from Lily so early in their life. She thought they'd never been apart until now.

"Well, when we left the hospital, you would not stop crying. You were so upset, crying as if you'd been injured. I tried everything to comfort you—rocking, walking, singing—but nothing would calm your cries. Then the nurse on duty called and told us Lai Song was the same way and was disrupting the entire nursery. She asked if I could bring you back up and let you stay with your sister to see if that would help."

Ivy laughed. Usually it was her doing the disrupting and it was amusing to hear that Lily had caused the commotion for once.

"Your father thought it was silly and wouldn't take you. So even though I was still sore from childbirth, I got a taxi and took you right back to that hospital, with you crying all the way there—so much that the taxi driver almost put us out on the road. I had to pay him extra to keep driving!"

"What a jerk," Ivy said.

"Anyway, we got to the hospital and by the time we reached the nursery, my ears were ringing from your high-pitched wails. Everyone stared at us, as if they thought I was beating you under the blankets. The elevator opened and your bawling blended in with another that I immediately knew came from your sister. I quickly went into the room, put you in the cradle next to her, and it was like shutting off a water spigot. Immediately you both stopped crying and went straight to sleep."

"You're making that up," Ivy said.

Fengniao laughed and took the empty carton from her hands, then pushed a small bottle of milk in them. "No, I'm not. Cross my heart. After that, you two were like perfect angels until the day you came home. And it never changed. As you grew older you still stayed close. You barely allowed me to care for my own daughter! You insisted on being her little mother, helping her dress and eat, guiding her around. You even struggled to do her hair when you were only three or so!"

Ivy had to admit, that story fit with how her own family described her and Lily when they were brought to them. Nai Nai said the same things about the way she cared for Lily. Maybe her mother wasn't such a liar after all. But she still would have been a murderer if Ivy had not woken up that night, and she couldn't forget that.

With the food in her belly and the milk to quench her thirst, Ivy felt a sudden urge to sleep. But she still didn't want to be alone, so she forced herself to stay awake.

"I'm so tired."

She felt her mother move closer to her, her voice thick with sympathy. "I know you are. And you've had a rough time of it,

Lai Sun. If you would let me tell you the truth, I could make you believe that I never intended to hurt you or your sister."

"Don't call me by that name. I'm not that girl anymore," Ivy mumbled, though not very forcefully. "And I don't need your blanket. Or your lies."

"Okay, okay. Just lay your head down and let me sing you the lullaby you used to like. Here, I'll cover you and you'll warm up in no time."

Fengniao tugged at her sleeve. Ivy tried to resist but her body felt so heavy. *She'd just lay her head down for a minute.* Being next to the woman was so much warmer than being alone. Part of her softened; she really wanted to know what lullaby she used to ask for. Any small remnant of the life she'd been deprived of was something she wanted—*needed*—to know, even if only to hide the memory in her heart, never to be spoken of again. She allowed herself to be pulled into a reclining position on the mat.

It seemed like weeks since she'd felt any real comfort and Fengniao's lap was too enticing to avoid. Ivy gave up and let her head fall, and soon felt her mother's hand stroking her hair. She was glad the room was pitch-black and she had to admit, the soft touch felt nice. She'd never tell Lily about her weak moment— she'd just let Fengniao continue for a few more minutes; then she'd tell her to leave. Vaguely, she felt the blanket being pulled over her until she no longer felt the chill of the blasting air conditioner from the vent in the ceiling.

The soft words from an ancient Chinese lullaby being sung, assuring her calmer winds were coming, to fear no more, were the last thing she remembered before she let a long-awaited peaceful sleep overtake her. With the song floating in the room around her, Ivy remembered it being sung to her long ago. Finally she let go of her need for control and allowed the memory to envelop her in comfort until she knew no more.

Chapter Twenty-Three

Lily stood at the kitchen sink, washing the morning breakfast bowls. For the first time, she alone had taken over the kitchen for Li Jin and directed the helpers to keep everything on schedule. Li Jin and Sami had come in so late the night before that both of them were sleeping in. With it being Saturday, it was a bit more relaxed than if they'd had to get everyone off to school. It was a perfect time to show everyone she could accomplish something and Lily couldn't help but feel pleased.

"Lily, I can't say enough how proud of you I am," Nai Nai said from her place at the table where she held Lan on her lap, feeding her a bottle.

"*Xie xie.*"

"No, really. Where did you learn to give orders like that and keep everyone so organized?"

"From Li Jin. I've been helping her almost every morning since we moved in here. I know the drill, Nai Nai." Lily had carefully supervised the morning crew through every task, making sure the table was set, the tea steeped, and even making the huge pot of congee herself before everyone else in the center had arrived for breakfast. Then she'd set the cleaning crew to work and shooed them out when all but the dishes were done. She wanted to do them herself—anything to keep her busy so she wouldn't have too much time to think.

"Lily . . . ," Jojo called out from the hallway. "You have a visitor."

Lily stopped, her hands still in the soapy water. A visitor? She'd never had a visitor in her life. Who was it?

"Oh, hello there," Nai Nai said. "Jojo, bring him around here. He can sit at the table."

"*Ni hao.*"

Lily recognized his voice immediately. It was Dawei. What was he doing here and how had he found her? She resumed washing dishes, feeling sweat break out across her forehead.

"Lily? *Ni hao ma,*" he said.

"I—I'm fine. How did you know where I lived?"

"I went by your sister's shop. Linnea gave me directions."

Lily heard the release of suction from Lan's bottle. Nai Nai scooted her chair back and stood. *Oh no, Nai Nai, don't leave me alone with him!* she thought, but didn't say it aloud.

"I'm going to take Lan out for a little fresh air. You two stay in here and visit. Dawei, take my chair." With that she was gone and Lily was alone with Dawei. She knew by her announcement that Nai Nai was also letting her know exactly where in the room the boy sat.

"Have you had breakfast?" she asked. He paused, then cleared his throat. "*Bushi,*" he said.

Lily felt a stir of pity, then got busy scooping the last bit of remaining congee from the pot into a freshly washed wooden bowl. She picked it up, dumped a ceramic spoon into it, and made her way around the counter toward the table.

"I can get that," Dawei said.

"No, stay there. I'll bring it." Her pity for his hunger was replaced with irritation at his offer. Didn't he understand she didn't want to be treated differently? She was more than capable of bringing him a bowl of congee. *Aiya,* she'd even cooked it!

He should've been there earlier to see her in action; then he wouldn't be doubting her abilities.

With her hand she felt the back of his chair; then she carefully set the bowl and spoon in front of him. She felt until she found the edge of the table and after making sure the bowl was a safe distance from it, she pulled out the chair next to him and sat down.

"So, what have you been up to?" she asked. It'd been almost a week since they'd spent the afternoon together and Lily wouldn't admit it, but she'd thought of him constantly.

He noisily slurped at the congee for a moment, then paused.

"Lily, I think I've found a buyer for your violin. I can take it with me, and if you give me a few days, I'll bring you back the money."

With those words Lily felt a wave of relief. She *would* be able to do something to get her sister home. All was going to be okay. Suddenly she felt like the most capable person in the world. Dawei knew how much she needed, and if he thought he could get it, then she'd just have to push away her first inclination to question him more. For once, she'd go on blind faith—literally.

After lunch Lily sat cross-legged on the bed as she braided her wet hair. The morning had flown by since she'd been so busy with breakfast; then her government-appointed tutor came by and Lily had begged off her afternoon classes. Now she was bored. Their room still felt weird without the energy her sister always brought to it. It was too quiet—almost eerie. And what once she had complained of being too small for them now felt like a massive empty space.

But Lily smiled as she thought about Dawei and how he'd reached over and touched her arm before he had left earlier.

Could he really like her? In that way? She wished Ivy were there so she could talk to her about him. But if he was right, and he was able to get as much money as he thought he could for her violin, then her sister would soon be home.

She tried not to think of the emptiness the absence of the violin created. It was usually so near her it almost felt like an extension of her own body. She'd almost reached for it several times before remembering that she'd sent it with Dawei.

She took a deep breath. She wouldn't allow herself to be sad. It was just a thing—not flesh and blood like her sister. And if the tables were turned, Ivy would do it for her, of that much she was sure. That was what sisters did—they gave up everything for each other if need be. And she could get another violin one day. It wouldn't hold the memories that Viola held, or have that history of being passed down from her Ye Ye, but she'd just have to give it a new history.

She heard the front door open in the hall and listened closely. It was Linnea. She could tell by her footsteps.

"Linnea?" she called out.

Linnea filled the door, then came to sit down on the pallet beside her.

"Lily, I have some bad news."

Lily felt her heart drop. Had something happened to Ivy? If so, why would Linnea come to tell her instead of Ye Ye?

"What? Tell me. Is it Ivy?"

She heard Linnea sigh. "No, it's not about Ivy. It's about your new friend—the one who came by my shop earlier today. I'm so sorry I told him where to find you."

"Dawei? What about him? I didn't mind him visiting."

Linnea reached out and took her hand. "I think he's a fake."

Lily snatched her hand back. "What do you mean? A fake what?"

"A con artist. A fraud. Lily, I asked him his whole name and when he left, I did all kinds of searches on the Internet and he doesn't exist."

Lily wouldn't let Linnea steal this away from her. The one time someone finally liked her, not her sister. This was *her* friend—made on her own, interested in knowing only *her*.

"He *does* exist. He competed in the Olympics."

"I'm sorry. But I looked at every list that named the Olympic teams and participants. He's not there. I even searched team photos in case he was there under another name. He's not in them. He lied to you."

Lily felt her throat thicken with tears; then she remembered the violin.

"Oh no!"

"What? Did he do something to you, Lily? Did he touch you?"

"No! I mean yes—but not the way you mean. But he said he had a buyer for my violin and I let him take it. He was going to get us the money to get Ivy home." Lily felt her world swaying around her. How could she have been so stupid? *So naive?* Ivy would've never allowed herself to be fooled like that. She felt her face flush with embarrassment.

"Oh, Lily. Ye Ye is going to be so upset."

"I know. He's going to hate me. What am I going to do, Linnea? We have to find Dawei." Lily jumped up from the pallet and felt a sob rising.

Linnea stood and put her arm around Lily. She hugged her close. "It's too late. He's gone. And it's not your fault. There are cruel people in this world. Ye Ye will understand. And if Dawei is still out there anywhere that Ye Ye can find him, he's going to be very sorry. He'd better be finding a rock to hide under for the next decade."

Lily let the tears slide down her face. First she'd lost her sister and now her violin. What were the gods trying to tell her? She pushed the thought away but it came right back and hit her in the face. *Maybe her birth father was right the night he'd whispered to her that her blindness was punishment for being an evil being.* Ivy thought she didn't have any memories from that time, but Ivy was wrong. Lily had some secrets—and that one swirled in her head, taunting her that it was her own fault her life was in shambles.

She turned away from Linnea. "Please go, Lin. I want to be alone. I have to find a way to tell Ye Ye what I've done. Just wait for me in the kitchen and I'll be there shortly."

Benfu shook his head and slammed his fist on the table. He felt his blood pressure begin to rise and his ears started ringing. They hadn't even gotten through the day and already he'd had a call from the official, Delun, that Ivy's fine had been raised. He hadn't even had time to tell everyone about her supposed escape attempt, and now they'd hit him with more bad news. The day was just getting worse.

"Benfu, don't you act like that. Lily was only trying to help," Calli said gently, still bouncing Baby Lan on her knee.

Benfu looked up to see the stricken expression on Lily's face. She had stood at the counter, pale as a ghost as she told her story. She was still standing there, waiting for a response from him, Linnea keeping her arm around Lily's shoulder for support.

"I'm so sorry, Ye Ye."

Benfu immediately felt ashamed at his burst of anger. "No, Lily, I'm not angry at you. I just can't stand the thought of that boy taking advantage of you because you can't see."

"I don't think it had anything to do with her ability to see or not see," Linnea said. "He would've done the same thing to Ivy. He was obviously after the violin from the start."

"But—" Benfu was interrupted by Li Jin as she made her way into the kitchen.

"*Aiya,* I really overslept. But what's going on?"

"That new friend Lily made wasn't really a friend. He swindled her out of the violin," Linnea said.

Li Jin dropped into a chair at the table. "Oh no. But how? Why the violin?"

"We were working together to find a buyer for it. I was going to use the money to pay Ivy's fine and get her home."

Li Jin dropped her head in her hands and mumbled something.

"What did you say?" Calli asked.

"*I said,* you didn't have to try to sell the violin because I got the money for Ivy's fine last night."

At the counter, Lily's face transformed and she threw her arms around Linnea. "She got it! Li Jin got the money! Ivy can come home. Let's go right now, Ye Ye, come on."

"Hold on, there. Where did you get that kind of money, Li Jin?" Benfu asked.

Li Jin sat up straight and Benfu saw her take a deep breath and pull her shoulders back. "Sami and I went to a shadow lender, like we talked about."

Benfu felt a rock of dread forming in his stomach. He thought he had successfully discouraged that idea when it had come up. What had his daughter done? Did she even realize the scope of making a deal with those sorts of people? And there was only one thing she could've exchanged. He ran his fingers through his hair a few times before looking up to see Lily making her way around the counter and starting down the hall.

"I'm going to change and get my shoes on. Ivy's coming home! Hurry up, everyone."

"We'll be ready in just a minute, Lily. Let me talk to Li Jin first," Benfu called to her, then turned his attention to his other daughter. "You gave them the deed to Rose Haven, didn't you?"

"No, I didn't *give* him anything. He's holding it until we repay the loan. And I got enough to get Sky out, too. We borrowed thirty thousand."

Thirty thousand? Benfu shook his head. How would they ever get their hands on that kind of money? He held his tongue. He was afraid to ask about the conditions of the loan, the interest, and even the time allowed for repayment. It wouldn't do any good to scold Li Jin for her actions. She was a grown woman, and after all, Rose Haven was technically her place. And she'd just jeopardized it for Ivy—for their family. Wasn't that what he'd wanted, for her to finally feel like she was a part of their family? Well, she'd just proven her loyalty, not just to him, but to her sisters and herself. He swallowed back a lump in his throat. He wouldn't let her see how moved he was by what she'd done.

"Baba, I know you're worried. But I got an idea while we were there. You know that empty building we're using for storage right now?"

Benfu nodded. The least he could do was to hear her out.

"It's just wasted space. But we can turn it into a hostel and start bringing in money right away. It doesn't have to be fancy; our customers will be foreign backpackers and university students traveling around China. I was up half the night when we got home, talking it over with Sami. I know exactly how to do it."

A hostel? Benfu had never considered that before but it made sense. Right now he was opening his doors to people for free— but there were those out there who could pay for a safe bed and shelter over their heads for a night or two. It might just work.

"A hostel sounds like a very good idea, don't you think, Benfu?" Calli asked. "I mean, we're already in the service business, we might as well start a side we'll be paid for."

"How much time do we have to pay back the loan?" Benfu asked.

He could see Li Jin shift nervously in her chair before she answered him. "Four months."

He took a deep breath. "That means we'd have to work really fast to even have a chance at this. We need to clean the building and paint it. Buy bedrolls and blankets. Oh—and we need to get approved for a permit—and that might take forever."

"Jet's father can help with that," Linnea said. "Calm down, Ye Ye. We can do this."

Benfu's mind was swirling with possibilities and instant lists of what would need to be done to make the building habitable. There'd need to be two areas, one for men and the other for women. There was an old bathroom there but they'd need another. And a common area with a television and couches was standard for hostels. And foreigners were needy people, so the place would have to look nice and hospitable. They might even have to offer meals. It was going to be quite an undertaking, but what else could they do?

"This is a good idea, Baba. And after the loan is paid back, the revenue from the hostel will help us take care of those under our own roof—the ones who have nowhere to go or money to get there; the ones who really need us."

She was right. He'd been spending more and more time worrying about what would happen when he was gone. How they would all survive. This could be the answer.

"Let's talk more about it this afternoon. Right now we need to go get Ivy and bring her home. Everything else can wait."

"Mama, just let me go to my room and get the money. I'll stay and watch Lan until Sami gets up so you, Lily, and Baba can all go."

"But don't you want to go with us?" Calli asked.

"No, there's no more room in the taxi, so I'll see her when she gets here," Li Jin said.

"Li Jin, one more thing before we go. I have bad news I haven't had the chance to share yet," Benfu said. "Because the officials believe there was an escape attempt, they have raised the fine to twenty thousand. There won't be enough for Sky, too. I'm sorry."

He saw Li Jin's face fall and he was proud of the compassion she continued to show to everyone around her. She composed herself quickly and met his eyes.

"Oh, Baba, that is terrible. But our first priority must be Ivy, I understand," Li Jin said.

"*Hao le*. Get us the funds then, Li Jin. We need to get going before Lily finds us still standing here talking." Benfu urged them along, anxious himself to get Ivy out of the clutches of the hospital administration.

Chapter Twenty-Four

Ivy woke up to find Fengniao gone and her Ye Ye's coat tucked firmly around her. The woman must have taken the blanket, as Ivy felt around her but did not find it. She sat up and rubbed at her eyes, realizing immediately her bladder was about to explode. She wasn't sure if it was day or night, but she was sure she'd finally slept soundly. She last remembered Fengniao rubbing her hair and singing softly. She felt her face burn with shame at the memory. Instead of holding firm to her anger, she had folded in a moment of weakness and allowed her birth mother to break through the walls she'd spent years building. She was glad it had happened in the dark, in a solitary room with no one else to witness it. Still, she felt an instant of regret that the woman was gone before she pushed it back and got her head on straight again.

Throwing the coat off, she crawled over to the door and pressed her ear against it. She hollered out, knowing no one would hear but unable to stop herself. She needed the bathroom.

Standing now, she crossed her legs and bounced up and down. Seriously, she could barely hold it. Her eyes watered as she tried to think of something else—anything else—to keep her mind off her urge to squat. She should never have drunk the milk Fengniao had brought and she didn't even want to think of the pork and rice. Her stomach was already begging for something new.

Pacing now, she began to replay the previous night in her head. Fengniao had told her more than a few stories of when she and Lily were little. She stopped for a moment, thinking hard. Ivy knew it was impossible, but the woman had sounded as if she held affection for them both. But she had tried to kill Lily, so why did it sound like she had loved her? Ivy felt so confused. She started pacing again.

Strange, for the last few days she'd stopped thinking about home so much. She guessed it was because she knew Lily was safe and that left her to concentrate on just surviving her own experiences. If anything, being away from her family had given her loads of time to think—figure out her life a bit. Maybe even examine all the hurt and resentment she'd been carrying and analyze if it was worth all the energy it took to keep it.

Finally she heard the doorknob turn and the door opened.

"Come on." A nurse stood waiting in the hall.

Ivy couldn't make out her face, since she was so blinded by the light, but she could hear and feel the impatience. That was okay, she was a bit irritated herself. The overwhelming stench of hospital cleaner in the hall was like a sucker punch and her stomach rolled.

"Finally. You sure took long enough. I'm about to wet myself." Ivy squinted in the bright light and held on to the door frame for support as she walked into the hall, then pushed her arms through her Ye Ye's jacket.

"Oh, I'm not taking you to the bathroom. You've been processed."

With that the nurse turned and brusquely led the way, Ivy following.

"Processed? What does that mean?" Ivy cringed. She didn't want to go to the reeducation center. She wanted to go back to the room with Mo. There she knew how to keep herself safe.

"I mean discharged. Your fine is paid and your family is here."

Ivy stopped in midstride and her heart beat rapidly. "Are you telling the truth?"

The nurse continued toward her station. "You'd better hurry before they change their minds."

"I can really go home?" Ivy muttered, starting after the nurse again.

She looked at every person as she passed, scrutinizing them to see if they were in on some sort of cruel joke and maybe they'd be taking her back to the isolation room after all. A nurse's assistant passed her, carrying a ceramic urine pot, her face screwed up in a disgusted scowl. An old man pushed a dust mop but he didn't look up. They all seemed oblivious to her sudden freedom. Ivy felt a tingle run up her spine. *It was real, wasn't it?* she thought.

Suddenly she remembered the night before and her joy turned to confusion. Should she say good-bye? She hesitated, then took a chance.

"Excuse me, is there any way I could see the patient you call Fengniao?" The least she could do was to tell the woman she was leaving. After the comfort she'd brought her the night before, Ivy owed her at least that.

The nurse stopped. "I really don't have time for this. Who are you talking about?"

"Her name is Fengniao. She does the laundry for this floor." Ivy hoped she wouldn't get the woman in trouble.

The nurse shook her head. "I've worked this floor every day for ten years and I can promise you we don't have anyone by that name."

The nurse started walking again, and Ivy followed. She was confused. Why didn't the nurse know who Fengniao was?

"Just one more question, please."

At the nurses' station the nurse used a heavy red chop to stamp papers on her clipboard; then she went around the other side and picked up a plastic bag. She let out an exaggerated sigh.

"What? Last question for the day. Spit it out."

"When I was caught in the laundry room with my friend Mo, it was the woman named Fengniao who was with us. They would have it in my records, right?"

The nurse looked back at the clipboard and flipped through the papers, reading entries. She finally pointed at one sheet in particular. "It says here that the orderly Cho caught you and another patient—your friend Mo, I assume—hiding in the laundry area. No other witnesses."

Ivy's head swam with confusion.

"Can I talk to Mo before I leave? Where have you put her?"

"You can go and meet your family now, or I'll personally escort you back to the ward to wait another week for discharge. While you're there you can catch up with your friend Mo all you want. What's your fancy?" She glared at Ivy.

That was an easy choice. Her loyalty was to her family, not the woman who'd abandoned them so long ago—a woman whom no one else knew of.

"Home."

"Then take these into the bathroom across the hall and put them on," she said, handing the bag to Ivy.

Ivy took the bag and looked into it. There she saw the clothes Lily had worn the day she'd been snatched by the police team. With the familiar garments in view, Ivy felt a burst of relief. She was going to get out of there! She turned to the bathroom and practically raced in, almost colliding with another patient shuffling out. The woman wore the same striped pajama clothes and didn't even lift her head to look at Ivy.

Ivy rushed around her and emptied the bag right on the floor, then quickly skirted into the toilet cubicle and did her business. Breathing a sigh of relief, she emerged and took off her Ye Ye's jacket and folded it, then gently laid it on the counter. She pulled the thin shirt over her head and threw it down. She untied the drawstring and the pants dropped to a puddle around her ankles. Ivy made quick work of putting on Lily's clothes and even her shoes that were at the bottom of the bag. Less than two minutes later, she emerged from the bathroom, the jacket in one hand and the soiled but bagged hospital clothing in the other.

"Here are the clothes." She set them on the counter. She hoped she never again had to see or wear a pair of striped pajamas in her life.

"Let's go. I'll transport you to the waiting room. Since you are underage, your family has already paid your fine and signed all the release documents."

Ivy had forgotten about her empty stomach and even the trauma she'd endured. She was going home! She practically glided after the nurse, stepping into the elevator behind her and crossing her arms over her chest to contain her joy. A small family including a mother holding her sick child and a man with his hand on the attached IV pole stepped back to make room for her.

The elevator seemed to take forever to go the few floors down. Ivy sighed once, twice, then another time before the nurse shot her a scolding look. Then Ivy held her breath as the first-floor number lit up and the doors began to open slowly. Immediately Ivy heard the tail end of a heated conversation between her Ye Ye and the officer who had originally brought her in.

"The government needs to go ahead and pass that law! People need something in place to control these shenanigans from you government officials to prevent you from sending innocent and sane citizens to the mental hospitals. This was a travesty, and you know it."

The chime indicating the arrival of the elevator stopped any response and the doors opened completely to show Ivy the sweetest sight she'd ever seen. There, standing together, were all her family members, their faces bright with anticipation as they waited to see if she was among the passengers.

Of course, a smile as big as the Yangtze River lit up her Ye Ye's face and her Nai Nai burst into loud sobs as soon as she saw her. Ivy could see the exact second Lily realized it was her getting off the elevator. Her sister took a step forward and Ivy ran to her, throwing her arms around her. They hugged each other and cried, and a second later were wrapped in the middle of their Ye Ye and Nai Nai's arms, one big pile of hugging and crying.

"I'm so sorry, Ivy. I should've never let you trade places with me," Lily whispered into Ivy's ear, through her sobs. She reached up and Ivy felt her hands on her face, searching it to be sure this was really her sister.

"I'm okay. This was the plan and we stuck to it." Ivy tried to comfort Lily but even she hadn't known what she was getting herself into. Still, she'd do it again if it meant keeping her sister out of harm's way.

They all stepped back to give her some room. Ivy put an arm around her Nai Nai and kissed her cheek, then smiled at the feel of the soft, crinkly skin under her lips. She inhaled the familiar scent and instantly felt reassured. *Aiya,* how she loved the woman!

Her Nai Nai used a crumpled handkerchief to mop at the tears running down her face as she studied Ivy.

"Oh, *Nuer,* what have they done to you?"

Ivy looked down at herself. "What? I'm fine. Just a little rumpled."

Ye Ye gave her a concerned look. "You look a bit confused. And you're skinny, girl. Let's get you home so your Nai Nai can fatten you up."

"Here's your jacket, Ye Ye. It kept me warm and gave me a lot of comfort in here." Ivy passed the jacket back to her Ye Ye and he held it to his nose.

He wrinkled his face. "Whoa, where they been keeping you—the pigpen?"

Ivy laughed and threw her arms in the air. Everything was funny now. She could laugh and run. She was free! She could even go outside to smell the sweet Wuxi air and with that thought, she started leading them toward the door. She was a happy girl—as long as she was leaving the large, cold building. Every other worry could wait. She was going home.

After the excitement of Ivy's homecoming had settled and everyone separated to their own rooms, Benfu made his way down the hall to say a final good night to Ivy and Lily. His old heart felt lighter just knowing the twins were back together and once again safe under his roof. And he wanted to congratulate Ivy again on the news from Lily's tutor. The woman had come by and said with Ivy's expertise and years of being Lily's guide that she'd make a perfect addition to their team of teacher's assistants at the school. As soon as her local classes ended for the summer, the school was offering her a full scholarship to get her certificate! Surprisingly, Ivy had even seemed open to the possibility of doing something that wouldn't involve Lily. His girls were growing up and he knew it was inevitable their lives would start to take different paths. It was his duty to encourage their independence while helping them to maintain that close relationship.

He heard their whispering and stopped just short of the door, wondering if perhaps he shouldn't interrupt. He peeked around and saw they were lying on their bed, searching the pockets of their handmade quilt, finding the little gifts Nai Nai had painstakingly sneaked in to welcome Ivy home.

Ivy pulled a tiny square of paper from one of the pockets and unwrapped it to find a shiny red button. She read the characters on the paper and laughed.

"What is it?" Lily asked.

"A button from Jojo. And the note says he's glad to have us both home at the same time so you'll stop moping around." Ivy stretched her arms high over her head and yawned. "It's so good to be back in our bed, Lily."

"It's good to have you back home, Ivy, and I'm so sorry for what you went through in that place. Thank you again for switching places with me, but next time, I'll have to deal myself with whatever life brings me," Lily answered.

Ivy looked around their sparse, but homey little room. "Where's Viola? I was hoping you'd play my favorite song before we go to sleep. I've missed hearing you play."

Lily rolled over, covering her face from her sister.

"Lily, what's wrong? Where's your violin?"

"Oh Ivy, I screwed up so bad! I made a friend while you were gone. I trusted him; he was so nice to me. He said he was going to help me sell Viola to get the money for your fine, to bring you home, but instead he turned out to be a thief and a liar. He took Viola and I haven't seen him since. Ye Ye was so upset, and I miss my violin so much. I know I'll never see it again!" Lily cried.

Benfu started to go in, to let Lily know not to worry about

him; she was the one who'd been wronged. But he kept his place, knowing they needed this time.

"Lily, don't worry. I'll help you find this so-called friend and make him get Viola back for you. Please don't cry. Right now let's just be happy we're both here and safe together again. I'm really exhausted and can't even think straight. We'll worry about your violin later."

Benfu watched them turn over and move until their backs were touching, their usual way to sleep. He felt someone beside him and he looked to find Calli there. She'd obviously wanted to say good night, too.

"Benfu, just look at them. They look just like the night we brought them home, all snuggled up next to each other. Thank the gods our girls are back together where they belong."

"I know, my Calla Lily, I know."

"When are we going to tell them? About their mother? It's just too eerie that the girls probably walked the same halls their own mother did so long ago."

Benfu shook his head. He didn't know when the right time would be, but in light of the twist of irony that had his girls ensnared in the same mental institution that their mother had died in, he and Calli had decided they were old enough to finally hear the truth. While Ivy and Lily never talked about the traumatic night that brought them to his family, Benfu had to wonder what they remembered of it.

He lowered his voice even more. "Let's let things settle down a bit first, m'love. It won't be easy for them to hear that their mother lost her mind, then killed herself after their father tried to set her girls on fire."

Chapter Twenty-Five

Li Jin laid the menu on the counter and poured herself a glass of warm water. She'd been listing supplies, creating recipes, and crunching numbers the entire morning to come up with what she thought would feed their crew at Rose Haven and a dozen hostel customers for a week at a time. Never in her life had she been forced to be so budget-minded. In her years past, it was only herself, and then her and Jojo she'd had to provide for. But now the responsibility of feeding so many fell on her shoulders. It wasn't an easy decision, but they'd chosen to include a simple breakfast with each night's stay to encourage patrons to choose their hostel over the dozens available in Wuxi.

The weeks had flown by and everyone had settled back into their normal routine plus much more in their frenzy to finish the hostel side of their property. Lily and Ivy had let all their slight bickering and push for independence go, and spent almost every spare minute together. Li Jin still thought Ivy needed to back up a bit and let Lily learn to do things on her own, and she was coming around. But it would take a long time before Ivy agreed that Lily didn't need her protection, after all they'd both been through.

Li Jin was getting really nervous about the money they'd borrowed to pay the fine and free Ivy from the hospital. Construction and finding usable secondhand furniture were taking longer than she'd thought and before she knew it, they were down to only a month before she was scheduled to repay the loan to the shadow lenders. Although the hostel was almost ready to open and everyone had pitched in to make it happen, she knew it was very unlikely they'd take in enough patrons to make the needed funds before the deadline. They were working almost around the clock, but would it all be for nothing? She was barely sleeping because thoughts of losing Rose Haven wouldn't let her be. There had to be something else they could do.

To add to her stress, Sami was getting even more unpredictable, sleeping through her days and then wanting Li Jin's attention at night. The constant roller coaster of her moods was beginning to deter everyone from approaching her until Li Jin was the only one left who would even attempt a civil conversation with Sami. Even last night, when Li Jin had tried to talk to her about the impending deadline of the debt they owed, Sami had only wanted to talk about herself and when they could go out again together. *She just doesn't get it,* Li Jin thought, and sighed.

Speaking of the self-appointed empress, she walked through the kitchen door, two hours late for breakfast and two hours too early for lunch. Li Jin swore under her breath that she would not prepare her something to eat. She needed to get her kitchen tasks under control and get over and help the others. And this time, for Sami's own good, Li Jin was going to get her involved.

"Sami, I really need you today. Can you help us with the painting over at the hostel?"

"I'm hungry, Li Jin. Fix me something, please." Sami sat at the table and laid her head on her arms.

Li Jin swallowed back the angry words that sprang to her tongue, and she concentrated on remaining calm. She didn't want to set Sami off. But still, some things needed to be addressed.

"Do you know where Lan is?"

"Lan, Lan, Lan. Why is it always about Lan?"

Li Jin stopped what she was doing and stared at Sami. She'd carried a sniffling Lan in the sack on her back—that she was quickly outgrowing—that very morning as she'd cooked breakfast for over fifty people. Now Auntie Rae had her. Every day others were taking care of her child and Sami didn't even care. It wasn't that Li Jin minded helping with Lan—she loved her to pieces—but it wasn't healthy that the baby spent more time with others than with her own mother. And Lan needed a lot of attention; there were many days she was sickly and just wanted to be cuddled. Sami needed to realize she had a responsibility, if not to Rose Haven, at least to her own child.

"It's not always about Lan. But since you don't want to help with getting the hostel side ready, the least you could do is get up and care for Lan so that Auntie Rae and I are free to go over there and work. You know with Lan's breathing issues we can't have her around construction or fumes."

That did it. Li Jin saw the moment the rage hit Sami in the straightening of her back and the glint in her eyes. She was almost sorry she'd said anything.

"Well, maybe if you all made *me* feel like a part of the family, I'd do more. Have you ever thought of that, Li Jin?"

For the first time, Li Jin lost her patience with Sami and couldn't bite back the words. "Sami! What more can we do? We've tried and tried. I just don't understand you. There are all these people around trying to embrace you and yet you still don't see you are welcome."

Sami lowered her head and Li Jin strained to make out her words.

"Even surrounded by all of you, I still feel alone."

Li Jin felt the anger evaporate. She sighed. It killed her to see Sami so bereft. "That's not the way it is. I'm here for you; we are all here for you." She wished with all her might she could find a way to break through to Sami and help her see the good things in her life.

Li Jin went around the counter to hug Sami. Sami stood and held her hands out to stop Li Jin from coming closer. "No, don't come over here, Li Jin. I don't need your pity. I don't need you at all, actually. Just leave me alone."

"Sami! What is going on? I'm sorry if you think I've ignored you, but I'm really worried about the debt we've got to pay. I didn't mean to take it out on you."

"Oh, I know. All you worry about is Rose Haven. That's clear to me now, Li Jin. I mean nothing to you or to your precious little family."

Li Jin stared, openmouthed, and listened to the venom Sami spouted before she turned and stomped from the room. Sami had never turned on her in such a way. Li Jin was stunned. *What had she said that was so terrible?* She shook her head. Her parents were right. Sami really needed some help.

Sami pulled her bag from the closet and began stuffing clothes in it. If Li Jin couldn't see how she felt, she'd just go and then they'd be sorry—they'd all be sorry. No one understood the way she felt. They didn't know what she'd been through or how she'd been treated. Even Li Jin was now settled in with her happy little family and could no longer relate. Once they'd walked a parallel path, but now Sami felt like the outsider in their sickening little pocket of happiness.

She slammed her fist into the mirror and felt a burst of satisfaction as it broke into shards of glass and covered their bedroom floor. She looked at her fist and marveled, a little sadly, that she hadn't even nicked herself. But she needed to get out of there before the sounds of the glass breaking brought some nosy face to her door.

She added a few more items and a pair of shoes and pulled the strap of the bag over her shoulder. Breathing deep to get herself under control, she sat on the edge of the bed and put her head in her hands. *She should leave, right?* That would show them that she didn't need them. *Or should she stay?* Now she couldn't even remember why she was so mad at Li Jin. Thoughts twirled in her mind, making her dizzy with confusion. If only she could hurt someone, like she'd been hurt, she felt like it would release all the ugly in her and finally let it go.

Suddenly she heard Lan's cry from down the hall. Then she heard Auntie Rae cooing to her to calm her. She lifted her head and listened to them.

Lan was *her* baby. Not Li Jin's baby and definitely not that old hag Auntie Rae's baby. Hers. But did she want the responsibility of a crying child to tote around as she searched for a new place to live? Could she really care for her? Well, Lan belonged to her, that much she was sure of.

She stood and added a few more articles to her bag. Then she pulled a piece of Li Jin's stationery from the bedside table and scribbled a note. She fought through the tears as she said her good-byes with the deeply scratched characters on the paper. Words were useless, though. She'd never been good with spoken words and now even written words failed to describe her feelings. How could she relay it when even she didn't know what she was feeling? All she knew was she needed to get out before she destroyed the entire house with her bare hands.

She didn't belong here with the good this family represented. She had done nothing to deserve it and the guilt of that discovery was eating her alive. She knew the truth was she deserved to be on the streets with the rest of the scum of the earth—those who forged their way through life using their cunning skills and experiences. Maybe one day she'd be able to change, but that day had not arrived.

She carried the bag and turned for one last look at the room she and her only friend had shared, then left. It was time. Time to show them all what she was really capable of.

Chapter Twenty-Six

"I can pay, but not with money," Sami said to the vendor as he passed her a steamed bun from his street-side stand.

His expression turned from confusion to acknowledgment as Sami stared deep into his eyes. She was hungry, and was willing to do anything to appease her growling stomach. Her funds hadn't lasted a week on the streets. She was starting to get desperate and she had only one other thing left of value—and it wasn't with her at the moment.

"I close up at seven. Do you promise to come back?" The young man couldn't have been more than twenty years old and Sami knew he'd cave in with just the thought of a stolen moment with a pretty woman.

"If you wrap me up a few of those, and throw in the milk, I'll be standing just over there at fifteen minutes till."

She'd scoped out this specific vendor early this morning and pinned her hopes that he would be the easiest to manipulate among the people on the street that early. She'd waited until the bulk of his morning business was done and he was looking at what were probably leftovers before she'd approached him.

One more second of eye contact and he let her take the bun, then quickly wrapped up three more. He handed them and the small plastic bottle of milk to Sami, then pushed the hair out of his eyes and smiled.

So easy, thought Sami. And did he really think she'd let him put his greasy hands on her body? She nodded her thanks and moved away.

"See you later," she called out, and sauntered down the street.

"Don't forget," he answered hopefully.

She crossed at the intersection and turned down a small alley. She ate one more of the buns before she arrived in front of the small row house. They'd spent one scary night under the arches of a busy overpass, reliving old times before Sami had found the place. She hoped the old woman who ran it wasn't anywhere in sight. Sami was supposed to have been out the morning before, but she'd squeezed one more night out of her. She opened the door and peeked in. Hearing and seeing no one, she entered and slowly climbed the stairs to the room at the end of the long hall.

It wasn't a hostel—she wasn't stupid. She knew that would be the first place Li Jin would look for her. Instead she'd asked around until she'd found a boardinghouse on the run-down side of Wuxi. For the same price as a hostel would cost, she'd snagged a tiny room only big enough for a bed and one tiny chest of drawers. Primarily rented to single migrant workers, the room wasn't ideal and she'd had to share the tiny bathroom with other tenants, but it was at least shelter. But now her deposit was long gone and Sami had promised payment today, but it wasn't coming. She needed to get her things and get out of there before the woman called in the police to get the money owed to her.

She opened the door to find Lan still sleeping soundly on the bed. She wasn't surprised. The damn baby had cried most of the night—and just about got her kicked out. She'd never seen so much coughing and sniffling, then gasping for breath. Sami wasn't a nurse; how was she supposed to know what to do? She'd walked with her for hours, trying to calm her until someone had banged on her door and yelled at her to shut the baby up or get out. Then she'd poured a tiny bit of the *bai jiu* someone had left behind into a bottle. When she'd stuck it in the open mouth, the child had coughed and sputtered but hungrily drank every drop. That had shut her up really fast, but by then it was almost morning. Sami had slipped away for some quiet and she didn't know what she'd do that night if it all started up again. If she were being honest with herself, she'd admit she could barely take the screeching cries without wanting to throw the child out the window.

Avoiding the bed where the baby slept, Sami took the bottle of milk and set it on the dresser. She'd feed it to her the next time the bawling started. Quietly, she gathered their things and packed it all into the bag. She looked at the baby and dreaded the moment she would awaken. She decided to chance a small nap and she slid in between the crack of the bed and the dresser, curling into a tight ball.

But she couldn't go to sleep.

She thought of Li Jin and the last look she'd seen on her face. Her expression said everything—especially that she hadn't understood why Sami had lashed out at her, refusing to acknowledge the kindness of her family. Sami didn't understand it, either. All she knew was that at that moment, she couldn't take any more. It was true that Li Jin was the only person in her life who had ever reached out to her while wanting nothing in return. And Sami knew she'd screwed up but the fact was, she just couldn't deal with kindness. Even from Li Jin.

That didn't mean she didn't care about her, though. She thought of the stress Li Jin was under and the looming deadline the shadow lender had set. And she knew those kinds of men— they'd take Rose Haven without a second thought to whose lives they'd uproot. At least then Li Jin would possibly have time for something other than caring for those people, wouldn't she? Sami was still confused. She knew her evil side would love to see Rose

Haven crumble to dust. But there was a tiny part of her that didn't want Li Jin to suffer more than she already had. There was nothing in her that hated the girl who'd shown her such unconditional acceptance.

But then, it wasn't up to her anymore to care. She couldn't do anything to help. She wasn't rich. She was broke. She couldn't help Li Jin and at this point, she couldn't even help herself.

She thought back to a few days before when a disheveled man had approached her in the street and asked her if she was willing to part with her baby girl for a price. Sami had walked away after giving him a tongue lashing.

But now it was time to go to plan B.

Chapter Twenty-Seven

"I've been all over Wuxi and even searched a few places in Suzhou. It's been a week and Sami is nowhere to be found," Li Jin said as she dropped more dumplings into the oil. Lily and Ivy had prepared the dough before they'd taken off to meet some new friends.

"You've got to just let it go. It is what it is," her Baba answered from his place at the table, then went into a discussion about providing toilet paper, sheets, and even towels to the upcoming patrons of the hostel.

Li Jin knew her father was relieved Sami was gone but she couldn't let it go. Even though she was needed at home, between meals and while Jojo was at school, she'd used up valuable time and money to try to find Sami and Lan. Was fate teasing her? Only just over a year before she'd juggled similar feelings when Jojo had been snatched from her life and she'd searched hopelessly for him. Now she felt just as fearful for Lan, as the morning Sami had pulled her daughter from Auntie Rae's arms, the baby had been running another fever and was having trouble breathing. Auntie Rae had begged Sami to leave her, but she said Sami was like a possessed demon and had left without a backward glance or one touch of sympathy for the baby who wailed in discomfort.

It was a puzzle. Why would Sami take Lan with her when all she'd ever tried to do was foist her off on everyone else? Just to prove she could? To punish everyone who loved her? It just didn't make sense and Li Jin was desperately worried for little Lan. Even though she'd like to think Sami could never hurt her own child, a part of Li Jin wondered if that was true.

"We can get the sheets from the local women's club. They don't have to be new—they only have to be clean," Li Jin's mother said. "And the good news is that Jace found us an old thrown-away pool table for the common room, and he's resurfacing it."

Her father started telling them about some of the offers he was getting on a few discarded machines they'd found underneath the piles of rubble in the warehouse. Offers that weren't enough to pay back their debt to the shadow lenders, but money that would be added to what they'd so far accumulated. Or at least, what they had left after paying for the few construction projects they'd financed for the hostel. It seemed to her that as fast as the funds came in, they were funneling out. Things had to turn around.

Their voices faded as they continued to talk about sheets and other things as if they were the most important thing in the world. And right now she had to admit, funds were important. They had to get the money to pay their debt. *But what about Lan? And what about Sky, for that matter?* No one had been able to come up with his fine money and Linnea had told her that Sky's mother was resigned to the fact that her son would not be coming home for a long time. Li Jin had tried to visit him again but they'd turned her away, saying Sky was in isolation.

Li Jin could only imagine what he was going through. Since the whole Falun Gong subject had been thrust into their lives, she'd found out a lot more about the persecution of anyone even remotely connected to the group. There were some scary rumors out there—even talk about organ harvesting from those imprisoned. Lots of horrible stories floated around, and Li Jin just wanted Sky out of there and safe at home.

"Li Jin. *Li Jin* . . ."

She snapped back to the present to find both of her parents studying her with worried faces.

"Oh, I'm sorry. What?" she asked. She realized she'd been completely lost in her thoughts of Sami, Lan, and even Sky.

"Your dumplings are burning," her mother scolded, but kindly. "And we asked you if you've got the numbers ready for your food-supply budget?"

Li Jin looked down to see the few dumplings had turned into blackened chunks. She sighed. She had a lot of food to prepare and couldn't afford the time lost or for the ingredients to burn.

"Yes, I've got some figures. Let me just get this batch done and I'll bring the paper to you." She spooned out the scorched dough and threw it in the bin. She needed to pull herself together. It was going to take some more brainstorming or they were going to lose Rose Haven.

Ivy sat across from Lily and took notes. She tried to keep the irritation out of her voice. Lily needed to concentrate.

"Dawei . . . Okay, and what year did 'Dawei' say he was on the Olympic team?"

Lily put her finger to her lip. "Um . . . he didn't say what year. I just assumed he meant the last time the Olympics were held. Ivy—we're never going to find him. I can't even tell you what he looked like."

Ivy nodded. "Oh yes, we will find him. Linnea already gave me a description and I promise you, we're going to get your violin back. That little thief is going to pay."

She'd been so glad to get home and then when Lily had told her about losing her violin in an attempt to get the money to free her, Ivy had just about gone crazy with anger. If it wasn't enough that the woman named Fengniao continued to haunt her in her dreams—as if she'd been real—now this Dawei character had swooped in and taken the one thing that meant the most to her sister. She meant to find him and he was going to give the violin back or he was going to lose a few limbs.

"Can you think of any other details he might have told you? The street he lived on? His family name? Sometimes when people make up stories, they use real bits of their past. We just have to sort through and see if there is anything that can lead us to him."

Lily shook her head. "No, he only talked about his grandfather but he didn't call him by name. And he said they'd lost their home a year before."

"Did he say—"

"Wait, Ivy! I remember something else. He said they lived on Yellow Lane Street."

Ivy was so excited, she jumped up from the bench. "That's great, Lily! We'll start there. Maybe someone knows him or his family."

If it took her a year, she'd get Viola back into Lily's arms and when all was as it used to be—settled down and calm—she'd tell her about Fengniao. Even if the woman wasn't real and had been a dream that came during her darkest moment, she felt it was time she and her sister examined and shared their memories. All of them.

Besides the memories, she wanted all the secrets exposed. They were growing older, and after all she'd heard Lily had been up to, she knew it was inevitable they'd begin growing apart. She also knew the less left unsaid between them, the better. Lily was her only blood family and she wouldn't let their past come between them.

Ivy settled back down on the bench. "Let's talk it over some more and you might remember more details."

They were interrupted by their Ye Ye as he came out the door.

"Ivy?"

"Yes?" She tried to keep the impatience out of her voice but she wanted to get back to writing down details while they were fresh in Lily's mind.

He walked out farther and stood before them, blocking the sun.

"You left something in the pocket of my jacket when you had it at the hospital. Look what I found."

Ivy squinted to see what he carried. She gasped. In the middle of his big, gnarled hand lay a tiny blue feather.

Chapter Twenty-Eight

Sami stood in front of the bed and unbuttoned the red silk dress she'd pilfered from the rack in the busy market only the afternoon before. She let it fall off her shoulders and to the floor, pooling at her feet. She looked down at her body and struggled to mask her expression of pride. She was glad to finally be her willowy self again, done with carrying the pregnancy weight from the child who lay sleeping across the room in the hotel closet.

A few feet away, the man groaned loudly, and Sami looked over at the closet door and hoped the baby wouldn't stir. She should be tired, seeing how Sami had kept her awake for hours, posing her to take photos from every angle possible. Maybe she'd even send one back to Rose Haven. She had to admit, the baby was a beauty, and as she'd come to know, beauty was very valuable in this world. The shadow lenders had unknowingly given her an idea that could prove profitable, and Sami had never been known to let an opportunity pass by.

Thinking back to her last night at the center, she could see Li Jin's face in her mind and hear the fear in her voice as they lay side by side talking in bed. She'd been so worried about losing Rose Haven to the shadow lenders. Then the next morning everything had blown up. She'd had a lot of time to think about it since and she regretted leaving, but what was done was done. She wouldn't go back.

It still irked Sami that because of that family—and all for one girl who wasn't even blood related—Li Jin was willing to risk her home. *Oh, to be so noble.* Other than Jojo, Sami knew that Rose Haven was the thing nearest and dearest to Li Jin's heart. She wasn't stupid, after all. She might have thought she took first place but over the last few months, Sami knew she'd been replaced by a piece of property. The truth was, Li Jin cared more for Rose Haven than she did for her, and that hurt.

Maybe if she'd had a home like that old Zheng and his wife offered to their girls, things would've been different—she would have been less . . . *less hardened.* Her own childhood couldn't have been more opposite than the fairy tale Li Jin's parents provided. Sami had been told from an early age she was nothing but a mistake, just another mouth to feed. She'd learned to stay in the shadows while her elder brother basked in his place as the coveted son. She'd thought all the time spent studying and receiving high marks at school would guarantee her a place in a university, a chance to do something with her life, but that vision had ended the night she was taken to the red-light district.

Nothing had prepared her for the day her own father had sold her to an uncle for prostitution. At only thirteen, her life had crumbled around her. Even her own mother hadn't tried to save her; she had stood in the doorway, ignoring Sami's pleading as her father led her away. Her mother was nothing like Lao Calli, though. Where Li Jin's mother was soft and affectionate, Sami had only known her *mufu* to be a skinny, bitter woman who walked hunched over as if she carried the world on her shoulders. Truth was, her mother was old long before her time, her youth disappearing along with her hope for a better life as she struggled to obey her strict husband. Sami had known without being told, even as a toddler, she'd find no comfort from the woman who'd given her birth. She'd marveled that in her situation and with her beauty, if she'd only been born much earlier, she'd most likely have been sold to a high official as a concubine. At least then she'd have been treated to beautiful gowns and succulent food—possibly even lived in a palace or some other extravagant home. She knew even then she would have had to be cunning to work her way to the top tier of favored concubines, but cunning was a trait she had mastered. However, fate had ruined her, dropping her in the wrong century where her beauty wasn't enough to pull her from poverty. Even so, she'd buried her nose in books. And through legends and folk stories, and then poetry, she'd fostered a desire to do more and be more than her mother had.

Now the old Sami, the smart girl with hopes and dreams, was gone. She'd disappeared underneath an excruciating half hour of sweaty rutting that had left her bruised and terrified, but no longer a child. But that was years ago and what remained of that girl was an empty shell. She knew this and welcomed it—embraced it even. It was simple; if she didn't allow herself to feel emotions, then she couldn't be hurt again.

But at least she was no longer forced to spread her legs. She'd taken back control of her life the night her uncle had beaten her and she'd fled. And because of that, she had Li Jin in her life. She couldn't forget the gods had given her at least one true friend. One person who understood what life on the streets can do to a soul—crumple it and leave it for dead. Would she be missed?

Get back in the moment, she told herself, pushing Li Jin out of her head. She reached up and caressed the jade stone that hung low on a necklace, burrowing between her breasts. It felt cool against her skin and she thought of the man who'd gifted her with it just days before. That wasn't all he'd given her, either. He'd bought her an expensive *qipao* to wear to the theater when he'd taken her as his escort. After their night together, he'd called her his soul mate and thought she'd be back to meet him again. Same place, same time next week, he'd said.

What a fool. But the few stolen moments with him had put her on the right track. No more hostels or boardinghouses for her. She'd found a way to live a better life, but before she could truly let go and let the darkness of her destiny envelop her, she had just a few loose ends to tie up.

"Guo lai." A different fool, but this one gruffly beckoned from where he sat propped up against a mound of pillows. He looked ridiculous, still wearing the shirt and jacket of his uniform while his hairless legs protruded from beneath. Sami swallowed her revulsion and concentrated on leading him to do what she wanted, but making him think it was what *he* wanted.

The curtains were pulled and only a sliver of afternoon light filtered through the crack in the middle—just enough to fall across Sami's breasts and give him the thrill she knew he wanted. He was just like the rest of them. They couldn't hide the excitement they felt when they saw her tattoo. The marks on her body added to the thrill of doing something forbidden they craved. This wasn't her first time with an official and she knew the routine. He'd cop a feel, make a few moves, and within five minutes he'd be snoring, then wake up in a panic thinking someone at the district had noticed he was gone. The tease was the longest part and how she really earned her money; the sex was really just an afterthought with the middle-aged fools who still imagined themselves young and virile. But just once she wished she'd feel something, too. Anything would be something, but here she stood once again, a cold shell of a woman.

Maybe this time she could change it up. Maybe this time, she could feel human. "Come and get me." She put one foot on the bed, knowing the sight of it would drive him crazy. Her feet were petite and still perfect, despite the many miles they'd traveled. After all, of all her features, her feet were usually the most complimented in the bedroom.

She stood glaring at him, just out of reach.

"No, seriously, come here. I have to be back on the beat in an hour." His leering smile turned down into a frown. Even with only a flash of his teeth Sami made out the dark spots from the tobacco he tucked in his cheek. She knew if she looked at his hands, she'd be disgusted at the fat sausages that passed as fingers. She was usually much choosier, but there was a reason she'd allowed this hairy monkey to borrow her for a fleeting moment. There was also a reason this time she'd booked the room and prepared it, instead of allowing her customer to lead her around. This time more was at stake.

"Are you deaf? I said hurry up," he growled, bringing her back to the present and out of her lingering thoughts of what this afternoon could mean.

He thought he could scare her. Well, he didn't know who he was messing with. Scaring her was just what she wanted. Fear was an emotion, right? She turned around and bent over, slowly waving her hips side to side. "I dropped something." She leisurely picked up her scarf and brought it up between her legs, rubbing it back and forth as the drool practically ran from the corners of his mouth. He reached for her and she stepped back once more. Then he lunged.

"*Aiya,* I said come here, dammit."

She struggled out of his grasp and put her heel right onto his crotch. She kicked back, knowing she made contact by the sudden grunt he made. He recovered quickly and grabbed her hair, jerking her backward onto the bed.

She smiled. He was furious. She felt a stirring—finally.

His face hovered only inches above hers and he glared down at her pinned under his thick arms. She laughed at his twisted expression. She'd ruined it for him.

"I shouldn't even pay you for this since you played the hard-to-get act," he said brusquely as he readied himself. No longer was he gentle or playful; now he obviously just wanted to get it over with before he became impotent again. But still, it wasn't rough enough for Sami. Oh, and he'd pay—he'd pay more than he knew.

Now to get him even more worked up. Since she'd lowered herself to his standard, she might as well squeeze all the thrill out of it she could muster.

"*Tamade.*" She spat out the word and glared up at him. If he was any kind of man at all, her cursing of his mother would bring out the devil in him.

A look of shock crossed his face, then turned to rage. He reached down and slapped her. "You've obviously forgotten who I am. I am at the top tier of the local division. Say the name *Delun* and others will cower." He looked down at his jacket, indicating his badge. Using his knee, he maneuvered himself until he hovered over Sami. "And my women keep their mouth shut and their legs open. Now do it, *chòu bidozi.*"

He thought calling her a dirty whore would bother her? She almost laughed. The instant warmth on her face from his strike spread down Sami's body, and she finally felt anchored, no longer just a weightless being. She ached for him to hit her again but he didn't. Still, he was no longer careful to keep his heavy weight from her and Sami relished the rough way he touched her, the way he used her. As he let loose a string of cursing and finally slid into her, she let her eyes close and savored the flash of pain. He pinched her breast and Sami sighed. He hated her, he was hurting her, and that made her feel a little less hollow.

Sami opened her eyes and listened for a moment. The room was now dark and she heard nothing from the closet. After the official left hours before, the slamming door had awakened the baby, causing her to cry until she'd grown hoarse and had finally quieted to a barely audible whimper.

Sami had stayed under the bed covers, holding her hands over her ears, unable to push herself to tend to the girl. It had taken hours for the child to stop crying but Sami had finally fallen asleep—used up and sore—nevertheless triumphant that she had gathered what she needed next.

She sat up and threw her legs over the side of the bed, testing their strength. She knew she'd feel wobbly, at the least, after the strenuous events with the sour-smelling Delun. He was a *diào sī,* but at least the room he'd paid for boasted its own shower and she couldn't wait to wash his scent from her body. She reached over and turned on the lamp, then staring at the closet door, she stumbled across the room until she stood before it.

She reached up and pushed aside the silk arrangement of flowers, feeling until her hand touched the cold metal of the camera. She thought briefly of the unsuspecting tourist she'd snagged it from, but he was the least of her concerns and was an idiot to leave his bag on the bench anyway. Maybe next time he'd be more careful.

She pulled the tiny camera down and checked the light. It still blinked. She'd wait until she got to the Internet café to remove the memory disc. The attendant at the mall had sold her a cheap thumb drive and all she had to do was save it to the contraption. Then it was hers to do with what she wanted, and she already had help lined up for that part. *Whoever said an uneducated girl was stupid? They obviously hadn't met her,* Sami thought, and smiled.

She heard a rustle from behind the closet door. Warily, she opened it and looked inside. Now silent but staring up at her with mournful, dark eyes, the baby had somehow found her fingers and sucked hungrily. She wondered if the child could wait a little longer, at least until Sami had taken a shower and washed her hair. Locking eyes, Sami felt like the little girl was beseeching her, with only a look. She felt something stir deep in her stomach.

"Aiya," Sami muttered, set the camera on the table, then bent down and picked the child up.

The baby's bottom felt heavy with wetness and Sami shivered in revulsion. She held her away from her body, wishing for Auntie Rae and her always-willing hands.

She sighed. At least it was better to do it before her shower than after when it would soil her hands again. She carried the baby to the bed and laid her down. The cool air of the room revived the child and she lost her grip on the fingers she was feasting on, causing her to get mad. Sami chuckled at the girl who was kicking and working up a fit. Her round cheeks reddened and her nose crinkled in dismay as she croaked out a lusty cry. *Maybe she has some of her mother in her after all,* Sami thought as she turned and went to the bag she'd set before the window.

She bent down and rummaged through, looking for a clean diaper. She was glad she'd swiped some from the storeroom at the center, as it wasn't an option to let the child remain naked under her split pants. Sami wasn't the type of doting mother who would chance being soiled on. She found a diaper and a clean pair of clothes and from the corner of her eye, she saw the baby begin to roll toward the edge of the bed.

Sami leapt at the child, landing next to the bed on her knees but catching her just before she fell to the floor. Now kneeling with the baby in her arms, she looked down to find a new expression on the little face. Amusement. *So she thought her little acrobatic adventure was funny, huh? She wouldn't have thought so had she gotten a knot on her head,* Sami thought as she stood and put the baby back on the bed.

"Let's get you out of these wet clothes." She bent over the baby and pulled the pants off, then unfastened the diaper, immediately covering her nose in disgust. The outfit that Li Jin's mother was so proud of making with her own hands now reeked worse than a pigpen. The baby had left her an unwelcome gift.

Sami stood and stared down at the child again. She was too much trouble, that was all there was to it. She was glad she'd gotten the photos earlier, when the clothing was still clean and fresh. Now the child was ruined. Sami wished she didn't have to touch her.

"Just for that, don't expect a bottle any time soon," she said to the girl. She then tried to remember when she'd fed her last. It had to have been around the morning hour, she thought as she saw on her watch it was now close to the time supper was usually served at Rose Haven. Her own stomach growled, reinforcing her discovery that it was time to eat.

Looking around, but of course, finding no one to pass the baby off on, Sami started again. She pulled out the soiled diaper and dragged it to the side of the bed where the child couldn't kick it off and make even more of a mess. Looking at the baby's red and raw bottom, Sami felt another burst of irritation that she'd probably have to spend money on tiger balm to relieve the rash. *More trouble.* Determined now to get it over with, Sami fit her with the clean diaper and then quickly pulled the dry pants on, picked up the baby, and returned her to the closet floor. The baby immediately began another long but hoarse wail, weakly vocalizing her dislike for the sudden darkness and repeat abandonment.

Sami walked away. She just needed to take a shower and then she'd feed her. She bundled up the dirty diaper and took it into the tight bathroom, ignoring the cries as she passed in front of the closet again. She pushed the diaper into the trash can and then started the water running. It would need a moment to get hot, so she quickly removed her clothing and stacked it on the shelf over the spigot to keep it dry, then leaned over the sink to peer into the mirror.

Under the smooth contours of her face, beneath the mask of beauty, she didn't like what she saw. But then, that was nothing new.

She turned away. Stepping under the showerhead, she forced her shoulders back and rolled her neck. With the sound of the water and the now-closed bathroom door, she was grateful the crying of the child was drowned out and she could relax under the steady stream of water, cleaning off the sordid remnants of her afternoon tryst. She tilted her head back and let the water pelt her face while she planned her next move.

Chapter Twenty-Nine

Though only just afternoon, it had already been a long day and Sami was tired. She felt like sleeping forever but she had just one more task to take care of. Earlier that morning she'd gone to the Internet café and found an overly eager teenage boy to help her figure out how to get the photos from her camera to a contraption he'd gladly let her borrow, something called a jump drive.

He'd even given her a crash course on how to send documents and attachments across what he called the World Wide Web. After only an hour there, Sami found her head was spinning with new information. However, she now saw why every Internet café in Wuxi was usually crammed full of the younger crowd, using computers to reach out of their own little worlds to fill their heads with fantasies, games, and pretend relationships. She could also see how it could be addicting to make believe for a short time that you were someone else—somewhere else—anywhere but in your real life being yourself.

Amusingly, the boy had chattered nonstop, telling her how his own father had hired an online gamer to specifically search him out on every Internet game, and assassinate him in each virtual realm he entered. The father had thought it was a sure way to get his son away from the computers and back to his search for a job, but the boy stubbornly continued to set up new profiles and create new characters, playing until he was found out and his persona was killed again and again.

From there she'd gone to the Kodak store, and now she was in possession of not only two sets of photos, but was also the proud owner of a new e-mail account with some privileged files attached.

She switched the baby to the other arm and whispered to her to hush. They'd not spent much time together the last few days because Sami had been lucky enough to run into the hotel maid who was more than glad to pick up a little extra money by babysitting. Sami had to alter her schedule around when the woman was off work, but it was worth it to be able to leave the baby behind.

But today the maid hadn't shown up. So here they were, mother and daughter, stuck together for the afternoon.

The baby lifted her head and with a wobbly neck, maneuvered until she was looking Sami straight in the eye.

"What? Why are you looking at me?" Sami said, feeling uncomfortable with the eye contact.

Just the night before she'd gone through some of the photos, the ones she'd taken of the baby after she'd finally bathed her in the hotel bathtub. Sami hadn't really known what to do, but she'd found just putting her in the warm water had brought a smile to the little girl's face and Sami had grabbed the camera. She'd gotten some good shots of her.

Now she turned the baby around so she faced outward, and the new viewpoint quieted her down. Sami continued to walk, looking for the post office. As they passed strangers, some reached out to touch the baby, exclaiming over her beauty. It didn't thrill Sami that she was basically ignored with the child's presence, and her irritation began to build.

"Soon, we'll see how many smiles your beauty brings you," she whispered.

They arrived at the post office, and after standing in the line for half an hour, Sami was able to send the package. She'd made up a return address, but no one was the wiser. She only wished she could be a fly on the wall when the recipient opened the envelope and viewed the enclosed photos. The thought of what his reaction would be raised Sami's spirits and she laughed. The baby heard the sound and thought it was for her. She laughed, too, and her sudden intake of breath caused another coughing fit. Her cheeks turned red as she struggled for breath.

Still, Sami didn't let it bring her down. If she could get a sitter at the hotel, she'd go out and celebrate. "Not much more time with me, little miss, then you'll be on your way to a new adventure."

Three days later Sami tapped her long, red nails on the side of the chair as she waited impatiently. The morning had been eventful and she was glad to have the worst of it over. Her second little visit with the official, Delun, had gone better than she thought it would and she'd left him feeling victorious. It was amazing how much a little discretion was worth to a deceitful man who fancied keeping up his reputation as well as his highly esteemed position. In a world of charades, keeping up the façade was expensive; and that was what she'd told him on her way out.

Now Sami was at her final stop of the day. So far she'd been left waiting too long in the stark room, and she was just starting to get irritated when he was escorted in.

She stood, surprised to see how different he looked. In turn he was startled to see her sitting there. They exchanged greetings and he took a chair at the table; then Sami got right to business.

"I'm glad to see you. I'm hoping you can make a delivery for me." She began to tell him how they could help each other, *if he agreed to her terms.*

At first he looked puzzled, but Sami was relieved to see that when he looked down and saw the baby sleeping on the blanket she'd laid down in the corner, a small smile crept over his face. "She's bigger than I remember. And she looks sickly. Is she okay?"

Sami nodded and pulled the photos from her bag, then laid them on the table between them. "Here's what she looks like when she's awake—make sure some of these go with her. And she's fine; she just has a little cold. But everyone we pass on the street feels as if they must stop and tell me how beautiful she is."

He looked at the pictures, then walked over to the child and bent down. He rubbed her downy hair. "*Aiya,* you're right. She is an undeniably stunning gem of a child."

"Yeah, yeah, I get it. She's pretty. So—can you do it?"

He sighed. "Tell me again why you want to do this, and if you are completely sure."

Sami looked down and shrugged. "I've done a lot of bad things in my life, why not one more?"

"I don't know you that well, but I can't imagine your unlucky path in life was from your own making."

"Oh, you just don't know. Nobody does. I've done things. Things I won't discuss."

Suddenly Sami felt the urge to throw herself into his arms, to prove just one embrace could start a spark. Maybe a man like him was just what she needed to turn her life around. She went to him and pressed her body next to his, but he backed away quickly and held his arms up in defense.

"What are you doing?" He looked around nervously.

She gave him her most seductive smile. "What do you think I'm doing?"

"I don't know, but listen, I'm not interested."

Sami shrugged and busied herself pulling out half the photos and shoving the rest back in her bag. She wasn't surprised. It was the way her luck had run lately. But a girl could try, right? She went to the baby and looked down at her. She realized she'd never said the child's name aloud. She'd kept her distance, but not out of selfishness. Something in her—perhaps a mother's intuition—was trying not to hurt the girl. But had she made the right decision? Was she about to rid herself of the only good thing she'd ever been a part of? She looked up at the man and despite her usual tough composure, she felt herself begin to tremble. Then she realized he probably thought it was because he'd rejected her.

She took a deep breath and let out a husky laugh. "Don't feel bad, you aren't the only one. No one wants me—except for a few sordid moments at a time. But I just realized something. What if I died today? Who would mourn me? Or welcome me to the afterworld? I have no one. I'll be just as alone in the next life as I've been in this one."

A look of pity crossed his face and Sami felt embarrassed.

"Who do you love most in this world? That is who you have, and whoever that is, you must always think of them before yourself."

Sami gazed at the baby girl again and was startled when her little dark eyes fluttered open and stared back. Once more, she seemed to be searching for something in Sami's face—something she couldn't give. Or could she? For the last year she'd thought there was only one person in the world she loved. But was it possible she loved one other?

She bent down and picked her up, then held her to her chest, this time holding her much differently than she ever had before. As the baby melted against her, Sami felt a strange fluttering in her heart and a catch in her throat. She moved until her lips were touching the downy little ear, and then she whispered, "Goodbye, little Lan. Go out into the world and make it your own."

With one kiss on the soft head—*her first and last kiss to her own daughter*—she handed her over to the man who stood waiting and watching. She turned away so he couldn't see the traitorous tear slide down her cheek and fall from her face. She never cried—making it a surprise even to her as she reached up and used her closed fist to wipe away the moisture.

She rummaged in the bag that hung across her shoulder, feeling past her wallet, her discarded bottle of water, and even past the envelope of photos until she found the folded note.

She pulled it out and through her tears she thrust it at him. With one last look, she left the building, leaving behind a piece of herself.

Chapter Thirty

Li Jin smiled as Jojo snuggled closer to her. "'And then they all lived happily ever after.'" She closed the book and set it on the nightstand. Since Sami had disappeared with Lan, Jojo had moved into her room to sleep with her. She was glad he didn't think he was too old for bedtime stories, as it was her favorite part of the day. Tonight was just a simple book she'd picked up out of their nursery, and was probably too young for him, but she'd chosen it because she was tired of reading the Harry Potter series the girls had hooked Jojo on. Tomorrow they'd pick it back up but tonight she wanted easy, mindless reading.

"Ma, where do you think Lan is?"

She looked at the empty cradle against the wall and felt her heart give a tug. "I don't know, Jojo, but I'm sure she's just fine."

Truly she didn't think that at all. She'd just about worried herself sick over the baby. They'd kept all her stuff in place, in the hopes Sami would come back, but as the days went on, Li Jin had lost hope.

Jojo picked up a pillow and punched it with his fist. "Sami didn't even like her. Why did she have to take her?"

Li Jin was surprised. She hadn't known Jojo had picked up on the way Sami treated Lan. "Sure, she likes her. Lan's her daughter. Sami just had to get used to being a mother, Jojo."

"Then why did she always let her cry? And she never sang to her like you did, Ma."

That was true, too. She wished she could go back. She wouldn't have gotten Lan used to the attention if she'd known one day she'd be taken away. Li Jin prayed with all her heart that now that Sami had her to herself, she was being a better mother.

"Jojo, do you want to go outside and look at the moon with me?" Li Jin didn't want Jojo to go to sleep on such a sad note. She wanted his dreams to be full of good things.

He crawled out of the bed and slipped his feet into his slippers, then followed her down the hall to the front door. Around them Li Jin heard the sounds of her sisters getting ready for bed. They passed Lily and Ivy's room and the girls' chatter sounded like two little birds rapidly exchanging gossip. She smiled and put her finger to her lip, exaggerating her attempt to tiptoe through the hall to make Jojo laugh.

"Shh . . . I just want it to be you and me," she said as she grabbed a quilt off the rack, then nudged him out the door before anyone else heard them.

They went to the bench and sat down, and Li Jin put her arm around Jojo and pulled him closer. It was chilly and she spread the quilt over them both. He burrowed under her arm and together they stared up at the magnificent full moon.

"This makes me think of Moon Harbor, where I met Nai Nai and Ye Ye," Jojo said.

Li Jin smiled. "That was a crazy but happy time, wasn't it? All those years it was just you and me, and now we have this big family."

She felt him nod. They were lucky. Even with the sadness Sami left behind by taking off without saying good-bye, Li Jin still had things to appreciate. Yes, they still might end up losing the center, and that made her sick, but she'd never lose her family again. They'd simply have to find a way to start over.

As for Sami, she still wondered where she was and worried for her, and especially for little Lan, but she wouldn't let it steal her joy. And maybe Li Jin didn't have the kind of love her parents had, that connection between a man and a woman, but she had the next best thing. She had a family who loved her and would do anything for her. Maybe someday she'd find her soul mate, but for now, she'd be content with what the gods had seen fit to give her.

"Tell me another story," Jojo said, snuggling closer.

Li Jin wanted to get his mind onto something else, so she thought for a minute. "Okay, I'll tell you the old legend about the Moon Goddess."

Jojo squirmed and she knew she had him. He was a sucker for fairy tales. He always had been.

"Many centuries ago all the young maidens in China would wait until the moon festival to pray to the Moon Goddess to bring them the man destined to be the love of their life. They'd offer up cakes and fruits, burn candles and incense, or anything they had to bribe the Moon Goddess with."

"Did it work?" Jojo asked. Li Jin smiled. He never could let her get through telling a story without breaking in to ask questions.

"It worked for many. But for some, their hearts weren't really in it, so the Moon Goddess didn't bring them anything but heartache for the next year. Then when the eighth month came around again, they'd start all over with the bribery."

"Next time I'll help you burn candles, Ma. But just in case, I just asked the Moon Goddess to send you someone."

Li Jin chuckled. Lately Jojo had hinted more and more that she should have a man in her life. When they'd shopped or gone to the park, he'd even pointed out a few fellows that he thought were good candidates. She was constantly reassuring him that he was the only man she needed in her life. But it was a perfect night for the story and Li Jin looked out over the courtyard at the moon shining brightly on the flowers that had finally bloomed.

She heard footsteps coming around the corner and her instinct was to get Jojo inside. It was too late for visitors. "Jojo, sit up. Someone's coming."

Jojo sat up and looked, then leapt from the bench and ran toward the figure.

"Jojo! Wait!" Li Jin could see a man but couldn't tell who it was, at least not until her son called out his name.

"Sky! You're back!"

Li Jin felt her breath catch. Sky was out? And why would he come here so late at night? She reached up and patted her hair down. She was dressed in ratty old nightclothes and she felt a blush creeping up her neck. She hoped he couldn't see her clearly in the shadow of the house.

Sky came closer and Li Jin could see Jojo hanging on to him as if he were a tree. She still couldn't see him clearly, but from where she stood, he looked so much slimmer. She rose from the bench and then she saw he carried something.

"Sky! I'm so glad to see you again." She began to walk to him and she heard a gurgle. A familiar gurgle. Her heart raced and began to pound so hard she thought it would jump out of her chest.

"Li Jin. I have someone here who wants to see you." He came close and held out the bundle.

Li Jin took it, then looked down into warm, dark eyes, and the lump that came to her throat blocked any words that might come. It was Lan. *Sweet, sweet Lan and she was safe.* She looked tired and a bit pale, but overall she appeared healthy enough. Li

Jin couldn't stop the tears from flowing as she held her to her chest, rocking her back and forth.

Swallowing hard, she finally found her voice. "But how? Where's Sami?"

"It's a long story, but Sami paid my fine. We spent an afternoon together and she said she wanted me to bring you a gift from her."

Sami. Of course. She'd found a way to win Sky over. Li Jin wondered if they were a couple now. She knew how convincing Sami could be when she wanted something.

Jojo held his hands up. "Let me have her, please, Ma." He sat down and Li Jin put Lan on his lap.

"Sami left you a note, and some photos, too." Sky reached into his jacket pocket and pulled out a scrap of paper with the photos. The first picture was Sami obviously taking a photo of herself and Lan as she leaned into the frame. Lan looked red-eyed and startled; Sami just looked determined. Li Jin looked at the note and recognized Sami's style immediately.

Sami had drawn a tiny black-and-white sketch of a garden filled with flowers in front of a simple house. Over the door of the home was a replica of their Rose Haven sign. In the garden, all the flowers were of the same height and type except for one that stood taller than all the rest. For that one she'd drawn an orchid and colored it in with lavender shadows. The flower was supposed to be Lan; Li Jin knew this and smiled. Above it she'd written only a few characters, a short note. It read:

> Buddha says, "Like a beautiful flower, full of color but without scent, are the empty words of him who does not act accordingly."
> I give my daughter to you, Li Jin, because you have a mother's heart, and she is the only gift I have for someone as dear as you are to me. I've also enclosed the deed to your home. Your debt

*is paid in full; consider it my gratitude for your showing me
what life could be. Maybe someday. Until then I'm wishing you
ten thousand years of happiness.*

Sami

Li Jin stopped wiping away the tears. There were too many.
The note sounded like a permanent good-bye. She looked at Sky
and he handed her two more pieces of paper. Her property deed
and the lender note stamped *paid*.

Sami wasn't coming back. Li Jin knew it in her gut and she
swallowed back an engulfing sadness. *Where was she? Was she safe?*
She couldn't say she was surprised; she'd seen Sami slowly
becoming more and more disillusioned with the simple life
they'd carved out in Wuxi but she'd hoped with time she
would've settled.

That hope was shattered but once again, Sami had shown her
loyalty. Li Jin didn't know how Sami had done it or where she'd
gotten the funds, but she'd given her back the home she knew
meant so much to Li Jin. And along with it, Baby Lan. It was a bittersweet moment. While her heart ached for Sami and the sacrifice
she'd made, it also soared with joy for Lan being returned to her.
The relief she felt was too immense for words, but she had to try.

"Thank you, Sky, for bringing her. And I'm so glad you're
free." She hoped she didn't sound too sappy and wished she
could take back her last few words. Sky probably wanted to get
back to Sami, wherever she was hiding. After all, she must have
gone to a lot of trouble to get him out of custody. Wherever she
was, Li Jin was thankful to her for sending Lan back.

Sky held out his arms. "Is that all I get after all the weeks I've
sat behind bars thinking only thoughts of you to get me through?"

Did she hear him right? "Me? Don't you mean Sami?"

Sky looked puzzled. "No, I mean *you*, Li Jin. She said you'd be like this. Turn the note over."

Li Jin flipped the piece of paper to find a short note scribbled on the back.

Also, I thought sending Sky to you would complete the picture. He is your airen, Li Jin. Accept it and stop being stubborn.

It was so like Sami to add a biting remark to camouflage her feelings. Li Jin laughed quietly; then she turned serious again. He needed to be warned. Bad luck seemed to follow her everywhere. She stared at him for a moment, swallowed hard, then said what she needed to say.

"It would be a mistake to fall for someone like me."

He shook his head playfully. "Don't you know by now you're the one I'm in love with? What do I have to do? Write it on a bridge? Come here."

Li Jin felt a rush of affection. She looked down at Jojo for reassurance, or maybe affirmation; she wasn't sure. She looked from her son to Sky, but still she felt unsure what to say or do.

Sky held his arms out and smiled teasingly. "Well, if you're going to be someone's mistake, I want you to be mine. You're exhausting yourself trying to put up walls, but Lao Tzu tells us, 'Sometimes we put walls up not to keep people out, but to see who cares enough to break them down.' Now for the next part in the story, Li Jin—*I* care enough."

"Go on, Ma," Jojo urged, grinning widely. "Can't you see? The Moon Goddess sent him."

So she did, Li Jin thought, *so she did.* Along with the realization she was no longer broken, but instead worthy of her own happily-ever-after, she let go of all her sworn oaths to never love again. When she entered into Sky's embrace, her body instinctively softened against his. It had been over a year since she'd been held by a man and she'd have thought it would feel strange, or be difficult because of all she'd been through, but it wasn't. For such a gentle man, Sky's arms were surprisingly steady and strong.

With Jojo and Lan behind them, Sky's arms circled around her, and, her head on his shoulder, it felt like coming home.

Glossary

Airen (pronounced I-run)	Soul mate/love of your life
Aiya (I-yah)	Expresses surprise or other sudden emotion
Anjing (Ann Jing)	A command to be quiet
Ayi (I-yee)	Auntie or a woman performing house help
Bushi (Boo sher)	No
Cha (Ch-aw)	Tea
Chengguan (Chung gwon)	Local police enforcement
Chòu biǎozi (Cho bee-ow-zuh)	Stinking whore
Dan ding (Dan ding)	Calm down/chill out
Diào sǐ (Dow suh)	Loser/douche bag
Dui le (Dway luh)	Right/correct
Erzi (Are-tzuh)	Son
Fengniao (Fung now)	Hummingbird
Gei wo qian (Gay whoa chee an)	Give me money
Guo lai (Gwoh lie)	Come here
Hao le? (How luh)	Okay
Hutong (Who tong)	Lane or residential area
Kuai (K-why)	Fast
Laoban (L-oww ban)	Manager or boss
Laoren (L-oww run)	Respectful way to address the elderly
Laowai (L-oww-why)	Foreigner
Li Jin (Lee-Jean)	Female name meaning beautiful, gold
Mei wenti (May when tee)	No problem
Meiyou (May yoh)	Don't have any
Mifan (Mee fon)	Rice

Mingbai (Mean bye)	Understand?
Nai Nai (Nie Nie)	Grandmother or other elderly female
Ni hao (Knee how)	Hello
Ni hao ma (Knee how ma)	How are you?
Ni ji sui le (Knee jee sway luh)	How old are you?
Nuer (New are)	Daughter
Qi gai (Chee g-I)	Beggar
Qipao (Chee pow)	Body-hugging Chinese dress
Reminbi (Rim in bee)	Money
Sanlun che (San loon chuh)	Three-wheeled bicycle
Shi (Sure)	Yes
Sui bian (Sway bee ann)	Slang expression for "whatever"
Tamade (Tah ma duh)	A curse word meaning "Damn your mother"
Waipo (Why po)	Grandfather
Wo Keyi bang ni, ma? (Woe kuh yee bong knee, ma?)	Can I help you?
Xiangqi (She-an-chee)	A form of Chinese chess popular in Asia and around the world
Xiao Jie (She ow jay uh)	Meaning "Miss"
Xia wu hao (Sha woo how)	Good afternoon
Xie xie (She she)	Thank you
Ye Ye (Yay Yay)	Grandfather or other elderly male
Yi bei cha (Ee bay cha)	One cup of tea
Zaijian (Zie gee an)	Good-bye
Zao (Zow)	A short morning greeting
Zou kai (Zoe kie)	Slang for "Go away"

Author's Note

Bitter Winds, book three in the Tales of the Scavenger's Daughters, was a fun book to write because once again, I pulled from memories of my time in China to create a story. My idea for Rose Haven came from a similar place in Anhui in which the owner of a bankrupt shoe factory truly did allow his property to be used to shelter the needy. Inspiration for Lily's story came from all I've seen and read over the last few years of how horribly beggars are treated in China. The catalyst was an online article and photo that showed an actual temporary iron jail constructed on a sidewalk outside of a festival, where the local officials had gathered and imprisoned beggars in 2011.

With regards to citizens being unlawfully sent to mental hospitals, after much public outrage, in October of 2012, China's legislature finally passed a long-awaited mental health law to prevent citizens from being involuntarily held and needlessly treated in psychiatric facilities. Stories of such abuse are rampant, and I'm relieved that perhaps China is on track to mend its soiled reputation when it comes to human rights issues.

I included the storyline involving Falun Gong because I find the controversy concerning it fascinating. Lily and then Ivy's predicament is very common and, as in their story, Chinese citizens want to avoid their names being recorded in official files as much as possible, even if it means doing time as penance. I do not support or speak against Falun Gong, as most of what I have read has been contradictory in nature, so it is difficult to form an opinion. I chose it because it is an interesting subject that fit well into this story.

If you enjoyed this book, a short review posted on Amazon or GoodReads would be very much appreciated. Also, please go to the Kay Bratt website to sign up for my newsletter to notify you of new releases, and come join me on my Facebook Author page!

Acknowledgments

First I'd like to thank my twin sister, Lisa. Our twinship provided a lot of background for the emotions and sense of loyalty Lily and Ivy feel toward each other. Our own experiences of maturing, and the inevitable process of growing apart that life demands, helped me to forge their relationship. To my husband, Ben, you were the role model I created Benfu from, and the kindness he seeps was inspired from how you truly are. Amanda, writing this series has kept me away from you most of your last year at home, but I hope when you read it, you will find it worthy of that sacrifice. To my Zachadoodle; as I created the character of Jojo, I used you as a model because you are the same age and I wanted Jojo to be just as awesome as you are.

Research for the mental hospitals in China came from many places, including CHRD's report, "The Darkest Corners: Abuses of Involuntary Psychiatric Commitment in China," which details the grim conditions and human rights abuses faced by these individuals [TheDailyBeast.com Aug 22, 2011]: "In practice, hospitals often admit patients taken there against their will simply on the basis of an allegation made by the police, other government officials, family members, or employers that the person might have a psychosocial disability," according to the report.

Thank you to Thomas Bickford, author of *Care and Feeding of the Long White Cane*. Your book was a crash course for me in learning how blind people traverse a sighted world. Thanks to Heather Tomlinson and Michele Coco. Your critiques were vital to helping me explore the daily challenges of being blind. Also to best-selling author Karen McQuestion, indubitably one of the coolest people in the entire universe, I wish her ten thousand years of happiness for being my mentor and critique partner. Many thanks to Lisa from TheGrammarGenie.com. Your developing skills helped me move the story forward and you did a fine job cleaning up the first round of my inevitable grammar snafus. Kate Danley and Gina Barlean, fellow authors and cheerleaders, thank you for spurring me on to finish this book when I felt like throwing in the towel, and your suggestions and ideas were most welcome and appreciated.

Once again I owe a heaping helping of gratitude to my editor and the rest of the team at Amazon Publishing. Terry Goodman, Jessica, and Nikki, without you, my stories might be wallowing at the bottom of a slush pile, or maybe just hovering on the wrong end of Amazon rankings. Charlotte Herscher, I'm still thrilled to call you my developmental editor because without your touch, I'd never get that final polish that marks a story as *ready to roll.*

The creation of a successful book is definitely a team project and I am grateful for every review and tidbit of encouragement my readers give me; it is because of them I continue to dream up characters who navigate the trials of life in an imperfect world. It is my hope that in their stories I can possibly capture a glimpse of the heart of humanity.

About the Author

KAY BRATT is a child advocate and author. She lived in China for more than four years, and because of her experiences working with orphans, she strives to be the voice for children who cannot speak for themselves. If you would like to read more about what started her career as an author, and also meet the children she knew and loved in China, read her poignant memoir, *Silent Tears; A Journey of Hope in a Chinese Orphanage*. Her works of fiction include *A Thread Unbroken* as well as *The Scavenger's Daughters* and *Tangled Vines*, the first two books in the Tales of the Scavenger's Daughters series. Kay resides with her husband, daughter, dog, and cat in a cozy cottage overlooking Lake Hartwell in South Carolina.